W9-BUY-583

DEPARTMENT OF SLAVIC LANGUAGES
HAMILTON HALL, COLUMBIA UNIVERSITY
NEW YORK, NEW YORK 10027

Konstantin
FEDIN

EARLY JOYS

★

NO ORDINARY
SUMMER

★

A NOVEL IN TWO BOOKS

FOREIGN LANGUAGES
PUBLISHING HOUSE
MOSCOW 1950

Konstantin FEDIN

NO ORDINARY SUMMER

A NOVEL IN TWO PARTS

II

FOREIGN LANGUAGES
PUBLISHING HOUSE
MOSCOW 1950

NO ORDINARY SUMMER

PART TWO

MERKURI AVDEYEVICH received a second summons to the Finance Department.

A month had not yet passed since his first visit to Ragozin, during which time he had scarcely managed to adjust himself to the idea that his life was in danger, and now here he was having to report again. He set out as though going to his doom.

But in spite of his gloomy expectations, Ragozin received him kindly and even spoke with a
shade of approval in his voice, though without
exhibiting any desire to prolong their conversation.
It turned out that the investigation carried on by
the bank had confirmed Meshkov's statement that
he had no money. He had indeed lost everything,
and the incongruous faith he had placed in the
"Liberty Loan" (which he had at first bitterly re-
gretted) now proved to have its bright side. He was
a beggar, and therein lay his good fortune. Never
in the old times had money saved people as effectively as an empty pocket now saved them, thought
Meshkov on realizing that the danger was past. He
was afraid to express this thought in so many
words, so he embellished it:

"How could a person help putting by a penny
for a rainy day in the old times? I hid nothing
from you, Pyotr Petrovich, and I couldn't have even
if I had tried: you remember only too well how
I lived. There's no denying the facts. But I never
did anybody any harm. Whatever I had I got by
putting aside bit by bit from the fruits of my
own labour, with only one purpose in mind: to
provide for my old age. Nowadays, even if I do
have one foot in the grave, I don't worry. I have a
corner to live in, I have a job, and when I'm too
feeble to do it, the Soviet government will look

8

after me like any other workingman. What else do I need?"

"All right. And on that we shall close our conversation, workingman Meshkov," said Ragozin, giving him a sharp glance, but trying not to show the curiosity of one conducting a cross-examination. But he added brusquely:

"You contend that you have no gold?"

"Yes, I do."

"Then there is nothing more to be said. You may continue at your job in the cooperative store without worrying. It's in a cooperative you're working, isn't it?"

Yes, Merkuri Avdeyevich was working in a cooperative, a fact which he was sure he had told Ragozin a hundred times. He bowed his way out graciously, happy that he had not met his doom after all, and that everything had turned out so well. Yet when he reached the street he definitely experienced a feeling of protest. Ragozin's encouragement—that he might continue at his job without worrying—only increased Meshkov's dislike for that job, which now he seemed to have received like a condescending favour from the hand of Ragozin. This favour weighed heavily upon him, because it added one more horror to the ten horrors lying in wait behind every corner. And of all of them, the horror of his work was the worst.

Not long before this, a couple of men had entered the store and demanded some merchandise for the trade unions. They had loaded a cart with the goods, signed the receipt, and calmly driven off. While he was entering the sale in the books, Merkuri Avdeyevich suddenly felt his flesh creep with suspicion that the order had not been bona fide. He rushed to the telephone and discovered that the trade unions had not sent for any merchandise. The order was false. Beside himself with fear, he rushed to militia headquarters. While papers were being drawn up he worked himself up into such a state that he was sure he would immediately be put behind bars and never again see the light of day. On returning to the store he found agents from the criminal investigation service waiting for him, and he nearly fainted from this new scare. But suddenly he discovered that luck was with him: it seems that the cart had driven into a yard at the edge of town, where it had aroused the suspicion of these agents. They had taken it in custody, and were now here at the store to investigate the matter. The innocence of Merkuri Avdeyevich was easily established.

He went to church and offered up a prayer of gratitude for having escaped this danger. But he had not escaped his fear. He was convinced that his job would be his ruin. After all, if chance had not come to his aid, who would ever have believed that Meshkov, the former merchant and property owner who, according to the present way of thinking, must by nature be dishonest, had not been mixed up with the thieves?

Oh no, it was impossible to continue at his job without worrying. And in spite of the fact that, thanks to Ragozin, this latest danger had passed him by, he was greatly depressed, and involuntarily turned from the path leading to the store where he should have gone, taking advantage of the fact that he was not expected back because of this summons.

All his life Merkuri Avdeyevich had preferred taking back streets. The late Valeria Ivanovna would walk along with him without saying a word until her patience gave out, when she would cry in vexation: "For the Lord's sake, why must you always pick your way among garbage heaps?" But even when he went out for a pleasure stroll he sought back alleys and empty lots. He was not proud, but secretive, and feared above everything else that by casting himself in the public eye he would cause people to remember that he was rich.

He turned off the main street, went down some bystreets and an abandoned boulevard lined with grey bushes, skirted a gulley serving as a dump for garbage and ashes, crossed it, and climbed a path leading to the cemetery. The day was as hot and dusty as usual, with the air rising in vibrant waves from the baked earth.

After saying a prayer at the grave of Valeria Ivanovna, he sat down on a mound. He often came here for comfort. In the spring he brought a spade with him to remove loose earth and reinforce the cross; on great church holidays he came to dispense charity to the beggars crowding about the gates. From among the crosses came the sound of a single voice chanting the burial service: "The heavens were awed, the earth stood in wonder...."

"The heavens might well be awed," thought Meshkov to himself. "And well might the whole globe stand in wonder! Just look what's happening! Just look! You can thank the Lord, Valeria Ivanovna, that He has already closed your eyes, so that they know no fear but the fear of God."

Calm in spirit and strong in his humility, he bowed to the grave and left the cemetery, making his way towards the hermitage in the monastery settlement.

This hermitage was better known as the country house belonging to the diocese. Behind the monastery began a woods which covered a slope and shaded the country house with young oak trees. Beyond the fence could be seen some low yellow buildings and the dome of a church. Quite recently the country house had been turned into a home for backward boys, formerly called boys requiring special attention. From morning to night the once quiet woods rang with shouts and yells. The gates of the hermitage, opened by the revolution, were now never closed, but since the woods were thick and the property extensive, there were still secluded corners where one might find solitude.

In one such corner stood a particularly isolated little structure in which the Bishop lived. He was a man unlike most members of the clergy. It would be wrong to say that he allowed himself to disagree with his superiors, or especially with church canons or ritual. He was orthodox in every respect. The only way in which he distinguished himself from others of his calling was in his manner of living. And even this would have been considered quite proper and called forth nothing but approbation had he been a simple monk. But his rank forbade his living in a manner which, while elevating a simple monk, could only disgrace so exalted a personage as a Bishop.

This contradiction created a peculiar situation. He lived almost like a beggar, as though he had no requirements other than those of the simplest novice. His admirers brought him many contributions, but he gave everything away in a prodigal and carefree manner. Knowing his weakness, the most various types came to partake of his bounty, including even the boys from the neighbouring home, who came mostly for the fun of it. His contempt for worldly goods inspired people with profound respect for him, and the number of his admirers grew quietly, but steadily. It was rumoured that here was one who was truly righteous, and people came to him to ease their consciences and repent. To be sure, his fame was not to be compared with that of legendary holy men, or even those of more recent times, to whom the people came in flocks, but still no one could deny that he was famous, or that his fame stemmed from the people's faith in his righteousness. But it was just this circumstance which caused church authorities to hate him and almost persecute him. The highest dignitaries, headed by His Eparchial Reverence, as well as the clerks of the Consistory, looked upon his simplicity as cunning, and upon his prodigality as a means of exposing the greed of the priesthood; they found that his pride fed on his popularity, and that his outward humility was dictated by an aspiration to sainthood. In a word, all that his followers accounted his virtues, his enemies accounted his sins.

For the first time in his life Meshkov allowed himself to defy the opinion of the church. On becoming acquainted with the Bishop, he was so completely won over that he denounced even those who harboured some doubt as to the monk's utter sinlessness, and as for the Bishop's enemies—he hated them for all time.

With utter humility of the spirit Meshkov entered the hermitage. He was filled with a resolution which he had long been seriously considering, but which only now had become firm and unshakeable. As he walked along the wall of the hermitage he kept thinking to himself that only an hour before he had fearfully walked a shameful path into the very lair of that servant of the antichrist Ragozin, whereas now he was fearlessly walking a holy path into the dwelling of the servant of God, and on his lips were praises to the Most High, and in his ears were the sounds of heavenly voices which seemed to be circling above his pious head.

He was met by a curlyheaded monk in shabby robes. He led him through the outer chamber into a second, where he first knocked, then opened a door with the words: "In the name of the Father, and of the Son, and of the Holy Ghost." Then he disappeared, but was back in a minute saying that the Reverend Father would receive him.

Merkuri Avdeyevich crossed himself before the icons, touched the middle finger of his right hand to the floor in a low bow, and entered for the blessing. The Bishop leaned forward in his armchair to greet him, excusing himself for not getting up because of his ill health. His face showed the puffiness of those suffering from heart disease, and it was covered with such a scant beard that the heavy oval was as visible as though he were shaven, and each one of the long grey hairs seemed to have been fastened separately to his yellow skin. He rarely moved his little eyes, but their colourless, watery transparency conveyed to them an expression of constant anxiety. The window in the wall was small, but since the sun was beaming down on the woods, the room was brightly lighted.

The Bishop dismissed Meshkov's enquiries as to his health with an impatient gesture of his joint-swollen hands and quickened the telling of his turquoise beads. He glanced at his visitor expectantly, indicating that he should waste no time in communicating the business which had brought him to the cell.

"I have come to ask your blessing on my decision, Your Reverence. I have long since had the desire to take the cowl. Now the time has come to realize this desire. I beg you to give me your blessing, Your Reverence."

Once more Merkuri Avdeyevich bowed.

"Are you sure you are not acting hastily?" asked the Bishop quietly.

"I am already sixty years old, Your Reverence."

"I see that. The cowl fits some lads of fifteen as though they were born monks, while the monastic garb sits clumsily on the shoulders of others even if they don it at a ripe old age."

"I am obeying the bidding of my heart, Your Reverence."

"Sit down if you please. And calm yourself. There is nothing to be upset about, if your decision has been made."

"It has indeed been made, Your Reverence. I live with the single thought of saving my soul."

"God help you. But it is not necessary to enter a monastery to save your soul. It is perhaps a greater service to the Lord to bear your cross in the world than inside our walls."

"I wish to lighten my cross...."

"I see. It is not easy to conquer hate," observed the Bishop with a sympathetic shake of his head. Again he leaned slightly forward, bringing his gaze closer to Meshkov's face, and said in a voice that was scarcely audible: "Reconcile yourself, and therein find salvation."

Merkuri Avdeyevich sighed and turned away from this white gaze, that was like a charged electric wire in sunlight.

"I lack the strength," he said humbly.

"In other words, it is weakness that leads you to this step?"

"Sin on my soul, Your Reverence."

"It is not weakness, but strength of spirit that our Heavenly Father demands."

The Bishop sank back in his chair as though he were exhausted, and stopped telling his rosary, letting his fingers come to rest on a large bead engraved with a cross. Suddenly he asked in a voice which was unexpectedly stern:

"So you would seek to escape the wrongs you suffer?"

"No," replied Meshkov firmly. "The wrongs I suffer only hasten the step. But the desire to enter a monastery was born in my youth. At that time I lived with some other salesclerks in the house of our master, and these clerks tried to convert me to the Old Believers—they were dissenters. I almost succumbed to their temptation, but a good man advised me to apply for advice to Jerome, the holy man of Athos Hill. I wrote him a letter, and he sent me a book and confirmed me in the Orthodox faith. After that I began to read holy books and experienced a desire to enter a monastery. But that same holy man advised me to postpone such a step until the death of my mother, after which, God willing, I could fulfil my desire. But while my mother was still alive I got married. However, even during my life as head of a family, I contemplated entering a monastery if ever I became a widower.

Now this time has come, and the grandson who was dependent on me will soon have a stepfather, so that there is nothing to keep me from entering a monastery."

"Very well," said the Bishop after a short pause. "Then give away your worldly possessions and follow me."

"There is nothing to give away," said Meshkov, starting up with new animation. "The last of my possessions which I valued, 'The Lives of the Saints,' I presented to you, Your Reverence. Anything else to be found in my room can simply be thrown away."

He glanced about the walls of the cell. The Bishop smiled good-naturedly.

"What are you looking for—your gift? I have already handed it on to somebody else. The other day a rural priest came to see me. He complained that life was hard; his parishioners no longer follow the ritual and the wellsprings of their bounty have dried up. They have forgotten their God. I felt sorry for him and said: 'Load your cart with these "Lives." Maybe you'll find somebody who will buy them.' It was clear the holy father had long since stopped reading 'The Lives of the Saints.' His nose was red as a cranberry, and he'll probably guzzle down the books, poor devil."

Meshkov slowly shook his head.

"Are you sorry?" asked the Bishop.

"It pleased me to think that you had my books, Your Reverence."

"There now," said the Bishop, still smiling, but in a tone of reproach. "You regret giving away not only your own things, but even other people's. Once you give something away, forget about it!"

"Sin on my soul."

"Hm. Which monastery do you wish to enter? Not much joy in the monasteries these days either: the brothers threaten to start fighting soon themselves, like the soldiers at the front."

"I should like to enter the monastery near Khvalynsk. Do you approve?"

"I know that monastery. A soothing place, very picturesque. But the Old Believers are right next door. And stronger than our brothers. See that they don't win you over!" said the Bishop with teasing jocularity.

"If it is necessary to come to the defence of the Orthodox Church, I am equal to it, Your Reverence. It was in this hermitage that I learned to bring shame to the dissenters."

"Well," said the Bishop in a tone of relief, "thus shall it be. God be with you."

Merkuri Avdeyevich said a prayer, dropping on his knees before the Bishop, who blessed him and allowed him to kiss his hand. As he was leaving, Meshkov hesitated and looked enquiringly into the flabby, sickly face of the clergyman, waiting for the latter to give him some sign permitting him to speak.

"What is on your mind?" asked the Bishop.

"Would you be so kind as to tell me the significance of the number 1335?" asked Meshkov warily.

For some time the transparent eyes remained motionless while the last traces of colour drained out of them. Then they narrowed, closed, and suddenly opened, searing Meshkov with a white-hot glance.

"What has led your thoughts into such channels?"

Meshkov answered with complete assurance, while remaining utterly meek:

"I read a book which compared the history of men and kingdoms with holy prophecy. And this book ended with the prophetic words: 'Blessed is he who awaits and achieves 1335 days.'"

"And who may have written this noble work?"

"A learned man, or so it seemed to me—one Van Beiningen."

"A German?"

"I don't know. I only know that the book was passed by the censor."

"What of it?" observed the Bishop in a tone of commiseration. "The censor, due to his lack of foresight, allowed books on Socialism to be printed."

"But this book is against Socialism, Reverence."

"That means little, for the Roman popes also are most bitterly against Socialism."

"But this book brands papistry as the most heinous of heresies."

"That too means little, for the Socialists also brand papistry in a most sizzling manner."

Merkuri Avdeyevich bowed his head in such abject confusion that it remained for the Bishop only to punish or pardon the wandering sheep. The great man kept silence until the full weight of his triumph was felt, when he laughed softly and struck himself over the knee with his rosary.

"Why import foreign devils when we have so many of our own?" he asked merrily.

Then his face became stern as he took one of the hairs of his beard and ran it between thumb and forefinger.

"When you go home, light the stove and burn up your Van... what's his name?" he said harshly. "And stop being so clever; don't think you can understand everything with that mind of yours, for it's far too simple. Prophecy must be accepted as the word of God, and not as arithmetic. Remember

22

this: in order that men should have some slight comprehension of the truth, the Lamb of God was forced to resort to the human tongue. What is our tongue? The insufficiency of our mind—that's what our tongue is. God says 'a day,' and we interpret it as meaning twenty-four hours. But maybe God's day includes the lives of all of our ancestors and descendants, like a kernel in a nutshell. How then, can you expect to understand what is meant by Biblical figures! It is not interpretation we need, but faith. Faith, and purity of heart! Remember what our Teacher Himself said about His second coming: 'And no man shall know the day or the hour, not even the Son, but only the Heavenly Father.' "

He sighed, once more ran his fingers down the hair, and ended in a milder vein:

"You have worn me out. Go now. When you begin your life in the monastery, tell your confessor about the sins you committed with that foreign heretic passed by the censor. Perhaps he will name some punishment in expiation. And now you may go in peace. A great ordeal lies before you. Farewell. . . ."

Merkuri Avdeyevich returned home as though walking on air. He was separated from the past by a great divide, and in his old age, as in his youth, the future seemed full of promise. To be sure, nothing remained of the past but a pair of old shoes with worn elastic in the sides, but even if by some miracle that past were returned, Meshkov could no longer be part of it. The blessing he sought and had been granted demanded that he denounce even his memories of what had been. He did not have to become a new person: he had already become that new person, or so it seemed to him, so profoundly was he impressed by the decisive and awe-inspiring step he had taken.

On reaching home he was met by a surprise. As a matter of fact, he had expected this surprise, and it only speeded the emancipation which from that day became his one purpose in life. This surprise delighted him because it set him free, but at the same time it saddened him because it meant that before Merkuri Avdeyevich had had time to take leave of his family, before he had had time even to tell them of his intention, they no longer had need of him, of his advice, of his aid....

The table was covered with a freshly ironed cloth dug out of the trunk, and everything was as fresh and ironed and festive as the tablecloth.

Lisa was wearing a white dress. Her hair was piled on top of her head in light, airy masses. She seemed taller. Once more a wedding ring sparkled on her finger—a new, slender ring that matched the one on the finger of Anatoli Mikhailovich. She had already finished preparations, and four chairs were waiting about the table. Vitya had also donned a well-ironed, still unspotted Russian blouse made of orange silk. Oznobishin was wearing a summer coat, whose metal buttons bearing the tsarist eagle had been covered with linen.

When Merkuri Avdeyevich appeared in the doorway, everyone became silent and motionless. Nodding to his daughter, he asked:

"Have you registered?"

"Yes, we have," answered Lisa.

He went into his own room, and a minute later appeared with a little icon in a tarnished frame, no larger than the palm of his hand. With this he blessed first Lisa and then Oznobishin, thinking as he did so that this was his second son-in-law by the same daughter. Then he patted Vitya on the head and said:

"Now you have a stepfather. Obey him like a father. He is the head of the family from now on, and has more authority than even your mother, understand? And I ..."

"Let's sit down at the table," said Lisa.

"Before we sit down," said Merkuri Avdeyevich unhurriedly but insistently, "I want to tell you something. You have brought about a change in your life, and I have decided to do the same. In accordance with a vow taken long ago, I am leaving you to spend the rest of my days in a monastery. I hope you will find it in your hearts to forgive me."

25

He bowed to his daughter and to Anatoli Mikhailovich. Lisa took a tiny step toward him and ran her hand across her high forehead.

"You never mentioned this before, father...."

" 'Think a lot, say little.' But once a thing is spoken, there is no going back. I no longer have to worry about you—you have married a good man. And Vitya has someone to look after him. Now it is time for me to be thinking about my soul. This is my constant concern, both waking and sleeping."

All three stared at him in embarrassed silence, as though they were ashamed. Finally Vitya asked:

"Grandad, will you wear a cowl?"

"Vitya!" said Lisa.

Merkuri Avdeyevich restrained a sigh.

"I shall turn my room over to you," he said to Oznobishin.

Anatoli Mikhailovich rubbed his feminine hands together and objected feebly:

"But that is unnecessary. Lisa and I need so very little...."

"I can't give you much," said Meshkov. "For that reason I have no fear in leaving you. And now let us continue our talk at the table."

He glanced at the food. There was a dark bottle of old port, and a sparkling bottle of vodka.

The delicate odour of the eatables, to which the eye had long grown unaccustomed, was irresistible.

"Just think, just think!" he whispered. "So here I am at my first Soviet wedding!"

He closed the door tightly and everybody sat down, he between his daughter and grandson.

"This is like an engagement feast," he said. "And when will the church ceremony be held? Without the blessing of the church, married life cannot be happy. Hold the wedding ceremony while I am still with you."

"But why should you make such a decision all of a sudden?" asked Lisa, with a vague feeling of guilt which she herself could not define.

He touched her shoulder, exhorting her to reconcile herself to that which was inevitable.

"It is not all of a sudden, my dear. But only today have I received the sanction of the holy father. And now ..."

He again turned his eyes to the table and smiled, saying in a lowered tone:

"Pour me some wine. It makes no difference now—I'll have a last fling. For all time."

They drank in silence, nodding to each other approvingly; they could not even remember when they had had such a feast, and gave themselves up wholly to the sensation. Vitya smacked his lips over

27

the port wine, which he was tasting for the first time.

"Where did you ever dig it up?" marvelled Merkuri Avdeyevich, rewarding Oznobishin with the glance of an ally. "Perks you up all right. Tastes just like the old stuff. Listen, there's a question I want to ask you as my legal advisor. Now that everybody has to work, how can I quit my job without any unpleasantness, eh?"

"You'll have to get sick."

"I understand. I've thought of that. But what shall I come down with?"

"That question refers more to medicine than law."

"But what if I'm well, in spite of my years?"

"You must find the sort of doctor who claims that there is no such thing as a person without any complaints."

"The sort who claims that everybody's sick from the day of his birth?"

"The sort who allows that everybody can be found ailing if circumstances demand."

"Who allows...?" repeated Meshkov, tapping his pocket and winking slyly.

"You guessed right," said Anatoli Mikhailovich, reaching for the vodka.

Merkuri Avdeyevich always became drunk suddenly, and he could never determine at exactly what moment he lost control over himself. He would take a sudden leap from the humdrum world into a world where colours were translucent, like stained glass. And this world boldly challenged him to action.

But Lisa had no difficulty in determining the moment. In childhood she had learned the signs of her father's drunkenness: his nostrils began to tremble and he parted his beard with a resolute gesture that expressed both injury and indignation. Lisa moved the bottle away from him. Her father looked at her in silent disapproval.

"I am still a—citizen of the world—a slave to worldly passions," he said in self-justification. "Once I'm a monk—the fetters of this world will fall off, and for the first time I shall know real freedom."

"That's true," agreed Oznobishin. "True freedom comes only when a man is emancipated from his own self."

"You think that's right—from his own self?" asked Meshkov sceptically.

"According to my way of thinking, that's right. For a religious person gives himself up wholly to the will of God."

"That's it. A man submits his will to the will of his spiritual advisor, and through him to the will of God. Therefore it would be better to say:

he becomes emancipated from his own will, but not from his own self. Only death can emancipate us from our own selves. From the fleeting nature of this life."

Merkuri Avdeyevich was so pleased with the way he had put it, that he reached for the vodka. But Lisa was quicker, and poured him only half a glass. He raised his beetling brows and again lowered them.

"Looks like you're wanting to take your father in hand," he said with restraint.

But at this moment there was a knock on the wall and somebody coughed. This wall was only a partition, put up to make a passage through the large room for other residents of the house. It was as thin as the sounding board of a guitar, and so the knock came as a resounding interruption to their conversation. Lisa half opened the door.

Out in the corridor stood Matvei, the old workman who lived in the house. He glanced innocently into the room over the top of his spectacles and murmured something to Lisa.

"They've come for some sort of an inventory, father," said Lisa, turning to her father.

"Inventory? What kind of an inventory?" asked Merkuri Avdeyevich, filling up the half empty glass of vodka and swallowing it down angrily as he rose from the table.

He pushed his daughter away from the door and cleaved his beard in two.

"What kind of an inventory?" he repeated. "What can you take inventory of when there's nothing left?"

"It's houses and buildings they be measuring," replied Matvei lazily. "Want to know how much living space there be. I said as you probably know the size of the rooms."

"Who asked you?"

"What difference does it make? You just tell them the measurements so they don't come poking around with their yardsticks."

"Why shouldn't they come poking around with their yardsticks? That's what they get paid for, isn't it?"

"But it'll take less time if they don't have to go through all the rooms."

"That's none of my business. The house doesn't belong to me."

"I see, I see, Merkuri Avdeyevich," said the old man with a short laugh. "But the worse it'll be for you if they break in on your banquet."

"Ban-quet?" said Meshkov softly, straining up on his toes to keep the old man from looking into the room. "Ban-quet?" he repeated with a squeak. "Aha! So that's what's bringing them spying into my room! A banquet! So that's their purpose in breaking into other people's apartments!"

"Why, now, should they break into the apartment when the whole house reeks of home-brew?" said Matvei with a contemptuous shake of his head.

"Home-brew?" said Merkuri Avdeyevich on a threateningly high note. "I'll thank you to know there's no home-brew here!"

"Father!" exclaimed Lisa.

But as though Meshkov had just been waiting for some slight protest to set him off, he began shouting at the top of his lungs:

"It's distilled tsarist vodka, I'll have you know! Tsarist vodka, and none of your vile home-brew! Get that? So now maybe you'll run and squeal that Merkuri Avdeyevich prefers tsarist liquor to your stinking home-brew! Well, go ahead and run! Squeal on Meshkov, you shameless old devil!"

"Phooh! It's you that'll be the shameless old devil!" said the old man, snatching the spectacles off his nose and going off down the corridor.

"Go ahead and run! Go ahead and run!" cried Merkuri Avdeyevich, slamming the door and rushing from one end of the room to the other. "Tell everybody that Meshkov is hoarding vodka with the tsarist eagle on the trade mark. That he's giving banquets! Celebrating weddings! Holding orgies! And not treating his tattletale neighbours to even a sniff! Go ahead and run! Fast as your legs will carry you!"

The old workman gave a sharp knock on the wall and bellowed from the corridor:

"Don't be upsetting yourself! Everybody knows what kind of an element you are!"

Meshkov pounded on the wall with his fists.

"How dare you! Element! It's not me, it's you that's a dangerous element. It's you who broke into my apartment! It's you who keeps poking your snotty nose in other people's doors! Who robbed me of everything I had? Who forced me down to the same level as the beggars? You! You! You spiteful rascal! You and the likes of you! Stripped me to my last shirt, to my last worthless bond! It was you who issued the loan on your own liberty, you swindlers you! It was you who got people to invest in it! It was you who recalled it! And still it's too little for you! You have to keep snooping around, seeing what you can still measure off for yourselves, what you can still grab up and swallow down! All right, keep swallowing down Meshkov until there's nothing left to swallow! Rip out his heart. It won't make you feel any better. There's no luck in bettering yourself at other people's expense. You'll never get rich! You'll never be the bosses!"

He ran over to the table and poured out a full glass of vodka which he swallowed in one gulp. For a second he stood gasping, then suddenly collapsed on a chair.

All this while Lisa had been standing and looking out of the window.

There had been a time when her father's shouting had terrified her. It had seemed that in his fury he was capable of striking and beating and killing. But now she felt not the slightest fear. She only pitied her father, and was ashamed of his futility. She remembered how meek and helpless he had appeared in her dreams. She should have gone to his aid, but an old estrangement prevented her. He was weak and pitiable, and Lisa was oppressed by a sense of her own superiority, but she could not make herself do anything for him. At the present moment her pity was mixed with anger that he should be shaming her so in front of Anatoli Mikhailovich. The noise her father was making caused her pain, but she was oblivious of what he was shouting. She thought only of her husband, who from this day on would be part of her family life, and was now undergoing so rude and abrupt an initiation. Without turning around, she sensed that Oznobishin was so taken aback that he was at a loss what to do.

34

When at last the silence brought Lisa out of her trance, she turned to find her father blindly trying to prop his elbows on the table while he muttered:

"What have I ever done to them? Why should they call me a criminal? Why should they torture me? Why should they humiliate me? How is my labour any worse than theirs? Everybody works to keep himself alive. Why should they grab up my crust of bread?"

"Calm yourself," said Oznobishin, tactfully moving the dishes out of range of the old man's shifting elbows.

The sympathy in Oznobishin's voice caused Merkuri Avdeyevich to melt. He became maudlin, and his tongue refused to obey him:

"Sin on my soul! I've sinned, but I'll atone for it! I'll atone! Forgive me, sinner that I am!... I'll go away.... Live without me. Like in olden times, when old people went off into the taiga... stole away into the crypts of the North Pechora Monastery ... I'll do the same ... bury myself in the woods... only I'm sorry to leave Vitya behind... forgive me... I'll spend the rest of my days praying for you... Oh Lord, forgive me...."

He struck his head against the edge of the table.

Lisa glanced at Vitya. Together they lifted Merkuri Avdeyevich and led him into his room. His body was strangely loose and light and small. They

3*

laid him on the bed. He clutched at Vitya and kissed him on the cheek. The boy removed his grandfather's shoes, then brushed off his hands and wiped his own cheek. He had never seen his grandfather like this before, and it gave him a new sense of his own superiority. He adjusted his orange silk blouse and glanced down at it. The silk was mussed, but still clean. Lisa drew the quilt up over her father and they left him alone.

Oznobishin hesitantly approached his wife and put his arm about her shoulder. Something kept her from meeting his eye. At last she forced herself to speak:

"You must forgive him.... He is good enough at heart. Only... he is... a despot."

"Of course I forgive him," said Anatoli Mikhailovich, hastening to comfort her. "It is harder for those who are proud, than for those who are not. It is necessary to understand...."

Suddenly she moved away from him with a deep, angry sigh, blushing with shame at her vexation:

"What talk can there be of pride! He is simply intolerant of everyone except himself!"

She sat down at the table and for some time fixed her gaze steadily on Vitya. Then she said guiltily:

"How glad I am that he is leaving us!"

Alyosha lay weeping on the grass under the lilacs. He knew every nook and corner of Dorogomilov's overgrown garden, and yet he was always discovering new joys in which to find comfort. Here he carried on imaginary conversations with his elders which he dared not voice in other places.

His wet cheeks touched the sharp points of the stiff, heart-shaped leaves. He accepted their prick as a mark of sympathy. Everything about him seemed friendly—the fresh shoots growing out of the roots and resembling miniature trees, the little beetles with designs like black-eyed faces on their red backs, the white seed pods of unripe mallow, reminding him of the linen-covered buttons on night shirts.

To this isolated world in the shade of the leaves it was possible to say: you understand how Alyosha is suffering, and you love him with all your heart, just as he loves you. But do you think Alyosha's father loves him? Not the least bit!

This was the second time Arseni Romanovich had invited Alyosha to go over to the sands with him. And the second time that father had said no. And that after all the fishing rods had been examined and made ready. After all the nets had been mended. After Vitya had managed to get hold of some new fishing hooks—little ones, as tiny as a hangnail, and big ones the size of Olga Adamovna's hairpins. Everything had been made ready. And then his father had again said no!

And what a float for his fishing rod Arseni Romanovich had presented Alyosha with! Made out of a great big striped quill from a porcupine! A black stripe and a white stripe. Its equal was not to be found anywhere along the Volga. To be sure one end of the quill had holes in it, and if the water came through, the float would sink. But Arseni Romanovich had hunted out a honeycomb frame up in the attic and promised to patch the holes with wax. The wax had grown as hard as flint, but Arseni Romanovich would melt it over a spirit lamp. True, there was no alcohol, so the lamp didn't burn. But they could put kerosene in it. Not long ago Olga Adamovna had got hold of some kerosene, and Alyosha knew where she had hidden it.

Olga Adamovna was the cause of most of Alyosha's misfortunes. She was forever saying that Arseni Romanovich would ruin their poor dear Alyosha. Naturally this was just because she was jealous—as though she could be compared with Arseni Romanovich! Nobody could be compared with him. If it was not for his mother, Alyosha could definitely say there was nobody on earth as dear to him as Arseni Romanovich. And if anyone should ask Alyosha what he wished to be when he grew up, he would answer—Arseni Romanovich.

He would like to be him all his life, though he knew only too well that he could never achieve anything so wonderful. As though he could ever know so much about everything as Arseni Romanovich knew! And where would he ever get a house like his, with a garden around it and a corridor bursting with so many things! And what about his carpenter's bench? And the lifesaver? And the flock of little boys ever following at his heels? Little boys would never follow at Alyosha's heels. And Alyosha would never be able to get a job like Arseni Romanovich's. Take Alyosha's father, now. He never got any job at all. And he surely must have wanted to. And Arseni Romanovich's hat? And his beard? How could Alyosha ever grow such a beard?

No, Alyosha realized only too well that he would never make an Arseni Romanovich. But if he could at least live with him, like the other boys did. Go roaming with him over the hills, and take trips to the sands. Freely, fearlessly, forever and ever!...

Alyosha wiped his tear-stained face and began to gather the mallow buttons. When he had collected a whole handful, he decided to eat them all out in the garden, where no one could see him. Otherwise they would immediately become panicky about Alyosha's stomach. Not long ago Olga Adamovna had brought a saucerful of black currants home from the market, and before Alyosha had even a chance to taste them his father had grabbed the saucer and dumped them all in the garbage can. "Next time, madam, bring home blackberries," he had said angrily. "It's easier to get the cholera from them!"

In general, father had begun to be afraid of everything. Suddenly he would announce that the whole family would die of starvation. Or he would sigh mournfully and say: "Nobody wants us, Asya!" Or he would mutter something wholly incomprehensible, such as: "Perhaps Alyosha will live to see something worth while, but you and I won't, Asya."

"If it gets hard for you to see, daddy," Alyosha had said on that occasion, "you'll just buy yourself a pair of pince-nez, like Olga Adamovna's."

"You adorable little idiot!" his father had replied.

Thinking these thoughts, Alyosha chewed the last of the mallow and came out from under the bushes onto the path. He raised his head and suddenly caught sight of a man in military uniform standing with his back to the open window of the corridor. He immediately recognized his close-cropped head and extraordinarily smooth back, and became frightened.

He brushed off his hands and ran home. His shoe came off, and he shoved his toe into it, smashing down the back in his terrific haste. He could hear his heart thumping like a sledge hammer.

In the corridor he found his mother and father talking with Zubinsky.

"I repeat that the question has been settled once and for all," said Zubinsky politely.

"But our fate is at stake," answered his mother quietly, looking at Zubinsky with enormous eyes.

"I am very sorry. I realize that all this is highly uncultured, but what can I do? The situation at the front is such that the devil only knows what we can expect, begging your pardon. I am merely carrying out orders. The day after tomorrow the house must be freed of its occupants. It has already been transferred to the military. I beg you to inform citizen Dorogomilov that this decision is final."

Zubinsky clicked his heels, put on his cap and saluted.

And for a second time Alyosha heard his stiff soles go pattering down the stairs.

Without saying a word, his father went into their room. Alyosha crept over to the door with bated breath. His heart was still racing. His fear

had not subsided. Zubinsky's last word—"final"—
did not die out like the striking of a bell, but grew
louder and louder, like the sound of an approaching locomotive. Now it was coming down the street.
Now it had entered the garden and was crushing
the trees. Now it had burst into the house and the
corridor and was smashing all the dear, beloved
things belonging to Arseni Romanovich. In a minute the floor Alyosha was standing on would collapse under its weight!

"So that's that," came father's fierce voice,
cleaving the silence. His father turned to his mother
and cried in a tone which Alyosha had never heard
before:

"Stop looking at me with your water-colour
eyes!"

He grabbed up his box of tobacco, flopped down
on the bed, and began rolling a cigarette with shaking fingers. His mother went over to him and softly
stroked his hair, as she did to Alyosha when she
wanted to soothe him.

"Don't lose heart," she said. "Take my advice.
Go right over to that despot Izvekov and paint our
situation to him."

"Paint!" mocked his father. "This is no time
for painting. It's time to start thrashing around
with a club! They won't listen to me anyhow.
Humiliate myself before that young upstart? Our

situation! This is no situation, it's a catastrophe! Just get that into your head! A cataclysm! A coffin! A grave! The stake! Death!"

"What do you mean, 'humiliate yourself?'" asked Alyosha's mother. "When it rains you take an umbrella, don't you? That doesn't mean you are humiliating yourself before the rain."

His father jumped up, and after standing silent for a minute, muttered peaceably:

"Where's my hat?"

He scooped up a handful of water from the washbasin, splashed his face, ran a wet hand over his hair, combed it and adjusted his tie. Then he took the hand of Alyosha's mother and held his lips to it for a long, long time.

"Please don't be angry with me," he mumbled.

In the corridor he caught sight of his son. Alyosha wanted to slip through the door to his mother, but his father caught him and lifted him high above his head by the elbows, as though he were still very small. Then he lowered him and kissed him on the forehead. Faint with happiness, Alyosha said:

"Daddy, daddy ... you won't tell Arseni Romanovich he said 'final,' will you?"

His father put him down.

"Go inside. Mother will explain everything to you."

Once out on the street, Alexander Vladimirovich felt very peculiar. He was not interested in the
people, he did not notice the heat, and even his
sense of smell seemed to be dulled. Everything
within him was concentrated on a single idea which
tortured him like pain. He called it—"the last hour
of one sentenced to death." His mind was simultaneously possessed by a fact whose significance
dominated everything else, and his desire to discover some meaning in this fact. The fact was that
he was sentenced to death. In his effort to discover
some meaning in this fact, contradictions kept growing and fading in his mind: at one moment he became reconciled to his sentence, at another he protested against it.

The civil war was also a fact. Without going
over the details of the war in his mind, Pastukhov
saw them in one inseparable whole, just as the
single word "death" suggests to a condemned
man all the details involved in his taking leave
of life.

He walked through the quiet city, but somewhere just beyond the city streets he heard a noise
which kept growing ever louder. It was as though
the erupting volcano of July was invading the
innocent silence of the city.

In July, Wrangel's Caucasian army slowly made
its way up the Volga to Kamyshin. More than a

month before, in an order issued at Ekaterinodar to the Armed Forces of South Russia, Denikin had recognized Kolchak as the Supreme Ruler of Russia, in reply to which the Supreme Ruler had sent the general a telegram in which he stated that he was "deeply touched." Soon after this act uniting the counterrevolutionary forces of South and East, Denikin entered the captured city of Tsaritsyn and after reviewing his forces there, signed a new order beginning presumptuously: "With the ultimate intention of conquering Moscow, the heart of Russia, I hereby order...."

This order was accompanied by detailed instructions as to the operations to be carried out by White generals. They read like a copy of the theoretical plans of that learned German wearing a badly tailored Russian uniform (General Pful, from *War and Peace*) who felt himself at home only when poring over a map. According to these instructions, Wrangel was to form a front extending from Saratov to Rtishchevo and Balashov, and continue the drive through Penza and Nizhni Novgorod in the direction of Moscow. Sidorin was to develop operations at Voronezh, Kozlov and Ryazan, as well as at Elets and Kashira. Mai-Mayevsky was to advance on Moscow through Kursk, Orel and Tula. In the south, the instructions demanded the taking of Kiev and Kherson, Nikolayev and Odessa.

Far in the northwest, Yudenich was participating in the general plan by marching on Petrograd.

At any moment the Whites were expected to cross to the left bank of the Volga in the district of Tsaritsyn-Kamyshin in order to join the Urals Cossacks. But at that time Vasili Chapayev was carrying out the order of Frunze to advance on Uralsk, and on the day before the issuing of Denikin's "Moscow Instructions" he began his drive. The Cossacks were defeated, and five days later they began their flight to the south. In another five days, on the very day specified by Frunze, Chapayev led his cavalry into Uralsk, thus ending the siege of the city. On the following day the Red Army celebrated another victory on the Eastern front: the city of Zlatoust was taken and Kolchak's forces driven beyond the Ural mountains, where they broke into headlong retreat into Siberia.

A person lost in the woods at night is fully aware that daylight and open roads exist. But that knowledge does not relieve his sense of being trapped in the dark. Pastukhov knew of Uralsk and of Zlatoust. He also knew that a counterattack on Tsaritsyn was being prepared by the revolutionary forces. But physically he was conscious only of the stifling proximity of the front menacing Saratov. The war was driving down on the city, the war was roaring beyond its gates, the war was swooping down on Pastukhov, and his Asya, and his Alyosha, and his vase of flowers, and his manuscripts, and his thoughts, and his expectations of the future, and his very life. History, the times, the calendar, the hands of the clock, all sentenced Pastukhov to war. Sentenced him to death. This was a fact.

How could he find meaning in that fact? Why should Alexander Pastukhov perish in a war which he had not caused, did not want, and from which he wished to stand aloof? Sentences are pronounced for some crime. For some guilt. What crime had he committed? Of what was he guilty? He was not a Red, so he was counted a White. He was not a White, so he was counted a Red. He was sentenced because he was neither Red nor White. Was it possible that the whole world was either Red or White? What was to be done if Pastukhov was burnt orange? Kill him! Or if he was ultramarine? Kill him! But why did not the Burnt Oranges and Ultramarines kill? Why was all the killing being done by the Reds and the Whites? Come to think of it, there were Greens who also did some killing. It was a curious detail that the Greens were called brothers—brothers who went in for killing—green brothers—deserters who hid in the woods. In the woods where Pastukhov was lost in the dark. He was lost, he was condemned. That was a fact. And it was impossible to find meaning in that fact.

47

One who has been sentenced to death may find some meaning in his death for others, but he cannot possibly find any meaning in his death for himself: his death may be demanded by history, by the times, by the calendar, by the hands of the clock—but never by himself. For himself—for Pastukhov, who is about to die—his death has not the slightest meaning. And his mind protests against the idea of his death.

But his mind seeks some sort of reconciliation with death, though he himself does not wish to be reconciled. He thinks like this: A person is faced with the fact of historical circumstances just as he is faced with the fact of his own nature. He is given an opportunity to fight with the forces of nature in order to prolong his life. But the forces of nature eventually conquer, and he dies. He is given the opportunity to fight for the prolongation of his life, choosing what he believes to be the most salutary environment under the given circumstances. But if he is unable to foresee what environment is most capable of protecting his life and he falls victim to a premature death, then nothing is left for him but to find some meaning in his sacrifice. To find meaning in a meaningless sacrifice. He is trying to find it. If a young, healthy, talented person such as Pastukhov considered himself to be, is sacrificed to no good purpose, people will come to recognize the senselessness of the sacrifice. They will kill one, two, five, ten Pastukhovs, and suddenly discover that there is no sense in killing them. They will discover that there is not only no sense in killing them, but that there is even waste and harm in killing them. They will understand this and come to their senses, and the sacrifice, instead of being meaningless, will assume significance.

But once again Pastukhov returns to his point of departure. It is true that some significance can be found in his sacrifice, but this significance holds only for those for whom the sacrifice is made, excluding those who make it. Those who sacrifice themselves "for their brothers" gain nothing. It is only the "brothers" who gain. Who are these brothers, these others, these friends? For whose sake is Pastukhov to be annihilated?

He thinks about his "brothers." Who are they? Asya? Alyosha? They will suffer great misfortune if he perishes. His Petrograd friends? They are scattered over the face of the earth and have no thought for him. The directors of theatres, troupes of actors? They would be more likely to regret his loss than profit by it. Who would receive any advantage from the wiping out of Pastukhov? Two or three pen slingers who suffered from Pastukhov's popularity. They would sign a joint necrology, and after wiping their crocodile tears, dance with joy that there would never again be a play by Pastukhov. Was he, then, to die only that they should have their dance?

No, Pastukhov had no friends. Perhaps his whole trouble was that he had no friends. Perhaps if he had some friends they would help him make up his mind which side to choose—what to sacrifice himself for if history, the times, the calendar, and the hands of the clock all sentenced him to death. A choice, a choice, that was what Pastukhov had to make! The meaning of his whole life, its very essence, boiled down to one thing— a choice.

It was with this sense of one condemned that Alexander Vladimirovich arrived at Izvekov's. He was made to wait in the reception room. He realized that they might slight him, and he was prepared to accept this slight. Even his bearing expressed resignation. But he was mistaken: no one had any intention of slighting him. In half an hour Izvekov rushed out all afluster:

"A thousand pardons: I was kept busy on the telephone. Come on in here. Do you mind if I have my dinner?"

Izvekov led him into a narrow little room next to his office, where he removed the napkin covering two plates. One of them contained millet porridge, the other an unripe apple and a piece of rye bread.

"Eat the apple," said Izvekov.

"No, thank you. I'm afraid I'm in the way. My business won't take much time."

"You're not in the way in the least," protested Izvekov as he lifted a spoonful of porridge to his mouth. "Have the apple. It's from our Soviet orchards in Rokotovka. Have you ever been there?"

"Yes. It used to be a beautiful place."

"It still is."

"Have you seen it?"

"No. But I can just imagine what it must be like now!"

Pastukhov was intrigued by this young man swallowing down cold porridge with as much relish as though it were the most exquisite of delicacies. But it was not so much Izvekov's appetite that aroused his curiosity (few people suffered from lack of appetite these days) as the fact that throughout the meal his face retained an expression of wariness which in no way seemed to interfere with his eating.

"These days it's all the same—the orchards are about as good as the truck gardens," said Pastukhov.

"About as good, or about as bad?"

"Suffice it to say that they're all the same. So

4*

far as I can see, human misery all comes from these teachings about levelling down. You can't create a form of life which is uniform and common to all, any more than you can create a form of happiness which is uniform and common to all."

Izvekov licked his lips and gave the impression that he was winking at his companion.

"Got an urge to philosophize, eh? Like in that story of Chekhov's. Well, come on. To begin with, let's expose one misconception. There's a difference between 'common' and 'uniform.' 'Common' refers to things which belong to everybody, but are not uniform. What is common may be diverse, but equally accessible to all. Everyone will choose his work according to his taste: one will become a gardener, another a surgeon, the third a ploughman or an engineer. But happiness will be equally accessible to all."

"If a person doesn't reject such happiness," observed Pastukhov.

"That will not be to his advantage."

"What is to the advantage of one, is not necessarily to the advantage of another. The war has proved that."

"That's just until everything is redistributed. Naturally it is to the advantage of those from whom surplus wealth is being confiscated to reject the happiness of those to whom it is being transferred."

Pastukhov observed a new shade of satisfaction in Izvekov's face—the rather gloating satisfaction of a person who feels his superiority. Izvekov ate the rest of his porridge with particular pleasure, as though he were rewarding himself for having answered his opponent so easily.

"Thoughts are a mere diversion," said Pastukhov disapprovingly. "Feelings are the motivating force of life."

"Thoughts too!" exclaimed Izvekov eagerly. "And perhaps thoughts are even more important, because they strive to guide feelings."

"That's not true," protested Pastukhov with slight irritation. "At first there was pain. Then a gesture. Then a cry. Finally the spoken word. Thoughts are born of feelings, and not the other way about. No, it is not the other way about. Anger, hate, and love, are always stronger than reason. We don't want war, but we cannot abolish it."

"We don't want senseless war—that is, war fought for evil ends."

"I suppose you want a war motivated by love? You want a good, kind war—in its aims and purposes—am I right? But that means you want to ennoble or enrich feeling with thought—the feeling which precedes thought, the feeling of hate, because war is inspired by a feeling of hate. And that feeling is stronger than the thought which you

53

would make its predecessor. The evil of war is stronger than the good of its aims."

Izvekov turned from his plate and gazed at Pastukhov with a harsh fixity.

"Whom do you mean by 'you?'" he asked in a low voice.

Pastukhov waited for a second before shrugging his shoulders and replying:

"I was not thinking of you personally. But since you used the word 'we' . . . I was speaking . . . in general. . . ."

"In order to separate yourself from us?"

"Is that forbidden?"

"It is your right. I only wanted to know whether 'we' were holding this conversation, or whether it was between 'you' and 'us.' Apparently it is the latter. Then I shall speak only of 'us.'. . . Yes, in this war we are inspired by hate. But it is not a blind hate. It turns on all things a keen eye—the eye of justice. We are waging the just war of the dispossessed who are defending their right to a life worthy of human beings. We do not want war. We want peace for everyone. But violence was used against us; we were forced to wage war. And we did not funk. We are fighting against war. For that reason, our war is not senseless and has no evil aims. It is, as you have put it, a good, kind war. It has great significance and noble purposes. It would be criminal for us to lay down our arms, for our enemies would show us no mercy. They would utterly crush us, and then further dispossess the dispossessed."

Pastukhov lifted his hand to interrupt Izvekov.

"I have never doubted the exalted aims of which you speak," he said very quietly, fighting down a fresh wave of the same suffering he had experienced on the way here. "I am not so naive, or, in the final analysis, so despicable, as to fear a fight which has some meaning. But I must confess that I am horrified to see how much evil man commits in the name of good."

Without answering, Kirill took the apple, easily broke it in two and handed half of it to Pastukhov with a smile:

"Try it."

For a long time Pastukhov gazed motionless, with deep-seated caution, at the juicy, greenish-white pulp of the broken apple.

"Apparently I'll have to succumb to temptation all by myself," said Izvekov, again smiling as he bit one of the halves in two.

His reference to the legend of our ancestors was so obvious that Pastukhov considered it unworthy of comment. He carefully watched Izvekov chew the apple along with a piece of bread. Kirill's angular jaw worked hard at the bidding of strong muscles. It seemed that he had given himself over entirely to his enjoyment of the fruit. Yet his glance still retained an expression of wariness and thoughtfulness. As he crunched the apple he remarked:

"You say you are horrified by war, but by war you mean revolution. At least that is what I gather."

"I mean the annihilation of man by man. Is it of any importance what this annihilation is called?"

"Probably you didn't take part in the war. The army uses the following term: 'expendable material.' Our code of morals demands that we place in the hands of the revolution this 'expendable material.' As a matter of fact, if armies have always had the right to expend property and human lives to wreak destruction in the name of victory, in the name of protection against the enemy, then why should the revolution be deprived of all property and of the right to dispose of human lives, when its purpose is the creating of a new world? A soldier is not held to account for the ammunition he fires, the homes he ruins, the wealth and the human lives he destroys, if he does all this in the interests of victory. Why then should the revolution have to account for every cracked plate, every broken arm, even if the damage is done to its obvious enemies?"

"Logical enough, but very brutal," said Pastu-khov.

"What about the world war, a war which I seriously doubt that you protested against before it was turned into a revolution. That war was bru-tal and *not* logical. Do you agree?"

Kirill looked at Pastukhov triumphantly. The Lord only knew where this unexpected debate might lead them!—thought Pastukhov, and he answered in a lazy tone, meant to convey that he was tired of the argument:

"Man is a creature given to explanation. He cannot rest in peace until he has explained what he sees, or what is taking place. But once he has found an explanation, he is willing to reconcile himself to anything at all."

"Not to reconcile himself, but to defend what he considers a true explanation."

This was becoming insufferable. The fellow ob-viously was enjoying the argument. After all, Pastukhov had not come here to juggle words at such a moment.

"Is it worth while risking your life hanging on to the steps of a crowded streetcar just for the sake of some kind of explanation?" he said wearily. "Wouldn't it be far more sensible to go respectably on foot?"

"Or to ride an ass?" added Izvekov teasingly.

Again Pastukhov shrugged his shoulders.

"It seems to me that in your search for explanations, you don't try to understand Russia," he said.

"No, I belong to those who try to understand in order to build a new Russia, as distinguished from those who try to understand in order to preserve the old Russia."

"I doubt whether it is advisable to throw over everything old in one fell swoop. And there are many who think as I do. I am not the only one."

"I know that you are not the only one," said Kirill with a short laugh. "According to the figures last month there were two hundred thousand like you. At present there are even more."

"According to what figures?"

"The figures of the Central Commission for Rounding up Deserters." Izvekov raised his hand to his mouth to hide a smile. "But there may be less. The Commission is apt to exaggerate in order to show how vigilant it is—catches them all up—doesn't let anybody slip by."

Pastukhov hesitated, indicating that an answer could hardly be expected. But suddenly he assumed a matter-of-fact tone, as though putting all joking aside, and expressed an opinion that only amused Izvekov all the more:

"I understand you are a Bolshevik. In that case, the latest decision of your Party obliges you to work with—comrade-deserters, if I am not mistaken."

"Your remark, as they say, is not without..." Izvekov sought a suitable word, but ended up with a laugh.

There was less amusement than challenge in his laughter, and Pastukhov realized that it was not always wise to have your little joke. He got up impressively and adjusted his coat.

"A deserter is one who violates his oath. I have not taken any oath."

Kirill also got up. Drawing his straight brows together, he measured Pastukhov from head to foot through narrowed eyes.

"When a city is threatened by flood, its inhabitants go out to build a dam without taking any oath.... And anyone who hides and refuses to help is a deserter."

Pastukhov took out his handkerchief, wiped his lips, and enquired with exaggerated politeness:

"Have you finished your dinner?"

"Yes," answered Izvekov. "Let's go into the office."

Once in the office, he remained standing behind his desk, making it clear that he wished to end this business as quickly as possible.

"I don't know whether you will wish to help me after our philosophical discussion," said Pastukhov in a strained tone. "My family has been put out on the street. The apartment in which we live has been taken over by the city military authorities for some sort of an office. The apartment belongs to Dorogomilov. Have you ever heard of him? He is being evicted along with us."

"Dorogomilov?"

"Yes. We must get out tomorrow. I have no idea where we shall go. I must ask you either to stop the eviction, or to supply me with some sort of a roof over my head."

The conversation now took a turn which required no philosophizing. Since the house had been taken over by the military authorities, Izvekov could not stop the eviction. As for supplying Pastukhov with new quarters, the housing situation was so bad that Pastukhov would have to depend on his own resources. Of course it was hardly to be expected that he would be able to find anything in twenty-four hours, but Izvekov saw no other way out.

"I beg your pardon," said Pastukhov in a hurt tone, "but what will the City Soviet feel like if tomorrow the citizens of Saratov see my family sitting on their baggage out in the street like gipsies?"

"That will not happen. The Housing Department is obliged to give you some sort of quarters, even if they are only temporary."

"In some barrack?" asked Pastukhov with a slight bow, as though in gratitude for the confirmation which he anticipated.

"Possibly," replied Izvekov coldly. "At any rate, you can be sure we shall not transfer any more houses to the Housing Department for the sake of supplying you with an apartment."

Pastukhov remained standing there like a monument to himself, motionless, his arms hanging, his whole figure seeming to have expanded. Suddenly he said in a broken voice, with a loud sigh:

"You will lead me to doing ... heaven only knows what!"

"I am not interested in what I shall lead you to doing," answered Izvekov quickly. "You are older than I am. You have a head of your own.... What is it?" he asked the shingled secretary who entered at this moment.

"They are waiting for you at the conference."

"All right, I have finished. I shall be right in."

"Good day," said Pastukhov under his breath, and walked out briskly without offering Izvekov his hand.

As soon as the door had shut behind him, Kirill ordered his secretary to get the Military Commissar on the telephone. He paced the floor while she turned the handle, banged the hook up and down, and gave the operator a calling down. Finally he himself took over the battle with the operator, eventually getting the commissar.

"Somebody just complained to me that you were putting one of our townsmen out of his apartment.... Yes, there is such a man: Arseni Romanovich Dorogomilov. You can find out about him from Ragozin if you wish.... What do you mean you don't know anything about it? Throwing a person out on the street and you don't know anything about it?... Why ask me? I'm the one to ask you who did it. They did it in your name.... What's that? You don't need any more space?... That's funny. Look into it, if you don't mind.... Naturally you've got more important things on your mind. So have I.... Please get to the bottom of it because it's not a very pretty business. And let me know the results."

Kirill slapped himself heavily on the thigh and went to the window. Pastukhov could not have made up the whole story. There he was in the distance, walking briskly away with the same injured and constrained air with which he had left the office. Now he looked even more scornful, his head was held higher, his right arm swinging imperiously, in time to his stride. No, such a person did not go in for idle talk. Such a person was convinced that it was not for nothing he occupied a place in the universe. People gave the road to such a person, for they respected him as one who knew his own worth. Obviously there was something wrong here.

Yes, there was something wrong. Pastukhov carried himself proudly. But that was his natural carriage, resulting from his habit of walking over the earth in a manner befitting his conception of his superior stock. But in his heart of hearts there was not a trace of his former self-confidence. The world had rejected and humiliated him. He kept painfully repeating one and the same thing: here you are, young and handsome, once independent, walking down the street with that same graceful swing to your step. But make no mistake about it: it is your last step. Take a last fond look at this well-formed, well-fed, one might almost say superb body which you are carrying into the unknown. It is your last look, your last hour. Say farewell to everything you see. Say farewell to yourself, for soon you shall cease to be.

Alexander Vladimirovich returned home in such a black mood that Asya immediately realized they had suffered defeat. He threw down his hat, snatched off his coat, and sank heavily into a chair. Never before had he seemed so ponderous.

"Well?" asked Asya with an apologetic smile.

"The serpent tempted me to eat of the fruit of knowledge," he said.

She smiled more playfully, but more anxiously:

"Well, and did you succumb to the temptation?"

"Brew me some fresh tea."

He poured himself such strong tea that she feared for his heart. After that he lay down and remained gazing up at the ceiling until dusk.

Then he took Asya out into the garden. They sat down on the overturned wheelbarrow which Alyosha was fond of pushing about the paths. They spoke unhurriedly about things that were equally clear and important to each of them. The decision was already formed, but they led each other to it warily, testing again everything they had lived through.

They would have been glad to reconcile themselves to the quiet of that abandoned garden where the mallow intertwined with bindweed to form a carpet under their feet, and the hollyhocks clung to the fence, and the poplars formed a canopy over their heads. To be sure, it was not Eden, but the very fact that they were being driven out made this garden dear to them. Yesterday's fugitives had become today's exiles. There was nothing left for them to do but seek some other spot as secluded as this. Once more they yearned toward Balashov, so desired and so unattainable, the refuge for whose sake they had left Petrograd. There, of course, the family estate still awaited them, as did Anastasia Germanovna's old parents; there they would find bread and shelter at the family hearth, and there no one would dare to violate the sanctity of the individual. They agreed to immediately set out for Balashov.

That evening Pastukhov informed Dorogomilov of their decision.

For the last week or so Arseni Romanovich had been in a constant state of excitement. Events roused his energy. He reproached himself with inaction. Alarm was growing in the city. People were making all sorts of preparations for the approaching danger, while he went on leafing through accounts and adding up figures as he had been doing all his life. He was angered by his inability to leave the beaten path. He received the news that he was to be evicted from his apartment without the slightest protest, for it brought him the secret hope that it would be just the jolt he needed to effect some great change in his life—perhaps his entering the army and even going to the front. Yes, he would change his faded coat for an army uniform. He would pull in his belt, take off his tie, and shave his beard and mane. He would prove a fine one at marching, for he had always been a tireless walker. To be sure, his life was already behind him, but whatever warmth was left in his body should be expended on a worthy cause.

"You don't say!" exclaimed Arseni Romanovich, when Pastukhov announced that on the next day he intended taking his family to Balashov. "Why, the fighting is going on only a stone's throw away from there! How can you—with the child! And the Whites are all around the place."

"In our situation, it makes little difference who is around. Once they've driven me to such a step. We need a house to live in," answered Pastukhov a bit superciliously.

Arseni Romanovich said not a word. He merely took a step backward, then silently hurried down the dark corridor to his own room without the slightest effort to seem polite.

Alyosha overheard that brief conversation. He was crushed by the manner in which Arseni Romanovich had turned away from his father. Never before had he seen such an expression of disapproval on the face of Dorogomilov. The child had difficulty in falling asleep, and all night long dreamed that he was being thrown down from a belfry, or over a mountain precipice, or off a ship's mast into the roaring sea, and he kept waking up in a feverish perspiration to hear his mother and Olga Adamovna wrapping dishes in newspapers and his father grunting as he pulled at the squeaky straps of suitcases.

Alyosha had held Vitya and Pavlik in the greatest respect ever since the moment he had caught them having an honest-to-goodness fight. He felt a deferential fear in their presence, as in the presence of beings who were incomparably superior to himself, and he was accustomed to telling them the truth at all times. For that reason, when the boys ran in to see Arseni Romanovich at the dinner hour on the next day, he was prepared to tell them everything. But when he found himself alone with them in the garden, he guessed that they already knew everything, and for some reason he was painfully ashamed.

Pavlik and Vitya gave him a glance that was even more alien than the one turned on him that unforgettable moment when they had first become acquainted in the study of Arseni Romanovich. Pavlik even sucked in his lower lip as though getting ready to spit. Vitya whistled a tune which Alyosha did not know, and which he therefore found extremely irritating. Finally Vitya seemed to take pity on the suffering Alyosha and asked contemptuously:

"Running away, eh?"

"We're leaving for mother's home. That's on a farm where grandmother and grandfather live," explained Alyosha painstakingly.

"You don't say! Why didn't you go before? Waited until it began to get hot here!"

"What do you mean, hot?" asked Alyosha.

"Just what I say."

"They're Whites," observed Pavlik scornfully.

"No, we're not," said Alyosha in a weak voice.

"Then why are you against Red Army men?" asked Vitya.

"We're not against Red Army men," protested Alyosha, and a tear sparkled in one of his eyes.

All three of them stood without speaking or looking at each other.

"Are you sore?" asked Alyosha timidly, taking a step toward Vitya.

"Why should we be?" snorted Pavlik.

"What's there to get sore about?" agreed Vitya. "You're little. They just cart you with them wherever they go."

"It's all daddy!" cried Alyosha bitterly, grateful to Vitya for understanding his situation. "I don't want to leave Arseni Romanovich ... or you either," he added, blushing furiously.

"Poor people are better," said Pavlik, as though opening Alyosha's eyes. "My father's poorer than yours, but he's better. Except he's a soak."

"What do you mean, a soak?" asked Alyosha.

"Goes on a bat when he's in the mood."

"Beats you?"

"No, drinks, you silly."

They remained standing there a while, until Pavlik said to Vitya:

"Well, let's go. What we waiting for?"

They left without saying goodbye to Alyosha, and he remained standing by the back stairs all alone, in front of the open door through which came the sound of heavy things being dragged out into the upstairs corridor.

To these upsetting sounds was presently added the clatter of steps on the stairs, and Arseni Romanovich appeared in the doorway. His coat was open, he was hatless and dishevelled, and he rushed past Alyosha to the gate. He already had his hand on the latch before he stopped and came back.

He embraced Alyosha's head and impulsively pressed it three times to his stomach, and then smothered the child with his cold and tangled beard. This violent, inexplicable siege of hugging and kissing lasted a mere fraction of a second, after which Arseni Romanovich once more ran to the gate.

When Alyosha heard it slam and click behind him and realized that he was left all, all alone, he raised his fists to his eyes and began to slowly climb the stairs, his little body shaken with sobs. He so clearly understood what had happened that he defined his suffering in words which until recently had been quite unfamiliar. It seemed to him that in his sobbing he was uttering these strange, despairing words. Actually he was only crying. He and his mother and father and Olga Adamovna were outcasts, and were fleeing to some unknown place. Everyone despised him because his father was worse than a poor man, and because he himself was worse and more cowardly than Pavlik and Vitya. Arseni Romanovich was the only one who pitied him. He pitied him and loved him, but was unable to save him and had left him for all time.

Alyosha entered the summer kitchen and stopped beside the stove. He removed his fists from his eyes and saw before him the lifesaver which he had found on first entering this house.

The marvellous object was lying in the same place. How many of Alyosha's fond expectations were linked with this lifesaver! Unrealized fishing expeditions, trips to the sands of the main stream, adventures in rowboats, possibly in sail boats, swims in the waves left by passing steamers, and best of all—campfires—the many, many campfires he had dreamed of building with Arseni Romanovich! Whenever Arseni Romanovich went boating with the boys, this lifesaver was their faithful companion. And now Alyosha took his leave of this faithful companion as though it were his lost hopes. He felt that he himself was lost, and that there was nothing on earth that could save him.

He stroked the rough painted cork and placed his wet cheek against the loops of rope attached to the edge.

Suddenly his mother's voice sounded in the corridor:

"Where's our Alyosha? Where's Alyosha?"

He wiped his eyes and cheeks and answered sternly:

"I'm here.... Only please don't shout."

Before the sun had set the Pastukhovs arrived at the station in the wake of their baggage. Dorogomilov did not go to see them off. Alyosha heard Olga Adamovna say to his mother: "He didn't have to go to the station with us, but he could at least have said goodbye. Ordinary decency requires that!" To which his mother had answered with her faint, meditative smile: "He is a severe judge."

Pastukhov conversed with no one. He was overwhelmed by the sight of all these people—life itself, violent and many-visaged—encamped on the station square. Just as in the spring, his family stood helplessly chained to a pile of baggage which had to be protected against this avalanche of human beings. But what amazing changes had taken place in the last few months!

First of all, there were incomparably more people. They formed a solid mass broken up into
smaller crowds and groups and clusters. Some of
them kept flowing in an endless stream into the
station, while others struggled against them in an
opposing stream, finally bursting out of the doors
in pressed bunches, like raisins.

Another thing which impressed Pastukhov was
the number of armed Red Army men. They were
also constantly moving in the human stream, now
in groups, now singly. Above the heads of the
people flashed silver bayonets. The soldiers pulled
their rolled overcoats off their sweat-stained backs
and dragged them around like harnesses, and the
sight of these overcoats, so incompatible with the
heat of the day, suggested the frosts of fantastically distant winter nights.

The square was encircled by families of refu-
gees sitting on their bags. A fluctuating hum of
voices rose from the crowd, and no separate sound,
however arresting—the crash of a falling teakettle,
the wail of a child, the shriek of a locomotive—
could dominate this hum. The noise was solid and
compact, and it seemed that even thoughts could
not be born independent of this many-voiced,
many-headed, multitudinous unity.

Quite unexpectedly a military man in brand-
new uniform appeared in front of the meditating

Pastukhov. He was thin and slightly sunburned, and seemed to have just emerged from the bath. The dimple in his chin broadened as he smiled. He gazed at Pastukhov with an eager, youthful glance, and waited for the latter's response.

"I suppose you don't recognize me," he murmured boyishly, made impatient by so long a silence. "I used to have a beard."

"A beard?" repeated Pastukhov.

"You're the one who showed us the ribbon that time," said Alyosha unexpectedly.

"That's right," smiled the officer. "Dibich. My name is Dibich."

"Heavens! Why of course!" cried Asya. "How you have blossomed forth!"

"It's just that I've recovered my health. For the first time in I don't know how many years I feel like a human being. And what about you? Setting out again? Haven't yet reached your destination?"

"I can see that you—have reached yours," said Pastukhov, bringing his glance slowly to rest on the red star decorating Dibich's cap.

"Yes," replied Dibich, still smiling. "I'm in the army again. Forming new units."

"Clerical work? Naturally they won't let you do any commanding."

The darts left Dibich untouched. He spoke eagerly, making no effort to conceal his pleasure in having met these likeable acquaintances.

"The commanding can wait. At present it's probably harder to make up new units than to fight a battle. Such a muddle! ... I was thinking of you a few days ago. Remember that soldier who almost had us arrested in Rtishchevo?"

"The fellow with the pale eyes?"

"Yes. He had only one eye—got a splinter in the other. Ipat Ipatiev."

"Well?"

"He came to volunteer in my unit. We recalled Rtishchevo and had a good laugh. 'Look what you almost did,' I said to him. 'Tried to put a fellow in the cooler who helped make the revolution.' While I was in the hospital I read about you in the newspaper," added Dibich in a tone of respect.

"You don't say," said Pastukhov as he pinched Dibich's belt buckle between finger and thumb. "Tell me this, are you really unaware of the fact that you have gotten yourself mixed up in a business that is doomed to failure?"

Dibich unhurriedly pushed his cap to the back of his head.

"Business?" he repeated. "This is no business. This is history."

"Well, you'll find yourself a victim of this history!" said Pastukhov sharply, and let go of the buckle, giving Dibich a little push as he did so.

"Perhaps," replied Dibich seriously, but then he narrowed his glance and said challengingly: "And what if I don't?"

"If you don't?" drawled Alexander Vladimirovich. "If you don't, then I'm crazy."

Dibich laughed.

"Have it your own way."

Asya's fine sensitivity to danger caused her to interrupt at this point. She turned to Dibich the face radiant with good will which he remembered from their first encounter.

"What are you doing here now?" she asked.

"I came with a company of infantry made up of new recruits. I have to take them to Uvek and put them on a steamer. The fighting is very close. Yesterday the Whites took Kamyshin. Have you heard?"

Pastukhov glanced quickly at his wife. She hid her anxiety under a playful smile as she said:

"I see you feel right at home in the station. Maybe you'll take pity on us poor creatures and help us get shipped off?"

"Where are you going?"

"To the same place we were going when we last met—home."

"Home?" repeated Dibich with a short laugh. "That sounds like a fairy tale. But are you really going to Balashov? Not easy to help you get there. But I'll try."

He disappeared in the crowd and was gone for a long time. It was almost dark when he returned and announced that he had spoken to the commandant of the station, who asked to speak with Pastukhov personally. Dibich took a hasty leave, explaining that his company had already entrained.

If at that moment anyone had told Pastukhov that he would have to spend ten horrible days crawling along in a freight train which spent hours, day or night, waiting at stations and on sidetracks, only to arrive at a place that was not his destination, he would have preferred setting up camp somewhere at the edge of the road, or on the grounds of the monastery, or even farther away, in Igumnov Gorge, under the trees of some orchard. But in blissful ignorance he bit his lip and insisted on having his own way. The family finally boarded the train and set off on their journey as though sailing down an unknown river on a leaky raft.

Once again Pastukhov landed in Rtishchevo, and this time found it crowded with railway cars, horses, field kitchens, hay, unfed cattle, broken-down automobiles, and countless people. Once again he applied to commandants, officials, and commissars, asking and demanding that he be given accommodations on the Balashov train. He grew worn and thin. Asya lost her vivid colouring and her smile became wan. Alyosha slept or drowsed with his head in the lap of Olga Adamovna. Everything about them was grey with dust and vibrant with the heat of the scorched steppes.

One morning the Pastukhovs woke up to find themselves travelling at full speed. With a clang of couplers the train went swaying down an incline between stunted black firs mixed with birches. No one could explain how their car had become hooked on to this train, where it was going, and how long it had been on the way. On reaching a little station, they discovered that the train they were attached to was headed for Kozlov.

"Who cares?" said Pastukhov. "It's been a long time since I've been able to make head or tail out of anything anyhow. What difference does it make where we land?"

Seeing the despair in Asya's face, he hastened to add:

"It's even better. We'll get to Balashov quicker from Kozlov ... through Gryaz, or whatever they call it."

He glanced at Olga Adamovna and suddenly shouted at the top of his lungs:

"Stop wiping your eyes, madam! You're living in a historical epoch and you're obliged to be prepared for anything, damn it all!"

* 20 *

Early in July the Central Committee of the Russian Communist Party (Bolsheviks) published a letter addressed to all Party organizations. The letter was entitled "All Out for the Fight Against Denikin." It had been written by Lenin and began with the words:

"Comrades! We are now faced with one of the most critical—probably *the* most critical moment of the Socialist Revolution. ..."

In this letter Kolchak and Denikin were recognized as the main, and indeed the only serious enemies of the Soviet Republic. At the same time it was pointed out that only the support of the Entente made these enemies formidable. And while recognizing the moment as most critical, the letter announced victory over all our enemies as an accomplished fact: "We have already vanquished all our enemies except one—the Entente, representing the all-powerful, imperialist bourgeoisie of Britain, France, and America. And, even so, we have already smashed one of the arms of this enemy—Kolchak. We are only threatened by his other arm—Denikin."

In order to intercept the blow of that still unbroken arm raised over the Republic, Lenin called upon his Party to adapt itself to the war, putting all the work of all institutions on a war footing. He proposed that any activity not absolutely essential from a military point of view be unhesitatingly curtailed for a time. He wrote: "In the war zone about Petrograd and in that enormous war zone which is developing so quickly and so menacingly in the Ukraine and in the South, everything and everybody must be in a state of mobilization; all work, all effort, all thought must be wholly subordinated to the war, and the war alone. Otherwise it will be impossible to repulse Denikin's onslaught. That is clear. And it must be clearly understood and given practical application."

This letter, filled with conviction as hard and sharp as a diamond, re-echoed throughout the land with ever increasing force. While touching on the future of the entire country and the fate of the entire revolution, every line of the letter seemed to strike at some special location, some definite fact, some unique situation that appeared to be as isolated as an oasis. Thus, for those absorbed in events taking place at Saratov, the location which the letter seemed to have in mind was clearly Saratov; the definite facts were the Saratov facts—the social facts of the Lower Volga region; the unique situation standing out like an oasis on the background of the all-Russian situation was the Saratov situation. In other words, people in Saratov who sympathized with the revolution accepted this letter as being addressed to the Republic in general, but to Saratov in particular.

Ragozin read the letter twice—once during office hours, the second time at home, by the light of a kerosene lamp, pencil in hand. After this second reading he wrote a two-line application to be transferred to war work.

He was summoned to the Gubernia Party Committee. A member of the Bureau of the Committee informed him that at the present moment it was impossible to release him from his position in the Finance Department: thanks to Ragozin's efforts, the work of this department was just being put in shape, and to change the chief now would spoil everything. Pyotr Petrovich was ready for these objections, which he found only natural. Out of his pocket he took the letter, all covered with checks and underlines and exclamation marks, and found a heavily underscored paragraph in the section entitled "Curtailment of Non-Military Work," which he read aloud:

"'Take, for instance, the Scientific and Technical Department of the Supreme Council of National Economy. This is a most beneficial institution, and one which is essential for the complete building up of Socialism, for the correct calculating and distributing of all scientific and technical forces. But is such an institution absolutely essential? Of course not. And at the present moment it would be criminal to assign to such an institution people who could and should be immediately transferred to Communist work *in or for the army,* in order to accomplish tasks which are immediately and vitally essential.'"

"Hold on there," interrupted Ragozin's opponent. "Do you think we haven't studied this document?"

"You may have, but let me read you a few more lines here: 'There are many such institutions and departments both in and outside of the capital. In our efforts to completely realize Socialism, we naturally founded such institutions. But we would be fools or criminals if, in the face of Denikin's formidable onslaught, we did not *reorganize our ranks* in such a way as *to suspend or cut down everything* not absolutely essential.' "

"Well, what do you wish to say—that now we can suspend the Finance Department?"

"Not the Finance Department, but me—from the Finance Department."

"If that were true, we would never have put you there."

"Everything in due time, in due time!" said Ragozin, lifting a finger over his head. "Are we against science and technical achievements? We most certainly are not. But this is not the time for such things. Am I right? It is simply not the time. ... And for the present, someone else can handle the finances. That is definitely stated here also. Look."

Once more he unfolded the letter and found another underlined paragraph which he followed with his finger as he read:

" '... we may even take the risk of temporarily leaving many of the curtailed institutions (or departments of institutions) *without a single Communist,* allowing them to be run entirely by bourgeois executives.' "

"Read further," said the member of the Bureau, taking the letter out of Ragozin's hand when the latter stopped. "What is said further on? 'This risk is not very great, since we are speaking only of those institutions which are not absolutely essential.' Understand? And your department is absolutely essential."

"I know how to read too," said Ragozin, getting up and walking around the desk, where he leaned heavily over the member of the Bureau, the better to impress on him the import of the passages he kept pointing to with his finger, though he no longer read them, but only retold their contents in his own words. "How is the question put here? Here's how: will it be fatal to close down some institution or to cut down its work by nine-tenths, leaving it without a single Communist? Who is responsible for answering such a question? Every department head in the provinces, or every Party nucleus. Am I a department head or not? Am I capable of answering this question, or must the Party nucleus answer it for me?"

"It has already been answered for you," said the member of the Bureau with some vexation, pushing off Ragozin. "And it was answered not by the Party nucleus, but by the Bureau of the Gubernia Committee. You wish to respond to the summons of the Party? Increase the money granted to those working for the war and take it away from those whose work has little to do with the war. At Zaton, for example, where our ships are repaired, there aren't enough metal-workers. Give them some extra cash and they may be able to find the workers."

Pyotr Petrovich stopped in an awkward pose, as though stricken with sudden pain, as he said:

"Why hasn't anybody said anything to me about the shortage of metalworkers at Zaton? I'm a metalworker myself."

"Harping on the same old tune! We take people away from work benches to place them in responsible positions, and you'd like it to be the other way about."

"I don't mean that. There should be a lot of old workers on the railway and in the depot who remember me—I worked there a good many years. We could switch them over to Zaton. Want to give me the job?"

"Why not? Go ahead if you want to. Only see that it isn't at the expense of your immediate responsibilities."

Ragozin gave a slight wink:

"I'll cut down my immediate responsibilities. Not by nine-tenths, perhaps, but let's say by eight. . . ."

"This is no time for joking."

"Oh all right," laughed Ragozin from the doorway. "By seven—seven-tenths—no more, honest to goodness!"

Thus he landed first in the depot, under the sooty, smoke-blackened arches of the workshops where the wind came whistling through breaks in the smudged glass, and then at Zaton, under the free expanse of heaven, where the angry chattering of the riveters competed with the wail of the electric saws and the rasping of files.

Only two metalworkers were found at the depot who remembered the old days. These men had a heart-to-heart chat with their old friend, but only one of them consented to help out at Zaton, because the work at the depot was enough to keep people going from morning to night without a moment's rest. But they both promised to persuade some of the younger workers to come to the aid of the rivermen.

At Zaton, Ragozin began by reimbursing the neglected exchequer of this enterprise, which was unable to cope with the extraordinary tasks presented by the war. While making the rounds of the ships, Pyotr Petrovich came to a tugboat which was being armoured. He undertook to help, and kept hammering away until the very evening. After that, a good part of his daily hour at Zaton was spent on this pet tug of his, plying tools which he had once handled very skilfully. With amazing alacrity the authorities accepted the fact that Ragozin was supervising the work at Zaton, and before he knew it they took him to task, declaring that it was a crime to allow the overhauling of the fleet to proceed at such a slow pace. He only pulled slyly at his moustache and said:

"Serves me right, fool that I am—begged myself into the criminal class."

Immediately after the fall of Tsaritsyn, detachments of the river war fleet that had carried on successful operations against Kolchak on the Eastern front were withdrawn from the basin of the Kama and sent to the Lower Volga. This coincided with the taking of the city of Perm by the Red Army.

The ships which arrived in the southern war zone offered artillery support to army units fighting on the banks of the Volga. But along with these units they were forced to retreat first to Kamyshin, and then another hundred and fifty versts to the north. At that time, the fleet which took part in the fighting consisted of some thirty or forty vessels stretching out over a distance of several versts and boasting an artillery of as many as a hundred guns. After the retreat, one of the detachments was again despatched far behind enemy lines for the purpose of smashing Wrangel's rear units. This detachment sent landing parties of sailors to sow panic among the

Whites, and bombarded Kamyshin and Nikolayevskaya Sloboda, causing the forces of Denikin,
then moving on Saratov, to waver.

These operations were accompanied by serious losses. The enemy subjected the river forces
to intensive air raids. A number of the ships had
to be sent up for repairs. At the same time other
ships were being overhauled or remodelled preparatory to being added to the Northern detachment of the Volga war fleet, assigned to the defence of Saratov. The city assumed the appearance
of a sea port, with warships at the docks,
Black Sea and Baltic Sea sailors on the streets,
and a peculiar naval regime unfamiliar to the
peaceful shipping of Volga towns.

The quiet tugs, accustomed from time immemorial to haul strings of barges good-naturedly,
and the barges themselves, with the bailer's wash
strung out on the rudderpole, were hurriedly
transformed into fire-breathing forts. The tugs
were turned into gunboats, the barges into landing craft or vessels for transporting infantry when
forcing the river. Some of the gunboats were formi-
dably armed—the best of them had two four-
inch guns, two three-inch antiaircraft guns, four
machine guns, a radio station and a range finder.

A tug turned into a gunboat lost its innocent
appearance. She flew the flag of the Red Navy.

She no longer tied up at landings, but weighed anchor. The riverman's jargon was supplanted by naval slang. She no longer measured her leisurely progress in age-old versts; miles was what was now entered in her logbook. Nor did observers exclaim admiringly: "Just see how perky she goes!" Oh no. Nowadays she clipped along at a good twelve knots an hour. The place of the skipper who once ruled the bridge was taken by a commander, and even the deck hands now exchanged their former title of rivermen for that of sailors.

There was only one man for whom none of the sailors could substitute on a Volga boat, and this man observed all the military innovations with a glint of amusement in his eye. "Go ahead and have your fun," he seemed to say, "but without me your fine fortress would get stranded in the twinkling of an eye! I'm the only one who knows all the twists and turns, the channels and shallows of Mother Volga." This man was the native-born Volga pilot and it was he who remained the soul of the river fleet, guiding it on perilous ventures through shallow water. Truth to say, in spite of their transformation, the gunboats themselves remained honest tugs at heart, never forgetting for a moment as they energetically splashed their paddles through the water, that they had a draught of something less than two feet and motors of twenty-five horse power.

It was to such a little tug that Ragozin became attached. The boat was named *Risky*, and this pleased Pyotr Petrovich. It had been armoured by volunteers from among the rivermen, and when the sailors came to take it over, they gasped in astonishment. Behind the deck railings a wide bulwark made of ordinary roofing had been raised, and the enclosed space strewn with oakum. Embrasures had been left in this formidable casemate through which rifles and machine guns could be fired. The bow and stern were exposed to accommodate two three-inch field guns on wheels which were in no way fastened to the deck.

"But listen, brothers," protested the sailors, "if you do any firing from this monitor of yours, the oakum will go up in smoke and your bulwark turn somersaults into the water. This is too risky even for the *Risky*. Come on, let's begin all over again."

An order was given to remove the roofing and re-armour the boat. Ragozin arrived when the work was at its height. He was overwhelmed by the enthusiasm of the rivermen—mechanics and sailors, stokers and longshoremen, who first had applied their simple Volga skills to the building of this little fort in defence of the Republic, and now were mercilessly destroying the work of their own hands, in order to rebuild it with newly acquired naval and military skills. It seemed to Ragozin that all his life he had been searching for just this kind of work—work bathed in sweat and blood, work to the point of exhaustion and collapse, work in defence of a truth new-found, whose application was being thwarted by the enemy. But he could not neglect responsibilities from which he had not yet been released, though he curtailed them—not by nine-tenths, or even seven-tenths, as he had threatened, but by some two-tenths—"just a wee mite," as he told himself. And when, after indulging in his beloved labour for a brief hour or so, he emerged through the gates of Zaton guarded by an armed sailor, his brow wet with perspiration, his hands stained with rust and oil, he was not exhausted, but only happily tired, and he felt no trace of irritation at having to return to papers where scarcely a word was to be found among the countless figures whose zeros elevated them to realms of astronomical abstractions.

But one day, on emerging through the gate and climbing into the worn and battered buggy which had served him as transport all summer,

Ragozin had a strange sensation that something was missing, as though he had left something very important behind but was unable to remember what; as though he had been holding something in his hands, and suddenly his hands were empty.

Some street urchins were playing at a ditch alongside of the road. The oldest of them kicked a piece of brick into the ditch, and all the others followed suit. This was not enough for the smallest of them. He took up a heavy brick and, straining with all his might, lifted it above his head and flung it into the ditch. For this feat, obviously designed to win the respect of his elders, they rewarded him with not so much as a glance.

There was something about this young hero which reminded Ragozin of Pavlik Parabukin.

"What if you take that road over the hill?" Ragozin asked the coachman. "It will lead us out onto the Simbirsk Highway, won't it?"

The coachman found no objection to taking the road over the hill, and to his own surprise Ragozin ordered him to do so.

He had not forgotten his decision to search for his son. But it returned to him in spells, now worrying him like an ache in the heart, now subsiding into forgetfulness. About a month ago he had driven out to the monastery settlement with the intention of sounding out the possible whereabouts of his boy. He was haunted by the thought that he was in a reform school. Where else could he be? He had been born in jail, and no doubt placed in an orphans' home. What kind of upbringing could he have had? In all probability he had landed in the streets and become completely demoralized. Might even be a pickpocket. How many such unfortunates hung about the riverbank, the railway stations and the market!

None of the children or the teachers at the reform school had heard of any child named Ragozin. To be sure, one of the teachers who had been there longer than the others seemed to recall a boy whose name sounded something like Remezov or Ragozin. But for some misdemeanour he had been transferred to the Gusyolka School soon after the teacher had arrived. Documents were not kept at the school, most of the old teachers had left, as had the children of older groups, and everything kept changing. The organizations responsible for children's institutions kept vieing among themselves as to which was more competent to supervise juvenile delinquents, for this supervision was simultaneously the task of the People's Commissariats of Education, Health, Justice, and Social Welfare. Naturally it was the easiest thing in the world to lose track of a little boy in such chaos, especially when the very existence of the little boy was questionable.

On leaving the Home, Ragozin met a puffy-faced monk taking a walk in the monastery woods. His eyes were fixed on the ground and he leaned heavily on his staff. On learning from one of the teachers that this was the Bishop, who lived next door, Ragozin thought with some vexation that the ordered tranquillity of ecclesiastical life went on undisturbed, while the devil himself would break a leg in the tangle of children's institutions. Yet priests and bishops were a thing of the past, while the children were of the future. Where was the logic?

Now as he jounced over the monotonous road to the village of Pristannoye, Ragozin recalled all that he had ever heard about the Gusyolka School. The very mention of it had once struck fear to the heart. So famed had Gusyolka been for its cruelty that its name was used to terrorize children into obedience, and anyone reputed to have come from Gusyolka was more feared by grownups than by children.

Soon some dreary stone schoolbuildings loomed into sight. The sparse grass of the yard

93

was protected by a gap-toothed fence enclosing vast grounds. In the distance shone the Volga. The sun-scorched hills of the right bank had turned to ochre.

The road led them into a large orchard and truck garden. Here everything was bright and fresh. It was the hour for watering the trees and plants, and boys and girls in grey shirts and dresses were hoeing about the apple trees. From a distance Ragozin heard their laughter; they seemed lively enough. Apparently the aureole of martyrdom surrounding Gusyolka had dimmed of late.

The director was away, and Ragozin spoke with a very young teacher out in the garden. Without the slightest presumption she declared that she knew as much about the school as the director, because she herself was a product of Gusyolka—had been reformed, and now was reforming others.

"Successfully?" asked Pyotr Petrovich with some scepticism.

"Of course."

When asked about the Ragozin boy she replied with such assurance that Pyotr Petrovich gave little credence to her words:

"He used to be here. He cut loose in the spring."

"What do you mean, cut loose?"

"The way any of them cut loose. I don't remember him very well. He was attached to the workshops, not the gardens."

"Do you remember how old he was?"

"About fourteen."

"Sheer imagination," thought Ragozin to himself, and asked her how to reach the office of the school. She showed him the way—straight ahead, then cut across the lot to the building on the right. But when he had taken only a few steps she called out:

"Only you won't find anybody there. All the office people are digging potatoes today."

He rode away having accomplished nothing at all. Apparently things were all mixed up and he was following a wrong clue. It was necessary to try a different approach, not from below, where the thousands of children looked as like as a school of minnows in a bay, but from above, where some beam could penetrate the mysterious depths and pick out the one little fish he required. The thing was to find this beam. Surely if he searched among archives, record books, statistical data, he would come upon some definite date and number pointing to that neglected, but undoubtedly delightful little chap who was the son of Pyotr Petrovich and his wife Ksana. . . .

Pyotr Petrovich came to the office late, and in a bad mood. There were many people waiting for him. A strange, expostulating couple forced their way into his office out of turn.

"Comrade Ragozin, what is going on here!" cried the man.

"Preposterous!" added the lady.

The male was a student wearing a grey jacket with gold buttons and a panama hat perched on long raven locks that made him look like a Moor. He sat down at the desk without waiting for an invitation, while his Amazon-like companion remained standing. In spite of her youthful face and figure, she bore herself with an air of vast importance.

Their protests were called forth by the fact that for five days they had been waiting for funds urgently demanded by the Department of Public Education for an exhibition of children's work.

"Do you consider five days a long time?" asked Pyotr Petrovich unfeelingly.

"Unheard of!" murmured the girl.

"... Urgent—and you keep us waiting for five days! Almost a week!" exclaimed the student indignantly. "You're jamming the works just when everything is nearly completed!"

"The jam isn't completed," burst out Pyotr Petrovich with a malicious grin.

"What do you wish to imply?... Just because of a few rubles!" observed the student's companion contemptuously, while the student removed his panama hat and shook back his artistic locks.

"The Department of Public Education has sent us, the ones responsible for this exhibition, to get the necessary funds. The exhibition is already hung, but we are unable to open it because we have no money for printing a catalogue and announcements."

"The money belongs to us, not to you. You are merely the cashier," observed the girl again, pronouncing the word "cashier" with the repulsion applied to things reptilian.

"We are opening a city exhibition of children's drawings and sculpture," continued the student insistently, "in order for the first time to demonstrate the achievements of labour schools and other educational...."

"Well, go ahead and open it," interrupted Ragozin. "What's that got to do with me?"

"Oh, so you think it has nothing to do with you? Then where is our money, which you have illegally withheld?" asked the girl angrily.

Ragozin pursed his lips as he answered:

"At present I can't let you have any money for that purpose, and I have no more time to talk about it. Goodbye!"

"Just a minute! All right, we'll do without a catalogue, but at least give us the money to have announcements printed," pleaded the student unexpectedly, his face losing some of its Moorishness as his brow relaxed.

"Print the announcement in the newspaper."

"But—but we don't have the money even for that!"

Ragozin laughed.

"What can I do, comrades?" he said. "Try to understand that there are demands incomparably more urgent than your childish fancies."

"Childish fancies?" exclaimed the stunned young lady, bringing her fists down on the edge of the desk. "You're so busy with your figures that you have no idea of what's going on in the world! You have become isolated from reality like a true bureaucrat!"

Ragozin stared. What was that ruffled little poppycock saying? As though she had a better idea of what was going on in the world than he had! Could it be that he was a—bureaucrat? But he had always had an entirely different idea of a bureaucrat—more potbellied, or at least flashing a gold tooth.

"The only thing you know how to do is to refuse requests," went on the young lady undaunted, "to interfere with revolutionary beginnings. We are founding a school on labour processes, preparing citizens of a new type for our Republic. It would be better if you had a look at our exhibition before you...."

"Don't worry, I'll have a look," Ragozin admonished. "I'll have a look at just what it is you're squandering our precious money on...."

He gave crude reign to his displeasure, and all but put the two of them out.

But there was a certain amusement associated with his recollection of this interview, and he was very much pleased when, a few days later, he received a handmade announcement decorated with red and green lanterns bearing a laboured inscription which he seemed to hear a childish voice reading: "Dear comrade, please come to the opening of our exhibition and see our drawings and sculptures."

"That's a lot prettier than printed announcements," he laughed. "And cleverer, too."

He decided that he would drop in without fail to see what those little tadpoles were up to. If he didn't watch out he might actually become isolated from reality. Once more he laughed and carefully put the invitation into his pocket.

21

The exhibition was held in the Municipal Auditorium in the centre of the city, and the opening evoked considerable discussion in a certain circle. The city had its traditions in art. It boasted a first-class art school and the Radishchev Museum, one of the oldest in the provinces. Artists were trained along European lines: the Museum halls were famous for their canvases of the Barbizon and the Bogolyubov schools. But the years just preceding the revolution had brought a storm of the most radical tendencies, so that the bright and succulent canvases of Borisov-Musatov seemed a bit too spicy in the broth served up by the latest experimentalists. Here were to be found even super-Matisses, who frightened the citizens of Saratov with their geometric puzzles executed mostly in two colours—red and black.

It was in this limited circle of painters that the children's exhibition created a stir. There were two themes on which violent arguments were held. The first concerned the method of teaching art. According to the new method, the teacher receded to the background, while the pupil took the fore. Children were allowed to express their conception of the world in their own childish way. The greatest stress was placed on free imagination. Imitation and copying were anathema, and drawing from life was in no way essential. The second theme .concerned the aims of art. Was it the purpose of art to develop taste, and if so, in what direction? Or perhaps everything depended on how accessible art was to the observer? Those who insisted on the esthetic-educational aims of art became involved in the age-old controversy of conflicting trends. Was the beautiful eternal? What was meant by "the development of art"? Phidias or Rodin? "The World of Art"* or the futurists? Those who claimed that art must be accessible to the general understanding were drowned in a sea of contempt: "What do you mean by the general understanding?" they were asked. "The soap wrappers of Brokar and Co. are as understandable as the canvases of the *Peredvizhniki*.** Where are you leading the younger generation?"

* The World of Art—A group of St. Petersburg artists who, from 1899 to 1904 published a magazine called *The World of Art*. This magazine was reactionary in tendency, supporting the theory of "art for art's sake."
** *Peredvizhniki*—Artists belonging to the "Association for Holding Travelling Exhibitions," the aim of which was to bring art to the masses. It was organized during the second half of the nineteenth century by such outstanding artists as Kramskoi, Repin, Perov and Surikov, who supported a realistic, democratic trend in art.

DEPARTMENT OF SLAVIC LANGUAGES
HAMILTON HALL, COLUMBIA UNIVERSITY
NEW YORK, NEW YORK 10027

In the end this handful of philosophers was lost in the crowd of people who had come to the opening simply because they wanted to know what was going on in the schools and whether the drawings of children could possibly be interesting.

Ragozin was amazed to find so many people. To be sure, most of them, like himself, had dropped in for just a minute. People had no time for such things these days. The war was knocking at the gates of the city, and here were grown-up people frittering their time away.

But he was even more amazed by the strange visual impression made by the large, light hall, with its walls splashed with colour.

He began to examine the pictures. At first glance they represented the usual drawings so familiar to those who have raised children— little houses with smoke pouring out of the chimneys, and surrounded by fences and trees, dogs and carts. Suns resembling sieves through which cranberries have been strained. Stars like snowflakes. Inky little men carrying tomato-red banners. War: flames spouting from the nozzles of guns and purple smoke enveloping the whole picture. More war: cavalrymen galloping on hornless white goats. Again war: a dead man stretched on turquoise grass with a letter at his elbow containing the words printed in infinitesimal letters: "From your son, Volodia."

Ragozin was used to seeking for the idea expressed in a picture. Here he was attracted by something else. Suddenly two similar pictures revealed to him what this something was. He saw a lemon-coloured camel standing in a desert as pink as diluted wine. A great sadness breathed from the picture. All the hopelessness of the desert and the loneliness of the animal was expressed in that combination of pink and yellow. In the next picture a crimson Arabian steed with a long neck was scaling a brown cliff. The horse was racing at an angle almost vertical, but the strength expressed in the crimson and brown left no doubt that it could scale the very heaven. This colour, which the little artist had transformed into light, was deeply emotional.

Ragozin went closer to these exceptional drawings and read the bold signature in the right-hand corner: *Ivan Ragozin.*

He stood looking at the camel and the horse and kept reading the signature and felt his hands and feet going numb, so that he was unable to move a step. A dreadful fear was born in his soul in that moment. Why had he always been so certain that Ksana had born him a son? Why had he kept telling himself that he must search for a son? Perhaps if he had searched for a daughter, he would have found her long ago.

But his eyes, smarting with strain, would see nothing but the signature beneath the horse and the camel. Everything around him became crimson-brown, yellow-pink, and against that ecstasy of light and colour he saw that name in firm, unwavering letters—Ivan Ragozin. His son was alive. He lived near by. From the wall of this exhibition he was extending his little paint-stained hand to his father. He was a capable child— perhaps even a talented child. Naturally. How could the son of Pyotr Petrovich and Ksana be anything but talented?

Kirill Izvekov made his way quickly through the crowd and took Ragozin by the elbow as he said loudly:

"What do you think of it? Isn't it fine?"

"Yes," replied Ragozin so mechanically that his voice seemed to come to him from the next room.

Suddenly he caught sight of Dorogomilov waving his rasping cuffs amid an encirclement of little boys. Among them was Pavlik's red head. Ragozin forced himself to move, grabbed the child by the hand and led him to the two pictures.

"Look. Do you like them?"

"Ahuh," said Pavlik. "Only the horse isn't real. I know who drew them. Pauper Painter."

"Why Pauper?" asked Pyotr Petrovich, offended. "How do you know?"

"Him and I hang out around the piers together, and along the riverbank. The fellows call him Pauper Painter. He paints all the time. He showed us his pictures. He has better horses than that one."

"All right. Now come here," said Ragozin, pushing Pavlik toward the drawings. "Read what's written there."

Pavlik read the signature and looked enquiringly at Ragozin.

"The same as yours," he said absent-mindedly.

"Is that his name?"

"He could sign any name he liked, I guess. But it's his work all right!"

"I want you to bring him to see me. Will you promise?"

"Where'll I find him? He's from a Home."

"Which one?"

"How do I know? He never told me."

"But you'll see him down at the river, won't you? Where's your meeting place? Give me your word that you'll bring him to me."

At that moment an old man in a disreputable pongee coat with bulging pockets stepped between Pavlik and Ragozin. He smiled broadly:

"I beg your pardon, Comrade Ragozin, but I should like to hear your impressions of the exhibition. For the newspaper. I sign my articles U. M. Perhaps you have read them?"

"Ah yes," said Ragozin in all seriousness. "Well, you may write that, as a well-known specialist in the field of painting, I consider this exhibition an event of great historical significance in the development of the new art."

Mertsalov dropped the hand holding his notebook. The parchment skin of his bald pate crept slowly toward his lifted brows.

"That should make a good article for you. It seems you are a very politically-minded journalist. Wasn't that your article which recently appeared under the title: 'Where Can One Buy a Fret Saw'?"

Mertsalov's mouth opened even wider, but his glance expressed anger and insult.

"Or maybe I'm mistaken?" cried Ragozin, moving up close to Mertsalov and suddenly adding in exasperation: "It was you who published that nonsense about Pastukhov having spread revolutionary leaflets, wasn't it? Well, do you happen to know that Pastukhov has run off to the Whites? You ought to be put off the paper. You're a...."

He turned away sharply without saying what he was, and immediately forgot all about Mertsalov. In searching for Pavlik in the crowd, he came upon the Amazon-like young lady who had argued with him about the money. He asked her to come over to the drawings of Ivan Ragozin.

"Do you know that little rascal?"

"Aren't they fine?" she asked triumphantly, throwing back her head with an expression which seemed to say, "I told you so!"

"Yes. Could you tell me how to get in touch with the artist?"

"I'm very glad that you're capable of distinguishing the good from the mediocre. Do you feel the noble simplicity of that line?" She energetically ran her thumb along the mane, spine, and tail of the crimson horse. "That is better than a folk drawing, because it is more lucid and generalized than a folk drawing. Do you realize that here we are at the very fountainhead of art, unsullied by various influences?"

"Yes, I understand all that," said Ragozin impatiently, "but there's one thing I don't understand: why don't you answer my question?

You have hung up all these pictures splendidly, but you don't seem to give a fig for who did them."

"All the work on this wall is by children in Homes. If you wish, I shall find out about the child who drew the pictures you are interested in."

"That's it. Those very pictures. That very artist. Do find out, my dear, and as soon as possible."

He shook her hand vigorously, and she flashed him her first smile.

"How about our money?"

"Can't do a thing about that money," replied Ragozin, also smiling. "Why do you need money now? Everything's done. And done very well."

He kept repeating this phrase as he hurried out, no longer noticing either people or pictures.

From that moment on everything seemed to come to a standstill for him, as though braked by the question: had he found his son or not?

Two days later, as he was returning from Zaton, he saw two little boys standing at the entrance of the Soviet. They were leaning against the fence of the front yard and chewing sunflower seeds. He immediately recognized Pavlik, and as immediately sensed who was with him.

"We've been waiting ever so long," said Pavlik reproachfully.

"Come along," said Pyotr Petrovich, forcing himself to move calmly.

Once they were in the office, he walked from corner to corner, deliberating what would be best: to seat the boys next to him, to have them stand while he sat down, or to have them sit down while he walked about. "What difference does it make, damn it all?" he thought, still pacing the floor. Suddenly he realized that he was having difficulty making himself look at the boy whom Pavlik had brought. He immediately came to a halt directly in front of them and tried smiling cordially. Pavlik glanced indifferently about him. The other boy remained imperturbable. His tousled blond head was high-browed, his eyebrows turned sharply upward at the temples, his brown eyes were round and prominent. He was thin, with long arms and legs, and he stood with his elbows out, as though ready to strike back.

"So it was—*your* pictures I saw?" asked Ragozin, conscious that he was not saying what he would like to.

"I don't know."

The boy's voice was roughly self-assured.

"Those pictures, now ... the one with that red horse. ..."

"Sure, it was your horse," said Pavlik. "What are you afraid of? Pyotr Petrovich liked it."

"Who said I was afraid?"

"I don't bite," said Ragozin, as though seeking favour. "It's true that I liked them. Very bright and nice ... and all that. ... What's your name?"

"Ivan."

"Ivan Ragozin, isn't it? And how old are you? Soon be ten?"

"Maybe even more."

"More," asserted Pavlik. "I'm almost eleven, and he's stronger than me."

"Really?" said Pyotr Petrovich as though in relief. "Let's see."

He gently touched the puny, childish biceps, and his fingers involuntarily lingered there until the boy freed himself and took a step backwards.

"Vanya," said Ragozin slowly. "Hm-m. Have you a father?"

"Must of had one," answered the boy with the cynical smile of a grownup.

"I suppose so," said Pyotr Petrovich awkwardly, and again began to pace the floor.

"Remember your mother?" he asked without stopping.

"My father probably does," said Vanya even more cynically.

He stood sidewise to Ragozin, his head thrown back and his elbows protruding more than ever. It was clear that he was used to being asked about his father and mother, and therefore had his answers ready. Pyotr Petrovich was taken aback by the boy's harshness. He was annoyed that he had such poor control of himself, and glanced angrily at the child. As he did so, he was struck by the exact resemblance his profile bore to Ksana—the same sharp little turned-up nose, the same round and prominent eyes. He almost cried out "My son! My son!"—words which all this time had been straining at the tip of his tongue; but he held them back.

"What did you have me come here for?"

"To make your acquaintance. A closer acquaintance," said Pyotr Petrovich, noticing the boy's faded grey shirt, the string serving as a belt for his pants, and the rundown heels of his shoes.

"Do you buy pictures?" Vanya asked suddenly.

"What's that?"

"I thought you were ... one of those who wanted to buy pictures from the exhibition."

"Are you selling yours?" asked Ragozin with a smile.

"A little cash'd come in handy."

"Come in handy for what? I thought you lived in a Home."

"Depends on the season. Now it's warm everywhere."

"And where do you get your meals?"

"Meals!" scoffed Vanya with a shrug of his shoulders. "What do you think I am, a boarder, to be eating meals?"

"You can always get enough to eat down by the Volga," said Pavlik with the air of an experienced ranger of the riverbank.

"At the fleet headquarters or some other place," added Vanya.

"Or at Gusyolka—seems you were there once too?" put in Pyotr Petrovich deliberately and unexpectedly.

Vanya frowned.

"Why don't you answer me? Were you at Gusyolka?"

"What if I was? They pinned the snitching of some slippers from the Home on me. Said I sold them at the market, so they took me to court. But some rat stole them from me, only I didn't want to squeal."

"All right. Let bygones be bygones. Where are you living now?"

Vanya folded his arms and slowly turned

his head toward the door, as though he were finding these questions boring.

"They're taking me back at the Home," he answered reluctantly. "Sent my papers there already."

"I see," said Pyotr Petrovich quickly. "Very well. Only I was going to suggest that you come live with me. I'm all alone, and we could have a good time together. You'd go to school ... and paint ... and all that sort of thing, understand?"

Vanya made no reply. Pavlik squinted at Ragozin and gave a low whistle.

"Phe-e-w! Don't I know something though!"

"There's nothing you could know!" Ragozin almost shouted. "I'm just making a sensible suggestion."

He stepped over to Vanya and placed his hands on his shoulders.

"Come back here this evening—all right?" he said gently. "Or if you'd rather, come right to my house—all right?"

He explained where he lived, trying to catch the boy's evasive glance. Pavlik watched Vanya suspiciously, as though fearing that the latter would succumb to temptation or violate some prearranged agreement.

"Here, let's shake on it: I'll be seeing you this evening," said Pyotr Petrovich insistently.

"Have to think it over," said Pavlik in the manner of a merchant wangling his price.

"I'll think *you* over!" threatened Ragozin, half jokingly.

But presently he was taken aback by Vanya's point-blank question:

"Why do you want me to live with you?"

Ragozin could not think of an answer on the spur of the moment, and in order to hide the hurt that rose in his heart, he slapped Vanya roughly on the back and said:

"Get old too soon if you know too much. Come around this evening and I'll tell you. That's enough for the present. Get along now."

He closed the door after the boys, but immediately opened it again and called to Vanya:

"Here, wait a minute!" He fumbled through his pockets and pushed some crumpled bills into Vanya's fist, saying: "Take this and buy yourself something to eat. But be sure to come this evening, hear?"

Cautiously he stood with his ear to the door, as though he could distinguish the boys' steps along the corridor and down the stairs. But he only calculated in his mind the time it would take them to reach the street, and then, without a moment's delay, rushed downstairs, jumped into his buggy, and urged the coachman to drive the horse on and on over an endless road.

When they finally reached the Home on the monastery grounds, Ragozin had them look up the papers belonging to Ivan Ragozin. A folder marked "Personal Documents" contained recommendations written by the boy's teachers, conclusions drawn by medical and school commissions, a decision passed by the Rights of Minors Department concerning Ivan Ragozin's selling of slippers belonging to the Home, and other impressive papers. Ragozin quickly listed through them and immediately forgot them, until he came to a worn, yellow paper bearing the tsar's crest and the seal of the Ministry of Home Affairs.

Ragozin's eyes bore into this paper in his search for one all-decisive word, but at that instant he could not have told what this word was. He rose and tried to read the paper standing, but once more he sat down. Taking his head in his hands, he forced himself to read it line by line.

The office of the prison addressed its crested paper to the orphan asylum on Asylum Street, sending along with the paper a male infant, to be fed and raised at public expense. The mother of the infant was one Ksenia Ragozina, a resident of Saratov, who had been arrested and put in jail, where she died of childbirth; according to the mother, the father of the child was her legal husband Pyotr Petrovich Ragozin, son of a peasant, accused of a crime against the state but never caught. The child had been baptized in the prison church and given the name of Ivan.

The infant Ivan now rose in the mind of Ragozin as a wide-browed boy with round eyes, and the feel of the warm, soft muscles of this boy's arm was still in Ragozin's fingertips.

"I am taking this boy to raise," said Ragozin to the girl who watched him leaf through the papers.

"Before becoming a child's guardian it is necessary to obtain permission from the Rights of Minors Department," answered the girl.

"What do you mean, guardian?"

"Do you wish to adopt the child?"

"I am his father," said Ragozin with happy, almost ecstatic challenge in his voice as he drew himself up to full height.

"That makes no difference. If you wish...."

"And it makes no difference to me what you wish to call me—the child's guardian or patron, or anything else. What must I do in order to get him?"

"Apply to the Department of Public Education. There they have a Social Rights De ..."

"Or maybe some other department?" cried Ragozin unceremoniously. "They haven't got the child, have they? I have him! Do you understand? I found him, understand? Found my son! Phooh, you and your departments!"

He jovially slapped the girl on the arm and rushed out to the buggy. He rode home, gave his landlady money and orders to prepare supper, and went back to the office. All the rest of the day he had the feeling that something was undone: he tried to remember whether he had forgotten to order something from the market, and made enquiries as to whether he could buy any food in the dining room of the office. He left the office early.

Vanya had not yet arrived. Pyotr Petrovich examined every dish, reset the table according to his own taste, took some bedding out of the clothes basket, and with the help of his landlady dragged a mattress into the room. Then he sat down at the table, figuring out what else he could do. Several times he walked over to the window, and even ran down to the gate. That night he could not sleep, and blamed himself for having let the child go away when he might have brought him straight to his room.

On the following morning he stayed away from Zaton for the first time. He realized that he had made a mistake in not asking for Pavlik's address, so that he might find out from him where to search for Vanya. This mistake could be corrected with the aid of Dorogomilov, and Ragozin himself was surprised that he had not thought of enlisting the invaluable services of Arseni Romanovich in the search for Vanya.

Dorogomilov was amazed and delighted by the story of the father and son. He recalled the remarkable pictures at the exhibition and the stories his little friends had told him about Pauper Painter. He assured Ragozin that the search for the boy fitted right in with his plans, and he would immediately do everything in his power to find him.

And sure enough, when Ragozin came home during his dinner hour to see whether Vanya had put in his appearance, his landlady met him joyfully with the news that the boy had come about an hour before; she had fed him and he had fallen asleep.

Pyotr Petrovich cautiously opened the door to his room and squeezed himself through it. He tiptoed over to the window sill and sat down.

Vanya was lying on the mattress in the middle of the floor. Pyotr Petrovich studied him

avidly. Flies were crawling over the child's bare feet, but he was sleeping too soundly to notice them. Cuts and scratches could be seen on his dirt-encrusted soles. The tips of his toes were squarish. Suddenly Ragozin recognized his own feet in those squarish toes and flattish instep. He came closer and examined Vanya's hands. The knuckles were slightly enlarged, the nails rather small and fanning out at the tips. They were a perfect duplicate of Pyotr Petrovich's hands, an exact copy on a smaller scale. It was strange to see how, for some reason, Nature kept reproducing old patterns, maintaining established forms on the earth. Vanya's face more nearly resembled that of Ksana, especially when his eyes were closed. Ksana had looked just as gentle and somehow meditative when she slept.

Pyotr Petrovich felt thirsty. He went over to the pail and accidentally banged the dipper. He glanced around quickly. Vanya was sleeping as soundly as ever. Ragozin covered him with the sheet, waved a towel to drive the flies out of the room, and hung a blanket over the window.

How would he open the conversation when Vanya awoke? He would say: "You are my son." And the son would ask his father: "Why have you come only now?" Then the father would have to tell him how he had been persecuted by the police, and how the boy's mother had died. And the son would say: "You saved yourself; why didn't you save my mother?" "It wasn't myself I saved," the father would answer, "but the great cause I served." "But you knew I was to be born. Why didn't you try to find me?" "Because that would have been to the detriment of the great cause." And the son would say: "That means you love the cause more than me. Why do you want me now? You went on living without me. I went on living without you. Why do you want me now?"

He would have to think very carefully about how to guide the conversation. Very carefully. The greatest danger lay in the possibility of frightening his son away. What did a father mean to a child who was used to considering himself alone in the world? Only too well did Vanya know the meaning of an overseer, the law of his elders, the ruthless ignoring of his own inclinations. Such knowledge had been hard pressed on him long before this utterly unknown, baldheaded man whom perhaps the boy found unpleasant, turned up and began to call him son. But his father should arouse emotions which none of his teachers were capable of arousing. His father should be an example to him, and a joy.

Ragozin quietly left the room. He wanted to buy his son some paints and a notebook while the latter slept. He told his landlady not to let the child leave the house if he woke up.

The first store had neither paints nor notebooks. Ragozin went to the centre of town. He was in a great hurry. Every thought that came into his mind was unexpectedly new, and his thoughts seemed to be in even a greater hurry than he himself. He discovered that up to now he had never considered the matter of child education. Oh, to be sure he had considered it, but only to the extent he had considered many other matters. It was one of the many questions which had been abstractly settled more or less satisfactorily. But at present Ragozin was faced with the necessity of constructing not a theory, but a plan of behaviour—his behaviour as a father. And this behaviour must be such that his son should find in it an answer to the question as to how he himself should behave. Naturally the education of children was the responsibility of society. A child would inevitably imitate the behaviour of the society in which he lived. And it would take time to build a society worthy of imitation. But Ragozin could not say to his son: "Wait a bit, son, we shall build examples worthy of your imitation, and then you will know how to behave. At present we are fighting a war for your future, and therefore we have no time to think of you. But as soon as we win, we shall give you our attention." That would be the same as saying: "You just stop growing for a while." Of course it was necessary to give a child everything needed for his development right now.

In the second store Ragozin was told that he was not likely to find paints anywhere, for there was a deficit in things of much more importance than paints. As for the notebook, he might be able to find one in a third store, where it seemed they had received a stock not long before.

Once out in the street, Ragozin could not immediately pick up his train of thought. Ah yes, he had been thinking that first of all it was necessary to clearly decide on the aims of education. For example, a Soviet citizen should prove himself worthy of his native land no matter where he found himself. Therefore this sense of worthiness should be nurtured in him every day, so that it should become a normal attribute from earliest years, remaining intact despite humdrum relationships. Or again, the Red

Army is trained to a feeling of brotherhood between commanders and the rank and file, to a sense of loyalty and mutual responsibility in battle. Apparently the school should cultivate a sense of comradeship, the home a sense of friendship, daily life a sense of courtesy, good manners, and consideration for others. Hold on there, said Ragozin to himself. Good manners? But that smacks of dead conventions. Friendship in general? Friendship as a cult? What hangover is that? On the other hand, is it possible to develop this great spiritual quality in a child if friendship is inspired only in individual cases, for definite purposes, with particular intentions? This problem must be settled before his son began making friends. It must be settled this very moment, before Vanya woke up. Perhaps the boy had already awakened? He must hurry. He must be prepared to answer any question his son faced him with. He must think of him—think for him. That was what he must do.

There were neither paints nor notebooks in the third store. "How do you expect to find any notebooks now, when the schools are on vacation?" Ragozin was asked.

Had he only dreamed that the walls of the children's exhibition had been hung with sheets of paper daubed with paint? The exhibition was only a stone's throw away, and Ragozin decided to drop in.

There he found his acquaintances—the moorish student and the young Amazon. They were having an argument, but turned a united front to Ragozin when he entered. He told them of his predicament. They replied that there was nothing to get excited about, everything was as it should be—paints and notebooks were distributed through the schools and Children's Homes, and the children were adequately supplied.

"But that's not enough," protested Ragozin. "What about homework, home drawing?"

"With our children, 'home' is a conception that will eventually die out," said the student.

"Homework is an old-fashioned teaching method," said the young lady.

"All of that requires discussion, and I should like to be brief: where can I buy paints for my son?"

"We're not in business," said the young lady testily.

"We are trying to destroy the sense of private property in children, and are against making children presents, like spoiled little darlings," said the student.

"One thing's certain," answered Ragozin, turning abruptly to the door, "you either know too much, or not nearly enough!"

He kept increasing his speed as he strode down the street on his long legs. Vanya must have awakened already. Presently Ragozin would see him. Unquestionably the most vulnerable spot for a child like Vanya would be his sense of freedom. His father must show that he had no designs on it. Nor must he probe deeply into his son's life, asking, questioning, trying to find out what was most dear to the heart of Vanya. On the contrary, he must first lead him confidently into his own life, telling him about his work, his struggle, and his vision of the future.

Suddenly Ragozin checked his steps. A fine beginning! Already he had neglected going to Zaton and to the office in order to run about town in search of some gewgaws. How could he explain that to Vanya? "I just let my social duties go hang today, son. I'm so glad to see you I can't even think of work." "In other words," his son would say, "if a person's awfully glad, he can let his duties go hang?"

Pyotr Petrovich was as embarrassed by this question as though Vanya had actually asked it. But after all, today was an exception. The only one in his whole life. And the lost time would be made up for with a vengeance. Now, as ever, work came first with Ragozin.

He turned the corner in order to tell them at the office that he would be detained another hour or so.

Suddenly a man walking in front of him (a rather clumsy person he looked to Ragozin) fell down. Apparently it was difficult for him to rise, and Pyotr Petrovich went to his aid.

"Thank you. It's nothing much. Slipped on a watermelon rind. There it is."

"Hurt yourself?"

"Just a trifle. My elbow," said the man, brushing off his white coat.

He glanced gratefully at Ragozin and gave a start.

"Well, this is a coincidence! It was you I was going to see! How do you do, Comrade Ragozin."

Pyotr Petrovich recognized Oznobishin.

"Why were you coming to see me? I am very busy."

"On a personal matter. I shan't take much of your time. If you wish, I can tell you right here, just stepping away from the entrance."

"About your affairs?"

"No, about yours," replied Oznobishin confidently.

"Mine?"

They moved away from the entrance and walked slowly past the front yard.

"Only I beg you to be brief."

"Only two words. First of all I want to thank you for your solicitude, as a result of which a misunderstanding was removed which had placed me in a very precarious position."

"But you actually were the Public Prosecutor, weren't you?"

"If I had been," smiled Oznobishin, "it is doubtful that I would be talking to you now—at least out here in the street. That is why I wanted to thank you for taking the trouble to remove those suspicions about my past."

"But what has that to do with my affairs?"

"You did not say so in so many words, but I gathered that you were greatly interested in learning the fate of your wife, and especially— whether or not she had given birth to a child, and if the child were alive."

"Ah," said Ragozin, coming to a halt.

"At that time I did not dare offer my services, but I swore to myself that I would do everything in my power to help you."

"Well?"

"After the most painstaking search I managed to find a document which throws light on

127

circumstances which, while being tragic, at the same time suggest the possibility of a happy ending. This document is now accessible. You may procure it."

"Where?"

"At the archives."

"Just what is the document?"

"Unfortunately it is a confirmation of the fact that your wife died in jail. It even indicates the place of her burial."

"Really?"

"Yes. But at the same time the document states that she died of childbirth, and accordingly that you have—or at any rate, there must have been a child."

"You don't say!" said Ragozin.

"However that may be, I can confidently assert that I have fallen upon the trail of your child."

"That's interesting. And where does it lead?"

"This will require further effort, which I shall be only too glad to exert if I have your support."

"Support for what?"

"For continuing the search."

"If I give it to you, can I be sure that you will follow up the trail?"

"Unquestionably!" exclaimed Oznobishin with something like inspiration. "I shall accept it as a matter of honour. I shall begin with the jail archives, with the year of the child's birth."

"And if I tell you that the trail will lead you directly to my apartment?"

"What apartment?"

"The apartment in which I live with my son."

"With your ... you mean to say you have found...."

Oznobishin seemed almost frightened. The colour faded from his cheeks, he raised his hands, and began to cautiously rub his injured elbow. But presently he leaned toward Ragozin and said with a sigh of relief:

"Congratulations! From the bottom of my heart! Is it possible? Have you really found your son? The very one who...."

"The very one," interrupted Ragozin. "But may I ask what has prompted you to go to all this trouble?"

"My only reason has been ... to be of service to you. To show my gratitude."

"There is nothing to be grateful for."

"I should be happy simply to serve you."

"That is not an easy thing to do. I don't accept services."

Ragozin raised his hand to his temple, bowed, and walked over to the entrance, turning on the steps to say with a short laugh:

"Slipped ... on a watermelon rind!"

As he ran up the steps he was met by one of the clerks from his department.

"Have you been to the Party Committee? They sent for you."

Without going up to his own office, Ragozin walked to the end of the corridor on the first floor.

He was greeted by that same member of the Committee Bureau with whom he had argued about how Lenin's letter was to be interpreted.

"Well, your wish has been fulfilled," said the member with a nod. "It has been decided to assign you to a military post. You are to be the division commissar of the Volga fleet. You know something about the situation there, don't you?"

"A little," answered Ragozin, sinking down onto a chair. "When am I to leave?"

"Call up the Military Commissar. The Division Commissar has fallen ill and you are to take his place. The fleet is expected to set out tomorrow."

"Tomorrow?"

There was hesitation in Ragozin's voice, and he glanced aside as he said:

"What about my department?"

"Why worry about that? You'll hand over everything to your assistant."

"In just a few hours?"

"I don't know. Maybe in just a few minutes. The Whites are at Lesnoy Karamysh."

"Well, goodbye then," said Ragozin, rising heavily.

"You sound disappointed."

"You're all wrong!"

"Well then, wish you luck!"

They shook hands.

Ragozin phoned the Military Commissar and was told to come immediately for his papers. He sent for his buggy and told the coachman to first drive to his house.

He purposely made a lot of noise on entering his room in order to wake up Vanya. The blanket he had fastened over the window before leaving was hanging from a single nail. The mattress was empty and the sheet thrown in a heap on the floor.

Ragozin turned to his landlady. She made a helpless gesture. She had heard Vanya get up and take a drink of water, and she had wanted to give him some tea, but when she looked into the room he had disappeared. She could not say whether he had gone through the door or climbed out the window. Her only fear was that he had stolen something.

Pyotr Petrovich shot her a reproving look, but involuntarily glanced about. Everything was in its place.

For a minute he remained in the room. It had become strangely empty and unfamiliar, as though he had never lived in it. He clearly saw that his entire behaviour had been a mistake: he should have told Vanya everything as soon as they met. Had the child guessed that he had acquired a father? What would become of him now? Could it be that everything was over forever?

Ragozin carefully folded the wrinkled sheet and put it under the pillow on his bed.

"Probably I shall be leaving unexpectedly," he told his landlady with some agitation. "For a time. I have one thing to ask you: if that boy comes back, please don't turn him away, but help him make himself at home. In my room. He's a good chap and should be looked after. You can be sure that I shall repay you for anything you do. Goodbye."

He ran out into the street and ordered the coachman to drive as he had never driven in his life.

At the office of the Military Commissar he was commissioned to the staff of the northern detachment of the Volga fleet. At staff head-quarters he was ordered to report at six o'clock the next morning to the gunboat *October,* which, at the head of the division, was anchored beyond the sands.

Ragozin spent that evening and the whole night turning over the affairs of the Finance Department to his successor. He drove down to the river directly from the office, which was now a thing of the past for him and could be dismissed from his mind just as he had dismissed many of his former jobs.

A navy launch took him to the Volga proper. He climbed on board the *October,* where he was met by the sentry on duty. An hour later he and the division commander began an inspection of the four vessels drawn up in a line along the sandy banks of the islands. The last of them was the gunboat *Risky.* The tug looked very pugnacious with its smokestack clipped off and the armour encircling the deck narrowed and painted grey-green, like the water. Although the crew consisted almost entirely of navy men, Ragozin met a few natives of the Volga with whom he had worked at Zaton, and this meeting with familiar faces on a familiar ship not only overjoyed Ragozin, but caused the sailors to tacitly accept him as "one of us." The news soon spread that the commissar himself had helped overhaul one of the ships in the division, and that this commissar could handle any workman's tool you put in his hand.

At noon a meeting of the division staff was held in the deck cabin, and for the first time in his life Pyotr Petrovich Ragozin saw how a war map was read and held a compass in his fingers. Then the commissars of the various ships made reports to him.

Towards evening, numb with exhaustion, he went out on deck, where for the first time he noticed the Volga, though he had been on it all day long.

The river was smooth and rosy, with the lowlands of the left bank gradually fading from pink to gold, while still farther away the granaries of Pokrovsk humped yellow in the sun like a caravan of camels.

Suddenly Ragozin had a vivid memory of a yellow camel standing in a pink desert—the drawing which had so moved him. In other words, such things actually could be seen—such colours, such emptiness, and—was it really possible?—such hopelessness. He felt a strange pulsing of his heart. It was time to rest; he had not closed his eyes for two nights at a stretch. Due to the inexplicable faculty of the mind to conjure several visions at once, the memories of his son expressed in that pink-yellow tone were accompanied by another memory: in the Neopolitan yellow of the sand and the rosy surface of the water, Ragozin recognized a repetition of that sunset hour when his and Kirill's fishing trip had been interrupted by the motorboat rushing to take them back to the city. Now he again clearly saw that motorboat, and rubbed his eyes, thinking that exhaustion was causing hallucinations. But on opening his eyes he even more distinctly saw the motorboat, which was cleaving golden wedges in the waves, like a double ploughshare.

"What's that, a motorboat?" he asked the sentry.

"Yes it is, Comrade Commissar."

The boat quickly approached, growing ever larger and noisier. At last it swung into a wide circle and sidled up to the *October*. The gunboat let down a gangplank, and Ragozin gazed at the man who climbed agilely up on deck.

"Kirill!" he cried, and ran over to him.

They met on the lower deck near the engine room and embraced there in that narrow passage filled with the smell of gasoline and burning oil. Ragozin led Kirill to his cabin. They looked deep into each other's eyes and smiled quietly in their joy. Ragozin's weariness vanished like a dream.

"What's that you have there?" he asked.

Kirill was holding a market basket.

"Mother's doings," he answered in some embarrassment. "I told her yesterday that you were leaving."

"Make me feel like a hospital patient on visiting day," laughed Ragozin.

"Don't be silly."

Kirill fumbled around in the basket until he pulled out a bottle, at which they both laughed again. They sat shoulder to shoulder on the narrow bunk as they poured out the wine and arranged the golden-brown *pirozhki* on a newspaper. They drank without a toast, merely nodding to each other, and as they chewed the *pirozhki* they glanced through the open porthole at the fiery mirror of the water, which seemed from this angle to stand higher than their heads, while the movement of the river seemed a hundred times swifter than it actually was.

"Leaving tonight?" asked Kirill.

"At midnight."

"I was afraid I might be late."

"You're not one to be late," said Ragozin, placing his palm on Kirill's knee.

"How do you like that—a civilian like you, beating me to it!"

"What's your hurry? Your time will come. They're keeping you for the most important job."

"What's most important? The task of every hour is the most important."

"That's right. The main task and then secondary tasks. The main one has to be taken care of immediately, while the secondary ones can wait."

Ragozin said this with a thoughtful concentration that made Kirill glance at him sharply.

"What's on your mind?"

Ragozin jumped up and stretched himself as was his habit, but the ceiling of the cabin was even lower than at home, and he struck his fists hard against it.

"Damn it all!" he cried, once more laying his hand on Izvekov's knee and pressing it tightly. "There *is* something on my mind. You'll forgive me I know—maybe I ought not to think about it now, but... I didn't have time to tell you. I've found my son."

Kirill looked at him in amazement.

"Yes, my son. Mine and Ksenia Afanasyevna's. She gave birth to him in jail. I found out quite recently."

"Where is he?"

"He ... you see I found him, but not entirely. He still has to be looked for. But that'll be easy, very easy." In his eagerness, Ragozin swung his whole body around to face Kirill. "If you could only do it. I had no time to arrange things. Something else came up, understand? I had just found him when...."

"I can't make head or tail out of what you're saying."

"Remember Pavlik Parabukin? He's a friend of his. Tell Pavlik to ... or even better, tell Dorogomilov that you're looking for Ivan Ragozin, understand? He'll do everything. He's got all the little boys in his hip pocket. You just go to him and tell him.... All right?"

Kirill had never seen Ragozin like this before. Pyotr Petrovich's face was a study in contradictions. He was so clearly torn between desperate resolve and apologetic entreaty that Kirill could not bear to look at him.

He pulled Ragozin's head down to his shoulder and said with feeling:

"I understand everything and will do everything. Don't worry. I shall find the boy and take him to live with me—that is, with me and Vera Nikandrovna. And I shall answer to you for him. That is, mother and I will. Are you satisfied? And get rid of the notion that this is a trifle, something of secondary importance. I consider this just as much a main task as that other main task for the sake of which you are leaving at midnight. And you can go off on that task with an easy heart, fighting now for your son as well as for the cause. And come back as soon as possible."

They continued sitting there and talking, calmly now, and it was dusk when they had their parting drink.

As they went past the engine room, along the narrow passageway to the gangplank, they met a titan of a sailor. He was slightly taller than Ragozin and so broad in the chest that he almost barred the way, even though he pressed his back against the wall. As Kirill squeezed past he looked into his face, which was almost on a level with the electric ceiling light; the orange glow illuminated prominent cheekbones, an exceptional solidity of forehead, and a scattering of freckles about the nose. The sailor smiled slightly, and the composure of his smile struck Kirill as familiar. He immediately recalled the sailor from Archangel whom he had met while visiting Dibich in the convalescent home, and he too smiled.

"Comrade Strashnov?"

"Are you coming along with us, Comrade

Izvekov?" asked the sailor, with a broad pronunciation of his "o's."

"I just came for a visit, but my friend here, Comrade Ragozin, is to be your chief. Take care of him."

"Do our best," replied the sailor.

"We'll hold you responsible if anything happens to him," said Kirill with a laugh.

"You can count on us."

"Good," answered Kirill, remembering that the sailor had said the same thing in the convalescent home, and that on taking leave of him, Kirill had felt refreshed, as though after setting-up exercises.

"Feeling all right now?"

"Forgot which side was hurt."

Kirill smiled and shook the sailor's hand.

After again saying goodbye to Pyotr Petrovich, he climbed down into the boat and cried out "Good Luck!", but the noise of the engine prevented his catching an answer.

For a long time Ragozin stood gazing at the receding light on the bow of the motorboat. It had become quite dark already, and the water had turned brown-black. The peaceful lights of the gunboats made corrugated reflections on its surface. The boats stood motionless. Here on the river the coolness of the August evening made

itself felt. More than two hours remained before midnight. It was necessary to get some
sleep. Ragozin returned to his cabin.

* 22 *

Under the trying circumstances in which the
Red Army found itself as a result of the spring
and summer advance of Denikin, the command
of the Southern front, in accordance with the
orders of the Commander-in-Chief, worked out
a plan of counteroffensive. The main idea of the
plan was to deliver the Whites a stunning blow
with the left flank of the forces comprising the
Southern front. These were to cross the Don
steppes in the general direction of Tsaritsyn and
Novorossiisk. With that aim in view, the two
armies which were joined to form the striking
force were assigned the main task of advancing
on Tsaritsyn and proceeding further across the
Don. The adjacent grouping (to the west) was
to support them with blows at Voronezh and
Kupyansk. In this operation the Red Army had
the advantage over Denikin in infantry, cannon,
and machine guns, but the Whites still had a
much superior cavalry.

The later plan, which actually sealed the fate
of Denikin, was presented by Stalin and under-

141

taken only in the late autumn. This plan proved that the earlier one, the main idea of which was a drive across the Don on Novorossiisk, was strategically wrong. This began to be evident soon after the August attempt to put this plan into operation.

In order to thwart the efforts of the Red Army, Denikin himself began a drive. He undertook two operations almost simultaneously, entrusting their execution to two old and tried servants of counterrevolution: the Cossack General Mamontov, and General Kutepov, of the Volunteers.

In August, the Fourth Don Cavalry Corps commanded by Mamontov and numbering about eight thousand men, with guns, and armoured cars, and supported by an infantry detachment numbering up to a thousand, broke through Soviet lines near Novokhopersk. The first task which Denikin assigned the corps was the taking of the railway junction of Kozlov, with the purpose of causing disruption deep in the rear of the Red Army's Southern front. Later he changed this assignment and sent the corps against Voronezh in order to break up the Lisky grouping of the Red Army to the northwest of Novokhopersk. Mamontov did not carry out the orders of Denikin, but as soon as he had crossed the front line he led his corps directly north, towards

Tambov. Denikin attempted to swerve Mamontov to the west, but was unsuccessful. With every day Mamontov led his corps farther into the rear and away from the forces of the Red Army, which were concentrated on the front line. On the eighth day of his march he took the city of Tambov.

From the very beginning of the unexpected and devastating raids of the Don Cossacks, all who were familiar with Lenin's July letter recalled with astonishment its unerring foresight. Exactly a month before the Mamontov break-through, Lenin wrote: "A peculiarity of the Denikin army is its abundance of Cossacks and officers. These are elements which, lacking the support of the masses, are extremely prone to make swift raids, launching on adventurous and desperate undertakings with the purpose of sowing panic, and causing destruction for destruction's sake."

Kirill Izvekov was also amazed by the concreteness with which events were foretold. It almost seemed to him that he and his comrades had been personally warned of the attack to be made by this very Fourth Don Cossack Cavalry Corps commanded by Mamontov, and it was unforgivable that they had not heeded the warning. It seemed to Kirill that neither he nor his comrades could find the slightest justification for having been taken off their guard by the Mamontov drive: they could hardly have expected the letter to state the very date and the location along the front line at which the breach would be made. In that letter Lenin had demanded the taking of exceptional precautions. "In fighting such a foe, military discipline and military vigilance must be exercised to the highest degree. To be caught napping or to lose one's head means to lose everything."

In thinking back over his work, Kirill was convinced that he had done everything he was capable of doing in the position he occupied. But at the same time he thought that he should have done much more, and that he and others had even "been caught napping," thereby allowing the misfortune of Mamontov's attack.

After Ragozin had left for the front, Kirill's conviction that it would be better for him and the cause if he were in the ranks of the Red Army, kept growing until it gave him no rest. This uneasiness turned into alarm when news came of a new break-through by the Whites.

In advancing on the central sector of the Southern front, the First Volunteer Army Corps under the command of Kutepov broke through the front at the point where the two Soviet armies joined, and after intense fighting forced one to retreat in the direction of Kursk and the other in the direction of Vorozhba. As a result, the grouping which was to have helped the Red Army deliver an auxiliary blow at Voronezh in the direction of Kupyansk proved incapable of doing so.

Notwithstanding all this, in the middle of August, five days after the break-through of Mamontov and three days after the break-through of Kutepov, the Commander-in-Chief of the Red Army and the command of the Southern front began a drive against Denikin according to the plan worked out before these changes had occurred.

Like the overwhelming majority of Soviet officials (including army men), Izvekov did not know that the drive being opened had not been properly prepared from the point of view of either organization or operation. On the contrary, he was overjoyed that the Red Army had begun action in the south, and considered it a good token and mark of strength that the drive had been undertaken successfully in spite of the countermovements of the Whites. The only thing which disturbed him was that responsibility for defeating the Mamontov cavalry had been entrusted to the command of the main striking force, which had designated two rifle divisions for this purpose. This could not help weakening the blow of the Red Army on the main direction—south along the Volga and toward the Don. With the greatest concern he followed the developments of the Mamontov cavalry, which was now trampling over fields and people in the region of Tambov.

As soon as the latest news arrived from the front, Kirill would drop his work and unroll whatever maps he could lay hands on, beginning with school maps and ending with detailed agricultural charts, trying to get a more exact picture of the movement of troops and guess the further development of operations. And his envy of Ragozin grew in proportion to the development of the first successes of the Red Army.

One evening Annochka found him lost in a study of these maps. She entered his office without knocking and stopped in confusion when Kirill took her for his secretary and asked her, without raising his head, what she wanted. The low shadows cast by the table lamp made the lock of hair hanging over his brow seem blacker than usual, while the light fell full on his chin and compressed lips, revealing the fact that he was not shaved.

"Well, what is it?" he repeated loudly, raising his head from the map.

Immediately he ran over and took Annochka's hands, and as soon as he had greeted her, said in a changed, hesitant voice:

"How is it you are here?"

"They told me I could come in.... Shouldn't I have?"

"Of course you should. That isn't why I asked. I just wondered where you came from. I was expecting you ... that is, I wanted to see you. About a certain matter ... very important...."

He spoke quicker than usual and was conscious that his tongue was getting twisted. He glanced at the map as a lifesaver, and once more seized Annochka's hands to draw her to the desk.

"I kept putting it off from day to day—simply had no time at all. How nice that you should have come yourself. Incidentally, look what's happening."

He held her with his left hand, while with his right he pointed to the map covering the entire desk.

"This is the Volga, do you see? This is where our fleet is now. In another day Kamyshin will be ours. Do you understand? Wrangel is backing up. Our cavalry is pressing him from this side." He indicated the west as he pressed Annochka's shoulder, pushing her to the left. "Budyonny's mounted corps. Heard about them? No? This is where they're headed. Against Sutulov's Don Cossack cavalry. If we knock them out, then...."

Once more he pushed Annochka and she stepped back. He glanced at her as he ended in lowered tones:

"Then everything will be fine."

He spoke to her only of what roused his hopes and enthusiasm, saying nothing about his hidden fears and avoiding looking at the northern sections of the map so that Annochka should also avoid them. All the while he spoke about the encouraging events on the Volga, he involuntarily thought about the menacing situation to the northwest of Saratov, in the region of Tambov, for by that time Mamontov's cavalrymen were already rampant in Kozlov and the direct road to Moscow had been cut off, making it possible to reach the capital only by a roundabout route through Penza. He decided that he must surely distract Annochka's attention from these depressing circumstances, and was convinced that it was them he was hiding from her and nothing else, refusing to admit that he was no less anxious to hide the disturbance her unexpected proximity roused in him.

He rummaged through the rest of his maps, placing a small one on top and again leaning toward Annochka.

"I just showed you the Kamyshin-Tsaritsyn direction. Now look further west. Our other grouping. Here's where the front was five days ago, do you see? And look what a wedge we've made. This red line. How do you like that? If we continue this way, in a week we'll be in Kupyansk. Look."

He wanted to draw Annochka toward the map, but she said:

"I can see all right from here. Only I don't understand why we'll be in Kamyshin in a day, and in Kupyansk only in a week. Look how far it is to Kamyshin, while Kupyansk is right next door."

"Of course," said Kirill, stepping aside. "That's not at all pleasant. But the main complication here is that ... the maps are on different scales." He touched his unshaven upper lip. "On a small map places that are far away look close."

"Then we ought to fight only according to small maps," smiled Annochka.

He laughed.

"You said that you had been wanting to see me," she said in a tone that was at once playful and matter-of-fact. "In order to give me a lesson in strategy?"

"No. Without any strategy."

"How can that be, once you're a strategian?"

"I'm a bad strategian. Otherwise I should fight according to small maps—at least with you."

"Are you intending to fight with me?"

"Not with you, but for you."

Again she smiled, not slyly and not playfully, but with the triumphant satisfaction of a woman who has achieved her purpose jestingly. But at the same time she seemed to check herself and reject the coquettish turn the conversation had taken.

"Have you really something you wanted to see me about?" she asked. "I have also come to you on an important matter."

"I want to speak with your brother."

"Pavlik?"

"About a friend of his—Vanya Ragozin. Do you remember Ragozin—the one you went to see about money that time—with Tsvetukhin? Well, he has a son. . . ."

"What a strange coincidence," interrupted Annochka. "I have also come about Pavlik. He has disappeared."

"Disappeared?"

"Three days ago he left the house in the morning and never came back."

"Have you searched for him?"

"My father reported it to the militia and has asked everyone he knew, especially along the river. . . ."

"Maybe Dorogomilov knows something?"

"Arseni Romanovich has spoken to all of Pavlik's friends, but in vain. Not a trace of him. It's awful."

"Oh of course, all sorts of ideas immediately come into your head—that he's dead, or kidnapped, or something even worse," said Kirill in a rough tone intended to encourage her. "But he's probably simply run away to the front. He threatened to do that, didn't he?"

"But that's no consolation! He's so little—something's sure to happen to him!"

"Do you really think they allow such little shavers to reach the front?"

"How can they help it, if that's where he went?"

She took hold of the back of the chair and sank down heavily, for one of her fragility.

"Listen, Annochka—" began Kirill, but she did not let him finish.

"It's all my fault," she said. "This could never have happened if mother were alive. She loved Pavlik so. And I have neglected him completely. After all, he's still scarcely more than an infant."

She buried her face in the crook of her elbow, still holding on to the back of the chair.

"You're only an infant yourself," said Kirill, coming closer.

This seemed to deepen her distress, and on the verge of weeping, her face still pressed against her arm, she murmured:

"I wanted to invite you to our rehearsal, soon we shall be having our dress rehearsal, but now I know I'll be a failure—I shall, I shall, I know I shall!"

He spoke more brusquely than ever, afraid that she would begin to cry:

"Don't go imagining things. As though a rehearsal was anything of such importance. You'll make a wonderful Luise, or whoever it is. And I'll clap for you. Just think—getting upset like that over some Luise or other. What I mean to say is—it's a cinch to play that Luise of yours. As for Pavlik—well, I had to hunt for one boy anyway, so I may as well make it two. You can be sure the militia will bring him back to you. He's not the first young hero to have set out this way."

Annochka raised her head.

" 'Not the first young hero!' All he needs is a good hiding!" she said, giving such a good imitation of Kirill's bass voice that he had to turn away to keep his composure.

"Tomorrow morning I'll have all the militiamen on their feet and we'll do everything necessary," he said in softened tones.

"Really?" she asked almost joyfully. "Do you really think I shall act my role well?"

He had not expected such a turn to the conversation.

"Why not, if you've been acting it well so far?..."

"How did you know that I was playing Luise?"

"I asked mother."

"So you didn't forget me after all?"

"No I didn't, after all."

"And that's why you haven't seen me for two months?"

"Two months? Impossible!"

"Seven weeks and three days."

"You counted them?" asked Kirill, more surprised than ever.

"And you lost count?"

He made a disconsolate gesture toward the papers and maps covering his desk.

"I understand," said Annochka. "No time."

Slowly she raised her brows, and there was so much disappointment in this involuntary expression that he could say nothing.

"I must go. Thank you. I'm terribly afraid for Pavlik!"

"I'll see you home."

"Oh dear no!" she objected, pointing to the desk with exactly the same gesture he had used.

"Just a minute," he said, looking about for his cap and not finding it. "I want to take a walk like we did that time to the melon farm."

"And then disappear for another two months?"

"All the more reason for wanting to. Come on."

Not finding his cap, he went out without it.

They were immediately enveloped in cool darkness—the evenings already bore a presage of autumn, which conferred upon them a sad and sombre charm. The air was brisk. Down the street came the clear, persuasive call of a boat whistle.

Kirill slipped his arm under Annochka's. Once again he was holding this slim hand, every little bone of which could be felt. The thought came to him that this hand must often reach out for support and often drop in weariness, yet he read a hidden strength in its sharp angles.

"Aren't you cold . . . without your cap?"

"That isn't what you wanted to ask," he said.

"Why should you think that?" she retorted, taking a few steps in silence, waiting for his reply.

"For some reason I always have to think up what to talk to you about," she went on when no reply was forthcoming. "I suppose that is because you don't want to talk about what is most important. Wait. You're sure to ask me now what is most important, am I right?"

"Well, what *is*?" he said with a short laugh. "At the present moment, the search for Pavlik is probably most important, isn't it?"

"Of course," she agreed a bit too readily. "But you didn't finish what you were telling me that time in the automobile, remember?... Don't you regret in the least having parted with Lisa?"

"Oh, so that is the most important?... I don't like turning back to things in the past."

"Quite recently she got married again. After you had already returned to Saratov. Did you hear? That's the present, not the past."

"But that's a present which shouldn't concern me."

"Shouldn't, or actually doesn't?"

"Are you such a stickler for fine points in general, or just in this case?"

"In general," she said stubbornly.

155

Once more he gave a short laugh, but without any merriment, and remained silent for a long time.

"In order to have done with this, since it seems to interest you so," he finally said in lowered tones, "I actually have ceased to think about Lisa. At first I forced myself to, and then it became a habit—not to think of her."

"Does that mean you still love her?" asked Annochka impatiently, with a jerk of her hand, as though she wished to remove it, but then had changed her mind.

"Why should it mean that? Perhaps the Lisa I once loved—so many years ago I've lost count of them—never existed at all."

"But that's nonsense," said Annochka with a shade of injury, this time actually withdrawing her hand from his fingers.

"Why nonsense? At that time we were young and had our dreams."

"If you once had them, you still have them. If not, you're simply fickle."

"That's it. Simply fickle."

This struck him funny and he laughed out loud, and Annochka softly slipped her hand back into his as though she had never taken it away, and they went on without speaking, only listening to each other, although there was nothing to hear but the even crunching of the dirt under their feet.

When they reached Annochka's house she was about to take leave of him at the gate, but Kirill said he would see her to the door. She went to knock at the lighted window and suddenly cried out:

"Heavens! Look at that!"

Kirill went over.

Pavlik was sitting on the bed. Even in the dim light could be seen the dirty tearstains on his cheeks. His red hair was sticking up like the feathers of a fighting cock. He kept winding a piece of string about his finger and jerking it off.

At the table opposite sat Parabukin, with the august mien of a parent calling his erring offspring to account. He was drumming on the edge of the table and angrily rolling his eyes.

As soon as he had let Annochka in he began speaking, without paying the slightest attention to Izvekov.

"Turned up at last! Hunger's a mean stepmother! Nobody but his father serves coffee in bed to that little swank. Who does he take after, eh? Heaven only knows his poor mother was a hard-working woman enough—and kept washing the little pig and cleaning him up. His sister's all anybody could ask for—she'll be the one to feed him in place of his mother. His father . . . well, as for his father. . . ."

Here Parabukin looked askance at his daughter and her companion, drew himself up and ran his hand briskly over his tousled hair and beard, and at that moment it could be seen that in spite of his efforts, he was having a hard time keeping his equilibrium.

"His father's no scoundrel either, all his life he's been suffering on account of this family. . . ."

"Wait, father," said Annochka. "Where were you, Pavlik?"

From the moment she entered she had been looking at her brother with eyes so radiant with love and hurt, with such unselfish reproach welling from the very depths of her heart, that Pavlik dropped his head on his chest and stopped twisting the string.

"What's there to wait for? I've already had a talk with him," said Parabukin, opening his calloused palm and exhibiting it with solemn pride. "He confessed all his sailor's dreams to me. Says he wanted to join the sailors. Well, I showed him a sailor or two!"

Annochka rushed over to Pavlik and pressed him to her. With a sense of relief he buried his nose in her breast. He shuddered and grew quiet, while once again his fingers began to wind the string.

"Hid away in the hold of a ship and sailed away to Uvek, where they rolled him out along with some barrels. 'Why did you do that?' says I. 'Because I wanted to see a sea battle,' says he. 'On what sea or ocean, be so kind?' says I. 'Oh that,' says he, 'is a military secret!' "

"How could you have, Pavlik?" said Annochka, still upset, as she smoothed his curls.

" 'I decided to lay down my life for the revolution,' he confesses at last, the rapscallion! What you going to do with an imp like that, eh?"

"What did I tell you?" said Izvekov. "The call of the times. Children hear it better than grownups: 'To the front! To the front!' "

At the sound of the stranger's voice Pavlik pushed away from his sister to glance at him sharply. The boy at once recognized Izvekov, and, encouraged by his support, darted a golden glance full of challenge and protest at his father.

"Been different if I'd been alone, but it was all that Vanka, the Pauper Painter. He fixed himself up in a motorboat going straight to the fleet out in the main stream, but he says to me: 'You stow away on the first boat going to Uvek. The fleet'll be taking on oil there and I'll pick you up.' I waited for two days but there wasn't any sign of the fleet. A lot the fleet needs with that Uvek!"

"Tsck, tsck! What unreliable companions you pick up!" said Izvekov in a serious tone. "I suppose that was Vanya Ragozin, wasn't it?"

"Who else? It's all very well for him. All the sailors know him."

"Aren't you the least bit sorry for what you did?" asked Annochka, starting away from her brother.

Once more he dropped his head: the worst rebuke for him was the sight of his sister's suffering.

Thus in so simple a way one of the fugitives was found, while the trail of the other was as clear as footsteps in the snow. Kirill had every reason to be satisfied. He was about to take his leave when Parabukin, deprived of his role of a righteous father, addressed him in a rather condescending tone:

"I beg your pardon, but do you work at the theatre along with my daughter?"

"This is the son of Vera Nikandrovna," said Annochka. "You know him, father."

Parabukin immediately descended to solid earth, adjusted his voluminous blouse, and went on in his best manner:

"It's mostly through your high position I know you, inasmuch as your name is signed to most of the decrees. As well as because I'm your subordinate, working as I do in the Old Goods Department."

"Oh yes, I've been planning to pay you a visit," said Kirill. "What's going on down there? They say you destroy books?"

"Not a page without official permission! Only in accordance with definite instructions. Church ritual books, handbooks of tsarist law, and such things. The capitalist press—reports of stock companies, for example, or advertisements."

"Didn't you make paper bags out of a geography book?" put in Pavlik maliciously.

"Keep your mouth shut. You're too young to understand such things. Not from a geography, but from a history book. A past history—gone for good. A cancelled history. Our people know a thing or two about book learning. If a book's worth anything it gets put to one side. If it's not worth anything it gets put to better purposes. The linings go to make inner soles for shoes. Printed pages make paper bags. Clean pages make writing paper."

"I'll be sure to pay you a visit. I'm very much interested in your department," said Kirill.

"Very educated people come to see us and don't think it beneath them. Make up whole libraries out of our books."

"Good," said Kirill with a smile as he held out his hand to Pavlik. "Goodbye, my little comrade-in-arms. You and I will do some fighting yet. There'll be wars enough in our lifetime to keep us busy. In the meantime, try not to cause Annochka any more trouble, do you promise?"

At first Pavlik hesitated to give Kirill his hand, but finally he raised it cautiously, keeping his elbow pressed to his side and turning his head away.

Annochka saw her guest to the door. She had regained her composure and had even attended to her appearance, running to comb her short hair while Kirill was saying goodbye to her brother.

"Will it be long this time?" she asked slyly as they lingered in the darkness at the open door.

"Until tomorrow. Do you want it to be tomorrow?" he suggested, remembering how long he had put off their meeting that other time and deciding not to repeat the mistake.

Once more he was amazed by the smallness and delicacy of her hand, and suddenly he bent over this hand, which had no peer in the world, and kissed it twice, quickly and awkwardly.

"Goodness!" she cried, retreating into the hall, adding from behind the door: "How prickly!"

He immediately walked away with his short, strong steps. He was stunned and happy that it had turned out like that—that he had kissed her hand. Formerly he could never have imagined himself kissing a woman's hand: he looked upon this custom as either a society mannerism or something demeaning, indulged in by people with whom Kirill had nothing in common. Whenever he had seen people kissing hands—at railway stations, for example—he had been repulsed, and would have laughed at the idea that some day he would imitate a gesture which he considered humiliating for a woman and degrading for a man. He found the kissing of hands particularly incongruous today, when women had been freed from all prejudices and abasements. If hand kissing were defended as one of the chivalries, then let the woman enjoy equal rights in this respect also, pressing her lips to the hand of a man as a mark of her favour. Oh no, Kirill was unquestionably against hand kissing. But he was made unconceivably happy by the fact that he had kissed Annochka's hand—the exquisite hand of this remarkable girl. His kiss had nothing in common with the affected kissing he despised. It was not

11*   163

Annochka's hand he had kissed, but some peculiar essence of her being, so bewitchingly concentrated in her hand; it was of course Annochka he had kissed, Annochka herself. Was not everything about her equally worthy of being kissed—her face, her neck, her mouth or her hand? To-morrow he would tell Annochka how he considered every inch of her body equally precious—tomorrow, tomorrow—how wonderful that it would be soon!

He returned along the same road they had just walked together, and at each step he relived the sense of her proximity, which was sharply brought back to him by the crunching of the dirt under his feet in the darkness of the empty streets. It had crunched in just the same way when they had walked over it together. It had crunched this way under *her* feet. He sang to himself, quietly and incoherently. He had no ear for music, but whenever he sang to himself he liked it, and it seemed to him that he was musical. Tomorrow, tomorrow, was the song he sang. Tomorrow, to-morrow, was the answer he gave to his thoughts about the kiss. Tomorrow, tomorrow. . . .

Kirill found several people waiting for him in his office. Some were sitting on the window sill smoking, others were looking at the maps Kirill had shown Annochka. He knew all these people and realized that some unexpected event must have brought them here.

"Where have you been so long?" one of them asked.

"Nowhere in particular. See, even went without my cap," he said, glancing at his desk and forcing himself to walk to his chair at his usual pace.

He immediately noticed a telegram propped up against the inkwell. No one said a word while he read it. His mouth tightened and he seemed to grow older. He folded the telegram in half and sank slowly into his chair.

"Don't sit down," he was told. "The chairman is waiting for us—he has called a conference."

"All right. Well, come on," he said in a tone that indicated there could be no doubt that they would all follow him, as though he himself had called the conference. Quickly he strode across the office and entered the next room.

* 23 *

Only toward the end of the following day did Kirill find time to send Annochka a note saying that it would be necessary to postpone their meeting for a day or two. When he wrote "for a day or two" he did not believe that it would be so, but he lacked the courage to write anything else. To be sure he added that he wanted dreadfully to see her, and believed that such a note, explaining nothing, would atone for everything.

It was impossible to predict what would happen not only two days hence, but even two hours. The conference lasted the whole night, and the telephone and telegraph wires were not silent for a minute. The city was threatened by another uprising, this time in the north, and this might lead to the cutting off of the last railway connection with Moscow, through Penza.

A former Cossack colonel named Mironov, now commander of a Red Army division of Don Cossacks, after forming a cavalry corps in Saransk, Penza gubernia, had refused to recognize the authority of the Revolutionary Military Council. Even before this he had ignored the Political Department of the division, and at meetings of his own summoning had tried to convince the Cossacks and the peasants that he was the one who would save the revolution, inciting them against the Soviets and the Bolsheviks. When he was summoned to Penza by the Revolutionary Military Council, he answered by arming his units and sending an ultimatum demanding that he be immediately allowed to go to the front. His aim was to join Denikin. The advance of Mamontov, which had reached the northernmost point at that time, offered favourable circumstances for a revolt, and an advance to the south made by the troops of Mironov, attacking the Red Army from behind, would be a signal service to Mamontov. Mironov had embarked on a traitorous adventure in the style of Makhno, who had gone over to the Whites in the spring.

After arresting and jailing all local Soviet officials, Mironov set out at the head of his Cossack units from Saransk for Penza. He sent agents ahead to rouse the peasants to revolt. He stopped for almost a day in the town of Makaryevskoye, and this gave the Soviet command an opportunity to draw up its troops to attack him before he had a chance to enter the front-line region.

Penza gubernia was announced to be in a state of siege. All power was placed in the hands of the Military Council, while revolutionary committees were set up in the uyezds. Village Communists armed with hatchets and pitchforks made their way to the towns, uniting to offer resistance to the traitorous division. Scouts were sent out. Workshops were set up for repairing weapons. An inventory of horses and saddles was taken. A list of volunteers for a workers' regiment was drawn up in Penza. A mobilization of Bolsneviks took place in the most quiet and remote corners of the gubernia. Hundreds of people took up arms.

Four days after Mironov left Saransk, some of his units were caught in machine-gun fire and put to flight while trying to cross the Sura River. Three days later some thousand of Mironov's men laid down their arms and sent delegates to the Red Army asking to be taken back into its ranks.

Mironov and the remainder of his rebels continued their march to the Southern front. They were not allowed to approach Penza, and detoured almost to the northern uyezds of the Saratov gubernia, advancing in the general direction of Balashov. Mironov's forces melted along the way. Unlike Mamontov, he proceeded cautiously, afraid to enter large towns. He lost some of his Cossacks in skirmishes, while others, not wanting to fight, ran off to the woods, and then dispersed through towns and villages. All the territory through which he passed was overrun with these bands, while Mironov himself and five hundred of his men were taken prisoner by Red cavalrymen in the Balashov uyezd in the middle of September, three weeks after he turned traitor.

During the first days of the revolt it was naturally impossible to foresee the course of its development and how soon it would be put down. It represented a menace to Saratov not only because the loss of Penza would mean the loss of railway connections with Moscow (at that time the direct route had been cut off by Mamontov, who was in the region of Kozlov), but also because the northern uyezds of the Saratov gubernia lay directly in the path of the revolt. Fires of rebellion might break out in these nearer, northern regions, while the southern sky was still glowing with Denikin's conflagrations. The uprising in the Penza district might at any moment become an uprising in the Saratov district.

The drive on the Southern front might be said to have just gotten under way. On the very day when the Mironov revolt broke out the sailors of the Volga fleet attacked Nikolayevskaya Sloboda, opposite Kamyshin, and on the next day Red infantrymen took Kamyshin. This only made Kirill more furious on receiving the news of the Mironov adventure. He was more stunned by this unexpected threat from the north than by Mamontov's break-through. The constant series of misfortunes besieging Saratov made Kirill liken the city to a sick man who scarcely managed to fight down one ailment before falling prey to another. The inhabitants of Saratov had just finished the "Trench Days," with everyone out to dig defences, when they were mobilized for a "Week for the Front." One crisis after another.

It was expedient to find new forces where it seemed all forces had been exhausted.

The city garrison, worn out by the efforts exerted to first put up a defence against Wrangel and then open an attack against him, could supply only a few small detachments for the fight against Mironov.

One such detachment was sent to the Khvalynsk uyezd. It consisted of about a hundred and fifty volunteers and new recruits, and according to the Military Commissar was "not so bad." The question of who was to be its commander had to be decided: Mironov's betrayal once more raised arguments about what attitude should be assumed toward former officers of the tsarist army now serving as military experts in the Red Army. In discussing who the new commander was to be, the Military Commissar mentioned Dibich, who had done good work in the forming of new units, but who had come only recently to the Red Army and had not been tested in battle.

"But I am not the one to speak about him," added the Commissar. "Dibich was recommended by Comrade Izvekov, who can probably tell you anything you'd like to know."

Someone said jokingly that if it was Izvekov who recommended Dibich, let him be the one to put his recommendation to the test: let Izvekov be made Dibich's commissar. This remark might not have been taken seriously if attention at that moment had not been concentrated on finding some exceptional and resolute person to whom authority even greater than that of a company commissar might be given—a person capable even of organizing and heading a revolutionary committee on the spot if circumstances demanded. The appointing of Izvekov to this seemingly unimportant position would solve a very important problem, and what had been said jokingly proved to be to the point.

Kirill said briefly:

"I saw how Dibich fought the Germans. He is a serious person and a courageous commander. He came to serve us rather than the Whites because of his convictions. I am ready to answer for him."

This ended the talk as to whether Dibich was to be trusted—not because none were to be found who would have been only too glad to dig up the history of this former tsarist officer, but because the subject of the conversation shifted to

171

Izvekov. He was immediately appointed commissar, and in the eyes of all he thus assumed responsibility not only for Dibich and the company, but for whatever might happen in the Khvalynsk uyezd.

An hour later Vasili Danilovich, already commander of the company, arrived to talk with Izvekov about the preparations for their expedition.

"Just see what it means for a fellow to be in the right place!" said Kirill in greeting. "Why, you've even got roses in your cheeks! And here am I, back with you in the same unit!"

"Only you've been promoted, while I'm not even up to my former rank," said Dibich.

"What are you complaining about? Here's your happiness being served up on a silver platter—in a week's time you'll be back home in Khvalynsk."

"And in grand style," laughed Dibich. "Sword in hand. Hope I don't have to do battle for my own home!"

"Well, what if you do? You're up to it," said Kirill. "Here's a pencil. Sit down."

He opened up a map of the Volga, and with amazing clarity recalled how Annochka had bent over that map and followed his finger as he had tried to pin her attention to events in the south so that she would not glance to the north. Now he folded under the southern half.

But it was not with the map they began. Dibich told what this company, described as being "not so bad," actually represented. The Red Army men had not finished even a rush course of training; less than half the volunteers were experienced soldiers, and there were not enough uniforms, boots, or rifles for the men. Kirill and Dibich began to draw up a list of necessary guns, equipment, uniforms, and provisions. They figured out how much time it would take to get ready, and it came out to three days.

"That's no good," said Kirill. "We'll have to cut it in half."

"What do you mean?"

"Just what I say. We've got to leave at dawn the day after tomorrow."

"I'm ready to leave right now, but not emptyhanded. Takes time even to collect pebbles on a beach. And we're faced with the job of rummaging through every corner of every warehouse in Saratov."

"Have to speed up our rummaging."

"But we calculated everything to the minute."

"Have to calculate in seconds."

"Easy to say. This isn't the first company I've fitted out."

173

"Our company is being sent on a special assignment."

"All the more reason why we should equip it properly."

Kirill threw Dibich a stern glance from under lowered brows.

"Listen, Vasili Danilovich, let's assume the battle's already begun, and in battle there can be no differences of opinion, can there?"

"This is no difference of opinion; it's simple arithmetic."

"Then simple arithmetic's no good. Let's try another kind. I'll take upon myself the most difficult job. What do you think will be the hardest things to get hold of?"

"We need two machine guns, don't we? And communications? But just try to get hold of any wire!"

"All right, I'll try. I'll answer for communications. If the worst comes to the worst, I'll simply yank out this phone," said Kirill, indicating the one on his desk.

"One telephone is not communications," objected Dibich.

"We'll get as many as necessary. Well, what else?"

They went over and over their list, dividing up the work. Then they turned to the map.

If the company marched along the highroad to Volsk and from there to Khvalynsk, it would mean covering some two hundred and twenty versts. Dibich estimated five days for the march, including bivouacs. A good steamer would make the trip in a day, but most of the boats had been despatched to operations in the south, making the chances of securing one very slight. For that reason Izvekov suggested taking the train to Volsk (which would double the distance covered, but curtail the time) and march from there to Khvalynsk. Such a journey would take three days.

"If the locomotive doesn't let us down," said Dibich. "Trains are fuelled with wood these days, you know."

"We'll chop the wood ourselves," said Izvekov.

"And if Mironov doesn't move south from Penza and cut off the railway somewhere near Petrovsk."

"What are we being sent for? We'll fight them wherever we meet them."

"We're being sent to Khvalynsk. Others will be sent to Petrovsk. We have to carry out our own assignment."

"The assignment is to smash Mironov, and wherever we do it will be all right."

"I disagree. There's a big difference between being forced to fight, and choosing the time and place for a fight. Our enemy has cavalry troops which are already on the march. We'll be ready to set out only in three days. It will be easy for them to anticipate our movements."

"Not in three days, but in a day and a half," corrected Kirill. "And there is more chance that we shall do the anticipating than that our movements will be anticipated, once we go by railway."

"I have no objections. Nobody knows what will happen within the next two or three days anyway," remarked Dibich dryly, and fell silent.

Suddenly he grew white and said impulsively:

"You just spoke of differences of opinion. Let's come to an understanding right from the start. Do you trust me or not? If you don't, then we're only wasting time—you better find another commander."

"I trust you," replied Kirill calmly.

"Completely?"

"Completely."

"Thanks. Then there's one more question. Which of us is to do the commanding?"

"You."

"I'm not asking who will lead the troops into attack, but who will determine the battle tactics—you or I?"

"You and I together."

"Which means that I'm to agree to whatever you decide on?"

"No. Which means that each of us will try to see the other's point of view and come to a mutual agreement. But don't forget that I require the same trust of you that you demand of me."

"And what if we disagree?"

Dibich gazed at Kirill with eyes burning with impatience. He was still white, and Kirill remembered his appearance when he had first entered that office so weak and ill, battered by fate and protesting with all the strength left in his exhausted body.

"You are now in the Red Army," he said, "and its rules and regulations are no secret to you. But I doubt that any differences can arise between us. In the first place, I don't doubt the superiority of your military knowledge and shall always depend on it. In the second place, you and I have the same aims."

Kirill moved toward him and said more gently:

"You can be sure I shall never injure your pride."

"Oh, that's not why I said it," burst out Dibich with a wave of his hand. "Simply to get things straight once and for all.... So that we shall never have to return to this question. And so that you will know I am staking my life on this."

"But why?" exclaimed Kirill. "We're not gamblers. Your life is needed for important things."

"I understand," said Dibich in another outburst. "But I want you to know that I shall always act only according to my convictions—never because of pride or anything else..., so that if you and I ever have a difference of opinion..."

"But why should we?" said Kirill, getting up and going over to Dibich. "Let's work together."

"All right," repeated Dibich. "Let's work together."

They smiled, conscious of a new upsurge of friendship, and rejoicing in it, as one rejoices in the experience of any fine new feeling.

"And here's something else I've thought of," went on Kirill. "If there should be any unexpected delay in our preparations, you can go ahead with the company while I remain here to finish up. Then I'll take a machine and catch up with you in Volsk."

"Where will you get the machine?"

"That's my business too."

"Well, I can see things will go well, once we have a supply agent like you!" laughed Dibich.

As he was leaving, Izvekov stopped him for a minute.

"I wanted to ask you if you knew anything about a fellow named Zubinsky," he said. "The Military Commissar is assigning him to us for communications."

"Formerly he was a regiment adjutant. A braggart. But he seems to carry out orders all right—at least here in the rear."

"The Military Commissar says he's as reliable as a brick wall."

"Does he think we'll be needing to rely on brick walls?" asked Dibich with a snort.

"Well, shall we take him?"

"We're short of people. I suppose we'll have to."

From that moment began their energetic preparations. The nights were sleepless and the intervening day merged with the nights, and everything was like a dream, in which you feverishly collect things, and the more you collect, the more there remains to be collected, as though you were working with fractions whose numerators kept growing and growing.

Zubinsky rode up and down the streets on a fine black stallion with a light tan English saddle. He was a born adjutant. He loved to take orders, carrying them out with an exactness and enthusiasm which was often harsh. He shouted at anyone he dared shout at, arrested anyone he had the slightest cause to arrest, and made such free use of the names of his superiors that one might think they were his subordinates, or at least his bosom friends. In his dashing sword belt, with the squeaking leather holster on his hip, he made a worthy rider for his steed. Without interrupting his labours for a second, he was forever preening himself: he would clean his fingernails when engaged in conversation, snatch off his cap to adjust his slick hair while his horse was galloping down the street, test the buttons of his uniform or the buckles of his accoutrements while signing documents. Wherever he went he kept cleaning and brushing and adjusting his clothes as though in preparation for a dress parade.

"Yes, young man," he said to a quartermaster sergeant who was at least twice his age, "if the warehouse doesn't let me have fifty field kits by thirteen o'clock, you'll find yourself behind bars for a good forty-eight hours, and that's as certain as the fact that we're living under Soviet power."

He took the greatest pleasure in carrying out his threats. Everyone knew this, and that gave him power. Under certain circumstances, the value of such a person was unquestionable.

On the eve of the company's departure Izvekov went to say goodbye to his mother. He asked the driver to go along the street where the Parabukins lived. He wanted only to have another look at the road over which he had so recently walked arm in arm with Annochka.

The machine poured a stream of white light ahead, cutting through the rough waves of the ruts in the road and illuminating the front yards like the light of a full moon. The trees seemed to be swiftly changing places, and Kirill could only guess what blocks they were passing. Suddenly he touched the driver's elbow and said "stop."

For a second he hesitated, then flung open the door of the car and jumped out onto the pavement.

"Wait here. I'll be right back," he said.

After the glare of the headlights, the yard seemed impenetrably dark—as dark as it had been when he had returned with Annochka, and, like then, he immediately noticed the lighted window in its depths. His impulse to go over to it was inhibited by a sense of propriety. But the desire to exactly relive those precious moments was so strong that he found himself slowly approaching and glancing over the top of the short curtain.

Annochka was alone, and the little room seemed larger than he remembered it.

She was standing by the bed. In the flickering of the lamplight her paleness seemed to wax and wane, as though the blood kept flushing her cheeks and receding. Her lips trembled. She was whispering something to herself. The slenderness of her neck was particularly noticeable, and there was a tautness of the tendons rising from her collarbone, as when a singer is taking a high note. It seemed that at any moment Annochka would give voice to the cry she was suppressing with such effort.

Presently she did cry out. She stretched out her hands and rushed across the room as though someone were mercilessly dragging her by those frail arms held out in supplication, and then she fell on her knees.

She fell on her knees before the little round table on which her mother's sewing machine was standing. She stretched her clasped hands towards this machine while incoherent protests rose painfully to her lips. She seemed half crazed, and it was unbearable to witness such despair.

Kirill grabbed the window frame, ready to rip it off and burst into the room. But he was deterred by a strange movement: Annochka turned toward the window and glanced calmly about the room, running her fingers through her hair with a boyish gesture, after which she returned to the table.

Almost immediately she covered her face with her hands for a second, then locked her fingers, rose swiftly and went to the window with the heavy step of one crushed by misfortune. Her thin girlish shoulders drooped under the burden of her suffering, while numb horror was expressed in her unwinking eyes. It was hard for Kirill to believe that Annochka's eyes could be so enormous and so dreadful.

With her twitching fingers stretched helplessly toward the window, she kept coming on and on, as though there were no end to that tiny room. Kirill stepped aside, into the shadows. He saw the curtain stir as Annochka touched it with the tips of her fingers. He heard her moan: "Stay! Stay! Where art thou going? Mother! Father! He is abandoning us at such a moment!"

Kirill ran his hand over his forehead.

"Thank the Lord!" he sighed with relief. "She's acting. Probably practising her Luise!"

He could not suppress a sudden burst of laughter, and knocked loudly at the door.

"Is that you, Pavlik?" came the quick answer.

"It's me!" he cried.

She said nothing as she let him in.

He noticed the flush that swept her cheeks, and his whole body sang with joy that his coming could disturb her so.

"How nice that you came," she said, as though confirming his joy.

"Weren't you expecting me?"

"When I received your note I thought you wouldn't come. Why are you in such high spirits?"

"Am I?" asked Kirill.

He had been laughing as he entered, and the smile had not left his lips.

"Let's say it's because I don't want to pull the sad face with which people usually come to say goodbye."

"Say goodbye?" she repeated in alarm.

"Yes, don't be frightened. Nothing special. I have to go away for awhile on a certain assignment."

"To the front?"

"Not exactly. A modest little operation."

"Against that Mironov?"

He was too taken aback to answer.

"What kind of a friend do you call yourself if you have secrets from me?"

"Secrets? Why call them secrets?"

"If you trust me, you shouldn't hide things from me."

She said this with such childlike reproach that he felt uncomfortable and moved away. But presently he turned back and took her arm above the elbow. She sat down at the table in front of which Kirill had just seen her on her knees.

"So you won't see our rehearsal," she said mournfully.

"I have already seen—how you rehearse. . . ."

She raised her brows.

"Just now," he added, still smiling.

"You must be joking."

"Not in the least. If you want, I shall repeat your lines," and he gave a rather unsuccessful imitation of how she had moaned: "Stay! Stay! Where art thou going?. . ."

She covered her eyes with her hand as she cried:

"You looked through the window!"

He stood motionless, frightened by her cry. She dropped her head on the table.

"How could you!" she murmured.

"I only watched for a moment, on my word of honour," he declared, not knowing what to do.

She straightened up and calmly ran her fingers through her hair with that boyish gesture.

"Very well. If you've already seen the rehearsal, you can come to the performance. You'll be back for the performance, won't you? Where is it you're going, after all? Didn't I guess correctly? In what capacity?"

Without knowing why, he answered:

"As Chairman of the Revolutionary Committee. Have you heard what that is?"

She studied him through slightly lowered lids before she asked:

"You love power above everything else, don't you?"

"And love of power is a deadly sin, isn't it?" he smiled.

"No, not if the power is exerted for the benefit of humanity."

"Well, our power is for the benefit of humanity. Do you agree?"

"Yes."

"Then I have a right to love power?"

"Naturally. It wasn't of that I was thinking—you misunderstood me. I asked whether you loved power better than anything else?"

He glanced at her sternly, but his expression melted, as though warmed by rays of light, and assumed an unwonted naïveté. It was his heart rather than his mind that told him Annochka found the substance of their conversation of little importance; it was only the nuances of feeling that mattered to her.

"No," he said, now giving himself up wholly to his emotion. "I understand what you mean."

Quickly she looked away, and as quickly turned back to him with an expression that was amazingly luminous and free of all doubt, and he went over and took her in his arms, simply and strongly, and for a brief moment they remained thus, gazing at each other motionless. Then she resolutely pushed him away, and he heard her say as though from a great distance:

"When you return—when you return—not now. . . ."

And for the first time that evening he saw her smile—that slightly mischievous smile of hers, with its sudden touch of sadness.

"It would be quite in order for me to repeat what you heard me say at the window: 'Stay! Stay!. . .'"

She went back to his extended arms, and he was conscious of the warmth of her face and its unfamiliar fragrance.

Some time later she saw him to the gate. The driver started up the motor, which roared in the silence of the evening, and there was something menacing and admonitory in this outburst. Annochka lightly brushed Kirill's ear with her lips as she said:

"I shall expect you without fail at the performance."

"Why did Tsvetukhin choose this play?" he asked unexpectedly.

"What do you mean, why? Because it's a play everyone can understand. It shows how people suffered at the hands of the nobility."

"Oh yes," he replied jokingly, immediately assuming the serious tone of a teacher encouraging his student as he said: "You are absolutely correct—anyone can understand that."

He pressed her fingers in parting.

Once in the machine he could not shake off the thought that he was going away and leaving Annochka with Tsvetukhin. Once more the thought of this man irritated him, and once more he tried to convince himself that there was no cause for irritation. It rankled him that for the second time life was confronting him with a situation in which all the advantage was on the side of Tsvetukhin. The latter remained behind while Kirill had to go away, and at a time when he wanted desperately to live—yes, he wanted this desperately, because his soul was radiant with the newborn conviction that he loved and was loved. Was it possible that Tsvetukhin was destined always to cast a shadow on the happiest moments of Kirill's life?

"Never! Impossible!"

"What's that?" asked the driver.

"I was just asking if you'd been driving long."

"Why? Don't you like the way I drive?"

"Oh yes, it's quite all right. Have you a good knowledge of motors?"

"Can't boast of it. But I manage to get along."

"Hm."

Vera Nikandrovna was not at home when Kirill arrived. She was at a meeting, but was expected to return any moment.

Kirill decided to pack his things. It took him some time to find his suitcase, which he finally unearthed under his mother's bed. He began to empty it, first removing the things quickly, then more slowly, finally stopping to examine articles which carried him back into the past.

A cherished diagram of a river steamer, showing both vertical and horizontal cross-sections in white lines on a faded blue background; portraits of Przhevalsky and Leo Tolstoy, two great minds so different, yet so alike, concentrating on studies of the earth itself, and of man, its inhabitant. These scraps of paper took him back to the days of his youth. He recalled how as a boy he had constructed imaginary boats and ships on which he had sailed to unknown lands of the future. He recalled how he had then sought actual roads leading to these lands, and how his seeking had been intercepted at the very outset. He remembered how his house had been searched, and how the gendarme had torn the portrait of Przhevalsky off the wall and tossed it onto the floor: the upper corners of the picture were ripped even now, and Kirill slowly straightened them with his fingernail. He remembered that the evening of his arrest had been his last evening with Lisa. And while he knew that the entire road he had travelled since that evening, and the whole path leading from his dreams to actuality had been trod in accordance with his own wishes, and that he would not have chosen any other path, it hurt him to realize that so often and for so long he had been left so utterly alone.

At the bottom of the suitcase he found a linen envelope containing photographs. They were old photographs. Here he saw himself as a baby, not more than eighteen months old, in a long dress with a lace collar. Probably Kirill's first memory was of finding himself in the presence of a man with a black beard who handed him a horse with a whisk-broom tail, and said "coo-coo" as he ducked behind a black cloth, after which he reappeared from behind the cloth and took away the horse, causing Kirill to protest with all the strength of his lungs. In the picture he was sitting clutching the horse with amusing ferocity.

Suddenly Kirill heard steps on the stairs. He quickly went into the next room. Only then did he notice that he was breathing quickly and loudly.

He calmed himself before re-entering the room in which he had been going through the suitcase.

Vera Nikandrovna was standing motionless next to the pile of things on the table. He approached and silently embraced her. For some time they said nothing, their eyes fixed on that disorderly heap of things that seemed to be participating in their silent communion. Then Kirill kissed his mother's cold, moist temple.

"Why don't you say when?" she asked, struggling to make the words come.

"Tonight. I don't know the exact time yet."

She led him over to the window and whispered, having suddenly lost her voice:

"Sit here a while—just a little while—with me. . . ."

It was very quiet, and they were acutely conscious of the odour of these old things and the warmth coming from the lamp, burning so evenly. The soft glow of the lamplight on the furniture conferred to the room the quiet charm of home.

For several minutes the mother and son sat there in silence. Then Vera Nikandróvna helped Kirill pack his things and they went out together. As they were saying goodbye, Vera Nikandróvna admitted that she had long been expecting this moment, and still it had come as a shock. Kirill realized this without her telling him, and he hurried to be off, so as not to put too great a strain on his mother's self-control. She stood watching the lights of the automobile recede down the road, and continued to stand there motionless in the darkness when they had disappeared.

At dawn Izvekov saw his company off. The men boarded the train with Dibich at their head. According to their agreement, Kirill was to leave by automobile sometime during the day and meet them at Volsk. He still had to obtain medicines, field glasses, and a supply of revolver bullets—things they had not been able to get hold of in so short a time. Zubinsky and Kirill's assistant, a Bolshevik who had volunteered in the army, remained with Kirill.

Not long before it was time for these three to leave, Zubinsky reported that everything was ready, but the machine was playing tricks, and it would be risky to start out with a driver of so little experience.

"A Mercédès in inexperienced hands is a dangerous thing. What if we get stranded on the road?"

"Can you suggest any way out?" asked Kirill.

"If you ask, they will probably let you have a driver who is a mechanic as well."

"Do you know of such a mechanic?"

"Yes—Shubnikov, who works at your garage. He's a first-class driver too. A regular sportsman."

Kirill was silent a long time before answering. He recalled the conversation he had had with his driver on the previous evening. It would indeed be foolish to set out for the front with a man who himself admitted that he could not boast of his knowledge of motors. But the name of Shubnikov called forth in Kirill a feeling of protest and dislike. He glanced sharply at Zubinsky. The latter stood at attention awaiting orders, and his eyes gleamed with the devoted willingness of one born to serve.

"All right, I shall phone," said Kirill, adding to himself, "The devil with him, once it's necessary."

A half-hour later the stenographer took down an order placing Victor Semyonovich Shubnikov at the personal disposal of Izvekov, as his driver and mechanic.

* 24 *

Many precious details could be unearthed in the biography of Shubnikov after his marriage with Lisa. Mertsalov, for example, found him a figure worthy of being portrayed in a chronicle of Russian morals just before the revolution. And among the lesser newspapermen, Mertsalov was considered a person capable of making a valuable contribution to such a work, of which Russian literature has all too few. But even a brief summary of Shubnikov's life would require a whole chapter. It will suffice if we here describe only one or two aspects of the life of Shubnikov, who represented that type of energetic but not too big businessman which has now become either extinct or converted.

He was one of the first in the city to own an automobile. With this machine, which looked much like a carriage, he frightened horses and sent small boys into noisy ecstasies. Street loungers made a point of imitating the rubber-bulbed horn which was attached to the outside of the body along with the hand brake and gearshift, mechanisms which looked for all the world like the levers of railroad switches. When improved models appeared, Shubnikov bought a new machine, hiring out his old one.

Among the smart, rubber-tired cabs clustered about the monument to the "Tsar Emancipator," this "self-propelled" wonder stood hour after hour, waiting for a customer in search of a thrill. The cabdrivers, blissfully unaware of the fate awaiting them in this ruthless motor century, laughed at the cardboard sign which the driver hung on his machine to announce his rates. They hobnobbed beneath a towering bronze peasant sower intended to illustrate the words from the tsar's manifesto: "Shield yourselves with the sign of the cross, oh true believers!" The taxi driver and his sign remained contemptuously apart on the other side of the monument, closer to Themis. In this case the goddess became less a symbol of Justice than of the objectiveness of History, since she did not even deign to raise the bandage over her eyes in order to take a peek at the clash of two epochs being enacted at her very feet. The cabdrivers issued victorious. Apparently Victor Shubnikov, true to his natural impulsiveness, overestimated the conquering power of mechanics, which as yet remained at a very low level of development. Those who had a zest for holding races with trolleycars, remained loyal to the cabs, and the taxi business went up in smoke.

Shubnikov remained at home during the war. The drafting commission exempted him as an epileptic. He actually did suffer fits of epilepsy, but only when he chose, and then only to the extent necessary to torture Lisa or rouse the sympathy of his aunt Daria Antonovna. In the company of military clerks and doctors, he hung about the Ochkin Winter Garden, and made friends of various commissaries.

In the second year of the war Daria Antonovna died, and Victor inherited her entire fortune. Now the last restraint on his conduct was removed. He went about with women more than ever and gave Lisa no peace with his exaggerated jealousy. As is often the case with vain, spoiled individuals, the slightest provocation could make him jealous to the point of actual suffering, to the point of tears and hysterics.

Finally Lisa left him. He immediately sought refuge in the law, cultivating the company of lawyers and law clerks, and had so far arranged things that he was expecting to have his wife and son returned to him any day, with compensation for the insult offered his masculine pride. But came the February Revolution, which delayed matters, and then the October Revolution, which meant that all the expense he had gone to in order to restore his domestic bliss was in vain.

It must be said that after the death of his aunt, Victor did not limit his activities to debauching and seeking to restore his family. Indeed, he now felt a keen necessity to do things on a large scale. In Moscow he bought a magnificent Mercédès, which confounded not only the rich flour merchants, but various government officials as well, who rode about either in carriages or in machines of prewar make. He built up his stables, sold his old horse and bought a pair of race horses, one of which immediately carried off first prize. He sold his collection of stamps and medals and money, as well as his sail boat, and bought a high-powered motorboat.

During a picnic on Green Island he agreed to join a company planning to build a textile factory. With the most serious of faces he attended meetings of this future stock company.

But one day in a jovial mood he made a bet with a drinking companion who happened to be a columnist from the Moscow paper *Early Morning*, that he would found a cheap paper which in two months' time would put all its rivals out of business. Once having undertaken this intriguing enterprise, he gave himself up to it heart and soul.

He collected a picturesque staff of red-nosed reporters with an amazing knowledge of the sombre, impassioned life of the wharves, barracks, markets, and flophouses. The columnist, figuring that it would be more profitable for him to lose the bet than to win it, undertook to write a serial detective story for the paper. Vasili Churkin, notorious highwayman from Orekhovo-Zuyevo, was painted in heroic colours. The paper collected songs and stories about him and printed a pseudoscientific article describing different versions of folk dramas and puppet shows based on the Churkin legend.

Victor did not feel any inclination to literary activity. Nor did he claim to be a highly cultivated person. It meant nothing for him to mix up Jacobean and Jacobin, and he kept this ever in mind. He steered his newspaper away from politics and adopted as his motto: "the people love a scandal." For that reason, all murders, bankruptcies, fires, society divorces, and accidents, were vividly written up by facile pens. The paper scarcely recognized the existence of the theatre, but the private lives of the actresses were constantly featured. The success of circus performers or of new films (referred to only as "movies") soon came to depend on the reviews printed in Victor's paper. Cheap as it was, the paper soon became very profitable for those who made a livelihood from human curiosity.

Victor frequently paid his staff by treating them to vodka at the "Volga Station." This beerhouse on the riverbank inspired such poetic feelings that it proved to be the best place for thinking up further adventures for the provincial Sherlock Holmes who kept subscribers intrigued. The publisher himself helped his fiction writers cook up new instalments. Victor soared to such heights when he had a jag on that he swore the only reason he did not write novels and verse was that he had no time, and when one of his companions took up the cudgel in defence of Apollo, Victor dazzled everyone with his one and only lyric, signed with the pseudonym of *Ubicon*. The poem began with the following lines:

> *Departing from the earth,*
> *The spirit rises higher, higher,*
> *And finds a second birth*
> *In space which quenches passion's fire.*

Soon, however, Shubnikov lost interest in the printed word and sold his newspaper, partly because it became unprofitable (just before the revolution the number of advertisements fell off), and partly because there was a slogan in the air bringing a presentiment of doom to swanky publishers whose spirits kept rising higher and higher. This slogan was: "All Power to the Soviets!"

With the inauguration of this power, Shubnikov's entire capital was confiscated by the state. Step by step Victor was deprived of his various bank accounts, of his stores, race horses, real estate, and his Mercédès. He suffered most from the loss of his automobile. He would have wept when they came to take it away had not the inexperienced driver found difficulty in starting up the engine. In a fit of contemptuous anger, the former owner rushed out and drove the car dashingly to its new headquarters. In parting, he kissed the windshield of his darling.

From that moment on he secretly followed its fate. He always knew in whose hands it was, and if by chance he saw the machine coming down the street, he would freeze in his tracks and stand gazing in its wake long after it had disappeared. He made friends with its drivers, advised them how to care for it, and was overwhelmed with grief when one day he learned that the Mercédès had been hit by a truck. He was invited to repair the damage and proved himself an able workman. A year or so after the revolution he was taken on at the garage belonging to the Soviet, and soon thereafter he won the reputation of being an expert mechanic.

Shubnikov's appearance coarsened. He still owned remnants of his foppish wardrobe, but he preferred wearing overalls. He substituted a toothbrush moustache for his curled one, and was wont to spread his oil-stained hands on the table and declare that nobody was having to teach *him* how to work.

Merkuri Avdeyevich was amazed to see how easily his former son-in-law assumed an appearance suiting the times. As long as Shubnikov still had hope that Lisa would return to him, he kept dropping in to see his son and bringing him toys, taking advantage of such moments to set the child against his mother. After the divorce he abandoned this game, and in his heart of hearts was glad that the revolution found him unencumbered by a family. But he continued to pay visits to his father-in-law. He was grateful to Meshkov for maintaining that Victor was in the right, even though his paternal heart softened toward his daughter. And while Shubnikov did not share Meshkov's views in general, he considered him a safe confidant, and to him alone did he speak with complete frankness. They tried to instruct each other, but while Meshkov sought salvation in submission, Shubnikov had no intention of capitulating, convinced as he was that soon this lesson in history would come to an end and people would once more assume their rightful places in society.

"You're no diplomat, Papa," he would say. "You don't understand what's going on today. As long as these people are on top, we've got to support them. It won't be for long. Let them imagine we're impressed by their genius. We'll bide our time."

"No, this is a punishment for our sins," objected Meshkov. "God's patience has at last come to an end. You say—'what's going on today.'

202

Do you think God punishes today and forgives tomorrow? Ah no, it's repentance we need, and submission. Take up your cross and work by the sweat of your brow for your bit of daily bread. Perhaps then the gracious Lord will show his mercy."

"Nothing new about work. You, for example, worked all your life, and what for? Work is just a form of self-defence, Papa. There's no brains goes into work, if you want to know the scientific point of view—nothing but sad necessity. And there's no sense in inventing a lot of highfalutin ideas about it."

"You aim to be slicker than *them*? *They're* slicker than we could have guessed at first glance, my boy."

"What's so slick about *them*, Papa? I fail to see it."

"The fact that they could snitch that buggy of yours right from under you and hitch you to it to haul them around in the bargain."

"I won't be hauling them around long."

"You mean they won't keep you hitched to it long—only until you drop in your tracks."

Sometimes these discussions led to serious quarrels, but Shubnikov would always come back to his father-in-law and start the arguments all over again.

Just before leaving for the monastery, Merkuri Avdeyevich unburdened himself for the last time to his son-in-law, and this conversation convinced him once and for all that his new son-in-law, Anatoli Mikhailovich, was much superior to his old one. Like Meshkov, Oznobishin explained the existing state of affairs as a punishment sent by God; Shubnikov kept insisting that it was God's business to mess life up for us, while it was ours to straighten it out the best we could.

"You'll never get me to believe that you like the way God's punishing you, Papa. And if you don't like it, what talk can there be of submission? That's just a lot of bosh."

"You're sacrilegious, Victor," said Meshkov in farewell. "And I am very glad that Lisa took your son away from you. Otherwise you would poison the child with your godlessness. And if you're not careful, you'll be getting your head chopped off."

"If it goes, it'll go for a high price."

"And who'll get this price? You won't be around to enjoy it."

"We'll see who'll be around."

Shubnikov's appointment to drive the Mercédès to Khvalynsk came like a bolt out of a clear sky. Scarcely had he heard the purpose of the trip when the battery ran down. He adored his Mercédès, but not to the extent of going to fight Mironov to preserve it.

Shubnikov was so well known in Saratov that his person was more secure outside the city. But this applied to what might be called peacetime conditions. The situation was quite different when it came to comparing the front and the rear. The worst thing that could happen in Saratov was that they would remember Victor's former wealth, or his newspaper, or his riotous living, while the bullets at the front displayed a ruthless indifference to a person's biography, be the war civil, or any other kind.

Zubinsky (Shubnikov's pal on nocturnal escapades with Commissaries) was of a different opinion as to the prospects offered by the front.

"Don't get excited," he said to Victor on observing the latter's fright. "Clever people have long since put out their candles and stuck the butts in their pockets. The game isn't worth it. If the Whites enter Saratov, the only thing they'll ask is: 'Did you work for the Reds?' And there you are. It'll be even worse for a cultured person. They'll say there was no excuse for you—you knew what you were doing. But if you find yourself up against it at the front— well, there's the woods and the fields, and farmhouses, and your lines, and enemy lines—in a word, plenty of choice."

"They don't play hares and hounds at the front. They shoot people there."

"What of it? Don't be a fool. Do some shooting yourself—go shooting off in your Mercédès," snorted Zubinsky, after which he removed a thread from his cuff and added in an authoritative tone: "In a word, the machine is to be kept in perfect order."

Victor realized that he was caught like a mouse in a trap, and there was no one to help him escape. On the contrary, at such a moment the authorities were ruthless. For that reason Victor Semyonovich delivered the car at the exact hour specified, energetically helped tie on the baggage, and saluted Izvekov with a flourish that was almost as impressive as Zubinsky's.

Kirill circled the machine.

"Everything in order?"

"A full tank of gas and a reserve tin. Two spare tires. The motor isn't quite what it should be. Badly worn. But as they say—God willing. . . ."

During the past year Victor Semyonovich had developed a smile which expressed something halfway between bootlicking and good-natured simplicity.

Kirill gave him a sharp glance.

"It's not God who'll be answering for it, but you," he said.

"Quite right. Just a saying, you know. . . ."

Zubinsky offered Kirill the front seat, but the latter declined, climbing in back alongside of his assistant. With a glance at his watch he ordered Shubnikov to start.

A long drive in a car offers plenty of opportunity to come to a new understanding of things, to review events with a calm glance. Wide spaces incline one to meditation.

The spaces beyond Saratov were monotonous to the point of being dull and even sinister. The thin woods at the edge of the city were succeeded by bare hills cut up by ravines. Settlements fringed by willows and poplars were scattered at distances of many versts from each other. The roads should have been lined with birches and the hollows filled with oak and evergreen woods—the yellow nakedness of this land cried out for refreshing forest shade. How the fields would revive if the constant wind from the steppes scattered cooling forest mist over their furrows, instead of searing them with drought! How the springs would sparkle in the ravines, how the dew would glisten at dawn, how the streams would murmur! The arid earth unrolling before Kirill yearned for such refreshment. And from earliest childhood Kirill had shared this yearning—had pictured this endless plateau covered with rich foliage. Now he smiled as he recalled the type of verdure he had then visioned. His imagination had transplanted him to exotic tropical parks which seemed suspended above the earth, protecting it with a canopy of luxuriant trees. These strange parks kept recurring to him as his imagination rebounded from harsh contact with the barren steppes into visions of a lacy tangle of lianas. The dreamer was not curious as to how this transformation was accomplished. Suddenly the steppes were covered with parks. That was enough. The imagination revelled in the fruit without asking who had planted and nurtured it. Gather and feast; the fruit is sweet, though it be the fruit of a distant future, while the wretched clay overgrown with wormwood is repellent. Now Kirill found that the tropical extravagances which had captivated his childish fancy amazingly resembled the petrified flora of rock strata. And he began to ponder problems which in childhood had lain without the pale of his imagination. He pondered the possibilities of such a transformation. What must be done in order to enrich the steppes? How could they be watered? What trees should be planted in the ravines and on the hills? What varieties would prove resistant to the hot winds? How extensively would the uyezd have to be irrigated in order to turn the steppeland into woodland? How could towns and villages be mobilized for the struggle to transform Nature? Could ten thousand people take care of ten million trees? Would ten million trees be enough? How much time would pass before the forest ceased demanding moisture and began to supply it? No, this was no dream of the transformation of the region, nor even an abstract pondering of the question. It was the solving of a problem by means of cold calculation. Dreams of remaking the future had become the actuality of remaking it; the dreamer had become the doer. "And still ... and still ..." thought Kirill whimsically, as the exotic fantasies of his childhood gleamed far, far beyond the oak forests he was now contemplating.

The road looped to the right and left, swinging up and down, unaware of boredom, unconcerned with problems. And the round hills, now clayey yellow, now chalky white, rose like sunburn blisters on the belly of the earth. Everywhere the harvest had been gathered in, and only here and there stood pale hayricks.

Zubinsky slowly turned his head, wondering whether he dared violate the prolonged silence.

"Comrade Izvekov, I wanted to ask you what I am to call myself?"

Loathe to interrupt the flow of his thoughts, Kirill did not answer at once, but sat studying the long face distorted with a twist. What kind of a person was Zubinsky? What had led him to choose the same path Izvekov had chosen? What united them—common friends or common enemies?

"Call yourself by your first name and patronymic," said Kirill at last, laughing shortly.

"I understand that," replied Zubinsky with a guffaw. "But I mean in respect to my official position."

"What do you consider your official position? What do you think your duties will be?"

"This is how I see it," said Zubinsky very definitely as he screwed to a more comfortable position with his elbow on the back of the seat. "I shall fulfil the duties of your adjutant. I shall write reports."

"What kind of reports?"

"Descriptions of battles. A diary of military operations. You, as commander...."

"I'm not the commander."

"I understand. But, speaking frankly, as the actual commander, you are the one who will give general orders; the commander will lead in battle; and I will write reports."

Kirill laughed loud and long, rocking with the movement of the car. Then he glanced so sharply into Zubinsky's face that the latter quailed, removing his elbow and straightening up.

"You will do whatever you are ordered to do by our commander, Comrade Dibich, or by myself."

"Of course, of course. It is my duty to carry out orders," said Zubinsky, with loss of confidence, but not of dignity. "Only I should like you to indicate just what falls within the sphere of my duties. Formerly an adjutant had duties in the regiment like, for example, being in charge of communications: sergeants, scouts, telephone operators. . . ."

"All right, I'll let you be in charge of them— except the scouts," interrupted Kirill quickly, once more giving Zubinsky a piercing glance.

Again they were silent for a long time. The swaying of the car lulled them to sleep, but the bumps woke them up. Every once in a while Shubnikov would mutter something under his breath, though his driving gave no cause for complaint. Once more Zubinsky turned around.

"I can't help admiring how quickly you equipped and sent off the detachment, Comrade Izvekov. Without any fuss or noise. A born organizer. Not many your equal."

Izvekov did not answer.

"You ought to have a whole army at your command, honest to goodness," continued Zubinsky. "Nobody could understand it: holding the position you did and then being put at the head of one miserable little company. . . ."

"Offended on my account?"

"Not exactly offended, but surprised. A waste of good material, as I see it. Big people should be entrusted with big jobs. Just look what success the world revolution's having. That's a field for you! But here in this backwater of ours— wasting your time on small fry."

"That's an interesting idea," said Izvekov. "Perhaps you have your own views on strategy too?"

"It seems to me," said Zubinsky ponderously, "it seems to me we ought to concentrate all our forces on fighting the counterrevolutionaries in the Ukraine, and when we have wiped them out, turn to the west. There we would be caught up on the wave of world revolution."

"That's interesting," repeated Izvekov. "In other words, we ought to turn our backs on Denikin and Kolchak so that they can join forces and knife us in the back from the Volga? Is that the way you see it?"

"Of course we'd have to sacrifice something by turning our backs on the east. But the fact that now we are turning our backs on the west will cost us even more: if we let the right moment slip past, it will never return. The wave will pass over."

"I can see you have a definite plan in mind, and one which has plenty of supporters. It's true the grass always looks greener in the neighbour's yard."

Zubinsky was about to object when the automobile gave a sudden jolt and veered to the side of the road, coming to a halt with a screeching of brakes.

"A blowout!" cried Shubnikov in exasperation as he flung open the door.

Everyone began to climb out of the machine.

They were high above a river winding lazily between sheer banks and peaked hills which seemed to be keeping watch over the surrounding country. The sun was already setting and the shadows of the hills gave everything a lifeless, funereal appearance. There was not a breath of wind stirring. Somewhere a snipe whistled sadly as it planed in the sky.

Shubnikov immediately set about changing the tire with the efficiency of a practised driver. Izvekov liked the economy of his movements. Zubinsky fastidiously rebuckled and adjusted his belt. Kirill's assistant, who had not said a single word throughout the journey, watched Zubinsky disapprovingly.

Several times Kirill glanced at his watch as he paced up and down along the edge of the embankment. They had already covered more than half the distance, but this holdup cancelled their achievement. Gradually Kirill became annoyed by Shubnikov's continued fussing. It seemed to him there was something intentional in his labours—it certainly was taking him more than the usual time to pump up the inner tube.

"Can't you hurry up a bit? Let's take turns," he suggested.

"All right," agreed Zubinsky, beginning to unfasten his sword belt.

As he watched his affected movements, Kirill was overwhelmed by a wave of disgust for his dandyism.

"So you have no wish to waste your time on small fry?" he said to Zubinsky.

"I wasn't speaking for myself. I'm a person who merely carries out orders, and one who, you might say, is robbed of all initiative by the very nature of his position."

214

"Oh I don't know about that. It seems you show plenty of initiative when you want to. What was the idea of putting Dorogomilov out of his apartment?"

"So they complained to you, did they? But it was the Military Commissar himself who had me do it. We need buildings for recruiting centres. I searched the whole town over. Actually the apartment of Dorogomilov belongs to the city. And it's very conveniently located."

"For you?"

"Not for me, but. . . ."

"Are you personally fixed up all right?"

"In respect to an apartment? Awful."

"So you took a fancy to Dorogomilov's apartment?"

"I don't see why I, a soldier serving in the Red Army, should have to live in a rickety hovel up in the hills . . ."

"While Dorogomilov lives in a comfortable apartment in the centre of town," finished Kirill.

"I wasn't taking the apartment for myself. That's just tongue-wagging. I only had the hope that the recruiting centre would give me one room."

"Did you inform the Military Commissar of your plans?"

Zubinsky shrugged his shoulders. He stood there in his sweater, carefully folding the coat he had just removed and placing it on top of his belt and holster at the edge of the road. Going over to the automobile, he took the pump out of Shubnikov's hands and turned to Kirill to say:

"You don't know me very well, Comrade Izvekov. Zubinsky always sees things to a finish before making any report. What sense would there be in my reporting to you now, for instance, that the driver is pumping up the tire? When the tire's ready, I'll make my report: 'Comrade Commissar, the machine's repaired; we can set out.' "

He began to pump energetically.

When they had been on their way again for about an hour, the motor suddenly began to backfire. Once more Shubnikov had to fritter about, this time with the spark plugs, and again everyone climbed out.

The trees growing in front yards almost met over the highway. People were out taking their evening stroll, and soon a group of curious youngsters gathered about the automobile.

Zubinsky sauntered over to some peasants who were standing apart. He seemed excited when he returned, preening himself excessively even for one of his habits.

"Have you heard some news?" asked Izvekov.

"All the news is as old as Methuselah's beard, Comrade Commissar. No news in a hole like this. I wanted to get hold of some milk. Won't sell it—only barter it for salt. If we could only hurry and get to Volsk. . . . How are things coming, Shubnikov?"

Victor Semyonovich complained that if there had been time to overhaul the motor before setting out, they would not be having these stops.

"Too bad—a trip like this'll ruin the Mercédès."

But soon the motor began to work and everyone climbed back in. Not a word was spoken. The road, now dark and cool, ran east. More and more often they drove through woods, sometimes thick ones. The driver turned on the lights. The world suddenly narrowed down to a ribbon of white light in which the telegraph poles grew slowly, then swiftly flashed past.

When they were so near the city that the lights of the station were visible, the motor again went dead. Shubnikov let out an oath. As soon as they extinguished the headlights the machine was completely engulfed in darkness. Victor Semyonovich raised the hood and bent over the motor while Zubinsky held a flashlight.

Suppressing his fury, Kirill walked up and down the side of the road, now folding his arms on his breast, now holding his hands behind his back. Suddenly he stopped.

The faces of Shubnikov and Zubinsky were caught in the motionless beam of the flashlight as they bent over the motor. With lowered eyes, Zubinsky was angrily muttering something to Shubnikov, who answered shortly, and with obvious displeasure. It was clear that they were not working over the engine. Kirill was impressed by Zubinsky's nostrils, so flaring that they almost turned inside out.

Kirill called his assistant and quietly told him to stand by. He himself went over to Zubinsky.

"We may as well take advantage of this delay to find out where the troop train is. Go to the station and make enquiries."

"Just as you say, Comrade Commissar."

"Give me the flashlight. I'll hold it for the driver."

"What about me? I don't know this road."

"You can manage. The lights of the station are visible."

Zubinsky went off without a word.

Kirill moved closer to the machine.

"Just what's the trouble here?"

"I can't figure it out," sighed Shubnikov despairingly.

"Try," replied Kirill.

"The spark plugs seem to be in order, but there's no spark. Nothing could be worse than these worn-out cars. Sometimes you're faced with a conundrum the devil himself couldn't solve!"

"Here, hold this," said Kirill, handing the flashlight to Shubnikov and bending over the magneto.

"Nothing wrong with the magneto," said Shubnikov quickly, deflecting the flashlight.

"Bring the light closer," ordered Kirill.

He began to remove the top of the interrupter.

"There's nothing to look at here—I've already examined it," exclaimed Shubnikov, reaching for the top.

Kirill pushed away his hand, took a wrench, and began unscrewing. Shubnikov switched off the flashlight. At that moment he felt a strong hand close over his fingers; the flashlight was taken out of his hand by Kirill's assistant, who had quietly slipped up from behind. The light went on again. Kirill calmly unscrewed the top and glanced at Shubnikov: the interrupter was missing.

Kirill's assistant turned the flash on Shubnikov. Victor Semyonovich's underlip was trembling and jerking as though he wanted to say something and could not.

"Who removed the interrupter?" asked Izvekov.

"Who do you take me for—my own enemy?" muttered Shubnikov in a voice that had suddenly gone hoarse.

"Hardly."

"I can't make a thing out of it," said Shubnikov, coughing and making a feeble effort to smile.

"I can make quite a lot out of it," said Kirill dryly. "Have you a revolver?"

"No."

Kirill felt his pockets.

"Get into the machine. No, not in the driver's seat—in back."

Victor Semyonovich meekly obeyed. The beam of the flashlight followed him while he climbed in and sat down. Izvekov and his assistant took up posts on either side of the machine.

For a long time no one said a word. A night bird skimmed over their heads with a noise like a sigh, then let out two unearthly cries. The grasshoppers choired in the fields. Cooling breezes brought the odour of hot bricks. From the station came the mournful whistle of a locomotive. The station lights grew brighter.

"You didn't think I knew anything about motors, eh?" said Kirill slowly.

"Of course I did," replied Shubnikov with relief. "I remember very well that you're a mechanic by training."

"You don't say! Then what were you counting on?"

"I swear I don't understand a thing!"

"In other words, it was Zubinsky who took out the interrupter? What were you talking to him about?"

"We weren't talking about anything. He bawled me out for not being able to put my finger on the trouble. Said he was the one had recommended me to Comrade Izvekov, and here I was acting like an idiot."

Once more there was silence, and the darkness seemed to thicken.

"Of course. You'd have to count on a person's not knowing the first thing about motors to go and take out the interrupter," said Shubnikov.

Kirill made no reply.

"It's silly to suspect me," said Victor Semyonovich reproachfully. "I set great store by my reputation. It's just that you hold a personal grudge against me, Comrade Izvekov. For personal reasons."

"What nonsense are you talking!" said Kirill.

"I thought it was nonsense too—just a trifle. Long since forgotten. But it turns out different."

"What does?"

"It turns out you can't forgive Shubnikov for having once stood in your way. But just think how long ago that was! Lots of water has flowed under the bridge since then. Looks like you're one to harbour a grudge."

"Drop this talk."

"It's been a long time now since I turned down what you and I once thought was our heart's desire. I left Elisaveta Merkuryevna, Comrade Izvekov. So you see there's no sense in trying to take revenge on me. Who knows— maybe my unhappiness with Elisaveta Merkuryevna saved you from a great disappointment."

"Enough I tell you! Shut up!" cried Kirill in fury.

Suddenly Kirill's assistant, who all this time had remained silent, growled menacingly:

"Shut your trap!"

At least a half hour passed before they detected the shadow of a man striding along the road in military style. Ever more distinctly they could make out his silhouette—his breeches flaring like sickles, with his slick calves the handles.

Kirill allowed Zubinsky almost to reach the automobile before he turned on the headlights.

The fellow squinted and shielded his eyes with his hand.

"It's me, Comrade Commissar," he said. "It's me."

"Well?" asked Izvekov.

"The troop train is expected to arrive in twenty minutes. How's the machine?"

"Thank you," said Kirill. "Hand over your gun."

"What do you mean?"

"Hand over your gun."

"You must be joking, Comrade Izvekov."

Zubinsky stepped into the shadow. Kirill whipped his revolver out of his pocket.

"Hand over your gun, I tell you!"

With slow, elaborate movements, Zubinsky began to unfasten the squeaking holster.

"Maybe you would condescend to explain to me just what has happened?" he asked in a challenging tone tinged with flippancy.

As soon as the holster was unfastened Kirill grabbed Zubinsky's gun.

"It's you who are to do the explaining. When I ask you."

The two men under arrest were ordered to roll the machine to the side of the road. It was necessary to abandon it there in the darkness for some time. Then the men set out down the highway—Izvekov and his assistant behind, with the latter's gun trained on the two up ahead.

They were still some distance from the station when a train roared past. From the number of cars, Kirill recognized it as Dibich's troop train.

The soldiers were busy unloading when the four men arrived at the station.

Dibich was as happy to see Izvekov as though they had parted years before, instead of on the preceding morning. Unexpectedly for both of them, Kirill and Dibich embraced.

"Everything's fine so far as the troops are concerned. Did you have a good trip?"

"Made the last lap under our own steam."

"Why? A break-down?"

"A slight one. We ran into that brick wall. Remember?" laughed Kirill.

"Brick wall?" repeated Dibich, puzzled. Suddenly he opened his eyes wide: "Zubinsky?"

"That's right. Please send a couple of horses to tow the Mercédès to the station. I think for the present it will be best to hand it over to the station guard."

Kirill recounted what had happened, adding that they would have to take the prisoners along, and hold a proper investigation of the case on reaching their destination.

"Our first loss in men," said Dibich when Kirill had finished.

"Our enemy's first loss," corrected Kirill.

"An achievement of our Security Service," said Dibich, glancing at Izvekov with an encouraging smile.

"A blunder of our Security Service," said Kirill, also smiling. "Fortunately we caught it in time."

"I should have talked you out of taking Zubinsky."

"It was my fault for being in such a hurry," said Izvekov brusquely. "We shall be more careful in the future. Now let's get busy. We must set out before dawn."

* 25 *

Early one morning, when they were within less than a day's march of Khvalynsk, Dibich's scouts met with a Red Army mounted patrol, from whom they learned that Repyovka, the nearest town, had been captured by an armed band of rebels. The patrol was part of a small detachment from Khvalynsk, sent to put down the rebellion.

Such rebellions were quite frequent. They were stirred up by reactionary political parties, which based their activities on the rich peasants and counted on the support of the peasantry as a whole. Sometimes these outbursts were sporadic, limited to a single town or volost. Sometimes they encompassed entire uyezds, or even gubernias.

Early in the spring of that year, a wide movement of unrest had spread throughout adjoining uyezds of the Simbirsk and Samara gubernias. It received the name of the Chapan rebellion. (The peasant coat which in other regions is called an "azyam" or "armyak," is called by the Volga peasants a "chapan." There is a humorous song which runs: "Did we go for a ride?" "Yes we did." "Did I wear my chapan?" "Yes you did." "Did I take it off?" "Yes you did." "Did I put it in the cart?" "Yes you did." "Then where is it?" "Where is what?" "My chapan." "What chapan?" "Didn't we go for a ride?" "Yes we did." "Did I wear my chapan?" ... and so on, all over again.) The Chapans were supported by Left- and Right-wing Socialist-Revolutionaries, who, under the pretence of defending the constitution of the R.S.F.S.R., spread the slogan "Down with Communist Control of the Soviets!" For greater mystification, the Chapans were given banners bearing the absurd inscription: "Down with the

Communists! Long Live the Bolsheviks!" The rebellious kulaks further strengthened their propaganda by challenging people to come to the defence of the Orthodox Church. Dolinin, commandant of the city of Stavropol and an adherent of the Chapans, began his first appeal to the peasants with the words: "The time has come for all Orthodox Russians to awake!", and ended with: "Arise in rebellion, for god is with us!" The commandant wrote the name of God with a small letter, as was then in vogue (apparently having in mind his professed devotion to the Soviets), but the struggle for the Almighty, for icons and other holy concerns, considerably bolstered the cause of the Chapans, and that same Dolinin wrote in one of his announcements: "I order all citizens to remove their hats on entering government offices, for that is the first duty of a Christian." The Chapan rebellion was suppressed by local forces a week after it broke out. But for a long time its echo resounded in remote corners of Volga forest and steppe regions.

The pious banditry of the Chapans was a part of the Russian Vendée, which never became united into a single force despite the many desperate efforts made during the civil war (along the Volga as well as in the Ukraine and the black-earth regions of Tambov) to turn the masses of the peasants into a bulwark of counterrevolution. Many of these rebellions were prolonged and bloody. But none of them was destined to have decisive significance. The Red Army firmly held the fate of the future in its hands, and the strongest enemy of the Red Army was the regular army of the Whites. Kulak revolts flared up and died down, smoldered or went out, according to events at the various fronts, and more often than not the rebellions were merely tiny coals scattered by the storm of war to distant villages.

As soon as Dibich's scouts brought the news that Repyovka was in the hands of the enemy, Dibich got in touch with the Khvalynsk detachment sent to put down the rebellion. The detachment was headed by a military commissar and a member of the Uyezd Executive Committee of the Soviet, both of whom had been informed of the company sent from Saratov. The meeting between the commanders of the detachment and of the company took place on a hill south of Repyovka, from where they had a fine view of the surrounding country.

Repyovka lay in a valley, bounded on north and south by sloping hills. The town boasted many orchards which in the west merged with the forests of the highlands. Along the east extended a line of hills which broke off sharply to form the steep Volga embankment. The valley was crossed by a wide highway connected with the northern and southern hills by a dirt road. This road, which appeared and disappeared among the orchards, formed a main street bisecting Repyovka. Field glasses gave a view of the market square in the centre of the town, with its volost administration building, inn, school, granary, and a church crowned by azure domes.

The position of the rebels in this hollow surrounded by hills seemed highly disadvantageous. The only thing in their favour was the orchards and the nearness of the woods. Inhabitants of neighbouring villages disagreed as to the number of the rebels, figures ranging from fifty to a hundred. Nor was it possible to identify the band. Some claimed that the rebels were Green, i.e., deserters who had emerged from the woods. Others said they were followers of Mironov. Still others asserted that they were kulaks from Repyovka who refused to hand over their surplus grain to the government. Probably the truth was a mixture of all these claims, although there was no news of the Mironov rebellion, except for rumours coming from Khva-

lynsk that Mironov had been defeated on the
Sura River and his cavalry had scattered.

It was decided that the company and the
detachment should operate jointly under Dibich's command and that a Revolutionary Military Committee be formed, consisting of Izvekov, the Khvalynsk Military Commissar, and
the member of the Executive Committee. Dibich,
accompanied by mounted guards, immediately
left to select a position for the troops, while
the Revolutionary Committee set about deciding
the pressing matters which immediately arose.

First of all, Izvekov reported on the sabotage of driver Shubnikov and former tsarist
officer Zubinsky. The affair was a matter for a
military tribunal. Under the circumstances, the
Revolutionary Committee assumed the powers of
a tribunal and undertook the investigation without delay.

The highest governing body of this little
front which had so suddenly sprung up among
the dozens of other fronts, found headquarters
in a peasant hut whose windows looked out upon
the undulating hills along the river, now basking in the warmth of a clear and windless mid-
day.

When Zubinsky was led into the hut, he was
met by unbroken silence. The prisoner had

grown noticeably thinner as a result of the march. He no longer wore his wide belt and holster, and the ruby star was missing from his cap, but his dusty uniform seemed to have been recently pressed and sat trimly on his erect figure. He fastened an unwinking gaze on Izvekov.

Kirill said:

"You are now facing a Revolutionary Military Committee, which is about to try you for a crime committed against Soviet power. State your full name and tell us your origin."

Zubinsky answered unhesitatingly. When he had finished, he raised his eyebrows and asked, with exaggerated subservience:

"Would you be so kind as to tell me what crime I am accused of?"

"You are accused of preconceived sabotage. With the intention of doing harm to the Red Army, you put an automobile out of commission—an automobile belonging to the company in which you served."

"In what way?" asked Zubinsky in surprise.

"Explain to the court how you did it."

"I can't explain what I didn't do."

"What was your intention in removing the interrupter from the magneto?"

"This is the first time I have ever heard of an interrupter. What is it? Maybe while sitting up front with the driver I accidentally touched something with my foot. I don't understand anything about machines. I only understand horses."

"Answer the question: what was your purpose in damaging the automobile?" asked the Military Commissar abruptly.

"How can I answer such a question? It would have been idiotic for me to damage the machine. I prefer riding to walking."

"We are now at the front," said Izvekov with calm insistence. "You are a military man and fully comprehend what is going on. There isn't much time to make investigations during an expedition. Answer briefly: what were you whispering to Shubnikov about while he examined the engine during the staged delay?"

"I didn't want to shout out that he was an ass. I told him he'd be in for it if he didn't find the cause of the breakdown. I was ashamed to face you, Comrade Commissar...."

"Don't call me comrade."

"I see. For the present you are Citizen the Judge, is that it? I told Shubnikov that I answered for him to Comrade Izvekov, because I was the one who recommended him."

"What was your motive in recommending Shubnikov?"

"He was considered a first-class mechanic. I thought he was. In addition to which I thought Shubnikov would be particularly careful with his own machine. He'd hate to have anything happen to it."

Zubinsky shrugged and the corner of his mouth curled slightly. Kirill cast a wary glance at him.

"What do you mean—his own machine?"

"The Mercédès belonged to him—before the revolution."

"Why didn't you tell me this before?"

Both of the other members of the committee turned to Izvekov simultaneously. He picked up a pencil and began playing with it, striking the desk first with one end, then with the other.

"For two days I was in the saddle without a minute's rest," answered Zubinsky. "There wasn't any time for thinking. I didn't suppose Shubnikov would let us down, but it turns out. . . ."

"How does it turn out?" asked the Military Commissar.

Izvekov was upset by the new information. He kept toying with the pencil. The fact that he had taken Shubnikov on the expedition seemed an indictment against himself. It was his duty to have made enquiries about Shubnikov, instead of waiving the responsibility simply because he found the driver unpleasant for personal reasons. To be sure, there had been no time. But it required no time simply to ask Shubnikov's relationship to the automobile. All this complicated the investigation. Or perhaps just the opposite. Perhaps it simplified it. What was the duty of an examining judge? To come to a decision by drawing his own conclusions? To explain to the accused the possible results of the trial? Whatever else he had done, Kirill had never prepared himself to be a judge. And here he was having to both examine and pass sentence. Formerly these functions, it seemed, had been strictly separated. Perhaps only in appearance. The passing of a sentence requires a preliminary investigation of the facts. Kirill had to investigate, and judge, and pass sentence. His conscience told him that this was his revolutionary duty. This was no inquest, no investigation in the former sense, no trial according to tsarist law. This was a judgment passed by the revolution. He was neither a coroner nor a prosecuting attorney. He was a revolutionary. It was his duty to think not of the letter of the law, but of the interests he served, the cause of the revolution. In which case the sabotage committed by Shubnikov and Zubinsky....

234

Suddenly Kirill interrupted the nervous movement of his fingers. He held the pencil firmly and glanced at the sharpened lead which had slightly soiled the tips of his fingers. He gave a slight smile.

"Well, how does it turn out?" he repeated as he took out his handkerchief and began slowly wiping the pencil marks off his fingers.

"It turns out that a mistake has been made," said Zubinsky, also smiling slightly.

"No—a crime has been committed," said Izvekov more severely.

"If it's a crime, at least it's not mine."

"Then whose? Be more explicit."

"I don't know. The two people involved are me and Shubnikov. I haven't committed any crime."

"Then you accuse Shubnikov?"

"I have no grounds for such an accusation."

"Have you known him long?"

"I used to go in for horse racing, and so did he. But then he became interested in automobiles and we rarely met. He's a sportsman."

"A sportsman!" cried the member of the Executive Committee unexpectedly, looking at Izvekov with an expression of regret and conjecture.

"It's impossible to imagine Shubnikov damaging the machine on purpose. Just as though I sprinkled ground glass in my horse's oats."

"But he damaged it nevertheless, didn't he?" asked Izvekov.

"Maybe he actually was trying to save his Mercédès," suggested Zubinsky in an offhand manner. "Afraid it might get shot up at the front."

"That's clear," put in the Military Commissar with growing impatience. "In other words, your evidence indicates that the automobile was damaged in order to prevent its being used at the front."

Zubinsky raised the padded shoulders of his extraordinary uniform.

"If I had had the slightest suspicion of such a thing, I myself would have been the first to stand Shubnikov against the wall."

"It seems to me everything's clear," said the Military Commissar.

The three of them exchanged glances and Kirill ordered the guard to lead Zubinsky away.

The examination of Shubnikov took place in a changed atmosphere stemming from the behaviour of the accused himself. Victor Semyonovich was jittery. He kept glancing at the guards as though expecting something to happen any minute, interrupted his own words and left sentences hanging in the air. It was as though he did not know whether to adopt an aggressive or submissive tone. One thing he clearly understood (as evidenced by the fear in his eyes)—his entire fate was at stake; in one moment his life could be extinguished as easily as a match. While recounting his age, birth, and such data, he stopped to ask incredulously:

"What kind of a trial is this—in the middle of an expedition? Trials are held in cities, under decent circumstances, according to proper form. Why, you haven't got even an inkwell here!"

It was explained to him that he was in the army, but he objected.

"No, I'm not. I was exempted for epilepsy. I'm an epileptic. I have an exemption card. Look."

Out of his vest pocket he pulled a pile of papers, old and new, which he scattered over the table in order to search for the card. He had difficulty making his hands obey.

The member of the Executive Committee gathered up the papers and handed them to Shubnikov, saying:

"There is one question I should like to ask the accused, though actually it does not concern the case in hand. Just for personal reasons—as one sportsman to another. Tell me this, Shubnikov—was Zubinsky right when he boasted just now that he took first place in automobile racing in Saratov?"

"That's a lie!" shouted Shubnikov, waving his arms. "He's lying! He never sat at the wheel in his life! He's no sportsman at all! Not even a real horseman. He always sniffed around, finding out what horse I was betting on. You can ask anybody in Saratov. That's why I say you've got to go to the city if you want to hold a fair trial. There are witnesses there. They'll tell you who came in first in the auto races!"

"Who?" asked the member of the Executive Committee.

"They'll tell you who. Shubnikov, that's who!"

"In other words, Zubinsky doesn't understand anything about automobiles?"

"The only thing he understands anything about is tailors," exclaimed Shubnikov contemptuously, catching himself to add in lowered tones: "Nowadays everybody understands engines. Easy enough to learn."

Without taking his dull eyes off Izvekov, he remarked with an oily smirk: "A person can understand engines without being able to drive an automobile. Maybe that's how it is with Zubinsky. I can't make him out."

"When you went in for automobiling, was it with your own Mercédès?" asked the member of the Executive Committee.

Shubnikov glanced at the door and hesitated. "Various makes."

"Did the Mercédès which you damaged once belong to you?"

"I didn't damage it. Why should I? And if you're such a sportsman you ought to know that the car isn't called a Mercédès, but a Bentz-Mercédès."

"Answer the question put to you: is that Mercédès yours?" asked Izvekov.

"No, it belongs to the Soviets," answered Shubnikov, once more raising his voice. "Zubinsky been squealing? Well, it used to be mine. And when it was mine it worked like clockwork."

"And then you damaged it?"

"Me! All me! Only me! If it wasn't for me the Saratov garage would be a graveyard. I'm the one does all the repairs, and you talk about me doing damage! I protect Soviet property. Soviet property spoils four times quicker than private property. That's a matter of statistics if you want to know. I warned the Comrade Commissar that the motor was worn out when we left. Who wore it out? Me? They hired me in the garage to take care of Soviet property.

239

It made my heart bleed to see what was happening to Soviet property when...."

"That's enough," interrupted Izvekov. "Zubinsky said that you removed the interrupter so that the machine could not be taken to the front."

"Zubinsky lied. Can't you see he's nothing but a windbag?" shouted Shubnikov, quickly drawing the back of his hand across his mouth. "He says I did something or other to the engine because he doesn't understand a damn thing about engines. It's all a lie."

"Once he understands nothing about engines, he couldn't have removed the interrupter," continued Izvekov. "In other words, he was right in saying that you did it. Do you confess to your guilt?"

Shubnikov glanced about and became silent for a moment. He began to wipe his mouth more and more frequently, as though the flow of saliva impeded his speech. His eyes darkened.

"If you refuse to explain why you did it, we shall have to depend on the testimony of Zubinsky. He said that you put the motor out of commission in order to spare your former property. Answer my question: did you intend to desert?"

"All right," said Shubnikov quietly, with a toss of his head. "All right. Zubinsky lied in order to cook my goose. He figured nobody would believe me because I come from the merchant class. All right. He's no proletarian either. All right."

"Speak more clearly."

"I'm speaking clear enough," said Shubnikov in a louder voice but still incoherently. "My oath on it. On the Bible. And write it down. Pencil'll do—doesn't matter. Take it all down."

He unfastened the collar of his shirt. Two white flecks of saliva appeared on his lips. He breathed loudly and his words came in a rush.

"Zubinsky wanted to desert to the Whites. I didn't. He threatened me—said he'd put a bullet through my head. So nobody would know. He said we could reach the Whites in a single night in the machine."

"When did he say that?" asked Izvekov.

"Back there when the machine broke down. The last time. They told him that the Whites were in Penza. The muzhiks are expecting them. That's what they said in that village. And they're headed for Saratov. The muzhiks said the Reds were done for."

"Who's headed for Saratov?"

"The Whites. Mironov and his followers. He hadn't time to explain everything. Was in a rush. Said it was too late to think things over.

241

That's all. And it was all him. Zubinsky. There you have it. Now let come what may."

Shubnikov gave a sigh that filled the hut.

"And did he order you to remove the interrupter?"

"He told me to put the machine out of order somehow."

"And you removed the interrupter?"

"Comrades!" cried Shubnikov. "Comrade Izvekov! Do you think I would do such a thing of my own accord? Only at the point of a revolver! Under threat of death! How could I refuse?"

"You could have informed me of this treason," said Kirill. "You were in no danger when Zubinsky left to go to the station."

"Zubinsky went off with the interrupter in his pocket," cried Shubnikov in a tone of despair.

For a moment everyone was silent.

"You deceived me and hid the truth about Zubinsky," said Kirill.

Shubnikov leaned over as though about to fall on his knees.

"I'm to blame for that. Only for that. I was afraid. I didn't think you would believe me, Comrade Izvekov. I thought you'd never forgive me anyway—for personal reasons."

"What personal reasons?" said Kirill harshly, his face slowly going yellow.

Once again the other two members of the Committee looked at him.

"I won't mention it in the present company," muttered Shubnikov with his would-be innocent smile.

"You're a scoundrel, among other things!" burst out Izvekov. "Do you confess that back in Saratov you and Zubinsky had a secret agreement to desert to the Whites?"

Shubnikov thrust out his hands protectively and held the pose for a second:

"Oh no! There was no secret agreement! What I've just told you is the sacred truth! I'm a victim of circumstances. Acted under threat of my life. That's all. Wouldn't ever have thought of doing such a thing myself. I'm a man of my word. Once I agreed to serve Soviet power I wouldn't go back on it."

The Military Commissar said solemnly:

"I think everything's clear. The accused purposely put the machine out of commission and confessed to having done it with his own hands."

"What do you mean—his own hands? My hands were forced! It wasn't me. I was just a victim. How can you put me in the same class as Zubinsky? What crime have I committed?"

"When sentence is passed you will know for what crime," said Kirill with a glance at the guards. "Take him out."

"What sentence?" blubbered Shubnikov, throwing himself on the table. "When the sentence is passed it'll be too late. I want to know now. So I can see who's to blame. If you call me a criminal, I demand meeting Zubinsky face to face."

"I find that superfluous," said Kirill to the other two members of the Committee.

"Superfluous!" shouted Shubnikov hysterically. "Maybe you think Shubnikov's very life is superfluous! Looks like you always found it superfluous, Comrade Izvekov! Can't forgive me for taking Lisa away from you, eh? So now you've got me in your clutches! Decided to have your revenge, eh?"

"Stop that talk," said Kirill quietly, interrupting the man's shouts.

"Shut my mouth for me, eh? Because of the grudge you bear me, eh? Oh no! I'm not one to let you get away with that!"

Shubnikov ripped open his shirt. His lips jerked and he glanced about wildly. Suddenly he paled and rolled up his eyes; with a cry he fell like a board on the floor. His body was twisted by convulsions, his head was thrown back, he seemed to have stopped breathing except for occasional hoarse gasps. All his papers fell out of his pocket and scattered over the floor.

Everyone stood up and watched him in silence. The Military Commissar slowly rolled a cigarette, lighted up, and squinted through the smoke at the prisoner's distorted face.

"Maybe he should be taken out—into the air?" asked Izvekov in a trembling voice.

No one answered him, and for another minute or two they remained standing there watching the prisoner. Then the Military Commissar said calmly, but a bit squeamishly:

"I've seen such types before. Some of them put on the show much more realistically—fool even the doctors."

He walked over to the window and threw back his head, filtering his words through tobacco smoke:

"Get up, Shubnikov. Everything's clear."

But Shubnikov only writhed the more.

"Put him out in the entranceway," said Izvekov. The guard stood his rifle against the doorjamb, grabbed Shubnikov under the arms, and dragged him out of the room.

In the conference that followed, all three agreed that Shubnikov's guilt was fully established, if only by the fact that it was he alone who had committed the actual act of sabotage. As far as Zubinsky was concerned, his participation in the crime was indicated by Izvekov's having witnessed the conversation between him and Shubnikov at the moment the crime was committed. The evidence brought by Shubnikov against Zubinsky might have been dictated by the desire to ameliorate his own guilt. It might even have been false evidence, offered as revenge on Zubinsky for having thrust the guilt on Shubnikov. In addition to the fact that the evidence against Zubinsky was insufficient (though no one doubted his guilt), the suspicion arose that such a person might be guilty of other crimes, the exposure of which might be prevented by too hasty a decision at present. For that reason it was decided to postpone the settling of Zubinsky's case and have him taken back to Saratov if circumstances permitted.

All three of the judges were in complete agreement on every point, yet when the question of the sentence arose, Izvekov unexpectedly announced that while he would accept whatever sentence was proposed, he himself would not sign the paper.

Kirill expected that his announcement would cause consternation. But when it was met in silence, he involuntarily dropped his eyes and became as silent as his comrades. With a great effort he forced himself to add, without waiting for their questions:

"I have personal reasons for refusing."

Instead of relieving the strain, his words heightened it.

"Both of you heard Shubnikov claim that I was settling a personal grudge with him. I wouldn't want you or anybody else to suspect that this was the truth."

"But you helped try him," said the Military Commissar at last.

"I didn't foresee that my right to try him might be questioned. Actually the accused has challenged the fairness of his trial."

"Humph!" snorted the member of the Executive Committee. "What do you care? Counterrevolutionaries challenge the fairness of everything—even the revolution itself."

"I'm not worried about what Whiteguards think about us. But a revolutionary cannot allow the slightest suspicion to arise that his actions are motivated even indirectly by personal considerations."

"What's it all about anyway—some love affair?" asked the Military Commissar unceremoniously.

247

Kirill always turned yellow when he paled, and this time his face assumed even a greenish hue. His eyes flared strangely.

"Exactly," he said, stressing every syllable.

"Steal your wife? He mentioned some Lisa or other, didn't he?"

"I'd rather not discuss it."

"Can it be that you're against the death penalty?" exclaimed the member of the Executive Committee.

Kirill walked over to the window. The other two followed him with their eyes, and all three saw Shubnikov being led across the street by the guard. His step was lively enough.

"There goes the fellow you're defending. Fit as a fiddle," said the Military Commissar.

Kirill swung around.

"It's not him I'm defending. It's us I'm defending."

"Want to come out of it with clean hands?"

"Isn't this a clean business? But it's in danger of being soiled by the misinterpretation that scoundrel is capable of giving. I have no right to allow such a thing."

"In a word, you're backing out," observed the member of the Executive Committee, and there was something caustic in his tone. "Letting yourself be taken in by his provocation."

Kirill strode over to the door and grasped the knob.

"If you wish, the Party can investigate my behaviour.... You ask whether I'm against the death penalty? No. In fact I think it's the only thing in this case. But I shall not put my signature to Shubnikov's sentence."

He kicked the door open and went out.

On glancing about, he saw no one from his company but a Red Army communications man sitting on the porch. The street and the yards and the hills beyond the village were empty. He crossed the road, passed two or three huts, and found himself in front of an orchard whose wattled fence was down. He entered.

Apparently the orchard was abandoned. In a hollow overgrown with thistles stood the remains of apple trees whose trunks had once bowed under the weight of their fruit. Gooseberry bushes viciously thrust out their prickly wands entwined with white-blossoming bindweed.

Kirill came to a halt near a broken apple tree. From a young stump, breast-high, sprang a large branch stretching up and out like a human arm, thickly garlanded with leaves. On one half of the trunk the wood pulp was exposed and drying up. On the other, a ribbon of bark had curled inward to protect the living heart.

Kirill placed one hand on the calloused remnant of the tree. It seemed to him that he was completely absorbed in his impressions of the abandoned orchard. But hovering above these impressions was the incessant thought that perhaps he had succumbed to a moment's weakness and that his comrades were right in saying he had evaded his duty. He would have to answer to somebody for his behaviour. Someone would be his judge, just as he had been judge for Shubnikov.

With amazing clarity Kirill saw Annochka's gaze fixed on him. Perhaps she would not say so, but undoubtedly she would think that Kirill hated Lisa's husband with a hate that was purely personal. Perhaps he would some day meet Lisa again. And though she would probably not say so, she would think to herself: it was he who brought about the death of my son's father. And perhaps even Kirill's mother, while remaining silent, would evade his eyes and think: it would be better if Kirill did not give cause for rumours that his actions are prompted by personal considerations. And would not the comrades who helped investigate the Shubnikov case remember that some intimate affair of Izvekov's was connected with it? Some love affair, as the Military Commissar had put it—something concealed, not for other eyes.

But had his refusal to sign the sentence any but purely superficial significance? Through his crime, Shubnikov had passed his own sentence. With all the strength of his convictions, Kirill believed that Shubnikov deserved the death penalty. Was anything actually changed by the fact that Kirill withheld his signature? Yes, many things were changed. By refusing to sign the sentence, Kirill exposed the calumny that Shubnikov had been victimized by Izvekov. He exposed a lie aimed at defaming a soldier of the revolution, and thus the revolution itself. Oh yes, Kirill was right.

Suddenly he was struck by a new thought: what if Shubnikov remained alive? After all, the judges might decide on a lighter sentence. In that case, would not Shubnikov gloat over the fact that his provocations had been effective?

Kirill's fist tightened about the broken trunk of the apple tree. The pain in his hand brought him back to earth. Once more he glanced at the single branch richly clad in foliage. It was strange to see with what a greed for life the stump thrust that solitary branch skyward. The tree was doomed, and this fact seemed to heighten the frenzy with which it clutched at existence, its last shred of bark feeding the only leafy bough with frantic lavishness. Would it manage to survive? No. For a brief term it would put forth new shoots, which would suck up the last remnants of sap, leaving the mutilated trunk to die and turn into a mere log. It would then cast off its withered leaves, never more to become verdant. If such a moribund orchard were to be revived, it would be necessary to dig up all the old stumps and spade up all the earth.

Kirill said aloud:

"No, of course he will get the death sentence. . . ."

Suddenly he heard a dull shot.

He looked up. At the foot of the neighbouring yard he saw a storehouse, and in front of the storehouse a Red Army man with a rifle. As Kirill turned, the Red Army man rushed to the door of the storehouse and began fumbling with the bolt. In a flash it came to Kirill that the prisoners must be kept there—it was in that direction that the guard had led Shubnikov after the cross-examination. Kirill ran to the aid of the Red Army man.

The storehouse was a sturdy log building with narrow openings under the roof serving as windows—one of those small, well-built structures for storing grain which the peasants build either next to the cattle shed, or at the extreme end of the yard.

Zubinsky and Shubnikov had been brought here in the morning, and for the first time since their arrest they had an opportunity to talk undisturbed. Not once after leaving Volsk, either when marching or bivouacking, had they been left alone.

The tone of their conversation before the examination was at first hostile. Shubnikov accused Zubinsky of having been in too much of a hurry, while Zubinsky threw all the blame on Shubnikov for having damaged the motor in such a clumsy, obvious way, as though he were the only one with a knowledge of mechanics. But, realizing that no amount of recriminations could change their plight, they made things up and tried to think of a means of escape. They decided not to tempt fate while things were quiet, but to wait until the troops were engaged in operations. The conversation then assumed a lyrical tone and Shubnikov became particularly eloquent in recalling the good old days. As he cheerlessly chewed some grains of wheat scraped out of the bin, he even exclaimed:

"How much talent has been gobbled up by this goddam civil war! Take me for instance! Real talent! But what's the good of it, when at the given historical moment all a person's gifts are spent on trying to keep out of jail!"

"Which you didn't manage," observed Zubinsky, heaping coals.

"Whose fault is that? Yours."

They began to quarrel again.

They were unexpectedly interrupted by the guard, who came to lead Zubinsky away. The latter managed to whisper to Shubnikov: "Don't confess no matter what happens!" On returning he said that they were being tried by a revolutionary committee, and that he had denied everything.

"Watch your step. Keep yourself in hand," he admonished Shubnikov.

After the examination they were not inhibited either by caution or by the hope that they might yet be of any aid to each other. They battled their despair with crude assaults on each other. Had they not done so, they could only have lain there shuddering with dread. They gave vent to their fear in fury. Shubnikov insisted that Zubinsky had double-crossed him.

"What're you raving about? I only told the truth. I said I didn't understand anything about machines, that's all."

"Oh no it isn't. You lied that you were the star racer. If that's true, then it turns out you're the one must have damaged the car."

"You damn fool. They just caught you in their trap."

"Don't try to get out of it. Who walked off with the interrupter in his pocket, eh?"

"How do I know what you've got your pockets stuffed with?"

"Well, I know what you had stuffed in your pocket. And Izvekov knows it too."

"You been squealing?" said Zubinsky almost politely.

"Do you think I'm going to let myself get shot on your account? Picked on the wrong man, you dude."

"Maybe you think I ought to get shot on *your* account."

"On your own account."

"Well, your excellence, you haven't yet made a thorough study of my pockets."

"You'll get what's coming to you. Turn about's fair play. Wanted to see me drowned, did you? Well, I'll see you to the bottom first. Now they know you forced me into it. And that you wanted to make a getaway."

"Thought you could buy your life at the price of mine, did you?" said Zubinsky coldly. "Well, to hell with you, you louse!"

In the gloom of the storehouse Shubnikov saw Zubinsky thrust his hand inside his uniform

255

under the armpit and immediately withdraw it. Victor Semyonovich had time only to open his mouth.

Zubinsky killed him with a single shot at close range, fired with exceptional skill. Then he took two steps toward the light filtering through the high openings in the storehouse. He swept his eye over his coat and riding pants and brushed them off with his left hand, raising his revolver in his right. There he stood waiting for the door to be opened by the guard, who was already fumbling with the lock.

Zubinsky fired as soon as the storehouse was flooded with light, but he was immediately thrown off his feet by the Red Army man, who struck him on the chest with his rifle.

At that moment Kirill rushed up and began to wrench the revolver out of Zubinsky's convulsive grip. Another shot rang out. Then Izvekov got possession of the gun. They turned Zubinsky over and twisted his arms behind his back. The Red Army man told Kirill to bring some bast from the pile lying outside the storehouse; with a long, moist ribbon of this bark they bound Zubinsky's arms.

Shubnikov lay face down with his legs wide-spread. The mortal wound in his head was almost bloodless.

Zubinsky's bullet had grazed the Red Army man's shoulder, and a red stain appeared on the sleeve of his uniform. Kirill was about to pick up the guard's rifle, but the latter stopped him.

"That's not allowed. Tell them to send somebody in my place, Comrade Commissar. I can't leave my post."

Kirill led Zubinsky into the hut.

Only now was the fact revealed that the prisoners had not been properly searched: a small pocket for the revolver was found sewed into Zubinsky's sleeve. The investigation of the incident took no more than fifteen minutes. The Committee decided it would be dangerous to hold the prisoner under guard here at the front, so in accordance with the crimes he had committed, he was sentenced to be shot.

They procured some ink from the company clerk, but the pen was rusty and dirty. Kirill cleaned it painstakingly.

He was the first to sign the sentence in his straight, legible hand, writing the "z" with a bold flourish.

* 26 *

On the next morning Izvekov and Dibich cantered out to the positions to inspect the placement of the company and detachment.

Dibich's plan, which had been approved by the Committee, aimed at encircling the rebels, taking advantage of the terrain. The Khvalynsk detachment remained where it had been when joined by the company—just moving a bit down the slope of a northern hill in order to take shelter behind a cemetery overgrown with birches. The company took up the main positions. Some of its squads were stationed beyond the highway to the east of Repyovka for the purpose of making a frontal attack. The rest were spread out on a southern hill whose wooded slopes merged with the forest to the west.

This upland forest was made almost inaccessible by its density and the absence of paths. The only road to it led directly from Repyovka and was in the hands of the rebels. At sunrise scouts detected enemy movements along this road: the band was retreating to the forest, leaving only a covering detachment behind.

It became clear that, in the first place, a complete encirclement could hardly be achieved due to the natural barrier on the west, and in the second place, the enemy was preparing either to give battle in the forest or to scatter in its depths. For that reason Izvekov suggested that they strengthen their flanks with the purpose of pursuing the enemy into the forest.

Dibich accepted this proposal and galloped out onto the highway to transfer several squads from the eastern line.

Remaining alone on the southern hill, Kirill dismounted and walked through the coppice down the length of the position.

The smoke of morning campfires had already dispersed, and the Red Army men—singly, and in threes and fours—were engaged in various chores. Kirill was astonished to see how unimpressive were these groupings, how slender was the chain their lines formed about the territory which was to be captured. While the company had been marching in a column along the road it had seemed a sizable force.

From behind some buckthorn bushes came the odour of dying coals, and at the same time Kirill heard a hearty, singsong voice saying:

"I had a pup once—smart he was all right. Used to hunt rabbits with him."

"Hold on there! What'd you take that with?"

"Trumped it, what d'ye think?"

"Don't try to fool me with talk about that pup of yours. Spades is trump and not clubs."

"Humph, spades!" said the hearty one. "Begging your pardon if it's spades. Spades we don't got."

Kirill took a few steps forward and peeped through the shrubbery. He saw two Red Army men sitting at some distance from the fire with their feet tucked under them like Tatars. They were having a game of "Fool," slapping down the cards on a trench shovel serving as table. He immediately recognized both of them.

On the first day of their march from Volsk these men had involuntarily attracted Kirill's attention; later Dibich had told him their story— the story of two soldiers who, in spite of the great difference in their ages, had become bosom pals.

During the war Ipat Ipatiev and Nikon Karna-úkhov had served in the same company and been wounded in the same battle. Ipat had been released from the hospital sooner than his friend, and once more landed at the front. Nikon found himself in Moscow at the time of the October Revolution, and before returning to his native village decided to make a little money by peddling. But however much he peddled, his money did not increase: its value fell more quickly than he could raise his prices. But he continued to hang about the city, and one day during a raid on the Sukharevka market, was taken up for vagrancy by a patrol of which Ipat, now a Red Army man, was one of the members. The latter helped him out of the predicament. Some time later Ipat went to the front to fight the

Czechs. He was wounded in the eye, sent to Moscow for treatment, and finally discharged. Nikon put him up in his room, and thereafter the two were inseparable.

Both were from the Saratov district, though from different uyezds. Ipat's village was in the hands of the Whites, while Nikon's was Soviet. On arriving in Saratov, Ipat learned that he could not hope to reach home, so he talked Nikon into volunteering into the Red Army. Nikon submitted reluctantly; he was sick of roaming. But Ipat was possessed by the spirit of proselytism, and Nikon succumbed, protesting, to his persuasions.

While observing Ipat and Nikon during the march, Kirill reminded Dibich of Tolstoy's division of soldiers into types—a division which had once greatly impressed him. Kirill and Dibich placed Nikon in the subservient category; Ipat in the dictatorial. But both Nikon and Ipat obviously possessed traits other than those of the traditional Russian soldier. Nikon was a calculating dreamer and submitted to circumstances in order to cherish his dream, which he hoped some day to realize. Ipat was the dictatorial type with definite peculiarities of the times—the type of dictatorial revolutionary soldier, essentially a Red Guard, whose ideal was a soldier-worker. Having crossed the Carpathians, retreated to Orsha, helped drive the Germans from the Ukraine and pursue the mutinous Czechs, he aimed to plumb the secrets of war to their very depths, and his attitude toward war was one of irritation, as though it were an obstacle which, willy-nilly, must be overcome.

As he gazed through the foliage at the card game, Kirill remembered Dibich's account of his first meeting with Ipat in Rtishchevo and the talk of Pastukhov which it had elicited.

"He is also from Khvalynsk," Dibich had said of the writer.

"But he didn't want to return to Khvalynsk," observed Kirill. "Ipat sized him up just about right. Did you know that Pastukhov had run away from Saratov to join the Whites?"

"I know that he left. . . ."

Without finishing the sentence, Dibich sighed with an air of guilty longing.

"He has a beautiful wife. When I get home I'm going to find myself some Asya. . . ."

He glanced shyly at Izvekov, turned his horse and galloped back to hustle the wagons, which were lagging behind the rest of the column.

In the meantime, the players continued smartly snapping down their cards on the shovel and talking away:

262

"There was a rich guy for you, brother," said Ipat, fanning out the cards he held in his hand. "So rich he would soak his sponge in beer when he took a bath. Uh-huh."

"Hey, you can't take a king with a queen."

"It's the jack I'm taking. . . . Then one Sunday he ordered his man to soak his sponge in rum. Ever tasted rum? No? Three times as strong as straight alcohol. Hundred and seventy degrees. So he sent him to the wine cellar to buy some rum. Bring it right to the bathhouse, says he. . . . And light it, so's it'll burn. The rum, that is. And then soak it. The sponge, that is. . . . Ho ho! There you are—the fool again! Seventh time, counting yesterday!"

"If you count yesterday, you're not so far behind me," said Nikon, throwing down his cards and stretching out, propped up on his elbow.

"But the score's in my favour. Pretty poor in ideas you are, brother. No wonder you went bankrupt back there in Moscow."

"Can't see as you've got so many ideas."

Ipat straightened out his legs and lay on his back staring up into the sky:

"I've got only two. One of 'em is how to do some hunting. The other is how to change life so's it'll be fair."

"You'll change it all right."

"*We'll* change it."

"How?"

"Here's how. Anything as can't be divided up goes to everybody. Take a horse: can't divide up a horse, so it goes to everybody—yours, and mine, and everybody's. And everybody has to plough and harrow. That's how I see it."

"You got a horse of your own?"

"Well, no."

"Naturally," said Nikon in a belittling tone as he too rolled over on his back. After a moment's consideration he asked:

"What about things as *can* be divided up?"

"Get divided up even."

Once more Nikon grew silent.

"I've seen that city of yours," he mused, intent on a new thought. "It's plain to me where all this hurly-burly comes from. Make over this, make over that. Like second-rate tailors."

"How is it you escaped alive?" asked Ipat with unexpected venom.

"I was wary, that's why. Hadn't been wary—bang!—they'd have got me quicker than it takes to blink. The city squeezes the guts out of a muzhik."

"What would he do without the city?"

"What would it do without him?"

"Need iron for a ploughshare? Off goes the smith to the city. Need teeth for the harrow? Off to the city. Need a rim for a cart wheel? Again to the city."

"It's trade you're talking about here. But who turns the wheels? That's the main thing," said Nikon slyly.

"Got to come to terms with the muzhik—got to go along with him hand in hand. Then everything'll be different."

"Hand in hand!" sneered Nikon. "Either the muzhik rules the roost, or his woman does. Hand in hand!"

Kirill stepped out of the bushes and said hello. The two pals struggled to their haunches.

"Comrade Commissar," said Ipat with evident satisfaction.

"Have a seat," said Nikon in some embarrassment, dragging his greatcoat over the grass and covering the cards with it.

"We just been having an argument," began Ipat with animation.

"Forget it!" said Nikon with a wave of his hand. "Who's interested in that bosh?"

"Hold on there now. Like as how we're making a union between the proletariat and the poor peasants," went on Ipat unabashed, adopting a vocabulary which he considered more appropriate for carrying on a conversation with the commissar. "Nikon here can't make out which of them's to be chief. He says either the husband or the wife's boss, but the two of them can't run the household equal."

"There's an old saying," answered Kirill. " 'It's the water runs the mill; it's the water tears it down.' "

"How's that to be understood?" asked Nikon cautiously.

"I see!" cried Ipat. "The people—it's them sets everything stirring. They have to be steered onto the wheel. If you let them run wild, they'll tear everything down."

"What you butting in for? Let the Comrade Commissar explain."

"It's true what he says," replied Kirill. "An intelligent, progressive force must do the directing. The workers are such a force."

"See?" burst in Ipat again. "Take the Whites, for instance. They're all for the landowners and yet they expect the peasants to back them up. Steer the people the wrong way. And so they get everything in a muddle."

Proudly he fixed his white gaze on Izvekov, awaiting further approbation. Kirill nodded to him. Encouraged, he allowed himself the liberty

266

of asking a personal question, like one who has won confidence.

"Anyone can see as you're a learned person. We were just wondering here: was there any personal reason brought you to the workers' revolution, or was it just like that?"

Kirill had no time to answer.

From the hollow came a rifle shot which echoed and re-echoed through the woods, and then from the outskirts of Repyovka a running fire was opened on hills and highway. Just alongside of the men, a bullet came ripping through the foliage.

Nikon jumped up, stepped back, but stopped and said:

"Get behind a tree, Comrade Commissar. You're in plain sight, standing there."

Ipat threw back the skirt of the greatcoat and gathered up the cards, stacking them as neatly as the worn edges allowed and putting them away in his breast pocket.

"Trying to find out our positions," he said weightily, drawling his words like an old man. "And making as if their setup was in the village, when all the while they're encamped over there."

He pointed with a crooked thumb to the edge of the woods.

"The commander himself is in charge of your flank," said Kirill. "My place is beyond the highway. We must finish off that band today."

"Whenever you say," replied Ipat in his weighty singsong.

He accompanied the Commissar to his horse and held the stirrup while Kirill climbed into the saddle.

Along the way Kirill met Dibich at the head of a group of soldiers who were being transferred from the highway. Dibich was in high spirits and cried out from the distance:

"The enemy's feeling fidgety. Can't stand the silence. Well, we'll do some talking soon."

Kirill and Dibich stopped for a minute to check their watches. Then the commander held out his hand, palm upwards; the Commissar grasped it with a resounding smack, and, smiling to each other, they went their separate ways.

Grey clouds came up at nightfall, settling over the earth in a dense curtain. It began to drizzle. This dense, windless rain, fine as a mist and stretching from horizon to horizon, was a new factor transforming their surroundings. The air became chilly, so that the soldiers lying at the foot of the road embankment reached for their greatcoats to protect themselves from the rain.

Kirill made the rounds, then selected himself a place in the centre of the line and lay down. Ever more often he kept glancing at his watch, whose hands moved more and more slowly.

The attack was to be begun by the right flank on the northern hill. The Khvalynsk detachment was given the task of first cutting off the road from Repyovka to the forest, then turning west and moving through the orchards to the forest edge. A frontal attack on Repyovka from the highway was to be begun at the same moment, with the aim of wiping out the covering detachment of the rebels, cut off in the village by the Khvalynsk detachment. The third, and decisive aspect of the operation was entrusted to the left flank, which was to approach through the woods from the south, surprising the main forces of the enemy.

Kirill clearly perceived the entire plan, and he had already examined the locality so thoroughly and fitted the action into it so painstakingly that he was convinced there could be no hitch in its implementation.

But as the moment when the right flank was to open fire drew near, Kirill's anxiety grew. The rain had dimmed the hills, and the forest was separated from Repyovka by a curtain of mist. As he gazed through his field glasses at the cemetery with its darkened birches, Kirill felt that it required increasing effort to remain lying there motionless and conceal his anxiety from the Red Army men.

"Where's the Commissar?" he heard a familiar voice say.

Kirill rolled over on his side without rising. Before him stood Ipat, one rifle slung over his shoulder and a second pointed at the disarmed Nikon.

"It's to you I've come, Comrade Commissar," he said in a loud voice, stopping at the foot of the embankment and holding Nikon by the sleeve.

"Who gave you permission to leave your post?" asked Izvekov quickly, nonplussed by what he saw.

Desperate resolution gleamed in the glassy, starting eyes of Ipat. His face was white and his head reared at the end of his scrawny neck.

"The Comrade Commander ordered me to bring you the deserter Karnaúkhov, to be done with as you see fit."

"What? A deserter?"

"Aw, come on," muttered Nikon, his eyes on the ground.

"Allow me to explain?"

"Be quick about it."

270

"His talk raised my suspicions more than once, Comrade Commissar. The village he was born in is not far from here, Comrade Commissar—in the next uyezd."

"Briefer."

"I'm brief. He says he fought through the whole war and came out alive and now to be having to give up the ghost when here he is, at his very front door, so to speak. . . . Every man, says he, whoever he is, leaves some trace after him. One carves his initials in a bench, another plants a tree. But what, says he, is to be left of us but a pile of stinking meat?"

"What has he done?" asked Izvekov with an impatient glance at his watch.

"I may have only one eye, thinks I to myself, but I can see clean through you. 'You going into attack or not?' says I. 'Go yourself,' says he, and cusses me out. 'I'm going to my village,' says he. Aha! thinks I, so that's how things are! So I snatch his rifle and says, 'No you don't, you rum deserter. It's not to your village you'll go, but to the wall! That's where!' And I hauls him off to the commander. The commander gives me the following orders: take him to the Commissar, and whatever he says goes. Shoot him, Comrade Commissar. To hell with the bastard," Ipat wound up heartlessly.

"That's clear—what else?" said Kirill, turning to glance across the road and back again at his watch.

"Aha! Hear?" said Ipat, with a menacing step towards Nikon.

"Planned to turn traitor to your comrades just before battle?" asked Kirill.

"He's made it all up, Comrade Commissar," pleaded Nikon. "He's a hothead."

"Made it up?" shouted Ipat in fury. "Made up the initials in the bench?"

"He's been hankering to put in a complaint about me for a long time. Don't approve of me. Well, so we had a quarrel. Nothing much, Comrade Commissar. Just to pass the time—like playing cards. . . ."

Nikon stood there uneasily, like a man in new boots, shifting his feet and only occasionally raising his eyes to cast a reproachful glance at Ipat.

"So you refuse to go into attack, Karnaúkhov?" asked Izvekov.

"What do you mean? That's my job, isn't it? I never was no worse a soldier than Ipat here."

Kirill was about to answer when a round of machine-gun fire cut querulously through the humid space. It was followed by the cracking of rifles. The shooting was coming from the right—Kirill immediately detected that. But he was unable to determine the direction of the fire. He inhaled deeply, and could not immediately exhale. It was as though a sharp pain had stopped the beating of his heart, and everything that he saw at that moment assumed extraordinary clarity and precise purport.

"Who are you fighting for, I'm asking?" said Ipat more condescendingly, but with a shade of contempt. "For yourself, that's who. Our offspring will be a new sort of people. Did I tell you that or didn't I?"

Kirill turned around. Gazing at these soldiers as though from another world, he mentally repeated the words last heard and uncomprehended, and suddenly their meaning flashed on him: "Our offspring will be a new sort of people." He climbed down the embankment.

"If you make a good showing in this fight, I'll forgive you, Karnaúkhov. If you don't, you'll have only yourself to blame."

He placed his hand on Ipat's shoulder.

"Give him back his gun. And keep an eye on him. I'm handing him over to you. And now—back to your places, and step lively!"

"I'll keep my eye on him all right!" sang Ipat joyously.

They loped in soldier fashion down the line of riflemen, pressing their elbows hard against the guns slung over their shoulders. But Kirill was not watching them.

Through the field glasses the cemetery appeared to be as motionless as before, but it seemed to be broken up into minute details which Kirill studied assiduously. He was interested in knowing whether the shooting was aimed at the village or the forest, but could not make it out, especially when scattered return fire came from Repyovka, followed by heavier, but less distinct shooting from the rain-veiled forest position of the band.

Kirill turned his field glasses on the village. During a pause in the shooting which immediately followed, he heard a strange screeching and saw a frenzied flock of rooks and daws plunging above the fields separating the highway from the village. Separate birds circled above the houses, scattering away from the blue domes of the church only to return, and their strange screeching and cawing mingled ever more urgently with the cracking of the rifles and the short rounds of machine-gun fire.

All that followed seemed to Kirill a consistent violation of the plan which he had so clearly visualized, and that despite his efforts to carry it out with uncompromising exactness.

The Khvalynsk detachment left the positions sooner than the time set. Against the background of birch trees, Kirill made out little figures running down the hill through the cemetery and disappearing in the greenery of the orchards. According to the plan, this was the moment when the attack from the highway should begin. But this moment arrived sooner than Kirill had expected, and with a feeling that nothing was happening as it should, he flourished his revolver above his head and glanced up and down the line as he shouted "Forward!" Not even his voice sounded as he thought it should. Kirill rushed up onto the road, crossed it, and plunged down the other side. Glancing behind, he saw his Red Army men scattering onto the road, looking fantastically tall and tattered in their flying greatcoats. Once more he cried "Forward! Follow me!"

He ran across a field, his ears strained, his revolver waving. Behind him and on either side he heard the heavy thumping of feet, while above his head the birds continued to circle and shriek. He was utterly unconscious of his body, though he kept stumbling over the ruts and furrows of the ploughed earth. He kept shouting something over and over.

They had already reached the centre of the field when they were fired upon from some sheds on the Repyovka side. Kirill glanced about as he ran. A Red Army man to his left suddenly stopped in his tracks, as though he had bumped into some invisible barrier at full speed; his entire body swung around and he fell on his back.

"Down!" shouted Kirill, swinging his arm and dropping to the ground. "Fire at the sheds!"

Before he had finished giving the command, and before all his men were down, a crescendo of rifle shots answered the enemy's fire. Kirill emptied his revolver into one of the sheds and reloaded.

The man next to him, a heavy, bewhiskered fellow with the peak of his cap twisted around to the back of his head, said:

"Shoot into the hemp. See it moving?"

He turned away from Kirill and called out in the calm voice of a worker on the job:

"Keep your eye on the hemp. And the gardens."

Kirill marvelled at such keen-sightedness: he could not at first distinguish the dark rows of hemp which in places rose as high as the roofs of the sheds. But the men had already sensed their target and were training rapid fire on it.

Kirill suddenly noticed a man jump out from behind one of the buildings and dash across an opening. With the physical lust of a hunter for his prey—with an unprecedented urgency not to miss—Kirill aimed at the runner, but he was gone in a trice. Two others immediately followed, then more and more, and the bewhiskered fellow remarked in a tone of disappointment as he clicked the bolt of his rifle:

"They're beating it."

Kirill jumped to his feet and his men did likewise. They overtook him in a rush toward the gardens, tossing their rifles over the wattle fence and themselves leaping or climbing over, then streaming down the furrows, tramping over the flop-eared cabbages. The thin line in which they had advanced now condensed into groups headed for the openings between the sheds. The shooting continued uninterrupted, and it was accompanied by spontaneous outbursts of "Hurrah!" sounding wild and ominous.

Kirill ran along with the others, and like the others he kept shooting and shouting. Down the street he saw several armed men running, and he instinctively sensed that they were enemies, but he was unable to shoot because he was reloading. On the way to this street he came upon two other men lying side by side, their faces buried in the earth. He jumped over them.

He was possessed by only one idea, namely, that he must lead his men to the market square.

and there, in the centre of the village, kill or capture all who resisted.

But on reaching the square they were again met by scattered fire. He quickly glanced about in search of a shelter for his men. At that moment, from behind the damaged administration building on the other side of the square rushed the men of the Khvalynsk detachment with the same shouts of "Hurrah!"

This was a truly incomprehensible violation of the plan. The detachment was to have cut off the forest road from Repyovka and moved against the enemy's main position without entering the village.

Kirill rushed over to the men from Khvalynsk to find out what had happened. But they paid not the slightest attention to him, continuing to dash across the square, loading their rifles and shouting. He thought of grabbing the last man of them, and began to wave his revolver at him. He nearly caught up to him at the administration building. Suddenly he stopped.

In the middle of the road, stretched across the muddy ruts, lay the body of a girl. Her arms were out-flung; she was clothed in a lavender dress, torn and rain-soaked and clinging to her slender body; her skull was cleft almost from the brow to the nape of the neck; her blond

braid mingled with the mud of the road. The upper part of her face—the uninjured part of her brow, her closed eyes and the bridge of her nose—were clotted with mud and blood. But beginning with the delicate line of her nostrils and including her chin and beautiful neck and lips which curved youthfully over white, even teeth—all of this was soft and unsullied, as though she were sleeping, and at any moment would give a deep sigh.

Kirill stared at the body with wide eyes. With inexplicable clarity he saw in her chin and neck, glistening with raindrops, the chin and neck of Annochka, when she gave her head that sensitive tilt to listen to something.

He heard the startled caw and scream of the rooks flying about the church domes, and a shudder passed through his whole being.

The square was empty. Red Army men were rushing in a crowd down the main street between the rows of huts, set wide apart.

So far Kirill had been checking what was actually happening with the tasks he had expected to carry out. Now, however, he was completely dominated by the single desire to wipe out all those who were responsible for shedding the blood of the girl lying in the mud. Impulsively he dashed down the street in the wake of his men.

It became clear that the covering detachment of the rebels in Repyovka had fled to the southern hill in the hope of escaping in the woods. Separate individuals, shooting and running for cover, began to appear on the slope. But they were mercilessly pursued.

After crossing the village, Kirill reached a country road, where he saw a wild-haired bandit in an unbelted blouse drop his rifle and throw up his hands. But at the next moment the man fell to the earth. Others began to throw up their hands, but the pursuers did not cease firing, and Kirill also continued to shoot, regardless of whether his enemies threw down their rifles or fought back.

At the same time, from the forest came the sound of battle, now solid, now intermittent, and judging by the distance of the firing, it was clear that Dibich's flank had begun operations.

Having caught his breath and regained his composure, Kirill ordered his men to round up those who surrendered. They led the first two prisoners to him. He turned away from their pitiable, fear-filled eyes.

"Mironov's men?" he asked, unable to unclamp his lips.

"No, no! Greens!" they both answered, eager to assure their capturer that their band rated lowest of all.

"How many rifles?"

"Less than a hundred."

"Machine guns?"

"Only one—a Maxim."

Having appointed a guard for the prisoners, whose numbers kept increasing, Kirill ordered the men to assemble and line up—those from Khvalynsk separately. From the number of Khvalynsk men he guessed without asking that a small group had been sent from the detachment to help take Repyovka. They had suffered no losses. Seven of Kirill's men were missing. The medical attendant reported that he had dressed the wounds of four who had been lightly wounded, and named the men. Then those who had been killed were enumerated, and Kirill was surprised by one of the names: Portugalov.

"Which was Portugalov?"

"He had light whiskers—the only one with such whiskers."

"A husky fellow?" asked Izvekov. He immediately identified the man as his neighbour in line who had shouted so calmly that they aim into the hemp.

Kirill gave a mighty oath and shook his fist in the direction of the firing.

"It's not over yet!" he cried to the ranks. "Avenge the death of our comrades!"

He ordered them to follow him.

Silently and out of step they recrossed the village, where the gates to all the yards were closed and bolted—all the windows sightless. In spite of the fact that they moved quickly toward the forest positions, the shooting seemed to recede and become less concentrated. On emerging from the orchards they met a runner whom Dibich had sent to find out what was happening in the village. Scarcely had Kirill begun to talk with him when a clatter of hoofs came from the forest road and Dibich himself appeared around a bend.

His was the first bright, even joyful face that Kirill had seen since fighting had begun.

"What's that—you coming to our aid? How are things with you? Everything over? Congratulations!" he shouted eagerly and all in one breath as he reined in his horse. "Any losses? Damn it all! Prisoners? How many? My fellows are combing the woods for the bastards. We sure did give it to them! Killed their leader. Took their machine gun. Everything according to schedule!"

As he watched Dibich, who gave him no time to reply, Kirill also realized, to his own surprise, that all had been carried out according to schedule. Only now did it become clear to him that what had happened had in no way been a violation of the plan, but an urgent and anxious effort to prevent its being violated.

"Why aren't you on horseback? Where's your horse?" went on Dibich.

"A fine thing if I'd led the attack over the field on horseback," said Kirill.

"Oh, that's right. I'm not quite normal," laughed Dibich. "Look what you've done to yourself. On your bellies, eh?"

For the first time Kirill examined himself. His chest and stomach, knees and legs, were caked with mud, and his hands were bloody with scratches. He could not remember having scratched them and certainly had felt no pain.

They had to move aside to make way for the prisoners being led out of the woods. Once more Kirill met eyes whose pleading glance expressed deadly terror. Dressed in rags and tatters, having lost all but the faintest vestige of soldierlyness, these men dragged along, a sombre procession of outcasts. And somewhere at their side Izvekov contacted another glance—a keen, proud glance, full of gay challenge. He recognized its owner.

Ipat Ipatiev was one of the Red Army men escorting the captured Greens.

"Allow me to report, Comrade Commissar, that Nikon Karnaúkhov fought shoulder to shoulder like a true Red soldier!" he called out, without slackening his pace.

"Is he alive?"

"Quite, Comrade Commissar."

"I'm glad. Tell him I'm glad."

Kirill smiled at Dibich and they both understood.

"Rescued!" said Dibich, also smiling.

After discussing further operations, Dibich rode away. . . .

Two days later the victims of this rebellion were buried in Repyovka. Before retreating to the woods, the band, supported by local kulaks, had taken vengeance on their hostages—the chairman of the Volost Soviet, the Food Commissar, and the local schoolteacher, the girl whose body had arrested Kirill's attention during the attack. They buried them along with the Red Army men who had fallen in battle.

Eight box-like coffins made out of unplaned boards stood on the porch of the church—the highest place in the locality, visible to all. Many people came from surrounding villages. Repyovka itself revived after the passing of the storm; from all the yards people issued onto the square, and groups of whispering children scurried among the crowd.

284

The day was windy, with intermittent rain. A lowered red banner swung heavily above the open coffins. There was something autumnal about the pine and birch wreaths with which the porch was decorated. The peasant girls had adorned the coffins with paper lace, cut out of old newspapers and yellow wrapping paper.

Kirill gazed for a long time at the delicate, lifted chin of the dead schoolteacher. Her face held a strange fascination for him; he turned away to cut off the sight, and raised his eyes. Dark clouds scuttled low over the earth, so that the vault of the sky seemed tacked down to the surrounding hills. It was as though the village lay at the bottom of a great bowl, from which billowing vapours arose.

Before beginning to speak, Kirill once more ran his eyes over the coffins. The wind stirred the blond moustaches of Portugalov, and it seemed that the serene face of the soldier was about to break into a smile.

Everyone became breathlessly still when Kirill pronounced the first word: "Comrades." But in spite of the stillness, he felt that he could not be heard. For the first time in his life he lost control of his voice. A lump rose in his throat.

Then the coffins were raised on men's shoulders and carried to the other side of the square, where the fraternal grave had been prepared to receive them. Three rifle salvoes were fired, once more frightening the birds, who had already forgotten their recent alarms. Unhurriedly the forest replied with rolling echoes. The people again donned their hats.

An hour later the Khvalynsk soldiers led the column of prisoners through the village, past the mounted Izvekov and Dibich.

The prisoners had managed to pull themselves together. They had regained something of the posture common to all soldiers, which made them akin in this respect even to their captors. Their step showed that their spirit was broken, but their horror of death had passed.

Kirill was somehow offended by the prisoners' resemblance to Red Army men; the sight of their faces repulsed him as much as ever, and filled him with a brooding malevolence. Frowning, he watched the column march out of Repyovka and along a country road to the highway leading to the town. Then he turned his horse about and without a word to Dibich rode away. The trial of the Repyovka kulaks was still to be held.

27

The rain-washed countryside was dazzling on that sunny day when Izvekov and Dibich set out along the highway to the north.

Splotches of autumn colour were to be seen on every hand, but this brilliance did not yet dominate the earthy-green landscape. The moisture of the last few days had caused the grass to revive and assume a May-like verdure. Against the bright meadows, the yellow boughs of the maples stood out in particularly sharp relief. Separate leaves of birdcherry hung in trembling crimson drops. The upturned earth of the gardens was purplish in hue, and against this heavy, languid colour vibrated the iridescent leaves of tousled cabbage-heads.

But all these details were lost in the limitless spaces which met Kirill's eye as he turned in the saddle at the end of a climb.

To the left extended the ridge which followed the river's course—now bare, now wooded—the beginning of the chalk cliffs called Devichye Hills stretching south to Volsk. Beyond them glistened the Volga. Against the western horizon were etched the jagged contours of the forest, whose depths became darker and more mysterious the deeper they extended into the highlands.

Below, just off the highway, lay Repyovka, nestling in the foliage of its orchards.

Kirill involuntarily started at the sight of this quiet village so picturesquely girdled by hills and woodlands, basking in the glistening purity of the morning, engulfed in a silence so profound that the crowing of a cock could be heard at the distance of a verst. It was inconceivable that this village, seemingly made for a life of peace and concord, had just been the scene of bloody violence horrifying those who had beheld it, and that Kirill himself had been part of this violence.

As he sat motionless in the saddle with the reins loose in his hands, he felt himself very small in the midst of these spaces which could not even be encompassed by the eye, and in the midst of the events, so vast in significance, in which he had participated during the last three days. At that moment he clearly realized that the fighting which had taken place somewhere in the vicinity of Khvalynsk would become lost in the general history of the civil war, just as the village of Repyovka became lost on the map of the world. But at the same time he realized with equal clarity that these events, doomed to oblivion, represented an integral thousandth part of those thousands of parts making up history. And thinking thus, he knew that these events in Repyovka, insignificant for the great majority of people, were of incomparable importance for him, representing as it were the entire course of history. And it was beyond his power to grasp the complete meaning of these events, just as it was beyond his power to encompass the space which he viewed from this hill. He remembered the saying: "War is better to hear, than to see."

Slowly he turned his eyes from Repyovka. Dibich rode up to him.

"How peaceful it is," said Kirill in order to take his mind off what he had seen in the village, yet continuing to think about it.

"Marvellous. And every step brings me nearer home," said Dibich joyfully, reining in his horse and also glancing behind.

Some Red Army men, all bent over and dragging their feet with difficulty, came straggling up the hill. There was only a small detachment of them—some fifteen men. It was now well known that nowhere in the uyezd had any permanent front sprung up; all the trouble was caused by small bands of Mironov's men who, after having been defeated on the Sura, were making their way to the Volga, raiding villages and inciting the peasants to revolt by means of threats and empty promises. For that reason Dibich's company had been broken up into detachments whose task it was to comb the immediate vicinity for these bands. The company was then to unite in Khvalynsk, to which the main detachment, headed by Izvekov and Dibich, was now making its way.

When about five versts from Repyovka, the detachment left the highway and continued along a country road. The road was frequently intersected by ravines overgrown with underbrush and small trees. Wherever it was lined by stretches of forest, gnarled oak roots broke through the surface, forming bumps and ruts which made walking difficult.

By the time they halted for the night, some of the Red Army men were so tired that they fell asleep without waiting for supper. Ipat and Nikon built a campfire. Little boys from the neighbouring village stood watching them, first from a respectful distance, gradually gathering courage to come nearer. The stacked rifles were the most fascinating object of contemplation.

Kirill lay on the grass with his hands clasped behind his head. Grey oak branches and lancet-like pine tips cut their silhouette against the sunset sky: The damp odour of mushrooms rose from the lowlands.

Ipat stopped his exertions at the fire, suddenly alert.

"Hear that?"

Kirill listened, but could make out nothing but the lowing of the cows being driven back to the village. Ipat winked slyly:

"Just wait—we'll make her talk!"

He got up, pressed his palm to his mouth, and began to howl in a thin, high voice. As the sound descended into the valley, it grew in volume, yet seemed in some unnatural way to be self-devoured, and changed into a deep, hair-raising roar. Ipat turned purple with the effort; his eyes started from their sockets, bloodshot and glistening. Suddenly he intercepted the howl with a repulsive sound, like vomiting.

Some of the Red Army men jumped up half asleep and cursed him roundly; others began to laugh. One of the little boys shouted in ecstasy:

"O-o-o! A real she-wolf!"

Ipat shook his finger at him and waved his comrades silent.

A minute later an answering howl came from the depths of the forest, beginning on almost exactly the same note as Ipat's. And in the same way the forest re-echoed with a roar which even more disgustingly ended in what seemed the throwing up of the beast's very entrails.

"It's the mother wolf," said one of the ur-chins with weighty condescension.

"Uhuh, it's her," confirmed another.

"Many of them here?" asked Kirill.

"No counting them. There's a whole litter at the branching."

"Is that far away?" asked Ipat eagerly.

His glance roved from Kirill to the children, to the woods where the wolf's howl still seemed to resound, then back to the children and Kirill. He had completely forgotten about his campfire, and his face expressed a contradiction of scattered and concentrated attention. The weighty child answered:

"Right near by. Just beyond the clearing there's a stretch of mushroom woods, and beyond the woods—the branching, where the forest stream splits up. That's where the wolf has its lair—at the very branching."

"Would you let us round them up in the morning, Comrade Commissar?" asked Ipat anxiously. "We'll get the whole litter. The cubs ought to be big by this time. And maybe the older ones still trail the bitch. I've been a wolf hunter ever since I was a little bit of a shaver."

This proposition immediately caused a commotion. Everyone began saying that of course it would be a cinch to take the whole litter—the only thing was to carefully figure out where to station the hunters and to get as many beaters as possible. It turned out that Ipat was not the only one who had rounded up wolves, or at least who boasted of it, and immediately arguments arose, interrupted by tall stories of wolf hunting.

"Have you been losing a lot of sheep in your village?" asked Kirill, again turning to the boys.

"Whee-e-e! Sheep and geese—that's nothing. The wolves killed a cow when folks started driving the herd out to pasture. The only thing they found was the horns and two of the hoofs. Even dragged off the bones."

"Why don't you kill them off?"

"What with—sticks?"

"Aren't there any guns in the village?" asked Dibich naively, with a glance at the smiling Kirill.

"There used to be. They took them all away in the spring—shotguns and rifles. After the Chapan rebellion."

"Were there Chapans in your village?"

"Oh no, we're Soviet," answered several of the boys at once.

"We don't have chapans, we have azyams," said the weighty lad, and his chums chuckled at his joke.

"Maybe you'll let us hold a hunt in the morning, Comrade Commissar," urged Ipat again. "I'll go first—snoop around and find out where they're located."

Kirill glanced at Dibich and saw that the commander was also not averse to a hunt. He, like the Red Army men, was watching Kirill expectantly, in the hope of receiving an affirmative answer.

"Sorry, but we'll have to put it off," said Kirill in a voice that all should hear. "We have a job that can't be postponed. The hunt will delay us. When the fighting's over we can hunt to our heart's content."

"Ekh!" expostulated Ipat, moving quickly off to one side and shouting to the whole camp: "We could wipe them up in one sweep! Simple as beans. Not like waiting for a bear in the oats!"

For a long time his expostulations could be heard, mingled with the exclamations of the Red Army men, who had been roused by the prospects of a treat they saw no reason for foregoing.

The night passed quietly except for two repetitions of the bloodcurdling howl, which sounded even more fearful than in the evening. Kirill was awakened, and he noticed one of the men shifting about as though he were unable to sleep.

Just before the morning roll call, Kirill observed that Ipat was missing. And then, one after another two communications men rode up with reports from the detachments. The enemy was nowhere to be seen in the vicinity, peace reigned in the villages, and their men were advancing normally.

After hearing these reports, Izvekov and Dibich returned to the detachment, and Ipat came running to meet them. He was a sight indeed— the peak of his cap hung over one ear, the buckle of his belt was twisted to one side, a button was missing from his collar, and it was clear that his boots had been wading.

"Right under our very noses, Comrade Commanders!" he burst out without stopping for breath. "Just past those birches comes a stretch of bilberries, and after them some oaks, and then a boggish stretch of pines, first just a few, then more and more, and right in the very thick of them—the wolves!"

"Wait a minute. Were you present at the roll call?" interrupted Kirill.

"Sure. Got back just in time to hear my name," answered Ipat with a sheepish smile.

"Smart of you. Who gave you permission to leave camp?"

"I didn't leave, Comrade Commissar. It's right here. Just the same as if I'd gone off on my personal business."

"Watch your step. Another time...."

"What a chance! The whole litter right in our hands. Too bad to let them slip through our fingers, Comrade Commissar, eh?"

Ipat gave Kirill an imploring glance, unable to restrain his longing.

Kirill had never been on a wolf hunt. But more than once he had joined Olonets peasant-hunters on their forest expeditions when autumn was at its loveliest. He fondly remembered wandering along the golden paths with a whistle between his teeth, calling to the fluttering hazel grouse, who answered him trustingly. Kirill glanced at the woods. The morning was grey, but windless, so that the yellow tips of the motionless birch boughs burned all the brighter.

"Is it marshy there?" he asked.

"Oh no!" exclaimed Ipat, sensing that matters had taken a favourable turn. "Not marshy! Just a bit dampish."

"How did you manage to sink up to your knees in a 'dampish' place?"

"'Up to the thigh, the Russian calls dry,'" laughed Dibich.

"I didn't sink. Stepped in a puddle. A little stream overflowed and made a puddle. I didn't notice it and stepped in."

"These wolves of yours will hold us up," said Kirill irritably, turning to Dibich.

"We'll catch up a dozen times over," answered Dibich. "Our route is the shortest. We'll be in Khvalynsk before any of the other detachments."

"Oh all right then, go ahead," said Kirill with a wave of his hand, checking his lenience with: "But mind you don't take more than two hours for it!"

"Don't worry about that! We'll have them in a jiffy!" shouted Ipat ecstatically, now pulling off his cap, now jamming it over his ear as he turned to the army men who clustered round him.

But it was not so easy to organize the round-up. None of the men who could use a gun would agree to become beaters, insisting that they be posted for the killing.

The men from the village were equally stubborn. When somebody called one of the muzhiks a fool, saying it would be only the worse for him if the wolves killed his cow, he calmly spat and observed:

"They've already killed it."

There began a hot discussion as to who should do the beating.

"Let the ones with the most cattle do it," said the poor peasants.

"Ekh, you thickheads!" exclaimed Ipat. "What's it to a kulak if he loses a sheep or two? But if you lose your only one, what's left to you?"

"It's decreed as the richest are the first to get called up for labour duty; let them be first as beaters."

Someone mentioned that formerly the hunters always treated the beaters to wine. At this the Red Army men flared up: they wouldn't mind having a drink themselves—in fact they deserved a treat for ridding the countryside of wolves! As though everybody didn't know the muzhiks had kegs of home-brew stored away!

It was only the children who were eager to help. But this also gave rise to arguments, and even to tears, for some of them were rejected as being too young.

At last both groups were ready—some thirteen beaters with sticks in their hands, and fourteen hunters. Ipat gave impressive instructions:

"Here's how we'll carry out this operation. . . ."

They listened without interrupting. He took on himself the responsibility of placing the hunters at their posts, and put Nikon in charge of the beaters.

After crossing the birch grove, the group broke up—the hunters turning to the left, the beaters to the right, walking single file and as silently as possible.

Kirill followed at the heels of Ipat. When they reached the bilberry stretch, some of the men stooped to pick the berries, but Ipat furiously shook his fist at them. They came to an oak coppice, then a thicket of waist-high pines through which they carefully pushed their way. Finally their boots began to quash through marshy ground. Ipat kept turning around to glare at his followers, and from the silent movement of his lips it was clear that he was showering choice imprecations on all who made the slightest sound.

Suddenly he came to a halt in a sedge-grown clearing. He beckoned to Kirill, and pointed to little mirrors of still water among the grass.

"The wells the cubs dug to drink from," he whispered. "See the marks of their claws around the edge?"

For some time he strained his ear into the silence, tilting his head and stretching his neck.

"Now we'll call to make sure where they are," he whispered.

Once more, as on the preceding evening, he placed his hand over his mouth and howled. Slowly this incomparable sound filled the glens and hollows, until it encompassed the whole forest, gradually dying away above the crowns of the trees. For a long time there was no reply. Then, like a distant echo, the long-drawn response of the beast was born in the depths of the forest and slowly rose to the heaven. It was the call of the she-wolf.

But the sound come to the hunters from an entirely unexpected direction. The wolf was behind them and outside the circle of the beaters. Ipat straightened, taut as a string, listening, and figuring whether matters could still be righted, and concluding that they could not be if the wolf had taken her young along.

Suddenly from up ahead came the dog-like barking of the cubs, vying with each other to answer their mother's call.

"They're here!" said Ipat, almost out loud.

He could scarcely restrain his rapture. The blood rushed to his cheeks and he nodded hastily to his comrades to assure them that everything would be all right.

The young wolves kept barking in a high falsetto with a suggestion of a howl, ever more bellicose, and approaching the hunters so quickly that some of the men involuntarily swung their rifles off their shoulders in readiness to meet them.

"They've come for food—their mother should be bringing it," explained Ipat in a whisper.

At that moment Kirill clicked the lock of his gun. The dry, metallic ring was not loud, but so alien to all woodland sounds that the wolves immediately became silent.

Ipat turned a furious glance on the culprit. Kirill was overwhelmed. He stood with his mouth hanging open, and drops of perspiration glistened on his forehead. For a moment it seemed that Ipat did not know what to do. Then he took himself in hand and hastily, though with supreme caution, began placing the hunters at their posts.

They stretched in a line along two overgrown paths, at the intersection of which Ipat placed Kirill, with Dibich next to him. This was a sure place: the trail worn by the cubs (their "beat" as Ipat put it) led directly to this spot.

Kirill was hidden by a low pine. Through an opening in the shaggy branches he had a good view of the path, and he set about studying the thick trunks of occasional oaks, a tangle of elder thickets, and some golden pines rising from the underbrush. There were almost no spruce trees, but Kirill's attention was drawn to a young one which had been uprooted and lay, scarcely longer than a man's length, alongside a decayed log.

His shame at having clicked his rifle had somewhat passed, though every once in a while, as he recalled Ipat's furious glance, he would be troubled by the unpleasant thought that if this hunt proved unsuccessful, he would be to blame.

Tired of holding his gun, he let it slip to his feet. The silence remained unbroken. A yellow-speckled titmouse inspected a neighbouring pine, quickly mounting the trunk. With a chirp it flew to the fallen spruce, then off into the woods, while a whole flock of such spry little creatures rose in its wake. Kirill's wet feet grew cold, and he glanced about for a place to sit down.

Suddenly the stillness was broken by a distant shot, which seemed to break up into a sigh and a whistle, and the sigh rebounded dully from tree to tree, while the whistle mounted boldly into the sky.

Kirill heard inhuman shouts rising unhurriedly and unevenly, as though gradually filling up the hollow of the woods and spilling over. At first it was possible to distinguish the shrieks of the boys from the halloo-ing of the muzhiks. But with gathering speed the yells, shouts, whistles, and the beating of clubs against tree trunks grew into a solid, indefinable roar.

"Hall—oo-oo-oo!"

The beaters came streaming toward the hunters.

A shot like a signal rang out; Kirill raised his rifle, leaned down to his opening, and began to scrutinize the bushes along the path as though they had just been put there. Every leaf and twig stood out distinctly, and the stillness of the trees seemed incompatible with the tumult in the air. It was as though the entire forest were being uprooted at once, and the mangled roots and the earth itself were moaning and shrieking with pain.

A single shot came from down the line.

For a second the moaning ceased, only to break out again with greater desperation. Kirill felt that every muscle in his body was taut. Suddenly he went cold: to his right, from where the single shot had come, began reckless firing.

It sounded as though children were lashing burdock leaves with whistling whip cords. Kirill felt the sting of every lash. He pressed the butt of his rifle against his shoulder until it hurt, and kept staring ahead, afraid even to blink, so that tears stung his eyes.

Something bright flashed under the felled spruce—under the star-points at its very tip. And immediately Kirill seemed to go deaf. For the moment there was no more shooting and shouting—the whole world was concentrated in that bright spot.

From out of a broad-browed face with clipped, wide-spaced ears, the two black-lacquer eyes of a wolf glanced down the path. The creature was creeping forward almost imperceptibly, its head drawn into raised shoulder blades.

Suddenly it gave a light spring and slithered above the spruce as though pouring its body across.

Kirill had already taken aim, but his finger pressed the trigger at the very moment of the jump. The squeal of the wolf came simultaneously with the shot. While still in the air the animal threw its head back over its haunches, as though biting at a pursuer. Then it fell. Twice it bit at its haunches, and tufts of fur were blown about by the beast's hoarse breathing. It crawled away to the left of Kirill, making quick little movements with its front paws and dragging its wounded hind quarters. Sometimes it whimpered like a puppy.

Kirill saw that the wounded wolf might get away, and raised his rifle for a second shot.

But it was dangerous to fire while the animal was crawling along the path, for Dibich lay hidden somewhere nearby. This moment of hesitation was sufficient to allow the wolf to crawl outside the circle, beyond the line of the hunters. It disappeared in the bushes.

Immediately after the shot, all of Kirill's senses again began to function. The shooting had stopped and the cries of the beaters died down. He left his post and rushed after the wolf. He glimpsed its fur through the foliage and heard its growls. The wolf was sitting propped up on widespread forepaws. Its fur bristled in a black brush down its spine. Its hanging tongue and purple mouth were covered with down. At that moment a shot rang out, and Kirill also shot, almost at random. The head of the wolf drooped and its body slumped slowly over onto the ground.

Everything was over. Yet Kirill did not move.

In leaving his post he had violated the rules. Dibich might catch sight of the wounded beast and shoot without noticing Kirill. That represented a definite danger. Only an immediate shot could remove this danger, though the final killing of the wolf could wait, the animal being too badly wounded to escape. And a shot would scare away other wolves which might be approach-

20—670

ing the line. But to the danger that Dibich might shoot without noticing Kirill was added the fear that someone else might finish off the wolf and take the trophy. Kirill must shoot.

Only now, when the wolf was dead, did Kirill begin to comprehend the lightning-like impulses that had led him to fire. And only now did he suddenly realize that besides all these impulses, he had been driven to fire by a subconscious fear of the wounded, frenzied, beast. And as soon as he caught himself in this fear, he was ashamed, and discovered that his body was bathed in hot sweat.

"Well? Is it done for?" came Dibich's voice.

There was so much joyful pride in the tone that Kirill was frightened: what if it were Dibich rather than he himself who had finished off the wolf? Actually Dibich had fired the first shot.

"Have you caught one?" asked Kirill, evading a reply; he still remained where he was.

"I should say so-o-o!" called Dibich with the same pride, and Kirill could hear the rustling of bushes close at hand.

At that Kirill broke away and rushed over to his kill. With pounding heart and wild joy he grabbed the wolf by the ear and raised its heavy, wide-browed head, only to fling it back on the ground.

"Oho, you rascal you!" he gloated, now kicking at the wolf's soft, empty belly, now shaking the coarse fur of its spine.

A beaming, enthusiastic Dibich issued from the underbrush. Taking the wolf by the hind legs, he turned it from side to side.

"So your bullet landed in the haunches, eh? I got mine with one shot—in the shoulder. Did you hear it?"

"Here's how it happened. . ." exclaimed Kirill, and began an eager, detailed account of how his first shot had caught the wolf on the leap, how the wolf had crawled away, and how he had finally finished it off. He omitted to say that he had killed the beast while cornered.

Several of the beaters were attracted by their voices, and came to gaze curiously at the catch. One of them had a bleeding cheek and a torn sleeve. He ran his finger over his cheek and said, showing the blood:

"Ripped myself up on these branches. You'll not be getting off with just a round of drinks, comrades."

"Ought to be glad we got rid of these devils for you," said Kirill merrily, giving the wolf an energetic thump with his boot.

"Some get the gladness, some get the sadness," replied the beater, pulling his ripped sleeve together and glancing at Kirill through narrowed eyes. "Seems you almost let the wolf get away, didn't you? It was pretty far away from the line when you shot it."

"What makes you think that?" asked Kirill, annoyed. Once more he recounted everything that had happened, his enthusiasm growing, rather than waning.

The beaters pulled up a young pine and stripped it of branches to make a pole, which they thrust between the wolf's tied legs, and then placed on their shoulders, to carry the animal away. Kirill followed behind, with the beaters who kept coming out of the woods to join him. He glanced in triumph at the black snout of the wolf dragging along the ground, and recounted with growing eloquence the story of his remarkable first shot, glossing over the second.

Four cubs had been killed. The hunters threw them in a pile. As like as peas, they lay in coats that had almost attained their winter colouring—yellow-grey with black markings on spine and paws, and downy white fur on flanks and belly. Their eyes were tightly closed, as though on leaving this earth, all four had disdained looking at it.

When the group of hunters and beaters began enumerating who had made the kills and how, somebody asked sarcastically:

"What about Ipat? Emptyhanded?"

They glanced about—but no Ipat was to be seen. They began to call. There was no answer. They began to argue as to where Ipat had been stationed. No one knew, for it was Ipat who had placed the others at their posts, and nobody had taken the trouble to enquire where he himself would be. Even the one who had been placed at the last post could not remember where Ipat had then gone: seemed he went to the right—but come to think of it, maybe it was to the left. Then they began to argue as to who had fired the first shot when the beaters began to approach. Everyone claimed it was someone else.

"What did you shart that shooting for?" enquired Dibich. "Used up all our ammunition—enough to defend a whole platoon. Fine hunters you are."

"We opened up a running fire, Comrade Commander, so's to get them for sure."

The frightened Nikon interrupted to say that in his opinion, it was Ipat who had started the shooting.

"When we started driving them in, right after my signal, suddenly I hears a bang!—and then a sort of a snuffle. Ipat! thinks I, beings as his gun's got a snuffle. Just a day or so back he was saying his gun's got a cold—a crack in the muzzle, it seems. So he fires, and then the boys start shooting for all they're worth down the line. Ipat fired from the end—the very last post."

The discussion had filled Kirill with such alarm that nothing was left of his triumph, or of his embarrassment at having missed, or of his shame for momentary fear. For the first time he seemed to realize that he alone answered for this hunt, and for anything that might have happened to Ipat. And not only to Ipat. He was responsible for every single person, beginning with Dibich and ending with the smallest of the village boys who had joined the hunt just for the fun of it.

After sending Red Army men to search the line along which the hunters had been placed, Kirill and Nikon set out for the spot where they figured Ipat might have stood. They examined every spot which might lure a hunter; they called; they listened to the distant voices of their comrades; and at last they came back to those who had searched the line. Ipat had not been found.

The beaters lifted the catch and set out, a long line of followers at their heels.

On the way Kirill said to Dibich:

"Could he possibly have been shot accidentally? Inconceivable! He's an experienced hunter."

"I have another idea," answered Dibich. "We'll probably find him waiting for us in the village."

Kirill stopped, uncomprehending.

"He probably ran away in shame: here he was without any catch after making himself out to be an expert wolf hunter and the initiator of the whole business."

"That's too subtle for him," said Kirill definitely, but the idea took root in his mind, and the closer they came to camp, the brighter burned the hope inspired by Dibich's words.

But they were doomed to disappointment. Ipat was not in the village. The news that one of the hunters was missing spread as quickly as the news that the Red Army men had wiped out a litter of wolves. It was impossible to set out on the march without making every effort to find the missing man, and after a short conference with Dibich, Kirill sent another searching party into the woods.

It was nearly noon. Kirill was sitting at the open window of the hut waiting for lunch. The wolves had been placed under the shed, and he could hear the children playing about them, and the furious barking of a little dog, excited by the scent of the animals but afraid to approach them. As often happens in Indian summer, the sky which had been overcast in the morning began to brighten, and soft, shadowless sunlight illuminated the earth.

At that moment Kirill noticed three men coming along the road leading from the woods. They were walking unhurriedly in a row. One of them carried a bundle in his hand, the other two had packs on their backs. As they came closer, Kirill could make out a fourth person behind, but he was constantly hidden by the forward three. Then he saw that the man with the bundle was pressing something to his chest with his free hand, and apparently it was heavy, for it caused him to lean over to one side.

When they had almost reached the village, the three men parted to avoid a rut in the road, and Kirill saw that the fourth man, about five steps behind, had a rifle trained on them. Kirill jumped up and leaned out of the window, for he had recognized the man with the rifle as Ipat.

Without taking his pale eyes off his captives, Ipat kept walking along heavily, with a slight roll which caused his rifle to swing rhythmically.

Kirill went out onto the porch. Peasants and Red Army men gathered at the gate, awaiting the newcomers in silence. Some children came running into the yard, stepping on each other's heels as they glanced behind.

Ipat led the men through the gate, and then strode forward in military fashion, dropping his rifle to his side. His tunic was open, revealing a glistening chest which seemed remarkably white in contrast with his sunburned face. His voice rang out:

"Here are three captives, Comrade Commissar. I arrested them in the woods. One of them got a wound in the hand as a result of attempting to escape."

Two of the prisoners were well on in years. They were bearded and hollow-cheeked and seemed exhausted. As soon as they reached the yard they slipped the packs off their backs— one of them a canvas sack, the other a bundle tied with rope. The third man also put down his bundle, leaning over with difficulty and immediately clutching his hand, which was wrapped in a bloody rag. Holding it high, he took off his cap, wiped his wet, bald head, and adjusted his glasses.

The moment that he bared his head and raised his bespectacled eyes to the Commissar on the

313

porch, Kirill started. lifted his brows, and leaned hard against the doorjamb.

The bald man continued to gaze at him through his steel-rimmed spectacles with no change of expression. Once more he gripped his wounded hand.

"Appoint a guard," said Kirill quietly, "and search them."

* 28 *

The incident which Ipat reported to Izvekov had taken place in the following manner:

Having taken up his position at the very end of the line of hunters, Ipat began to cast his eye in the direction from which the cry of the she-wolf had answered his howl. He figured that she should come to the aid of her young, and he was not mistaken. Sensing something wrong when the yelping of her cubs suddenly broke off, she came creeping back to her lair, drawing ever closer to the line. She dashed back as soon as she heard the cries of the beaters, but Ipat had seen her and shot. The idea that the honour of catching the old wolf might fall to him, made him abandon the roundup. He found traces of blood on the bushes into which he had shot and set out in pursuit. The further he went, the fewer became the blood stains, until they disappeared

altogether. But Ipat pressed on. He continued long
after the shouts of the beaters had died down,
and at last he found himself in the very depths
of the forest. There in a hazel thicket he caught
sight of an object which at first he took for the
wolf, and was about to shoot when he saw that
it was nothing but an old sack. Alongside lay a
pack and a bundle, and behind them crouched
three men. Ipat made the men come out and gather up their things, then he took a firmer grip
on his rifle and led them through the woods,
replying to their protests with the time-worn
phrase: "That's none of my business." Considerable time was lost in figuring out the proper
direction to take. While passing a gully, one of
the men threw himself over the edge. Ipat fired,
wounding him in the wrist, and threatened to
shoot again if he did not climb back. He gave
the man time to bind up his hand with a shirt
taken out of his bundle, and after that the
march out of the woods proceeded without further incident. Later the sun came out, and this
enabled Ipat to find his way unerringly.

Before being locked up in the shed, the prisoners had been asked where they were coming from and where they were bound. All three
replied that they had left Khvalynsk to go to
the other side of the Volga. When Ipat told Ki-

315

rill this, the latter decided to take the prisoners back to Khvalynsk, first questioning them as to the motives of their journey. One of the men was said to be an old resident of Khvalynsk, and Kirill ordered him to be brought into the hut first. Without telling Dibich what he had in mind, he asked the commander to be present at the examination.

The guard led in a sedate, bearded old man with a woollen muffler tucked into his worn vest. He told Kirill that he was a Khvalynsk artisan with relatives living in Irgiz, across the Volga, to whom he was now making his way. To Kirill's question as to why he should have been hiding in the woods with his companions, he replied that all three had been frightened by the shouts and the shooting, and had decided to hide until it was over. They had chosen the path through the woods as a short cut. When Kirill tried to find out who his companions were and whether the old man had known them for long, the latter replied that they were new people in Khvalynsk, but he was acquainted with them—one of them had even lodged in his house.

"The wounded one?" asked Kirill.

No, the old man scarcely knew the wounded one. His name was Vodkin. He had come to Khvalynsk some two years before, apparently from Penza, and was the owner of a little house on a sizable lot purchased on his arrival.

"In other words, he moved to Khvalynsk after the revolution?"

"Seems so. Or maybe it was during the war."

"I understand that you are going to join your relatives. But those other two—do they also have relatives in Irgiz?"

According to the old man, it was quite by chance that they were travelling together: he and his lodger had set out for Irgiz because things were more peaceful there, and Vodkin had joined them in order to bring back some bees: the regions across the Volga were famous for their bees. He had made the acquaintance of Vodkin when the latter came to have the rims of his glasses changed (the old man did a bit of jewelling on the side).

"He used to wear gold rims?" asked Kirill.

"Seems to me they were gold."

"And who is that lodger of yours?"

The lodger was a devotee of the Orthodox Church who had come to the Seraphimov hermitage with the intention of becoming a monk, but as yet had not been accepted, due to the fact that the monastery was overcrowded. The monks were hard pressed—more and more people kept coming to join them, but their quarters

317

were small. The name of this lodger was Mesh-kov.

"From Saratov?"

"Yes."

"Merkuri Avdeyevich?"

Dibich, who had been carefully following the conversation, could not make out who was more astonished—the old man at hearing this question, or Izvekov, on receiving an affirmative answer.

Kirill sat motionless, as though it required a tremendous effort of will to force his mind back from some great wandering. After ordering them to lead the old man away, he said to Dibich:

"I thought there was only one old acquaintance of mine among those three, but it turns out there are two. Hm."

"What sort of an antique is that Merkuri?"

"Simply a version of the good old Russian name Merkul. Well, we'll see..." mused Kirill.

They brought in Vodkin. He swayed on his feet, one hand pressed to his breast.

"Couldn't I see a doctor? My hand is troubling me," he said, dropping down onto the bench.

Kirill studied him for a long time. He was a man of over sixty with a peculiarly shaped head: the sides caved in, while the back and forehead bulged. Yellowish eyelashes fringed his fixed, sullen eyes.

"The medical assistant will bandage your hand for you," replied Kirill after a pause. "Why did you try to run away when you were arrested?"

"I thought I had fallen into the hands of a bandit."

"Then it was from fear?"

"Yes. They say that followers of some sort of Mironov are crossing over from the next uyezd."

"How did you ever find the courage to set out in the midst of such horrors?"

"Necessity. I was promised some bees from the other side of the Volga. I am a beeman."

"Oh, a beeman. Have you been one long?"

"Not very. One has to have some sort of an occupation in one's old age."

"And what might your former occupation have been?"

"I was a solicitor in Narovchat."

"In the court?"

"For civil affairs—a private solicitor."

"Only for civil affairs?" queried Kirill after a moment's pause.

"Exclusively."

"Have you any documents?"

"Didn't they give you my documents? They took them away during the search."

319

"Have you a passport?"

"Yes."

"What data does it bear?"

"You might have a look. Nothing in particular. Born in Penza. Residence—Narovchat. Occupation—clerk. I began as a clerk, so that's what remained in my passport."

"So before moving to Khvalynsk you lived in Narovchat?"

"Almost all my life."

"Did you ever live in Saratov?"

"I was never in Saratov. I was in Simbirsk and Samara. In Penza of course. Once I went to Moscow—to see the Tretyakov State Picture Gallery. I'm fond of painting."

"What is your name?"

"Vodkin. Ivan Ivanovich Vodkin."

"Only one name?"

"What's that?" asked the man in surprise.

"Sometimes people have double names. That is, the same person has two names."

"Ah, yes. It happens, to be sure. In Khvalynsk, for instance, there's a man named Petrov-Vodkin—half of it like mine. Maybe you've heard of him. He's a rather well-known painter."

"There now, you see?" said Kirill, getting up. "What an excellent example. And almost the whole name coincides—not only half."

"Why do you say it coincides?" asked Vodkin in an offended tone.

"The first half of his name begins with 'P'."

Kirill could scarcely restrain the triumph in his voice. Vodkin grabbed the blood-stiff bandage of his left hand and once more began to rock back and forth.

"Does it hurt?" asked Kirill, studying the man's fingers.

Dibich nervously turned to the window.

"Yes," answered Vodkin patiently, adding with more marked injury in his tone: "I don't understand you, Comrade Commissar. What is it you're trying to find out? This is no way to behave toward Soviet citizens. Arrest them for no good reason and then refuse to offer medical aid. That's against the law."

"You should know the law!" blurted out Kirill crisply. "Don't worry, you'll be given medical aid. The law will be carried out. Only not the law you used to carry out."

"You can't reproach me with anything. I may have been only a petty official, but I was always ready to defend what was right."

"There's no denying that you knew how to defend," said Kirill, keeping his eyes on Vodkin's hand. "Your grip was tighter in those days. You had nice long polished claws then."

Vodkin stopped rocking and shook his head.

"You're trying to make me out as someone else. Or perhaps you've really made a mistake."

"Not at all. I'm taking you for just who you are."

With a glance at his dirty fingers and a wan, meditative smile, Vodkin said:

"A person has to do all sorts of jobs these days, like a muzhik. I never used to have such dirty hands."

"I'm afraid they never were very clean."

"I don't know what you're referring to. . . ."

"Although to be sure, you always used to look much more trim—gold spectacles, for example."

"I never wore gold spectacles."

"Oh, didn't you? When you moved into this secluded little Khvalynsk you had to change everything—from your wardrobe to your passport. But you had no time to change your spectacles. Probably were in too much of a hurry. Those spectacles you're wearing now—didn't you get them in Khvalynsk? Spectacles can be changed, even if a bit late. But there's no changing your head. That's where the rub comes in."

Forgetting his wound, Vodkin raised his hands in protest, but immediately pressed his bandaged . hand to his breast once more.

"It seems you are indeed making a great mistake in respect to me, Comrade Commissar."

Kirill jumped up, kicking back his stool and sucking the air through his teeth as though about to let out a cry. But instead of crying out, he pronounced with great distinctness and even greater calm:

."Our biographies have become entangled, though actually they have nothing in common. You tried to give a fitting introduction to mine, I shall try to give a fitting conclusion to yours." He paused for a second, then added, as though tapping it out on a typewriter: "Lieutenant-Colonel Polotentsev of the Gendarmes!"

"My God! What a horrible mistake!" whispered Vodkin, covering his face with his sound hand.

Dibich, who all this time had been under a painful strain, awaiting some unexpected revelation, let out a gasp and made a gesture towards Kirill.

"There is no mistake whatever," said Kirill, gone yellow, and quieter than ever. "This man has always been a master of pretence. He is an actor. I know him personally. It was he who shipped me off to the Olonets gubernia."

21*

"If you are certain of this, I am amazed at you," said Dibich hurriedly. "Why bother to put on this show? Does it amuse you?"

"Obviously not," said Kirill with a short laugh. "It disgusts me. And yet, when you stop to think what these gentlemen did not so long ago . . . and what some of them are still doing . . . upon my word, you can almost find amusement in scenes like this."

Polotentsev uncovered his face. It remained unchanged, except that his pale yellowish eyebrows had climbed above his spectacles. He said in saccharine tones:

"I well understand that your blind mistake may cost me dearly, and yet I must try to keep up my courage, however difficult it may be. If you sincerely take me for a—a gendarme—then—but the gendarmes were beasts! Fiends! How can you. . . . I beg your pardon, I addressed you as 'comrade,' but now that you have so unwarrantedly accused me . . ." (he laughed noiselessly, through his nose) "probably in time there will be new forms of address corresponding to 'Your Honour,' or 'Your Highness.' Maybe 'Your Justness,' or 'Your Arbitrariness,' or something like that, heh-heh! . . . Well, Your Justness, it hardly becomes you to follow the example of the accursed past—the example of those fiends who allowed themselves to take advantage of defenceless people who. . . ."

"Couldn't restrain himself," laughed Kirill, interrupting Polotentsev's tirade. "The old spleen bubbling up. I remember only too well what an ironic gentleman you were. And not without wit, damn it all—not without wit. It gave you away no less than that bump on your head."

"The idea of all this may be intriguing," protested Polotentsev modestly, "but rather childishly intriguing. Too unfounded; based on a legally unconvincing, false identification offered by a single person. No direct evidence whatsoever. And I assure you that none can be found."

"We'll find it all right, once we get you to the place of your former residence. Not in Narovchat, of course, but in Saratov. Narovchat will not identify you as Vodkin, but Saratov will be sure to identify you as Polotentsev."

"You will succeed only in causing me undeserved suffering."

"Oh, not undeserved!" exclaimed Kirill with profound conviction. "Anything you like, but not undeserved!"

Four Red Army men with Ipat at their head came into the hut, bringing the contents of the packs and bundles. On the table Ipat placed the men's money, documents, a steel watch, and a silver one with a winding key; then he took from Nikon the tin can the latter was holding with awed veneration, and placed it with the same veneration at a respectful distance from the other things.

"No weapons were found on searching the prisoners, but here we have something of first-rate importance," he reported, tapping the tin can with his fingernails and casting a significant glance at the Red Army men.

Kirill made as if to draw the can over, but it did not move, and he raised enquiring eyes to Ipat. Ipat thrust out his lower lip and gave a little nod with his head, as much as to say: just wait and see!

The tin can was ordinary enough, with a sturgeon pictured on the lid and a trade-mark reading: "Astrakhan Caviar." But its weight was extraordinary. Kirill lifted the edge of the lid, and immediately dropped it.

"On whom did you find this?" he asked.

"It was in here," said Nikon, indicating a ripped pillow. "All covered up with feathers."

"Belongs to the fellow you haven't examined yet," explained Ipat.

Kirill nodded to Polotentsev.

"You're the one who brought him here, Ipat; you're the one I shall hold responsible to see that nothing happens to him," he said. "I order you personally to stand guard and watch him like the apple of your eye."

"I'm particularly watchful of my eye—I've only got one left."

When Polotentsev had been led out and Nikon and the other Red Army men were sorting out the prisoners' things, Dibich winked at the tin with a smile and said:

"What is it—some infernal machine?"

Kirill called the Red Army men. They gathered around him. He placed his palm on the table and overturned the can on it.

Gold coins spilled out and over like an overflow of grain. He carefully withdrew his hand. A dull metallic ring hung in the air as the pile spread out and became immobile.

"Mother of mine! Thousands!" gasped Nikon.

"A nice little nest egg!" exclaimed another Red Army man.

"Merkuri—there's your Mercury for you," muttered Dibich.

All eyes were glued on the gold. Only Kirill glanced in consternation at each of the men in turn. Then he walked over to the window and stood there a second before returning to the table.

"You could never guess what memories this calls up," he said to Dibich casually, with a smile. "It explains many things—many, many...."

He touched the gold, which again slid out over the table with a faint ring.

"Mother of mine!" breathed Nikon through soundless lips.

The third prisoner seemed completely crushed when they brought him in. His body was lost in the folds of the suit hanging from his shoulders, though it was clear the suit had been made for him, and not without taste. His unkempt hair and beard had grown into a tangle, increasing the just-woke-up look of his crumpled, vapid face. But his eyes under their shaggy brows glinted with a strange, quiet ecstasy, as though he were gloating over the triumph of indubitable justice.

With a dart of this glance at Izvekov, the prisoner sat on the edge of the bench, ignoring the gold.

"Meshkov—Merkuri Avdeyevich?"

"Yes."

"Has it been long since you left Saratov?"

"Over two weeks."

"Did you come here on a visit, or to live permanently?"

"I planned to live permanently."

"Why did you leave your native city?"

"Because I wished to enter a monastery. But on arriving, I found no accommodations. The cell I had been promised was occupied, so for the time being I took a room in town."

"Apparently the room didn't please you?"

"You mean, why did I set out again? I was uneasy. News came that the fighting was approaching Khvalynsk. I sought seclusion in my old age, and feared that my desires might be thwarted."

"Who did you think would give you peace and quiet beyond the Volga—the Cossacks?"

"Why the Cossacks?" asked Merkuri Avde-yevich in a tone like an obeisance. "I didn't dream of such a thing."

"But the Cossacks are beyond the Volga."

"I didn't plan to go that far. I wanted to get only to Irgiz—they say that place is beyond reach of the war. Though to tell the truth, the town's not much to my liking."

"Why not?"

"Most of the people there belong to the Old Faith. My landlord also turned out to be a blockhead—he's the one talked me into going. I'm only sorry I let him put such an idea into my head."

Kirill nodded toward the gold.

"Yours?"

"Yes," said Merkuri Avdeyevich, not only withholding his glance, but even turning further away, though there was apparently no doubt in his mind that it was about the gold he was being questioned.

"Hiding it from Soviet power, eh?"

"You can only hide something which is being sought for. Nobody ever asked me for it. So I didn't hide it—just saved it up."

"For the salvation of your soul?"

"I planned to present it to the monastery."

"Why did you change your mind?" unexpectedly put in the Red Army man who had been carefully watching Merkuri Avdeyevich. "If you'd given it to them, they'd probably have found you a cell quick enough."

Meshkov meekly ignored this remark.

"We must hand you over to the court," said Izvekov.

"Just as you say."

"But now we shall count this gold and draw up a document for you to sign."

"Just as you say," repeated Meshkov indifferently.

He closed his eyes and remained sitting motionless on the very edge of the bench, as though merely resting a second before getting up and leaving. It was impossible to guess his thoughts, though of course they must have been centred on the coins, especially when a jingle and clink indicated that they were being counted. Kirill and Dibich undertook to build them into even little piles. Meshkov could not avoid thinking of the money; the thought of it kept trailing or running ahead of all other thoughts, like a man's shadow. He kept comparing the present with the past. In the past, the more money a man saved, the more he acquired. The money contained within itself an element of growth. The most difficult thing was to get hold of the first coin; every additional one came more easily, as Rousseau once observed (Meshkov was in no need of reading him to be in full agreement on this point). But nowadays, the more money a man had, the less he was left with, for the more they took away.

And now they were taking away Meshkov's last gold. This was in very truth the last. He had hidden the coins away one by one when the last of his wealth was disappearing. He had hidden them from everybody. It would have been against his nature not to have had something hidden from everybody, even from the holy spirit. He had not mentioned them to the late Valeria Ivanovna, nor to Lisa, nor to his Father Confessor, nor even to the Bishop, who had given him his blessing on entering the monastery. He had said nothing about them in the Finance Department, though cold chills had run up and down his spine when Ragozin had asked him whether he had any gold. If it were possible for a man to hide his actions from his own self, Meshkov would never have let himself know about the caviar can, for fear of giving away the secret in some moment of weakness. He had hidden it under his mattress and taken it away in his pillow on leaving home. He had stuffed the can with cotton to prevent a telltale jingle. He had placed his cheek on it when sleeping, and found it softer than any feathers, and the coins had whispered as he drowsed: "We're yours, we're yours, we're yours!" And now the secret was out. The account was closed.

Yes, the account was closed. Dibich began to write out the document. With a stub of pencil Kirill jotted down the figures on the board table, and after a little multiplication, said:

"Altogether five thousand, six hundred and forty rubles. Is that right, Citizen Meshkov?"

"No," answered Merkuri Avdeyevich quietly. "That's not right. Miscounted."

"What do you mean?"

"Just that. You miscounted. You shouldn't have dumped them out. There was room for just nineteen coins on the bottom of the can. Each pile was thirty ten-ruble coins in height, in other words, three hundred rubles in each pile. Thirty times nineteen is five thousand seven hundred rubles, and not five thousand six hundred and forty. Unless, of course, six of the coins got lost—in the counting."

"Phooh, damn it all! Six coins! Go ahead and count them yourself!" cried Kirill, his face darkening with annoyance.

Merkuri Avdeyevich moved closer. Something caught in his throat as he glanced at the coins, and he was seized by a prolonged fit of coughing. Then he said, as though speaking to himself:

"If the surface of the table is even, it is a simple matter to check whether there are one hundred rubles in each pile. But the cracks make for unevenness. One board is higher than the other. Here, for example, is a pile that is not the same as the others, did you notice it? That's because it is standing in a depression. For that reason it contains an extra coin. And here's another. Will you allow me to recount the money?"

"Go ahead."

Meshkov moved one of the piles toward him, pressed it between finger and thumb and turned it over, so that it fanned out, with a little ting sound. He cupped his left palm under the edge of the table. With the third and index fingers of his right hand he took two coins at once, slipping them into his left palm with such speed that everyone gaped in astonishment.

"Eleven," he said, sending an extra ten-ruble piece ringing onto the table.

He unerringly found the miscounted piles, separated them from the others, and recounted them until he replaced the six coins making the full hundred. His fingers seemed to have grown younger.

"Think of that!" marvelled Nikon, overwhelmed by such virtuosity. "His fingers go whirring like a grasshopper."

As though suddenly roused, Merkuri Avdeyevich frowned at Nikon. His expression had lost all traces of the quiet ecstasy with which he had entered the hut. His eyes were now dark and brooding, and all his sober thoughts seemed to have vanished.

Everyone watched him in silence. He turned slowly away from the table and gave a sudden heave of his shoulders as he leaned over the bench.

"Plucked," said the Red Army man. "Too bad to part with your toys, eh?"

"Is the count correct or not?" asked Izvekov in a curt, almost angry tone.

"Mine is right; yours is wrong," whimpered Merkuri Avdeyevich so softly as to be scarcely audible. "Fifty-seven with a hundred in each. Just as it was. Oh Lord, just as it was."

He grabbed his head in his hands, shaking with sobs.

Dibich wrote the sum in the document—five thousand seven hundred rubles. They began to replace the money in the can, fumbling in their haste. Too much time had been spent on this business. They handed Meshkov the paper for his signature. He pulled himself together and signed without protest.

As they were leading him out of the hut, Kirill asked him one more question:

"Did you know that wounded companion of yours in Saratov?"

Meshkov paused.

"I answer for no one but myself," he replied.

"Obviously everyone answers for himself. But I think it will be held to your credit if you name him."

Meshkov hesitated.

"He hasn't mentioned who he was."

"He probably has good reason for not mentioning it. But I am asking you, not him."

Once more Meshkov was silent.

"He's nothing to me," he muttered, even more hesitantly. "But why should I go telling tales? Sin on my soul if I make a mistake."

"Don't make a mistake."

"Well, I'm not afraid of the truth. I'm not sure what his rank was, but it seems to me I remember him as a lieutenant-colonel in the gendarmes."

"Polotentsev?"

"Yes," said Merkuri Avdeyevich quickly. Dropping his eyes, he slipped through the door.

Kirill glanced at Dibich.

At last they set out on the march. The sun was already sinking. The prisoners walked up ahead of the column. Behind came a cart with the wolves. The dogs of the village, their fur bristling, escorted the column with furious barking.

Ipat walked alongside of the mounted commander and commissar. He saw that they were not inclined to speak, and he too remained silent.

Dibich glanced about with the fresh gaze of a man returning to his native haunts after a long absence and discovering familiar scenes in spite of the changes wrought by time. He hummed a simple tune, as he had been wont to do as a boy. As they emerged from the forest, his seat in the saddle gave him a fine view ahead, and a meditative smile played about his lips whenever he recognized some familiar woodland path. The hills were feathered with maples, a tree which loves a slope. Ever more frequently they came to villages, and the road widened, indicating the proximity of a town.

Kirill sat swaying in the saddle with closed eyes. He was not sleepy, but did not wish to be spoken to. The Repyovka events had faded in his mind, eclipsed by this unexpected and almost fantastic clash with the past, this coincidence of two interviews, either of which was sufficient to transport him to the days of his youth and absorb his thoughts for long. But at the same time there was some persistent connection between all his recent impressions: the exposing of Polotentsev, the Meshkov gold, the body of the girl in the road, the wind fluttering the paper lace of the coffins on the shoulders of the pallbearers, the wolf biting at its wounded haunches, the executed Zubinsky and the murdered Shubnikov, the forgiven deserter Nikon, and the hearty Ipat, with his musings on a just way of life. All of them were interdependent, like willow wands woven into a basket, and it was as impossible to dwell on any one of them without touching on a second, or a third, as to withdraw one wand from a basket without disturbing the others. Kirill realized that in these few short days he had overcome all obstacles in his path and had correctly solved all the problems with which he had been faced. He was, moreover, more confident than ever before that he was capable of overcoming much greater obstacles, and that perhaps there was nothing on earth which could bend his will. He asked himself if he was satisfied with his behaviour, and answered that he had every reason to be satisfied. And having answered thus, he was faced by another question: why, then, did he feel depressed? And this new question remained unanswered. He kept repeating it to himself, but his mind could offer no answer, and his spirit remained oppressed. He constantly saw before him the people with whom he had just had dealings, whose fate he had decided, and again he asked himself whether he had made no mistake, and was convinced that he had not. Yet he was sad in spirit.

He opened his eyes on hearing Ipat give a plaintive sigh.

"What's the matter, Ipat?" he asked with a smile. "Feeling blue?"

"I'll be dreaming about how I chased it, and that's God's truth!"

"How you chased what?"

"That wolf bitch. Her carcass is probably laying somewheres in the bushes right now. What a pelt to lose! And all on account of those bastards, god damn them!"

He shook his fist furiously at the prisoners.

"If we had such things as awards, I'd give you a medal for those bastards," said Kirill.

"That bitch is worth more to me than any medal. I've got two Orders of St. George knocking about in my knapsack as it is."

After a minute's pause, he glanced sharply at Kirill, as though trying to read his thoughts.

"You just write me a certificate, Comrade Commissar, saying as I've rendered services to the workers' and peasants' army. I'll put it in a frame and hang it up in the best room. Let everybody see it." (Here he gave a sly little squint.) "And you still owe me something for that wolf. You and the commander too. The posts I stationed you at were sure fire. I knew what I was doing!"

"You can have the pelt from my wolf if you're so bent on squaring accounts," smiled Kirill again, and pulled on the reins to overtake Dibich.

"How are you feeling, Vasili Danilovich?"

"Wonderful!" said Dibich, and half raised himself in the stirrups with a movement which broke his horse's gait and set it dancing, preparatory to breaking into a trot.

"See that road over the mountain?" continued Dibich, pointing to a line of hills covered with dense forest glowing dark in the sunset. "Up there where those pines are tipped with gold. About a half a verst on the other side there's a hollow, then some more hills with an Old Faith monastery tucked away in one of the gulleys. A little further on you come to the Volga, and the beginning of the town. And there in that town. . . ."

"Well, what?"

"That's where my home is," finished Dibich quietly, in some abashment.

While speaking to him, Kirill had expected that he would enquire who Meshkov and Polotentsev were, and was prepared to tell him something about his past. But apparently Dibich had lost all interest in the prisoners. Had these men been in no way connected with Kirill, he would not have minded Dibich's indifference: this former tsarist officer had agreed to fight the enemies of the revolution and was conscientiously fulfilling his duty; it would have been foolish to have asked anything more of him. But when Kirill had pointed to the can of money back there in the hut, he himself had broached the subject of his past by mentioning how many things the Meshkov gold explained to him. By spurning Kirill's confidence, Dibich as much as said that a person's private life was his own personal business, and Kirill found this harsh and hurtful.

"In other words, we'll soon reach Khvalynsk?"

"Not more than twenty minutes at a trot."

"It's probably quiet here—the bandits wouldn't dare approach the town."

"Naturally. There's little chance of our meeting anyone. I don't know about the other detachments. Probably they'll also come through without any clashes."

"Are you pleased?"

"With what? Haven't seen any serious fighting yet."

"And would you like to see some? I was asking if you were pleased you'd joined us."

"The Reds? These soldiers suit me. And these commissars."

The dimple in Dibich's chin flattened out and almost disappeared as he gave Kirill a fond smile.

"So far I just sort of sense this," he added. "Can't explain exactly why they suit me. Couldn't give a philosophical analysis, so to speak."

"These days philosophy is action rather than abstraction. Find out where you stand politically by participating. Then everything will come clear."

"So far as that's concerned, things are clear enough," said Dibich, continuing to smile. "I think I've settled everything in the right way."

Kirill was infected by his companion's light-heartedness. At this moment Dibich seemed utterly frank and unreserved.

"Oh come on! You're just happy to be home again!"

"Five years! And what years! Just imagine!" exclaimed Dibich, adding timidly, in a boyish tone: "Maybe you and I can steal an hour to have a look at that mother of mine, what do you say, Kirill Nikolayevich?"

"Why should I butt in?"

"You won't be butting in, honest to goodness. She's a wonder, my mother. You'll see!"

"No, it'll be better if I take over the command in your place, and you. . . ."

Kirill took a long look at Dibich's agitated face, then suddenly said:

"If you like, ride home now and come back tomorrow morning. By that time I hope the whole company will be assembled."

"Really?" said Dibich, almost in fright.

He reined in his horse and leaned toward Izvekov. His eyes were shining, but he seemed hesitating whether to believe his own ears or not.

"Afraid to trust me with your company?" laughed Kirill. "If anything happened to you in battle, I'd be obliged to take your place. But there's no battle now. Go ahead. Another time I'll be the one to go and leave you behind. Incidentally, you owe me an extra furlough. For that German—remember? I haven't had it yet. Well. . . ."

Kirill held out his hand to the commander.

Dibich ordered the detachment to halt and announced that he was turning over the command to the commissar and that he would join them in the town at eight o'clock the following morning.

He shook Izvekov's hand, struck his horse sharply with the reins, and rode past the detachment at a trot that set him jogging in the saddle.

Soon he entered the woods. Keeping to a steady trot along the lonely road, whose over-hanging branches often caused him to bend down, he crossed the summit and descended into the hollow. Here there were open stretches which allowed him to occasionally spur his horse to a gallop. But when he reached the next hills, the road dwindled to a mere path arched by intertwining maples. Dibich sprang off his horse and led it by the reins.

One of the slopes gave him a view of an orchard spread over the hollow between two hills and wrapped in the shadows of approaching evening. The smoke from two or three chimneys curled among the apple trees. These represented the most isolated hermitages belonging to the monastery. Long, long ago Dibich had come here with his playmates to catch songbirds.

He walked faster and faster, stretching his legs, which had become cramped from riding. A few steps ahead of him there was a sudden turbulance in the foliage, which immediately quieted down. The horse started and pulled at the reins in fright. Dibich unfastened the holster of his revolver. He heard a short sound, morbidly unpleasant, then the woods seemed to revolve about him like a merry-go-round, swaying sleepily. "Impossible!" was the cry which rose to Dibich's lips, but his voice failed him. Everything went black before his eyes. . . .

. . . Presently he saw a hawk emerge from the foliage and soar into the sky. It noiselessly flapped its dark, triangular wings, tilting its little head

344

to glance at the path with black buttons of eyes. A bit further along Dibich noticed fluffs of down, and then a heap of speckled feathers which he recognized as belonging to a heath cock. At any other time he would probably have stopped to search for the victim in the bushes, but now he did not even slacken his pace. There flashed through his mind a remembrance of having once before seen a hawk destroy a heath cock on this very path.

He emerged from the maple woods and jumped into the saddle, riding past the scattered hermitages and the monastery shrine without a glance. As soon as the town came into view, he whipped his horse into a gallop down the hill.

At the end of a long line of identical log buildings fronted by little yards, there rose a silver poplar, one lower branch of which still hid the roof of a yellow house.

Dibich reined in his horse. His heart pounded painfully, as though he had run the entire way. He decided not to ride up to the house, and tied his horse to a neighbouring fence.

The gate stood open. He entered the yard. The front porch was densely shaded by grapevines which had climbed to the very roof. A thin stream of smoke curled out of the chimney. The yard was overgrown with cherry trees, whose leafless, neglected branches swept the ground. The boardwalk leading to the house was rotting away, and had lost its squeak. The well had settled on one side. A china doll with broken arms lay in the dog kennel.

Dibich quietly entered the house. A samovar stood on the floor in the kitchen. The burning wood splinters whistled merrily through the tin pipe thrust into an opening in the stove, while lacy patterns of orange flame showed through the cracks. Everything in the house seemed musty and toy-like, so that Dibich ducked his head on entering the room which he remembered having been called the parlour. All the objects about him were dear and familiar, yet he had to make their acquaintance all over again. The dust of old age seemed to have settled over the entire house, like the ashes of a spent fire.

A night light was burning on a chiffonier. Formerly his mother had placed this tiny lamp beside her bed. Dibich glanced into the bedroom. The same white counterpane. He returned to the parlour and held the lamp up to the photographs.

He saw himself, strangely smooth-faced, in student uniform, holding a cigarette between the tips of his fingers. During his imprisonment he had lost the habit of smoking. He had left his student uniform with his Moscow landlady. A thousand years separated the present Dibich from this lad in uniform. Opposite hung an unfamiliar picture of his sister arm in arm with a pompous-looking man who greatly resembled Pastukhov.

Someone entered the kitchen. Dibich turned around. His breast contracted with a pain he had never before experienced. A tiny woman glanced at him through the pompon-bordered portieres of the doorway. Without being frightened, she lifted her head in astonishment, and Dibich recognized in her the Moscow landlady in whose care he had left his student uniform on entering military school.

"Can it be Vasenka come home?" asked the woman, still holding on to the curtain whose pompons trembled in her grasp.

"Where's mother?" cried the tortured Dibich.

"Didn't you see her, my boy?"

"Where? Where could I have seen her?"

"As soon as she got your letter saying you were in a hospital in Saratov, she tried to reach you. For a long time she had hopes of getting a boat ticket, but nothing came of it. It's been a week now since she set out in a cart."

"Why didn't she wait for me?"

"Ah, my dear, she was worn out with waiting for you."

347

"And my sister?"

"Your sister got married a long time ago."

"To him?" asked Dibich, pointing to the photograph.

"To him. The Pastukhovs are also from Khvalynsk."

Dibich saw the discontented Pastukhov, drawn to full height, his arm in that of his inexpressibly lovely wife, whose face was lighted by a bright, but slightly guilty smile.

"That's not my sister. That's—Asya. You're deceiving me."

"Why should I deceive you, you blessed boy? Here, I've brought you your student jacket. Try it on."

"You're lying! You're lying!" cried Dibich with insufferable pain. "Mother! Where are you?"

"Now don't you go shouting. Better calmly tell me, so's I can tell your mother, how long it's been since her Vasenka joined the Red Army?"

He felt an impulse to dash at the woman and remove her from his path, but suddenly she grabbed the portieres and pulled them together, leaving only her nose poking through the opening. There she hid, with one eye glancing out and the pompons shaking with her silent laughter.

Dibich jumped through the window onto the porch, tore aside the tangle of grapevines, and dashed through the yard.

He untied his horse and flung the reins over its back. The street was dark, but transparent, as though blown from bottle glass. No sooner had he placed his foot in the stirrup than the horse reared and galloped ahead. He could not mount, and kept pushing off with his right foot, feeling a numbness entering his fingers, and the saddle slipping on the horse's back, and a searing head wind smothering him, smothering him unbearably.

"But no, the war is not over . . . Izvekov is waiting for me. I'll be there, I'll be there!" he whispered through his teeth, in horrible expectation of losing his grip on the saddle. Already his body was dragging along the ground.

His fingers weakly relaxed, he let go and fell, but was brought back to his senses by a terrific kick in the chest from the horse's hoofs. . . .

He lay alone in the path under the thick canopy of maples. His horse was gone. He glanced at the sky through an opening in the branches and thought to himself that the hawk had flown away. At that moment his breast was rent by piercing pain and he moaned:

"A nightmare . . . a nightmare. . . . Bandits!"

He felt himself with a sticky hand. The holster of his revolver was empty. He crawled, gasping, along the path until he came to the slope. Exhausted, he turned over on his back, with his head hanging down. Some pebbles, disturbed by his movement, rattled down the hill. He had an inverted vision, like a reflection in water, of the apple orchard and the scattered hermitages belonging to the monastery. It was here he had come long, long ago, with his little playmates to catch songbirds.

"Mother!" he managed to gasp. "Mother! Oh God!"

There was a rush of blood to his throat. He choked, and again lost consciousness.

* 29 *

"I am most grateful to you for your trust, and for the honour," said Pastukhov with his official smile, "but it is quite by chance that I happen to be in the city, and it would hardly be proper for me to participate in so august an undertaking."

"But my dear Alexander Vladimirovich," protested a gentleman whose beard and hair comb placed him in the category of the elect whose necrologies were printed in the *Niva*. "But my dear Alexander Vladimirovich!"

Two other leading figures of the city of Kozlov who had come to ask Pastukhov to become a member of the delegation being sent to General Mamontov, shrugged their shoulders despairingly.

"You cannot be a chance figure in our city, any more than in the whole of civilized Russia."

"I assure you that your name is known even among our officers," ardently confirmed the gentleman from the necrologies. "To be sure, I am speaking of the progressive group of officers. And perhaps your name will quicken in even the General those finer feelings which, under the pressure of the war, are in a state of somnolence, if I may so put it."

"At least, which the General has rarely given expression to during his campaign of liberation," bitingly added another of the leading figures.

"And on which we must base our sole hope," said a third with a sigh. "And for that reason we beg and implore you not to refuse us."

Pastukhov blinked at Asya expectantly.

She too was sitting here in this room with a balcony facing the dusty square. As was always the case when she was particularly moved, her beauty became irresistible: her lifted lashes seemed to curl back more noticeably and a crystal tear sparkled on her delicate lids.

The four men encircled her in respectful expectation.

"I think, Sasha, that if you can be of any help—even the slightest. . . . After all, it is a nightmare what these terrible people are doing! Let the General—or anyone else—put a stop to it!"

"They break into bedrooms," burst from the representative of the elect, "to steal—even the linen!"

"Only you must know, gentlemen, that under no circumstances will I agree to head the delegation," said Pastukhov with a decisive wave of his hand.

"Oh no indeed, Alexander Vladimirovich! The delegation will be headed by a well-known educator. And, mind you, he too refused at first. But at last . . . the feeling of civic responsibility. . . . We ask you only to be a member of the delegation. Only a member! Only to lend your support!"

"All right, I agree to be one of the mob," joked Pastukhov condescendingly.

They all smiled at him gratefully, but once more his manner cooled.

"Furthermore, no petitions, gentlemen. I'm against them. Nothing in writing. And without tears and exclamation marks."

"Oh yes. Yes indeed. Only orally. But imperatively, I should say—am I not right, gentlemen? No requests, but a firm demand to protect our city and its peaceful population from unrestrained pillage. To put an immediate stop to it."

"And to all this violence," said Asya with a shudder, raising her hands, with outstretched little fingers, to her temples.

"I have no objections," repeated Pastukhov.

"Be prepared to leave at any time, Alexander Vladimirovich. We shall let you know the minute the General consents to receive us."

The visitors began to make their bows, but the youngest of them, the one who had made the biting remark about the General's liberation campaign, lingered behind.

"Allow me for just a minute ... on a personal matter...."

"I shall see them out," said Asya, going into the hallway and leaving her husband alone with the young man, who waited nervously until the door was closed.

"Maybe you have some—er—verse you would like to show me? Are you a poet?" asked Pastukhov sympathetically.

"Oh, not at all! Although it's true ... in the newspaper line. They talked me into joining this delegation too. But to be frank, I wanted to ask your opinion as to how you intend behaving in case—in case they return?"

"The Bolsheviks?"

"Exactly."

Pastukhov blandly examined this prudent young man, as though he found him an object worthy of study. The object had unmatched ears— one of them small, the other enormous, with a long, attached lobe, as though specially designed for listening, and to Pastukhov's mind came the phrase: "All the better to hear you with, my dear."

"It is quite possible that the Whites will hold out here no longer than in Tambov. A mere raid. And no power except a temporary administration will be set up. And then *they* will come," said the young man.

"You consider that possible?"

"Extremely. They will come and find out that you and I paid a visit to the General."

"But our visit is in the interests of the masses," said Pastukhov by way of justification, interrupting his study of the object.

"Try to prove that then! The masses!"

Pastukhov wiped his face with his hand, removing all traces of worry, and blurted out an idea which had suddenly dawned on him:

"You know what would be highly original? To hide in a lunatic asylum. That's it. Buy a sack of flour and go in hiding. One sack will last a long time. The very thing. Take refuge among the lunatics," he repeated as though actually convinced of the brilliance of his idea.

"Is that advice for me, or do you intend following it yourself?"

Pastukhov gave his visitor a hearty handshake and saw him to the door, laughing to himself.

"What a loathsome creature!" he murmured on returning.

He went out onto the balcony.

Past the brick façade of the former Commercial School on the other side of the square rode a cavalcade of Cossacks with sacks and bundles tied behind their saddles. They flew by in a cloud of dust, brandishing their whips, letting out wild shouts and whistles. Some of them jealously hung on to the loot flung over the cruppers of their horses. A stolen bolt of gingham came unwound and streamed in a bright blue ribbon behind one of the riders.

"Sasha! Sasha! Have you lost your mind!" exclaimed Asya, pulling him into the room and slamming the door to the balcony. "They might shoot! Standing there in plain sight!"

"The devil only knows what's going on," said Alexander Vladimirovich in disgust as he took to pacing the floor.

From the moment the followers of Mamontov had dashed into the city and begun plundering, he had been filled with horror, but at the same time with a strange curiosity as to what changes the new situation would bring to his family. His excited expectation of something unprecedented reminded him of the state of children on Christmas Eve, but fear dominated his curiosity, for Pastukhov knew that blood was flowing, and that the rivulets were creeping ever closer to his latest refuge.

The house in which the Pastukhovs had been living for over a week belonged to a tradesman whose son was director of the municipal theatre. The idea of applying for aid to the theatre belonged to Anastasia Germanovna, and it turned out to have been a good one: the director was familiar with the name of Pastukhov, and it tickled his pride to be able to do him a favour. As a result, the Pastukhovs found themselves encamped in two very decent rooms not far from the city's central thoroughfare.

Gradually they adjusted themselves to their rather monotonous life, realizing that their wellbeing was as fleeting as it was accidental, yet enjoying it while it lasted, with eyes closed to the future. Their presence here was as much a matter of chance as their presence in Saratov had been, but it was made easier to bear by the realization that now they were one step nearer to the final denouement, in which they firmly believed.

Alyosha did not like the new place as much as he had liked Dorogomilov's, and felt disconsolate. He found nothing imperative about accepted routine, and for him, as for all children, order and accident were equally a part of natural law. He assumed that his mother and father had gone to Saratov, on the Volga, in order to live with Dorogomilov, and on leaving his house had not immediately joined Alyosha's grandmother and grandfather because it was necessary first to spend some time with the director of the theatre in Kozlov. He found it more interesting to play in Arseni Romanovich's garden than in the director's yard, but he accepted his playing in both Saratov and Kozlov as perfectly natural, and a mere extension of his playing in Petrograd. Olga Adamovna was still at his side, as were his mother and father; they fed him, washed him in a basin or a washtub, cut his nails and scolded him—in other words, life went on normally, sometimes brighter, sometimes duller, but always in accordance with natural law, without any haphazardness.

For Alexander Vladimirovich and Asya, the last two years of their life had been made up exclusively of violations of natural law by ceaseless diversions from the norm. Some contingencies they found tolerable, others excruciating. But even the fact that it was necessary to bathe Alyosha in a basin or a washtub instead of a bathtub represented for them a devastating blow at immutable order.

They both knew that a sense of humour did much to make hardships endurable, and they strove to reduce things to a joke.

Neither of them had ever before lived in these parts. They were acquainted with Tambov only through Lermontov's *The Treasurer*, to which they added Myatlev's *Madame Kurdyukova*. For them, the horse fairs held at Kozlov were sufficient to convey the Tambov atmosphere. Asya, who had a good memory for verse, gave an apt recitation of Madame Kurdyukova's puerile extravagances, and Pastukhov laughingly repeated them:

> "*In my dreams again I see*
> *Those delightful leafy bowers,*
> *Overgrown with vines and flowers,*
> *Where the ardent Kurdyukov,*
> *First professed to me his love.*"

Once while sitting on the balcony revelling in the somnolence of this provincial town, they gave themselves up to the tranquil thoughts born of a starry night, when reminiscences merge with hopes and aspirations, and one wonders whether he should live for the future, or accept the present as the whole happiness.

"A falling star," said Asya. "Did you make a wish?"

"No, did you?"

"No. I'm never quick enough."

For a while they were silent.

"At last the dust has settled," said Pastukhov. "Do you catch that scent of peonies? The common folk call them 'Mary Roots.' Can they still be blooming somewhere?"

"I do seem to smell it," said Asya. "But it's too late for peonies."

"It's a strange scent. A mixture of roses and horse sweat."

"You have a queer nose. You always break down scents into something fine and vile."

"I don't break them down, I simply guess their compound. Scents can no more be broken down than feelings. Anyone who attempts to break down feelings into their component parts either loses them or has never had them. Feelings are always a combination of good and bad.

If you subtract the rose or the horse sweat from a peony, it will no longer be a peony."

"There is nothing bad in my feeling for you."

He stroked her knee.

"You are a physical woman. Primarily. You have properties. Like the stars. They have no qualities. They are neither good nor bad."

He laughed.

"Lord, what idiocy I'm talking!"

He leaned over and kissed her languidly on both eyes.

Again they sat without stirring for some time, until Asya observed, as though the conversation had never been interrupted:

"Did you know that 'How delicate, how lovely were the roses' is also Myatlev's?"

"Just imagine his having tempted Turgenev! How does the rest of it go?"

She recited:

"How delicate, how lovely were the roses
About my door. How soothing to the eye!
How I implored the bitter winds of autumn
To stay their icy breath when passing by!"

"What kind of a life must that have been?" she marvelled. "How must people have lived, and what must they have been like to have written such verse!"

"With such rhymes!" said Pastukhov. "If Gibshman had ever recited those roses with a straight face at 'The Wandering Dog,' the poor creature would have rolled over on its back laughing."

"The indivisibility of feeling," sighed Asya. "Your 'Dog' rips up everything. And everybody stands quietly by and watches for fear of being laughed at. Not a single integral feeling is left for art. Your 'Dog' finds it funny that we should contemplate the stars. Funny that we should recall the lines of Myatlev. Funny that we should love each other. For him, everything is funny."

Pastukhov snorted without answering. The tapping of his nails on the iron railing of the balcony seemed to suggest that they drop the subject. But he himself continued it.

"Never have I been able to give a final answer to the question: What is art? I have devoted my entire life to it, yet I don't know what it is. For the sake of convenience I assume that everything is clear. Otherwise it would be impossible to create. If you really understood, you would strive after perfection. But art cannot be perfect. It contains more fumbling and mistakes than science or anything else dealing with the ideal."

"Never mind, my friend, you make beautiful mistakes."

They heard someone running. The sound came from the distance, where the shadow of the cathedral loomed into the night sky. It entered the square, grew louder, and in the faint starlight they both caught sight of a dark figure making straight for their house.

"Why is he running? Let's go in," whispered Asya.

"Wait a minute. Maybe he's been robbed."

But they left the balcony and continued to listen from inside the room. The gate creaked and then there came a knocking at the door.

"Where are the matches? He's come to us," said Pastukhov, feeling on the table.

They had no time to light the lamp.

Their young patron, the director of the theatre, ran up the stairs and burst into the room, pressing his hand to his heart.

"Come downstairs. To father's apartment. I'll tell everybody at once."

He gasped for breath. When they reached the stairs he could no longer restrain himself—his news choked him and found outlet in one panic-stricken word:

"The Whites!"

Alexander Vladimirovich burned his fingers on the spluttering match. They stopped in the darkness.

"Come along, come along," urged the director.

Once down stairs, he pulled the curtains tight over the windows and had everyone sit down. His mother—a slow woman who was hard of hearing—waited in anxious bewilderment for what was to follow. His father, in vest and rolled-up shirt sleeves, folded his hands on a thick, illustrated magazine. He glanced over the pictures and let his eyes come to rest on the library of the Rumanian Queen Elizabeth—Carmen Silva.

"The Don Cossacks are in Tambov. The road is cut off," announced the gloomy herald, when the rather theatrical preparations were finished.

Then he told them that an actor had escaped from Tambov on a shunting locomotive which risked collision by driving off down the left-hand track when cavalrymen from Mamontov's corps had already taken over the town. The actor had made the rest of the trip in a peasant cart, and then a freight train. In Tambov the Cossacks had immediately started pogroms. They were catching Bolsheviks and stringing them up on telephone poles. They were torturing the peasants in the villages as in the days of serfdom. Fires had broken out everywhere, and Mamontov's men forbade the extinguishing of them.

"Who are they?" asked the mother.

"Whites."

"Where could they ever have come from?"

"The General brought them. A Whiteguard General."

"Oh, a General," said the mother, crossing herself (Pastukhov could not make out whether from fright or relief). "But why should the people go rushing about like a chicken without a head?" she added, with a glance at her husband.

"We must keep quiet. We must stand off to one side," said the father, without raising his eyes.

"They may put in their appearance here tomorrow. Cavalry troops," said his son.

"Probably this is—the end?" ventured the flushed Anastasia Germanovna.

"The end of what? It's all the fault of these learned people. Just look how many books," said the father, nodding at the library of Carmen Silva.

Pastukhov could have accepted the nod as being indirectly meant for him. He drew himself up, but lowered his eyes as he answered:

"It's not the books that are responsible for this barbarity. It's not the learned people who thrash the peasants. Reason cannot be called to answer for insanity. But you are right in saying that we must stand off to one side. We must calmly wait to see what turn events will take."

He rose. There was a certain grandeur in his bearing, and his aphorisms sounded well even to himself.

"If it is possible to wait calmly," said Asya, also rising.

"Why are you getting up? Here, I shall put up the samovar," said the mother, passing her fingers over her lips and slowly turning about in her chair (her deafness simplified life's problems by at least reducing their number).

But the Pastukhovs returned to their rooms. They stayed up until dawn discussing the prospects, calming and alarming each other in turn. Only once did Asya attempt to jest: glancing out onto the balcony when it was already getting light she said:

"The scent which you took for peonies turned out to be more of a compound than you thought, Sasha. It also contained an element of gunpowder."

"At least I was right about the horses: it smelled of Cossacks."

. . . .

If we view the Mamontov raid through the eyes of an ordinary citizen of Kozlov (who first heard rumours of the sudden seizure of Tambov by the Whites, and then saw the conquerors on the streets of his own city) we get a remarkable picture.

From the very moment of the founding of Soviet power, this region had known no other. The South, scene of innumerable changes in government, was far away, and it seemed that here the army was quite capable of defending the new life. The gubernia was pure Russian and was located not on the borders, but adjacent to the central regions. In the eyes of the entire population, therefore, it was part of the unified national nucleus which represented the very foundation of the new state. In other words, it was Russia itself, the Russia which had set up the Soviets and was fighting in their defence.

The news of the fall of Tambov came like a bolt from the blue. At first nobody in Kozlov—neither the civil authorities, nor the workers, nor the average citizen—could make anything out of what had happened. How could a whole corps of Whites have penetrated two hundred and fifty versts behind the front lines, cutting off with one blow the road to Saratov and Balashov? Had there been a battle, and if so where, and when, and why had it been lost?

On the following day there came a stream of information from Tambov, but the stream was murky: the news only shocked, without elucidating.

Staff headquarters of the Tambov fortified district were the first to spread rumours that the situation of the city was hopeless. The commandant himself openly stated that the enemy was marching twenty regiments against Tambov. No measures were taken to defend the approaches to the city; no preparations for street fighting were made. And yet no order to retreat was issued. This caused confusion among the units of the garrison and baffled everyone.

On the day before the arrival of Mamontov's forces, carts and automobiles crowded in front of railway warehouses and freight yards. Everything was loaded, whether it was needed or not, including broken chairs and office furniture. Soon the carts and automobiles stretched out in two long lines, and it was clear to the inhabitants that this meant flight. Panic ensued. The chief of a defence detachment, deciding that the panic must be put down, opened machine-gun fire on the houses of Soviet Street, and then he himself escaped in an armoured car.

The Cossacks raided the railway station. Students of an infantry school opened fire, but without any significant result. Tambov fell. Red Army men, unreleased from their posts, fought to their last bullet and died where they stood. Communists offered individual resistance and were also killed.

Without interrupting their march, Mamontov's troops swerved to the west and advanced on Kozlov.

These were the main facts which the citizens of Kozlov learned about the fall of Tambov, the centre of their district.

The Kozlov city authorities attempted to organize resistance. They tried to convince the people that they had sufficient forces. An artillery brigade of Bolsheviks was despatched to a position some thirty versts outside the city. A group of Don Cossacks appeared near Nikiforovka. The brigade opened fire.

But at the same time, the authorities hesitated, awaiting orders as to how to act. Their communications were contradictory, their actions confused. They shipped bank capital to Moscow, but failed to evacuate a hundred carloads of valuable goods. They asked "whether it is worth while evacuating the various departments of the Soviet, and if so, which departments, and where to send them." And in the same letter they said: "As for the various departments of the Soviet and their workers, they will naturally carry on until the last moment." They reported that "all Communists and local forces have been mobilized and are at their posts." Yet the very author of the despatch admitted that no one knew where these posts should be. "We can scarcely boast of putting up strong resistance for the simple reason that, unfortunately, our reconnaissance is unable to definitely establish where, and in what numbers the enemy is operating, and with approximately what forces he is moving on Kozlov. All of that remains unknown. . . . Please inform us as to the situation in Morshansk, for we have heard that the enemy has directed part of his forces against Morshansk and Ryazhsk."

Lack of resistance was due not only to poor reconnaissance. It was not only the enemy who gave cause for alarm. Plenty of cause was to be found on the home side as well.

The fact was that the city received no answers to all the letters sent to Staff Headquarters asking what measures were being taken to defend Kozlov, and whether there was any hope that the city would hold out. The Staff Department was already entrained and ready to leave, having previously evacuated its effects, while the Staff of the Southern front had left Kozlov the minute the city was in danger, and was now in Serpukhov. All the inhabitants, as well as the authorities, knew this very well, for they had witnessed everything with their own eyes.

Under such circumstances it was difficult for the city to offer resistance. It fell five days after the capture of Tambov.

A newspaper sponsored by Mamontov was immediately published.

Playing at democracy, the General allowed the paper to be called *Black-Earth Thoughts*—a rather grotesque title for even a democratic publication. On the second day it made the following announcement: "After resisting the Cossacks for three days, Red Army men and Communists abandoned Kozlov. The city was entered by General Denikin's Don Cossack army, with General Mamontov at the head. Most of the Communists were immediately wiped out, while the Red Army men either surrendered or fled and were pursued by the Cossacks...."

By this time, Mamontov's capture of Kozlov was already past history for the inhabitants. They remembered that at about three o'clock of the

preceding day they had heard a pounding of
hoofs coming from the Turmasov Plains and beyond the Voronezh River; that at exactly three
o'clock the White General himself, sitting none
too firmly in his saddle as a result of a sizable
luncheon, had appeared with his suite on Yam-
skaya Street; that the people had stood silent
and motionless in front of their houses; that sim-
pering girls had met them at the crossing with
a bouquet of flowers; that a bearded Cossack
had accepted the flowers and held them stiffly, as
though afraid they would burn him; and that
the church bells had rung that evening with particular insistence.

All of this had become a mere remembrance.
Because while *Black-Earth Thoughts* were being
posted on the fences, other events were taking
place in Kozlov—other scenes were being enacted
on its streets.

The Jewish quarter was raided, as were stores
and warehouses. Simple people placed icons in
their windows as protection. The Cossacks, after
first making sport of captured Jews, slashed them
with their swords. They ripped the bloodstained
clothes off the dead bodies, which they then dragged
to a yard where mounted guards prevented
the people from counting the number of their
victims.

They searched for and appropriated anything of the slightest value. They rolled barrels of wine and honey out of cellars, broke them open, drank and ate, shovelling honey into the mouths of their horses. They rode about peddling cloth. They robbed the tills of all the stores. They led the horses out of all the stables.

The railway station shook with explosions. The tower went up in the air. Bridges were blown up. Locomotives were driven into each other and went rolling down the embankment. The air was filled with the smoke of burning railway cars. Special brigades were sent down the tracks to destroy the switches.

A Cossack band played in the park. The young girls went walking with Mamontov's men. Petty officials appeared in wrinkled frock coats that had just been taken out of trunks. From the railway beyond the cathedral came the tap-tap of hatchets, chipping poles to be turned into gallows.

Mamontov received the commanders of his divisions: Generals Postovsky, Tolkushkin, and Kucherov. He confirmed appointments to the provisional city administration. He signed orders to confiscate horses, to organize a militia from among the civil population, to supply the members of this militia with white arm bands. He examined the loot taken from the churches—gold vessels and precious stones removed from icons—and indicated what was to be consigned to the transports and what was to be placed in his personal baggage.

Along the main street he held a review of his corps. Troop after troop of cavalry went cantering past, guns lumbered by, armoured cars and trucks loaded with machine guns went sputtering down the street, and a detachment of Cossack infantry strutted past in ceremonial march.

Mamontov reviewed the parade on horseback. In a blue uniform and enormous black gauntlets embroidered in gold, he sat with his red-banded cap pulled low over his eyes. He held the reins in such a way that all might see the gold embroidery of his gauntlets. He gave a supercilious glance at the crowd, then turned sharply around and raised a black fist to give an angry tug at his moustache: the crowd was not ecstatic.

That was the Mamontov raid on Kozlov as witnessed by the average citizen, whose comprehension of events stemmed only from what he personally saw and knew. . . .

If we look at the Mamontov raid in the light of a knowledge of succeeding events, its significance in respect to the entire civil war becomes more clear.

On withdrawing from Kozlov, Mamontov held a church service on the public square. It was accompanied by an elaborate ringing of church bells, and when the service was over he announced to the vestured priests who crowded round him that he would now march on Moscow, "to save the capital from the red menace."

The movements of Mamontov's corps after the taking of Kozlov justify the contention that if he dared not venture on anything as preposterous as a raid on Moscow, he at least intended to frighten people with the idea of such a raid. His corps advanced into the Ranenburg district, approaching roads leading to Pavelets and Tula.

Mamontov deliberately threatened to march on Moscow, and there was cunning as well as braggadocio in his threat. He well knew that his one great advantage lay in his cavalry, which was capable of swiftly shifting its course in any direction, and therefore of falling on whatever towns were most vulnerable—towns whose small, poorly equipped garrisons were intended only for local defence. Two factors prevented Mamontov from proceeding unimpeded toward the capital: the passage of time, which enabled the towns to strengthen their defence; and the mass resistance of the workers from industrial districts around Moscow, with Tula, Red arsenal of the proletariat, at their head. Mamontov realized that he would *inevitably* be forced to turn back to the south and join the White front. For that reason he found it even more important to make a show of proceeding north, towards the capital, in order to disguise his true tactics and weaken resistance in the regions he actually intended penetrating.

He quickly shifted his march from a northwest to a southwest direction. After Ranenburg, he raided Lebedyan and Elets. This was followed by a sharp deflection to the southeast, crossing Zadonsk along the broad highway leading to Voronezh.

Instead of weakening, the resistance of Soviet towns lying in the path of the Don Cossacks grew ever stronger. The helplessness shown at Tambov, at the very beginning of Mamontov's venture, had become transformed into such effective resistance that it was impossible for the General to subdue Voronezh, from which he was forced to retreat after spending only one day in the city. The battles at Voronezh represented the last phase of his march. Mamontov turned back, and this would have been the end of his efforts had not Denikin sent the Third Cavalry Corps of Lieutenant-General Shkuro to the aid of the Don Cossacks. Two weeks later this corps, its black banners waving, broke into the city and accomplished what had been beyond the power of Mamontov.

How was it that some cities resisted Mamontov, while others surrendered without a fight?

Mamontov's first successes were the result not only of the unexpectedness of his attacks. Betrayal played an important role.

With the connivance of the Commander-in-Chief, the command of the Southern front almost ignored the order to create reliable fortified districts at all strategic points. The defence of Tambov and Elets was completely neglected. While Soviet reconnaissance was ineffective, White reconnaissance supplied its army with all essential information. It was known, for example, that traitors in Tambov military units and institutions would give Denikin's men a proper welcome.

On the morning when the students of the infantry school had attempted to defend the Tambov railway station the Cossacks had knowingly shouted to them: "You may as well surrender! You have nothing to shoot with anyhow!" And they were right: on the previous night, former tsarist officers had stolen the locks off all the guns and, headed by the commander of the unit, joined Mamontov. The operative unit of the fortified district was entrusted to the commander of a separate rifle brigade, who immediately went over to the Whites. Instead of seeking an engagement with the enemy, the head of the armoured detachment fired on the city, under the pretence of bringing it to order. The commandant of the region himself sowed panic by spreading the rumour that twenty White regiments were moving on Tambov, when actually there were only two and a half thousand horsemen, i.e., three regiments. Nevertheless, the city was surrendered without a fight.

Only three days later did the city of Lebedyan learn of the fall of Tambov, and then only through the same sort of muddled rumours that came to Kozlov. The city made an attempt at defence. It was aided by Ranenburg infantry and cavalry detachments. But all these attempts were purely local, without support from the Staff of the Southern front, which abandoned Kozlov as soon as the city was threatened. It was later frankly admitted by Tambov organizations that "many wise measures proposed by the fortified district met with extraordinary opposition from the command of the Southern front."

The Whites sounded out the possibilities of treachery in the camp of their opponent, encouraging it as a supplementary factor operating against the Soviets and in support of Mamontov.

But with the passage of time, the basic advantages of Mamontov's methods of manoeuvring diminished. The element of surprise lost its effectiveness, for the towns energetically prepared to meet the Cossacks, and local governments became more vigilant in respect to traitors.

Furthermore, other factors began to work to the advantage of the Soviets and the disadvantage of Mamontov.

The first of them was the demoralization of the Cossack detachments, a demoralization which quickly set in and grew apace. Looting and pillaging corrupted Mamontov's men to such an extent that they refused to obey their general's orders; even in Kozlov they had ignored Mamontov's decree prohibiting the robbing of the population. It would be wrong to consider that the issuing of this decree had been mere hypocrisy on Mamontov's part: he himself went in for robbing, but at the same time he could see that his soldiers were much more enthusiastic about looting than about fighting. The carts with their booty took up more of the road than the troops. And this demoralization greatly decreased the fighting spirit of the entire corps.

Another factor hindering the development of Mamontov's first successes was the hostility of the Soviet population. Mamontov's hope of winning the support of the peasants was doomed to disappointment. The peasants did not support Mamontov, and Cossack looting and violence served only to make the village more hostile to the aims of the counterrevolution.

The results of the changed situation made themselves felt when Mamontov turned southward.

At Zadonsk his central column met with the first serious resistance. The city had managed to launch a conscription and form detachments which were organized into a regiment numbering more than one thousand five hundred men. The staff of the Voronezh fortified district, displaying decisiveness in preparing for resistance and resourcefulness in directing operations, helped create the Zadonsk regiment. Separate companies of this regiment demonstrated a heroic willingness to fight to the last breath. But the defenders of the city adopted tactics of field fighting requiring extensive reserves and considerable artillery, while the Zadonsk fighters had only eight machine guns, and no reserves whatsoever. Scattered as they were in thin ranks over a wide area, they necessarily relinquished the field of battle to the Cossacks. Under the circumstances, they should have adopted tactics of street fighting, but this was not done.

As a result of the thorough preparations made for self-defence, Voronezh met Mamontov's men with forces superior in both moral and military qualities. The battle of Voronezh lasted four days, and despite all their efforts, the Whites succeeded in taking only separate sections of the city, from which they were subsequently routed in street fighting. This accelerated the retreat of Mamontov's corps to the line of the Southern front. . . .

In order to lessen their responsibility for having allowed Mamontov's forces to penetrate Soviet territory, members of the Staff of the Southern front and the Revolutionary Military Council of the Republic represented the whole thing as merely the "pseudo successes" of the Whites. Obviously there was nothing "pseudo" about the enormous damage inflicted on more than a dozen cities subjected to raids, or about the suffering of the women and children, or the destruction of railways and stations, the blowing up of warehouses, the disruption of Soviet economy. Nor were the human losses suffered by the people and the Red Army limited to the large numbers of those who fell in battle against the Cossacks. The desire to depreciate the significance of Mamontov's devastating raids could stem only from the pricks of conscience suffered by those who abetted Denikin in his fight against the Soviets.

At the same time, the true significance of the raid was greatly exaggerated by the counterrevolutionaries, and by the White and foreign press, which sought to place a halo about the heads of the counterrevolutionaries.

The Whites considered Mamontov's raid to be an important strategic operation. But what, in the final analysis, did Denikin gain from it? The Mamontov raid estranged the sympathies of the population in the fighting districts. It accelerated the further growth of the Red cavalry, which with amazing speed was transformed from the Budyonny Corps (which at that time was successfully operating against the White cavalry southwest of Saratov) into the First Mounted Army. And finally, it threw the spotlight on unreliable elements occupying responsible posts in the command of the Southern front, as a result of which Lenin and Stalin interfered in the work of this command. It was this interference which determined the outcome of the war with Denikin.

Such was the actual political and military significance of the Mamontov raid. This raid demonstrated the weakest aspect of Denikin's strategy—its political flaccidity. It expressed the very essence of Denikin's undertaking, which Lenin defined in his July letter as a mere *adventure*. It was in very fact "a desperate undertaking with the purpose of sowing panic, and causing destruction for destruction's sake."

. . . .

Pastukhov was not certain that he had been right in agreeing to be one of the delegation sent to Mamontov. It was a political measure, and he avoided politics, convinced that they bred only trouble. But in the first place, Asya had approved of this measure, and in the second, there was no time to think about it. Scarcely had he donned his best suit and laid out his favourite coat (with the white fleck in the weave), when they came for him. The General had requested that the delegation put in its appearance immediately.

As Asya kissed Alexander Vladimirovich goodbye, she made a tiny sign of the cross on his stomach, where he would not notice it.

Mamontov was staying with the staff of his corps in the Grand Hotel on the main street—the only large hotel in the city. Now it was surrounded by armed Don Cossacks, both mounted and on foot. The delegation was met at the entrance by two cornets, who expressed doubt as to whether the General would be willing to see so many petitioners (there were eight in the group). But it had cost the members too much effort to decide on such a fearful undertaking, to abandon it now, at the very threshold. The noble gentleman who had urged Pastukhov to join the delegation became particularly flustered:

"But my dear sir! Allow me to read the list of names. Representatives of only the most dependable circles. It would be quite impossible to exclude a single one of them."

Pastukhov made the acquaintance of all the representatives, and took his place beside the head of the delegation, a weighty man with blue eyes that seemed forever apologizing. Pastukhov liked him. Apparently he was in a state of great excitement, for while waiting to be admitted to the rooms occupied by the staff, he kept scratching into his grey beard, then, catching himself, would stroke it nervously.

Finally the delegation was led upstairs to the Colonel who served as the General's personal adjutant. He glanced at the list of the members, asked who headed the delegation and which of them was Pastukhov.

Alexander Vladimirovich placed one foot forward and slightly bowed his head. The Colonel fixed him with his eye, and after a moment's consideration, waltzed into the next room with a clinking of spurs. Presently he reappeared, leaving the door open and announcing: "The Com-

mander is awaiting you." The eight delegates
filed past him one by one.

Mamontov was sitting at the desk poring over
some papers. They could see only the close-clipped
lawn of the top of his head and two bristling
pine cones of moustaches.

Behind him stood a young Cossack with his
hand on his silver sword hilt. Two more Cossacks were stationed behind the delegation, which
formed a semicircle at a respectful distance from
the desk. No one invited the members to sit down.

For some time after they had taken their
places, they stood waiting in motionless expectation, but Mamontov went on with his papers.
Suddenly he raised his head and swept his eye
from one end of the semicircle to the other,
as though verifying their ranks.

"With whom have I the pleasure?" he asked
without rising.

"General Mamontov!" began the head of the
delegation, taking a deep breath and advancing the
tiniest step forward. But Mamontov interrupted him:

"Who were you before the revolution?"

"A councillor of state."

"Then you should know that I am to be addressed as 'Your Excellency.'"

He took first one, then the other moustache
between his fingers and twisted them sharply to

right and left, so that they stuck out all the more impressively.

"Tell me the names so that I shall know with whom I am dealing," he said to the Colonel.

"A list has been presented," replied the latter, stepping away from the door.

"Let me have it."

The Colonel placed a sheet of paper on the desk. Mamontov leaned over it and asked, as though he were the only person in the room:

"Who are they anyway?"

"The most various sort, including even Reds," said the Colonel.

"That's a fine thing! Coming to me! A Bolshevik deputation!"

"Among them is a man named Pastukhov. He's a Red," said the Colonel with obvious relish.

"Which is he? Which is Pastukhov?" shouted Mamontov, once more running a sharp eye down the line.

"I am Pastukhov. But the Colonel has taken me for someone else," answered Alexander Vladimirovich without moving, trying to make his voice sound convincing.

"Here it says you are a writer. Is that true?" asked the Colonel.

"I am a St. Petersburg playwright. A dramatist."

"Then what are you trying to deny? With my own eyes I read an article in a Bolshevik newspaper stating that you had been in the Saratov underground movement," said the Colonel.

"That was a mistake, or perhaps even slander," said Pastukhov, his tongue going wooden.

"I have no time to investigate mistakes!" cried Mamontov again. "Lock him up! Daring to show his face to me! An intellectual, the bastard!"

Someone tugged at the coat Pastukhov had thrown over his arm. He glanced about. A Cossack took him firmly by the arm. Pastukhov stepped aside and tried to say something, but they were already leading him away.

He heard a voice, which he seemed to recognize as belonging to the gentleman from the necrologies, crying: "Your Excellency ... the merchants ... the clergy ... former officials. ..." and Mamontov's shouted retort: "Gone Bolshevik!"

And then a change took place in Pastukhov's powers of perception. Everything became strangely merged, as in a dream, yet the fusion would occasionally be rent by blinding flashes of insight.

He saw a high cheekboned Cossack turning a paper in his bronze fingers. This paper had some fatal connection with Pastukhov, but he did not clearly know what was written on it. The Cossack said to somebody: "What is he, an S.R.—that swell there?" Then a cornet with a tuft of black hair hanging over his eye, tapped the calf of his leg with his riding crop as he said to an officer in uhlan uniform: "What did that building across the street used to be?" "A girls' school." "Damn it all—those were the days—the pretty little creatures from those private schools!" Immediately Alexander Vladimirovich seemed to rise up in front of himself like another person, who was also Pastukhov, but quite separate from himself. This individual went walking down Moscow Street between two mounted Cossacks. He was carrying the white-flecked coat over his arm and glancing about him. Pastukhov had often strolled down this long street to the turn leading to the station. He recognized it now, but it too seemed to be another Moscow Street, along which they were leading this other Pastukhov. Some Cossacks came trotting toward them, singing as they rode, and as soon as they drew abreast of Pastukhov, one of the men turned in his saddle and whistled like a *djigit*. The whistle was so piercing that it caused Pastukhov physical pain. It seemed to him that he had been struck over the head by a whip, and this illusion was so strong that he clutched his forehead. Suddenly he caught sight of the flat wall of a building pierced by dreary rows of windows, and he recalled that at the turning to the station stood a jail with a rusty sign under the roof reading: "Prison Castle." Pastukhov remembered it because he had marvelled at the incongruity of the word "castle." But this other Pastukhov, who was now approaching the gate to the "castle," recalled the word without the slightest astonishment, and with the firm conviction that this adventure must inevitably end in the "castle."

A sense of reality returned to Alexander Vladimirovich when he was jammed into the cell. He was indeed jammed in—not led in, nor shoved in, nor thrown in. He found himself part of a solid mass of human bodies, and he immediately coughed from the stifling odour. No, it was no odour; it was merely one element of an environment incompatible with the human olfactory sense. The effect of this environment was such that a change took place in the colour of Pastukhov's skin, as he noticed on lifting his hand to his mouth. This environment acted on the pigmentation; a person turned earthen from lack of air.

At that moment he thought with great lucidity of Asya and Alyosha, and only now did he wholly comprehend what had happened to him. He realized that neither Asya nor Alyosha would ever see him again, for he was doomed. In realizing this, he probably moaned, for someone next to him asked mockingly: "Don't like it?", and gave a coarse laugh. He made no answer, foreseeing that his endurance would be put to more cruel tests.

Here, as in every other place where people are gathered together, there developed interrelationships depending on the strength of some and the weakness of others. In this noxious dumping ground of human bodies reigned an order of which Pastukhov became aware as soon as his blood had adjusted itself to the new conditions of respiration. It turned out that there were not as many people as he had at first imagined; or perhaps it would be more correct to say that the cell turned out to be incapable of accommodating the numberless horde which Pastukhov had imagined when he was first squeezed into their midst. Later he counted forty-eight people in a cell with twelve bunks built in two stories. Here were clerks and workers; old prisoners who had been released on the first day of the Mamontov raid, and then rejailed; respectable old men and shy youths with innocent eyes. One group stood near the door, another sat on the floor, and a third occupied the bunks. At the conclusion of a certain period of time, those who were lying on the bunks took the place of those standing at the door; those who had been sitting on the floor crawled up on the bunks; and some of the people who had been standing, sat on the floor. This revolving of positions at regular intervals was the order which Pastukhov observed. It was supplemented by the fact that three or four individuals saw to the enforcement of this regime without themselves falling subject to it. They merely lay on the bunks and ordered the others about, for they were the strongest of the species.

It was some time before Pastukhov was given an opportunity to sit down. During an argument as to whose turn it was, he heard the same coarse voice which had addressed him earlier say: "He's just come in out of the air. Let him stand!"

At first Pastukhov had even preferred standing. His eagerness to observe everything that came within range of his senses could in no way stop the intense activity of his mind. Involuntarily he noticed the most minute details of his environment, and at the same time asked himself questions which seemed to have no connection with what his eyes saw, his ears heard, his body felt.

More insistent than all others was the question: why, in the final analysis, should he perish? After all, he had *done nothing*. If he had *done* anything to justify his being called a Red! In his desire to curry favour with the Bolsheviks, Mertsalov had made a Red out of Pastukhov. But he had made him a Red only in the eyes of the Whites. In the eyes of the Reds, he remained the White he had always appeared. And the Whites had thrown him into the "castle" as a Red. Was that what Mertsalov had wanted? But the devil with Mertsalov. What had *fate* wanted of Pastukhov by entangling him in this snare? What was the truth? Wherein did it lie? Actually Pastukhov had *done nothing* to violate his sense of what was just. Why, then, had Justice turned her face from him?

Could it be that he had had a mistaken conception of what was right? And could it be that this mistake was a crime against Justice for which the goddess was now punishing him? Had he no right to err? Dared he not indulge in the luxury of a mistake? Merciful God, could it be that here, in this stink, in this cesspool, Pastukhov must search for new solutions to problems he had solved while yet a student?

"Don't you like it?" came the coarse voice.

"I'll try. I'll try to begin all over again," said Pastukhov to himself, swaying on his swollen feet.

... I was born into this world regardless of my own choice and to the astonishment of my growing consciousness. I was greeted by two laws, in the making of which I had no say. One of them was a biological law whose demands were rooted in my body cells—"I want to live." The other was the social-historical law presenting the ultimatum: "Either you will live in subjection to me, or you will be annihilated." If I should attempt to live isolated from humanity, I would become a beast. I am doomed to live among my kind. I accept this as the inevitable. I accept it as something laid down before I ever made my appearance in this world. I accept the world as something arbitrarily forced on me. . . .

An unpleasant, unfamiliar inner voice, somewhat resembling the voice which kept insulting him in the cell, interrupted the course of his thinking: "Do you accept the world along with this dungeon they've shoved you into?"

"I was as innocent when I sat in my bird's-eye maple study as I am now, sitting in this dungeon," Pastukhov answered to himself. "Which was more just—to allow me to sit in my bird's-eye maple study, or to shove me into this dungeon?"

"If you consider the world as something forced on you, why seek justice?" asked the unpleasant voice. "You didn't seek justice when life was easy. You thought of justice only when life became hard. Then you must admit that the demanding of justice on the part of those for whom life is hard has more foundation than the ignoring of justice on the part of those for whom life is easy."

"I never questioned anyone's right to demand justice. I always recognized the noble nature of such demands. I only supposed that those demands exaggerated the role of the social order in achieving justice. In any form of society a man has to struggle for existence, in this one as well as in that one, and I'm not sure under which form the struggle is easier."

"It was not necessary for you to engage in any particular struggle while sitting in your bird's-eye maple study. Your existence was taken care of by that order of society which you accepted as arbitrarily forced on you. You were quite content with that arbitrary enforcement. But others were not. Listen to yourself: you are always speaking about yourself—I, I, only I!"

"It's not my fault that I am doomed to live. I make far less claims on the world than it does on me."

"On what are your claims based? The world is no more responsible for your being alive than you are. But you want to receive without giving."

"What do you mean—without giving? What about my art?"

"You yourself called that a 'beautiful mistake.'"

"No, it wasn't I who called it that. It was Asya. Poor Asya! How she will suffer when I perish! Ah, Asya, how many mistakes! How many mistakes! Beautiful mistakes? Damn it all, that's mere affectation. Haven't I believed all my life that art, more than anything else, is governed by laws reflecting nature, the prototype of art? Take this building, for instance. It is ugly because it has no head, no shoulders, no thighs. Anyone can see that, and all agree that this building is ugly. Oh, if man could only build life unerringly, according to laws of art, like nature—perhaps then we should have a happy society."

"Aha," came the unpleasant inner voice again. "So now you are seeking a happy society! You no longer accept the world as arbitrarily forced on you, but intend constructing it according to your own will. Go on, go on—keep following that path. Maybe it will lead you out onto the highway...."

"Go on, go on. Sit down. Yes, you—the newcomer! Fresh from the big out-of-doors! Worn out with standing there, eh?"

At first Pastukhov did not realize that the shouts were addressed to him. He felt himself being pushed away from the door. With difficulty he bent his knees and let himself down onto the floor. Little by little a blissful oblivion crept over him: he drowsed, his chin on his chest.

Thus he merged with the bodies revolving within this cell: thus he began the existence common to all the inmates.

Once he had heard of the various diversions resorted to in prison in order to kill time and preserve the faculty of thought. Prisoners taught each other foreign languages and undertook the study of various sciences. On thinking over what he might teach, Pastukhov discovered that in spite of the extensiveness of his general knowledge, he knew nothing thoroughly. One subject was forgotten, another had been dropped half-learned, a third had never been really understood, while a fourth left impressions only of general conclusions. His knowledge of foreign languages was sufficient only to allow him to chat with a Frenchman about wine and food, and with a German about the weather and the high cost of living. But there was no occasion to regret his shortcomings as a teacher. No one cared to listen to lectures, and he himself lacked the strength to give them. The inmates were never given an opportunity to bathe, or to breathe clean air, but he gradually became reconciled to the dirt, for the aching of his body was worse than the dirt; the hunger was worse than the ache; and the uncertainty was worse than the hunger. Just as his sense of smell had been blunted by first contact with the stench, so other senses gradually became dulled, leaving only his hearing morbidly keen to the slightest rustle in the corridor of the "castle."

Early one morning, on awaking after sluggish sleep, he caught sight of a little grey insect approaching him clumsily—now hopping, now crawling along the outstretched legs of his neighbours. Pastukhov shuddered. It was frightening and repulsive that he had to lie helplessly there on the floor and allow vermin to crawl over his body as though he were a corpse. He recognized the insect as a cricket, and while immediately recalling all the good tales associated with this benign denizen of the hearth, he could not overcome his repulsion. Meanwhile the cricket kept hopping and crawling nearer. It resembled neither a locust, nor a roach, but was a combination of roach and locust, which made it all the more loathsome. It hopped on Pastukhov. He jumped up, shook it off, and crushed it with his foot, experiencing childlike fear and revulsion. For some time he continued to scrape his foot over the spot, and could not conquer his aversion.

Time passed in a series of dawns and dusks, noons and midnights, but all hours were monotonously alike, and filled for Pastukhov with an unwanted brooding which he called the struggle between body and soul. He awaited the end, and had already lost track of the passage of time when one day he heard a great commotion outside the door.

It was at first incomprehensible—a growing roar that came echoing down the corridor, interrupted by a great banging and clanging. Before the door was opened, someone in the cell cried out in a wild, ecstatic voice:

"The Reds."

Everyone jumped up off the bunks and floor and began pressing toward the door, causing a crush which was unbearable even for these people, accustomed as they were to cramped quarters. They shouted and hammered with their fists on door and bunks, causing a tumult which drowned out the noise outside their cell.

Expectation transformed the faces of the prisoners, lighting them up with a will to action.

"Open the do-o-or! Friends!" Such were the cries that came from the cell, and more and more vehement became the shouting, and more and more furious became the pounding, until light poured in where the door had been, and bayonets flashed in this light, and beneath the bayonets appeared caps bearing the red star.

Immediately the noise subsided, because everyone froze to the spot, unable to believe his own eyes, and for a second there seemed to be more space, and in that second Pastukhov heard a young voice cry out:

"All who're here on account of Mamontov, come on out!"

Again there was noise and a crush, and Pastukhov shoved forward, unconsciously straining all his muscles to push past those who were pushing him.

Somewhere in a downstairs corridor he found himself standing in line, and without knowing how, he landed in front of a desk behind which a Red Army man was sorting through papers.

"Who might you be, citizen?" he was asked.

(However dirty and wrinkled Pastukhov was, his appearance was notable.)

"A theatre worker," he answered.

"Ah, theatre!" laughed the fellow behind the desk, and handed him a slip of paper, saying, "Well, you may go."

He walked through the yard with the paper in his hand, glancing at those who had also been released, and it seemed to him that their faces were stupid with joy, and he felt that his face must also look stupid and joyful, and he was deeply moved that this was so.

He was stopped at the gate.

A guard of Red Army men was leading some prisoners into the yard. Among those in the first row was a weighty old man who kept nervously scratching into his unkempt beard. He looked at Pastukhov with blue, apologetic eyes, and Pastukhov recognized the head of the delegation to General Mamontov.

His mind turned a somersault. It seemed to Pastukhov that he was going insane. But presently someone asked him for his paper; he handed it over, went out onto the street, raised his eyes to the carefree sky, and set off down the pavement on shaky legs, but with tremendous gusto.

At a crossing he saw a man and woman intent on hammering something to the frame of a shop window. He stopped to regain some strength in his knees and glanced through the broken window into the store. It was empty, but in the show window stood a row of glass jars sealed with wax. Pastukhov felt a pleasant dizziness, and the necessity of genial conversation.

"What are you trading in?" he asked.

The woman looked at him without answering; the man went right on with his hammering.

Pastukhov took up one of the jars and read: "Horse-radish." With a grunt he began to decipher an incomprehensible word printed on the label in Russian letters. He wished to make some witty remark, but his brain refused to be roused from blessed inactivity. When he had made something out of the word, he said:

"Strange, isn't it? The language used to be so long and cumbersome: 'Tambov ... Gubernia ... Retail ... Cooperative ....' And now—all in one breath: 'Tamgubretacoopunion.' And there you are."

The man put down his hammer and asked:

"You just come out of there?" nodding toward the jail.

"Yes."

"Anybody can see that."

"You may take one if you like," said the woman.

Pastukhov gave a hopeless gesture: his coat, with his money in the pocket, had remained in the "castle."

"Help yourself. Nobody buys them anyway."

A mischievous glint came into his eye as he thrust the jar into his pocket and gave the traditional thanks of a beggar: "God will bless you for this." He walked away with his old independent stride, conscious of the same pleasant giddiness and of reviving satisfaction in his own artistry.

He increased his pace as he approached his house, and finally raced up the stairs like a little boy.

Asya let out a little scream and grabbed him about the neck. Alyosha came running from the other room; the child stood speechless for a moment, then rushed over and hugged his father's leg. He was the first to break the silence:

"You've got a beard, daddy," he said, looking up with eyes shining like his mother's.

Alexander Vladimirovich lacked the strength to utter a word. He gasped from the embraces and his own emotion.

Alyosha felt the jar in his pocket.

"What is it, daddy? This—what is it?"

Pastukhov drew it out of his pocket and handed it to Asya. She was nonplussed. Holding the jar in one hand, the other still about his neck, she glanced deep into his eyes in search of response to the one feeling which now overwhelmed her. He wanted her to read what was printed on the label so that they could laugh together. He still felt the urge to jest, but his first words were pronounced in such a way that even Asya, who was accustomed to his manner of talking nonsense with a serious mien, took them in earnest.

"Alms to a convict," he said.

Touched with gratitude, she hugged the silly jar to her breast. Then Pastukhov, with characteristic spontaneity, burst out laughing and grabbed the jar from Asya, tossing it onto the table and muttering through his laughter:

"Later ... later you'll have time to investigate that sauce!"

Still uncomprehending, and unwilling to comprehend anything but her happiness, she tried to answer his laughter with a smile.

Olga Adamovna appeared timidly in the doorway, wiping her eyes with a handkerchief. She was fully aware of the fact that she was intruding, but she could not restrain the desire to witness this remarkable reunion.

Pastukhov solemnly walked over and kissed her hand. She broke out in red blotches and her curls began to bob. She retreated and closed the door.

He called after her:

"Olga Adamovna! A bath—I implore you—as soon as possible! Do you think you could arrange for me to have a bath?"

By the time the turbulence rising from such deep-seated emotion had subsided and the power of rational thinking had reasserted itself, so that Pastukhov could give a brief account of himself and Asya could listen to this account—by that time Alyosha was already back with his toys and Olga Adamovna was struggling with a smoking kerosene stove.

As he paced the floor with a glass of tea in his hand, Pastukhov noticed the loose pages of a book on the bed.

"Were you reading?" he asked.

"Yes. I cried over it, but kept on reading," answered Asya, with an ephemeral smile that seemed to ask forgiveness for such an admission.

"What is it?"

"A conglomeration. From different parts of *War and Peace*. Strangely enough, I was glad the pages were mixed up. It made it all the sadder."

26*

She sat on the bed and began leafing through the papers.

"There's one place here. . . ."

She gave up searching for it.

"But I'll never find it in this mess."

"What's it about?"

"It's one of those places I used to find boring. I always skipped it. But this time I started thinking about it. . . . The place where he speaks about history."

"I know it. I also thought about it while I was in there."

"Really? Maybe at the very time I was reading it. You know—where he says it is obsolete to consider history something created by the will of man."

"Yes, yes. And that it is impossible to hold that point of view of history and at the same time recognize the authenticity of laws of statistics and political economy, which are in direct contradiction to such a point of view."

"How well you remember it!"

As usual when her husband thought out loud, Asya followed him fascinated.

"Well, what else?" he asked.

She paused.

"At first I thought he was right, but then I disagreed with him."

"Disagreed with Tolstoy?"

"Yes. It seems to me that a new view of history has triumphed. Isn't that true? Nowadays they contend that the evidence of history corresponds with that of those other sciences Tolstoy mentioned—that is, with statistics and natural science. Am I right?"

Again she was silent, and there was a dual expression in her eyes, as though she felt guilty for having introduced such an abstract subject of conversation, and at the same time had an irresistible urge to express herself and was proud to be doing so.

"Well?" he repeated.

"It seems to me that just as man formerly submitted to history, while interpreting it falsely, so now he submits while interpreting it correctly. History directs his course, like an instrument. Don't you agree?" asked Asya, the duality of her expression becoming more marked.

Pastukhov gulped down his tea, took a chair, and sat down opposite his wife. He did all this with the greatest deliberation.

"Don't you agree with me?" she asked again. "I kept thinking about you constantly, Sasha, and about us. I couldn't sleep, and that is why I read so much. But I kept coming back to that place in the book. And I developed my own point of view. Maybe it does not contradict Tolstoy's. I don't know. But for me it seems to go further. I asked myself what the conclusion must be, once the course of life is directed by history and we are its victims."

He looked straight into her eyes, and it seemed to him that that strange expression of guilt was veiling an underlying sharpness. Apparent weakness and hidden strength—these were the contradictions dwelling in the familiar features of Asya's face, now faintly smiling, now slightly hesitant, and appearing to him at this moment more beautiful than ever before.

"What must the conclusion be," she continued eagerly, "if, regardless of whether we interpret history falsely or correctly, we remain its victims? Submission. That's the only conclusion. Am I right?"

"A damned clever lady," he said seriously, but so that she could accept his praise as a jest, which she preferred doing, laughing excitedly.

He went on speaking without responding to her laughter, laying special emphasis on every word:

"Let us for the present disregard the fact that we must not confuse history with the course of events we ourselves are living through, and which will become the object of study only after a passage of time. At present I do not wish to analyze which interpretation of history is false, and which is scientifically sound. I live according to my own experience, do you understand? —and never has life provided it in such variety. This is history in which I am one of the participators. Is that clear? And you must understand one thing: I have not the slightest desire to be a victim of history. I don't wish to be a victim of anything, damn it all! Nothing at all!"

Pastukhov got up, pushed his chair away with his foot, and again began to pace the floor.

"There is no trick to understanding that what is happening in St. Petersburg, in Saratov, in Kozlov, and I don't know where else— to us and to our Alyosha—is part of the course of history. The trick lies in discovering the motivating force behind it all. It is necessary to identify yourself with whatever is propelling history forward. Mamontov is also history. But I'll thank you to let me keep as far away from such history as possible. If I must submit to the course of events regardless of circumstances (which I think you are quite correct in asserting), at least it is within my power to choose which of the various forces influencing this course I shall submit to. A victim? If I die a glorious and honourable death, I am a hero, rather than a victim. And if I stretch my legs in a lousy dungeon for no reason under the sun, I am also not a victim—I am just a damn fool!"

He stopped in some annoyance.

"There, you see? Seems that I too can make speeches."

He caught sight of Alyosha hugging the door-jamb and gazing at his father with an expression that was both proud and frightened.

"What are you doing here?"

"I thought you called me."

"Called you?"

"You cried out 'Alyosha!'"

"Don't come close to me, I need a bath. Go back to your playing," said Pastukhov, somewhat touched.

Asya's glance was dimmed by that inspired tear which always went to Pastukhov's heart, and he avoided looking at his wife in order to preserve the driving force of his resolution.

"Do you remember the conversation I had with Dibich at the Saratov station? Now I see that Dibich was right. Even if they die, people like him will belong to History, spelled with a capital letter (his own words, if you remember), and not to the so-called wreckage of history. I too have no intention of floundering among wreckage. Why should I, for God's sake?"

In the appreciation of some new force rising within him, he straightened his shoulders and thrust out his chin.

"Not a bad bit of wreckage," he said playfully.

Asya shook her head approvingly, but somewhat thoughtfully.

"He's a nice person, that Dibich," she said.

Pastukhov stopped and blinked at her, losing track of his thoughts. Going over to the table, he finished his tea in one gulp.

"You love to have people melt under your water-colours. Dibich went into ecstasies whenever he looked at you. Even old man Dorogomilov did some sighing. . . ."

She pushed back the hair on her temple with her little finger.

"It's just lovely when you get jealous!"

Again he pushed over his chair and sat down opposite her.

"My choice is final. Do you understand? I made it in there—in that local branch of Dante's Inferno. I resolved that if I ever got out alive, the first thing I would do would be to write a letter to Izvekov confessing to having been an ass. And to Dorogomilov too. I want them to know that I am not a Whiteguard."

He said this firmly and somewhat triumphantly. Suddenly he leaned toward Asya and lowered his voice.

"I had one frightful and repulsive moment in there. Listen. . . ."

And he described to her, illustrating with gesticulations, how the cricket had crawled onto him and how he had smashed it with his foot. Asya's face reflected the aversion expressed on his own as he recalled this unforgettable experience.

"The most disgusting aspect of that insect was the fact that it was neither roach nor locust, but a sort of hotchpotch. In addition to which there was something inexpressibly self-satisfied and important about it, as though the horrid creature fancied itself a beauty. It's impossible to look at such a thing without shuddering. Whenever I remember it the chills run up and down my back. Br-r-r!"

He rubbed his hands together, jumped up and shook himself. Several leaves of the book fell on the floor. He picked them up.

"There is nothing on earth worse than a hotchpotch. And it seemed to me that my own position, seen in that light, was loathsome."

"Sasha!" cried Asya, genuinely frightened.

He tried to arrange the leaves of the book in an even pile. They scattered in his hands.

"I imagined what I must look like to others. What I must look like to an intelligent person. And I made my choice. And once it was made —can you believe it?—even in that cesspool— doomed, and awaiting the end—I felt incomparably more free. Do you understand? To perish because of some fool misunderstanding is not even funny. It is humiliating. I resolved that if I must die, I would shout at them (I often imagined myself doing it): 'Yes, I'm a Red! I'm a Red, damn it all, and I hate you from the very depths of my soul!'"

Once more he noted the excited face of his son in the doorway.

"Daddy," said Alyosha softly, "do crickets bite?"

"No," answered Anastasia Germanovna with a slight smile. "Crickets don't bite. And don't interrupt daddy and me."

She got up with the intention of soothing her husband, or perhaps of preventing him from taking some dangerous step. He averted her movement, as though seeing in it a threat to that wavering structure he had just reared, fearing that it might collapse.

"And I'm not running off anywhere else," he cut in impatiently. "That's done with. I can understand Dibich's running away from a prison camp. He had to reach home. But I don't have to. I'm home already. You and I are home, do you understand? And we must share the fate of our home."

With shy insistence she took his fingers in her soft hands, opened his arms, and put her head on his breast.

"Darling. But I agree with you entirely. Entirely."

He freed himself. He wanted his structure to stand complete, to put an end to this wearying struggle between body and soul, and, most important of all, to be convinced that his decision had been made independent of outside prompting or pressure—that he had acted as a free agent. He feared objections, and at the same time did not want Asya to agree with him too readily. He could not admit her priority in a decision which was to change his entire life.

Finally he succeeded in arranging the leaves of the book, and said, while smoothing out the torn edges:

"You actually support Tolstoy's opinion if you consider that the whole problem resolves itself into a mere submitting to circumstances. I disagree with him. If the choice lies with me, then of my own free will I contribute to the development of circumstances. The sum of such free choices is one of the forces determining history. In other words, to a certain degree history is created by the free will of man. By *my* free will."

"That is just what I was going to say," whispered Asya, hugging his head. "Of course you are free in all your actions.... Like the prodigal son who came back to his father's house, you and I are also free to return to the fold. With bowed heads. Bowed heads don't get chopped off."

She ruffled his hair, and he wanted to turn away, but suddenly he burst out laughing in the old way and they looked into each other's eyes, pleased with each other, and somehow younger.

"So it turns out you have everything your own way?" said Pastukhov, with a scarcely perceptible wink.

Olga Adamovna glanced in and said, with the distraught expression with which unexpected holiday guests are announced, that the director of the theatre and his mother had arrived.

"Just to congratulate you! Just to congratulate you!" exclaimed the director, pumping Pastukhov's hand. "What luck! How do you feel? You certainly did give us some bad nights—ask my mother here! But things looked pretty bad—no denying that!"

"I hardly know what to say," replied Alexander Vladimirovich with a wan smile. "I don't remember in just which of Stendhal's novels he says of his hero: 'Misery made his soul accessible to art.' So you see things can turn out for the best after all."

"Did they beat you in there?" asked the director's mother, pushing the hair off one ear.

"God was merciful," he shouted back jovially.

She crossed herself.

"Excuse me, but I must be off to the theatre," said the director. "We're putting on an 'Apotheosis.' Such enthusiasm—you can't imagine."

"What did you say you were putting on?"

"An 'Apotheosis.'"

"Who wrote it?"

"Nobody. The members of the troupe are making it up as they go along. Music and singing and all the rest of it."

"Wait a second," said Pastukhov brusquely, catching the director by the sleeve. "Wait. I'll write an apotheosis for you. I'll call it 'Liberation.'"

He turned a magnanimous glance on all of them.

"Alexander Vladimirovich! We'll—why we'll —the whole troupe'll kiss your feet!"

414

The director ran to the door, shouting incoherent exclamations on the way.

"What's that he's saying?" asked his mother.

"They want to kiss my feet," yelled Pastukhov in her ear.

"Ah-h! That's right. We thought we'd never see you again.... I've heated the bath for you."

Alexander Vladimirovich squeezed her shoulder.

"How about some birch twigs to beat me into a perspiration. Have you got some birch twigs?" he shouted.

"I have some, but they're pretty well worn— like a broom."

"Thanks even for them. Thanks even for a broom, mother."

"Go ahead and sweat yourself, God bless you...."

"I'll scrub everything out of me once and for all," said Pastukhov with a loud sigh when he was again alone with his wife.

They went out onto the balcony. He glanced from one end of the empty square to the other.

"What a day! And what a wonderful, sourish smell the street dust has! Ah, Asya, Asya!"

Once more he took a deep breath, filling the vast expanse of his chest.

30

Ragozin's external appearance remained unchanged even after he became one of the crew of the *October*, and this distinguished him from the sailors; but everyone found this perfectly natural, and he himself did not attribute any particular significance to the fact that he did not look like a seaman. He still wore a Russian blouse buttoning down the left side, a suit coat, and a flat cap pulled down over his eyes, often with a curly wisp of hair caught over his temple. But as if to make up for all that, he walked with a more pronounced roll than any sailor. His former swaying gait became emphasized, perhaps because he seemed to have become younger now that he had abandoned his hopeless battle with finance and gone to live where the wind blew free over the Volga.

The squadron soon became accustomed to his tall, stooped figure. He often appeared among the men, though at first he had to spend much time in the headquarter's cabin, familiarizing himself with the affairs of the war fleet and reorganizing political work in accordance with changing circumstances.

Ragozin landed in the flotilla a few days before the beginning of the August drive of the Soviet Army southwest of Saratov. He was neither a soldier nor a sailor, and could handle only one weapon—a revolver, a weapon familiar enough to Russia's working people. Confident that a man is always in the right place if put there by his Party, he assumed the responsibilities of Squadron Commissar without the slightest doubt that, given enough time, he would be equal to them.

Among the crews of his ships were sailors from the Baltic, from the Caspian and Azov seas, mariners from the far north, and Volga boatmen. All the members of this aquatic tribe had years of sailing experience behind them; most of them had been through the war, and seemed specially designed by nature for life on shipboard.

The diversity of types was compensated for by the unified rules and regulations of the war fleet, as well as by the fact that an example was set for all of them by the Baltic sailors, who brought to the Volga the double glory of having fought the German fleet in the Baltic, and defended the revolution in Petrograd, from whence the famous battleship *Aurora* sent the first volley echoing throughout Russia to usher in the October Revolution. Everyone considered it his duty to imitate the Baltic sailors—their selfless bravery in battle, their pointed witticisms when off duty, even their manner of wearing their pancake hats in a line parallel with their brows rather than cocked over one ear—a style which made them look less jaunty, but more inexorable.

In addition to gunboats, the Northern detachment of the Volga-Kama flotilla included floating forts mounted with naval artillery, and auxiliary vessels: hospital and repair boats, cutters, landing and aviation craft and minelayers. On the day when this armed, colourful armada of big ships and little ships, smudging the shore and the sky with the black and brown and grey smoke of their stacks, pounding and puffing with their motors, clanking their anchor chains through the hawseholes, flashing signal flags from their bridges—when this complex floating bastion stretched out over the versts in preparation for operations and Ragozin passed the leading gunboats in a motor launch taking him to Staff Headquarters, his heart leaped in his breast. For the first time the true strength of the Red front was revealed to him with irresistible visual force, and it was as though in this formidable array he perceived the majesty of the whole people, streaming forward to claim their rights.

Ragozin scooped up a handful of sun-warmed water, took a swallow, wiped his brow with a palm uncooled by the water, and, for want of a better means of giving vent to his feeling, shouted to the man at the wheel: "How about a smoke?", though he had long since given up smoking.

From the moment that squadron Staff Headquarters had opened the envelope containing the order to go into attack and the signalman had played the gay flag pattern conveying the squadron commander's order to follow in a single column, Ragozin had not once entered his cabin. His presence on deck, or among the silent, serious sailors at the guns, or on the command bridge, with a pair of field glasses at his eyes, filled him with tense excitement. He was certain that the first battle would be decisive, and he found something incongruous about the serenity of the shores, the tints of the sunrise, delicate as the plumage of bullfinch, and the smoke of hearth fires wreathing above the villages. The sun rolled up in a full disc over the meadow side of the river, causing the high bank on the other side to come to life. Flocks of sheep and herds of bullocks raised clouds of dust as they climbed the hillsides. They were army cattle, being driven away as a sign that an attack on land was being opened at the same time as that from the river. The swirling dust on the shore seemed to call to the plumes of smoke from the gunboats: "Shoulder to shoulder, forward to victory!"

But these swirls of dust attracted the attention of the enemy. Two triangles of aeroplanes quickly came to meet the fleet, growing in the cloudless sky from insignificant sparrows to great ravens, and filling the air with a menacing roar. The foremost triangle flew above the riverbank, the second over the river. One after another the first bombs exploded, throwing up fans of earth. Dust billowed on the hillsides as the cattle scattered in every direction.

Three-inch antiaircraft guns began to bark. The boats manoeuvred. Towering wineglasses rose from the Volga with each bomb burst, disintegrating in showers of rain. The gunboats were tossed on conflicting waves.

Some of the engine-room crew of the *October* came up on deck. Everyone watched the planes circle and return. This time all six of them chose a course over the water. The bombs fell thickly, but the ships had taken advantage of the pause to move apart. Antiaircraft fire increased, filling the sky with the soft explosions of cotton stars. The planes were forced to climb, but again they circled, and again returned.

One of the bombs came screeching through the air and struck the water near the *October*. The deck of the gunboat was swamped by a frothing inundation; the ship answered the explosion with a groan issuing from its very entrails, while the clink of shattered glass came from the pilot's cabin.

A young sailor was blown off the bow into the water. They threw him a rope from the stern. He scrambled back on deck like a cat. There he stood with the water streaming from him, his middy and pants plastered to his rubber-like body. Glancing at the retreating planes, he shook his fist and cried:

"I won't forget this!", adding an oath that could be heard all over deck.

Strashnov, who had come up out of the engine room, was standing behind Ragozin when the explosion took place. He wiped the wave off his yellow, smudged face and growled in a bass voice:

"Fond greetings from the Entente!"

Ragozin wiped the back of his neck and said calmly:

"The dear allies."

"Are those birdies of French make?"

"Churchill's efforts," replied Ragozin, then, turning to Strashnov, said sharply: "Is this where you are scheduled to be?"

"We've got both watches on duty," responded Strashnov, his face averted.

Ragozin said nothing.

All during the raid he remained near the antiaircraft guns, watching the unfamiliar work of the gunners. He was afraid to miss some important moment demanding his aid, and his attention was fixed with such unprecedented concentration that it absorbed all other faculties. Only when the aeroplanes disappeared over the horizon did he realize, from head to toe, as it were, that the moment had been a tense one. If even one of the bombs had struck a ship, the loss would have been enormous. He was amazed that the antiaircraft guns did no harm to the aircraft, which flew away with mocking imperturbability, and he did not know whether the guns had been well manned or not, or whether this could even be called a battle. But the crew silently set about putting the ship in order, and Ragozin also remained significantly silent, pretending that such clashes were nothing new to him.

The gunboat *Risky*, which had been sent ahead, drew close to the enemy shore and sent out a boatload of scouts. The sailors climbed up onto the roof of a damaged house.

On either hand stretched the steppes, strewn with a monotone carpet of sunburnt grass. The level spaces were cleaved by a low elevation approaching the river at an angle. To the right of this elevation could be seen lines of infantry, drawn up facing the south. To the left extended a ridge of hills resembling barrows. The air was so vibrant with heat that it was difficult to make out the true contours of the barrows from the mirage. Through their field glasses the sailors began to make out moving figures clustered about certain points distributed over the ridge.

Suddenly they had a clear picture of the artillery positions of the Whites.

The scouts jumped down off the roof and rushed back to the gunboat, which set out full steam ahead, under cover of the bluffs along the riverbank. But before it could reach Staff Headquarters and impart the information gained by the reconnaissance, the enemy opened fire on the vessels.

The gunboats began to descend the river, with the intention of attacking the Whites from the rear. Their return fire increased. Other ships came to their assistance. One of the floating batteries opened up. The booming sighs of its guns added to the roar of the cannonade. Kite balloons rose into the air like bubbles in water. Evanescent as glowing clouds, they hung in the transparent sky, signalling artillery corrections.

On rounding a wide bend in the riverbank, the *October* came upon a gorge like a mountain canyon, one end of which joined the river, while the other penetrated far into the steppe, finally striking against the foot of the barrows. Through this gorge they could get a fine view of Denikin's batteries, which were firing uninterruptedly.

Before Ragozin's eyes rose that animated target, standing out in naked clarity, which they must destroy. In the golden haze above the steppe he could see the flash of the guns, the dust raised by the firing, the belches of earth caused by the shells from the gunboats—as though someone were digging a trench with a giant spade and tossing the dirt into the air.

The *October* trained a four-inch gun down the gorge, which was like a corridor leading into the rear of the enemy. An order was given, followed by a shot. The ship shuddered.

Ragozin braced his elbows on the railing and gazed through the field glasses. Had he been able to observe himself at that moment, he would have been astonished at the tautness of his body. The metal rod on which his elbows rested bent under his weight as he stood there leaning forward, his feet wide apart. Without such a straining of muscles he could scarcely have mastered the extraordinary feeling which he was experiencing for the first time in his life. It was a feeling of winged fury, drawing him toward the spot where the earth was being blown up in clumps and scattered in golden dust. He gazed fixedly into the shining distance, sending his fury along with the shells which left the ship one by one for the enemy's batteries.

Suddenly the firing began to die down. The *October* stopped shooting altogether. Ragozin dropped his glasses and rushed for the bridge.

"What's happened? Why are we silent?"

His voice sounded bird-like after the roar of the guns.

"Our infantry has gone into attack along with a landing party," shouted the commander.

Ragozin glanced at the riverbank.

Along the strip between the water and the foot of the embankment ran a ribbon of sailors from the landing party. One by one they vanished between the steep walls of the gorge. Several machine guns were being pushed and pulled by groups of men.

Once more Ragozin returned to his field glasses. Slowly the dust settled on the barrows. Ever less frequent became the flashes of gunfire. Up on the hill appeared a ball of smoke which grew ever larger until the dull boom of an explosion engulfed the steppes. Someone shouted on deck:

"They're blowing up their guns!"

Ragozin could see the landing party, now very close to the White positions, clambering up the steep sides of the gorge, the men lending each other a helping hand. Now the forward group stood upright on the plain. Now they were hauling up the machine guns. Ever more sailors reached the top, adding to the number lined up on the steppe. The first machine-gun round was fired. Then the air was pocked with distant rifle fire.

"Go after them!" shouted someone impatiently.

Suddenly dozens of voices from among the sailors crowding the deck began yelling:

"Give it to them! Let them have it!"

Ragozin turned his glasses on the barrows. Across the steppes horses were galloping away with the guns. At almost the same moment the Red infantry went into attack, strung out in a line that looked like fence palings against the sun. The landing party of sailors rushed to cut off the retreating Whites.

Ragozin glanced up at the bridge.

"They've routed them!" shouted the commander, waving both arms unintelligibly.

Ragozin looked at the sailors. They too were waving their arms and laughing and shouting and swearing as they watched the shore, and their faces were beaming with that naive, arrogant happiness which comes of success.

Suddenly Ragozin caught sight of Strashnov opposite him again. The sunlight glistened on his oil-stained face, and the sailor was grinning contentedly.

"The first step is the hardest," he said.

Ragozin frowned.

"What are you following me about for?"

"I'm here in case—well, in case something has to be fixed up on deck."

"What do you think you are—my nursemaid? It's me who's looking after you, and not the other way around, understand?"

"What's wrong? I'm just acting like everybody else. . . ."

"No you're not," interrupted Ragozin with unexpected venom. "I don't need your kowtowing. I'm no general, to have you trailing at my heels."

He turned abruptly and walked off. He was irritated, as though under some obligation. His men had silenced Denikin's artillery and the sailors had joined the infantry in pursuing the enemy, while he had just stood by and watched through his field glasses. This had been a real battle, which had ended in victory. But what had Ragozin contributed to this victory? And what was he expected to do during a battle anyway? Stand and watch?

"Kowtowing!" he growled indignantly, with a vicious tug at the shoulder strap from which the heavy glasses were swinging. He climbed the steps to the bridge.

As soon as his cap appeared above the last step, the commander—a flabby, middle-aged naval officer—greeted him with:

"Things are going fine, Pyotr Petrovich, things are going fine!"

427

The commander barely touched his cap with his left hand, giving only the appearance of raising it; and without actually crossing himself, he hinted at such a gesture with his right.

"God be with us."

He turned on Ragozin a glance that was official, and at the same time enquiring. Pyotr Petrovich twisted the neglected rings of his moustache. He made no objection to this observance of old tradition: why should the commander not cross himself as long as things were going well?

"We just got a radio message from the flagship," said the commander, half reporting, half confiding the news. "The advance is spreading over the entire front. The squadron is to go full speed ahead, wiping up the enemy along the shore."

"Mustn't get separated from the infantry," said Ragozin, with the air of a seasoned veteran.

"What have we got eyes for, Pyotr Petrovich? Have to keep our eyes open."

The officer tapped Ragozin's field glasses respectfully. He was pleased that the Commissar was not talkative and did not object to the commander's habitual manner, which was slightly paternal.

"In other words, full speed ahead?"

"Full speed ahead, Pyotr Petrovich. I am about to give the order."

On that day, assault forces of the Soviet Southern front opened up an extensive drive according to the plan of the Supreme Command, a plan which was first crowned with success, but later led to defeat and the loss of the initiative.

The failure of the frontal attack of the Southern front against the White Cossack Army became clear to the auxiliary group operating at Kupyansk within two weeks, and to the armies advancing on Tsaritsyn within three weeks. The auxiliary group, having wedged deep into White territory and taken the towns of Valuiky and Kupyansk, had left its battle-weakened flanks far behind, and faced the danger of being completely encircled. All efforts to eliminate the threat to the flanks presented by the Don Cossacks and Shkuro's Kuban cavalry proved in vain, and the whole group was forced to retreat as far as, and even beyond, its original position, sustaining heavy losses in the fighting. Fierce battles in the direction of the main drive at first brought the Red forces no few victories, but the group as a whole soon scattered over a wide front and was incapable of carrying out its assignments. On approaching the outskirts of Tsaritsyn, one of the armies was attacked by a manoeuvring group of Wrangel's cavalry. It proved incapable of withstanding so concentrated an attack and retreated north of the city.

But this drive proved the remarkable fighting qualities of the soldiers united under the banner of the revolution.

Particular valour was displayed along the line of the main drive, where Soviet infantry operated in conjunction with cavalry and the Volga-Kama flotilla.

The mounted divisions were united into a Cavalry Corps commanded by Budyonny. While constantly drawing reinforcements from the countryside, and uninterruptedly forming new units, this corps fought fierce battles with large forces of White Cossacks and inevitably emerged the victor. Near Kamenochernovskaya the corps defeated the Don Cossack Cavalry of General Sutulov, while three days later it dealt a crushing blow to the enemy near Serebryakov. Quickly shifting its positions, the brief battles of the corps seemed to anticipate the famous expeditions of the First Mounted Army of the near future.

The left flank of the army moving on Tsaritsyn was buttressed against the Volga, where it was supported by the river flotilla, newly created by the Soviets. During this operation, Russian sailors won undying fame for their fearlessness and self-sacrifice.

Ragozin soon lost the feeling that he was not contributing his share. On the contrary, it became clear that he was essential to the squadron, which demanded that he exert ever greater effort in order to unite the will of all these people and direct it toward definite tasks. Operations became more complicated and protracted: now it was the sending out of a landing party, now laying a curtain of fire to support an infantry attack, now a risky reconnaissance into enemy territory. At the same time, repairs had to be made without interrupting operations; the number of wounded was increasing; the store of ammunition was decreasing; and irreparable human losses were being sustained.

There came a moment when Ragozin perceived the very essence of his task, which heretofore he had carried out without any particular consideration. The essence of this task lay in preserving the true fighting spirit of the men, no matter what had to be done.

A strange thing had happened during the taking of Nikolayevskaya Sloboda. While the *October* was firing at the retreating Whites to cover the landing party of sailors already entering the streets of the town, the gun on the bow was blown up by the explosion of a defective shrapnel shell.

The commander of the gun crew was killed. He was a young sailor, who always kept his gun "on the ready," and was therefore himself nicknamed "Ready." Everybody loved him for his jolly disposition. The blast seared the faces of two other men in the gun crew and blew the squadron commander off the bridge, as a result of which he suffered a slight concussion.

The command was given to turn the vessel about and shoot from the stern gun. But the gun crew, frightened by the death of their comrade and convinced that the entire lot of shells was defective, could not bring themselves to continue firing.

During the battles of that week, Ragozin had learned something about handling the guns. He went to the stern, ordered the crew to retire, while he himself loaded and fired. After sending off three shells he turned around. Behind him stood the shamefaced gunners. Ragozin said:

"Well, go ahead, fellows, there's nothing to be afraid of. The shells are perfectly safe."

The crew rushed to the gun, took aim, and began firing with such fury that the tube grew hot.

As soon as Ragozin moved off to one side he realized that his shirt was clinging to his body, and it seemed to him that it was not he who had fired the gun, but some other person whom he was bound to obey in everything.

In looking back over all he had lived through during those weeks, Ragozin found that the strain he had been under belonged to a class which does not draw strength for endurance from moments of relaxation, but rather from the progressive increasing of the strain.

But at the same time two things occurred, apparently of no great importance, which Ragozin nonetheless found memorable, and which transported him from the tense world of actuality into a world of scarcely tangible disquietude. It was as though Ragozin had long been living in a house with curtained windows, and had grown so used to it that the house seemed spacious. Then suddenly one of the curtains was removed, and through the window he unexpectedly saw azure expanses with trees reflected in water, the whole scene bathed in a light which was entirely different from that within the house. Then the curtain was again drawn and once more his eyes grew accustomed to the house, which seemed as large as ever. But his memory retained the impression of different dimensions, of those spaces and trees, and of that unusual light.

In reporting the situation aboard the *Risky* on the evening following their first battle, the Commissar of the gunboat happened to mention the fact that the sailors had taken some youngster on board, and now it was necessary to put him off, for he kept poking his nose into places where he did not belong, and there was danger of his being injured.

"Where did they pick him up?" asked Ragozin, adopting the Commissar's casual tone.

"Back in Saratov."

"A big boy?"

"No. Just a kid. Couldn't be more than twelve."

"What's his name?"

"I don't know. They just call him the kid."

Ragozin clutched the edge of the bench, as though about to sit down, but instead of sitting down he straightened up and turned away, saying brusquely:

"Don't you know your own crew by name?"

The Commissar laughed.

"Call a tramp of a kid one of my crew?"

"What's that ship of yours anyway—an open house?"

"Well, I'll sign him out," said the Commissar, putting an end to a conversation which he obviously considered trifling.

Ragozin said nothing for a stern minute.

"Put a lad on shore to die of hunger? That's barbarous, brother. A sure way to turn the youngster into a tramp. Transfer him to the hospital ship. At least he'll be fed there. And more or less out of danger."

The thought of this boy did not occupy Ragozin's mind for long, but it had thrust in abruptly, as though someone had grabbed him by the shoulder and roughly spun him around. The waif had turned up on the *Risky*, a boat associated with Ragozin's search for Vanya, and the coincidence revived his worry about his new-found and new-lost son. Ragozin did not wish to convince himself that once more he had fallen on Vanya's trail. But in the most vulnerable corner of his heart brooded the sense of another life, isolated from everything that now absorbed him, and the existence of that imaginary life was as painful as some inconsolable injury.

Events quickly distracted him from his heartache. They demanded that he don the defensive armour wrought by the nerves when a person is constantly faced by danger to which he must become callous. He was conscious of wearing such armour, and did not find it burdensome. And yet, at a time when he was most proud and pleased with his invulnerability (just after having loaded and fired the gun which he expected to be blown up any minute by another defective shell), Ragozin found himself stabbed once more by memories of his son.

The squadron was descending to Bykov Khutor, famous throughout the Lower Volga as the "watermelon capital." The morning was wondrously quiet, or at least it seemed so, after the roaring battles for Nikolayevskaya Sloboda and Kamyshin.

At this spot the shore was higher than at most places along the left bank, and the motionless willows and the lush grass of the embankment were greenly reflected in the water. While awaiting information from the scouts sent to Bykov, the ships stood opposite some watermelon farms on the shore.

Boats loaded with watermelons and manned by village boys were rowed abreast of the gunboats. The boys shouted across the water to the sailors, who replied with echoing laughter. A brisk trade was carried on. Watermelons were tossed on deck from the rowboats, while little paper parcels containing salt, matches, cigarettes, and chunks of bread, were thrown down from the gunboats. Upon the waves danced crescents of watermelon rind, which the sailors had gaily slung away.

Ragozin stood staring at the water with that happy wonder experienced by a city dweller on suddenly lifting his eyes to see feathery cloud strata floating in blue expanses of sky. Yes, there was this wonderful, eternal quietude of sky and water, and the boys' voices filling this quietude with youthfulness, and the riverbank luring with a tenderness only the earth can hold for man. And all this together—the Volga dotted with watermelon rinds, the voices ringing in the silence, the lovely morning—again brought Ragozin to thoughts of his son, and of a life with his son which would be so unlike his former life and so utterly divorced from his present life. The armour which proved effective in shielding him from thunder, was impotent against silence, and once more his heart was pierced with pain.

A distant cannon shot roused the spaces. It was followed by another. The frightened boys in the boats scrambled over the heaped watermelons back to their oars. The sailors took long hooks and helped them push off. The oarlocks began to squeak, the water gurgled beneath the oars, which, in Volga fashion, were dipped in short, deep strokes. And then a shrapnel shell exploded over the very surface of the river.

Ragozin saw the little rowers duck and then, terrified by the explosion, begin to beat the water frantically with the heavy oars.

He ran to the bridge, swearing under his breath. No, not even a fraction of his mind could be released for meditation. All of this was merely a phantom—the serenity, the languid morning, the alluring tenderness of the riverbank. There could be no laughter, no childish banter, on an earth ruled by the thunder of guns. The gun crews took up their posts, the paddles of the wheels noisily slapped the water, the signalman sent his alarming despatches into the air. . . .

For some sailors, the Tsaritsyn drive was a ceremonial march, for others it was an uninterrupted series of fierce battles. As in all fighting, it is the lot of one section of the army to deliver and receive decisive blows, while it is the lot of other sections to take part in only light clashes, or to enjoy victories won for them by their comrades. So in the operations of the Volga flotilla, thousands of sailors proceeded from one fierce battle to another, while thousands of others knew only light fighting, or no fighting at all, rejoicing that the enemy took to flight without offering resistance.

The partisans and landing troops which dealt Denikin a blow at Dubovka, paid a high price for their victory. Their path was barred by cross fire from the White batteries. The landing troops attacked the enemy shore guns from the rear, routed the infantry sent to defend these guns, destroyed the batteries, and turned toward Dubovka, into which they forced their way. According to those who actually participated in this landing operation, the battle for Dubovka was a bold flanking manoeuvre, demanding exceptional courage and taking a high toll of human life. According to those who did not actually participate in the battle, the taking of Dubovka was just another one of the numerous victories won by the landing troops.

But among the crews of the flotilla, there could be no difference of opinion about the battle for Tsaritsyn, in which all the sailors participated, and which brought the drive to an unhappy end.

The three-day battle for Tsaritsyn began with the storming of the city, supported by hurricane fire from the ships. A series of defeats resulting in the withdrawal of Denikin's troops seemed to indicate that the enemy's strength was on the wane. Fires on the outskirts of the city could be observed from the gunboats: the Whites were burning everything they could not take with them, preparatory to evacuating the city. The method of coordinating operations of the flotilla with those of the infantry, a method which had so far proved effective, was to be applied at Tsaritsyn on a scale never before attempted on the Volga. All of this seemed to ensure success. Yet events took a different turn.

The section held by the Whites along the riverbank was captured by a landing detachment of sailors supported by artillery fire from the ships. The sailors attacked and took the French factory.

To the right, along the outer circle of trenches, operated one of the most famous infantry divisions of the Red Army. In preparing his defence, Wrangel united some three cavalry corps into a manoeuvring group. So the Soviet division met with a flank counterattack from superior forces of cavalry. At the same time the sailors, encouraged by their victory, proceeded independently from the factory to the city, and broke into Tsaritsyn. The Soviet division was forced to withdraw. Then the Whites threw their forces against the sailors and cut off their retreat from the city. In putting up desperate resistance, the greater part of the sailors was killed.

It was clear that the Whites had the advantage. At their disposal was a large railway junction, a cavalry capable of quick manoeuvring, and a reliable reconnaissance. But the fighting did not cease.

The flotilla stopped the Whites with curtain fire. Again and again Red units went into attack. Denikin's troops used everything they had against them, including tanks and aircraft. The British and French weapons sent to aid Denikin, here found a wide field for application: the aviation made as many as twelve mass attacks a day, dropping hundreds of bombs, especially over the water.

The air was filled with the roar of battle. Only the volleys from the floating forts and separate salvoes from particularly large-calibred guns could be distinguished above the general bombardment. The ships moved directly against the outer circle of White trenches, thus calling down upon themselves merciless artillery fire.

From the deck of the *October*, Ragozin saw the *Risky* become disabled: two shells, one after the other, struck her first in the hold, then in the deck. Launches rushed up to remove the wounded. The damaged deck began to smoke. The *October* asked if its aid were needed. The *Risky* replied: "We'll manage, thanks. Lick the Whites."

Soon the forward gun on the *October* was put out of commission. To save time, it was decided not to turn the ship about, but to replace the damaged gun with the gun from the quarter-deck. But the bolts had rusted and the nuts refused to be unscrewed. Mechanics came to saw them off.

Ragozin watched Strashnov wield a riveting hammer. His right shoulder blade moved like a cannon ball beneath his giant shoulder, whose muscles were clearly visible under the striped undershirt he was wearing.

"Powerful devil," muttered Ragozin in a sudden surge of admiration. Like all the others, he was absorbed in his work, oblivious of the missiles coming from the shore, deaf to the booming of the cannon, to which his ear had already become accustomed: the *October* had fired almost three thousand shells, and many of the other gunboats had done likewise.

When the gun had been hauled to the foredeck, fastened in place, and put into action, Ragozin

slapped Strashnov on the back. The latter wiped
his forehead on his rolled-up sleeve, glanced at the
smoking scene about him, and said approvingly:

"It's 'golka' all right!"

"It's what?"

"'Golka', I say!"

The slang meant nothing to Ragozin, but he
felt that there was no word in the language capable of describing this three-day madness of shooting
and explosions. So he merely nodded his head with
the same expression of approval.

Toward evening of the third day the squadron
received orders to send shock groups of volunteers
from every ship to the assistance of the sailors on
shore. More men than necessary volunteered from
the *October*, and Ragozin left behind those whom
he considered indispensable on board. Strashnov
wanted to go. Ragozin ordered him to remain. But
when the launch put them ashore and the sailors
formed in line, he noticed a giant of a chap, half a
head taller than anyone else, dressed in pea jacket
and leather cap: Strashnov was glancing casually
off to one side, and Ragozin pretended not to notice
him.

The reinforcement was divided into two pla-
toons of fifty men each and immediately despatched
to the front line. Ragozin and his platoon found
themselves in a place held by remnants of the

detachment which had taken the French factory. This stretch of wasteland, littered with rubbish and crisscrossed with trenches, was slightly elevated above the steppes, across which the sailors lay in a zigzag line.

The dust raised by the ships' firing hid the White positions. It was much quieter here than on board the *October*, but it seemed to Ragozin that he and the earth were being rocked no less than on shipboard.

He was lying uncomfortably in a foxhole protected in front by a mound of earth, but open on both sides. He kept his eye on a similar mound to the right which had been pointed out to him as the point from which the commander of the detachment would give the signal to go into attack.

The sun set in clouds, which it lighted with that lurid hue foretelling windy weather. Everything on the earth, including the clayey trench mounds, reflected the sunset. Ragozin counted a dozen British field bags scattered over the ground, where they had been abandoned by retreating Whites.

As soon as the artillery fire died down, he saw a tall man crawl up onto a mound, suddenly straighten to full height, and raise his arms above his head. Ragozin also crawled out of his hole, also jumped up onto his mound, and, raising his arms in the same way, leaped off and charged ahead.

The rest of the men began to rise, and Ragozin noticed that their formation was more compact than it had seemed to him while they were lying down. He looked to see if they were bringing the machine guns ("Maxims" which had been mounted on wheels just before coming ashore), and was reassured by seeing the guns come bounding along at the same rate as the sailors. He looked to see whether his platoon was keeping up with the one on the right, and was again reassured, for the sailors formed a single line. He glanced at the safety lock on his gun, to make sure that it was released, and found that it was. He checked whether anyone had forgotten to attach the bayonet to his gun, and found not a gap in the teeth of glistening steel in front of the charging sailors.

As he checked these details, he kept looking ahead into the wasteland stretching calmly away, tinged with the darkening sunset.

Presently he noticed a reddish-yellow cloud of dust slightly to one side of the advancing sailors. Then he heard voices to the right of him shouting orders down the line. At first he could not make out the words, but finally he recognized cries of: "Lie down!" "Fire at the cavalry!" He too began shouting to the left:

"Lie down! Fire at the...."

Just in front of the cloud of dust he saw a line of squat horses with flying hoofs. Like glowing wires flashed the sword blades above the heads of the riders. The Cossacks were pouring in a solid stream over the steppes, drawing nearer with every moment.

There came a volley of rifle fire, followed by the competitive rattle of machine guns.

Breaches appeared in the cavalry lines. Their compact formation was broken up into clambering groups of horses in some places, into thinned ranks in others. But the stream kept pouring on, growing ever larger, and already the hammer of hoofs was transmitted through the earth to Ragozin's body, as though his heart no longer beat in his breast, but in the very soil.

New volleys caused new jams and sent some of the riders scattering. Here the horses began to rush ahead, there to lag behind.

Ragozin could already distinguish the colour of the leading horses and saw them tossing their heads into the air. Suddenly the metallic wail of the machine guns rose to a screech, and he could plainly see Cossacks falling out of the saddles now and again, their crazed horses either charging on riderless or plunging to the earth themselves.

Then Ragozin heard the iron tread of hoofs seemingly just alongside of him, and not at all from the direction he had expected. In an extremity of fear he glanced about and shifted his revolver to the left.

In full view of his entire platoon, a group of furious horsemen rode out from behind some ruined shacks and went dashing into the wasteland. There were about a hundred of them, mounted on massive steeds, with a sailor in flying pea jacket and pancake hat riding at their head, waving his sword in the air. His grey mount kept tossing its head protestingly. The ribbons of his sailor hat flew about his head and his jacket flapped against his knees. He stood up in the stirrups. His mouth was open. The hundred in his wake shouted "Hurrah!"

Formerly Ragozin had only heard of mounted sailors who fought side by side with infantry detachments. Now he was seeing them in action. They galloped on their heavy steeds like true horsemen, but each one of them seemed to be rushing into hand-to-hand combat. The wind and the lurching of their bodies sent everything about them swirling and fluttering.

The end rider passed close to Ragozin. The latter looked into the sailor's face, which was twisted in frozen laughter, and heard his extraordinary cry:

"Steer to the left, brothers! Follow me! That's the way!... To he-e-ell with them!"

"Ah-h-h!" sounded in the wake of the galloping hundred. "Ah-h-h!"

The firing stopped. The enemy cavalry, scattered by the shooting, now turned and fled with gathering speed. The sailor-horsemen were by this time on their very heels, swords flashing in the air.

At that moment the line once more rose to attack.

Ragozin had the feeling that the defeat of the Whites was as good as accomplished—that it only required a little time and a final effort to completely break their resistance and take the city.

The sight of the mounted sailors confirmed this feeling, and as he looked down the line, Ragozin saw that his platoon in no way lagged behind the cavalry—was just as fierce and tempestuous in its onrush, just as monolithic.

The sailors came running behind Ragozin, some with their hat ribbons streaming, others bareheaded; some with their middy collars billowing out, others in only striped undershirts, soaking wet, like swimmers; some in flying leather jackets, others coatless with cartridge belts crossed on their chests.

"When such people go forth, it is only to victory," thought Ragozin. "And there's our victory—just up ahead."

447

At last they got a clear view of some segmented trenches at the far end of the wasteland; these were the White positions, and a low roar crescendoed down the line: the sailors were crying "Hurrah!"

At the same time he again saw the mounted sailors close at hand, galloping in scattered ranks across the wasteland, and behind them came a new wave of Cossacks which had risen out there where the routed cavalry had so recently rushed in retreat.

Then from the trenches came a burst of running fire.

Ragozin stumbled and fell on his face. He tried to get up. It was as though someone had placed his boot on his shoulder and was holding him down.

"Let me go!" he shouted, but his mouth was plastered with clay, so that even he could distinguish nothing but a garble.

He twisted his head and viciously spat out the dirt.

Twenty paces away galloped the sailor in the flying pea jacket who had led the hundred against the Cossacks.

Just when Ragozin recognized him, the sailor pulled on his reins with all his strength and fell back on the croup of his horse. Immediately he let go of the reins and was shaken off onto the ground, one foot catching for a second in the stirrup.

Like a circus horse, his mount reared on its hind legs, pawing the air with its front ones. Its dappled grey flanks reflected the sunset with a rosy shimmer, and it seemed to be vertically mounting the sky. For a second Ragozin imagined that the creature was small enough to be placed on a sheet of paper. Then it expanded and galloped away into the steppes.

In the tumult about him, Ragozin most clearly distinguished cries of "Commissar!" "Commissar!"

He twisted his head still further to see who could be treading so heavily on his shoulder.

He peered into a not unfamiliar face with prominent cheekbones, dilated nostrils, and a heavy chin dominating all other features. The person grinned and shouted into his ear.

"Where're you hit? Where?"

Ragozin did not understand what the fellow wanted, but immediately recognized him as Strashnov, and somehow this made him glad. He wanted to shout an answer, but managed only to grunt:

"I'll manage alone," and again tried to rise.

Excruciating pain in shoulder and collarbone forced him to lie quiet.

"What do you mean, alone? None of your obstinacy now. Humph—alone!" muttered Strashnov as he turned him over and slipped his hands under Ragozin's back and knees.

He picked him up like a baby and started running. Ragozin was conscious of nothing but daggers of pain which made him faint. Strashnov increased his speed, bending under the weight of his burden and the fear that the Cossacks would overtake them before he succeeded in getting the wounded man to safety. The galloping of the horsemen sounded louder than at first, and once more a volley was fired.

When Strashnov had almost reached the water's edge he caught up with some stretcher-bearers. They finally took Ragozin to the *October* in a motorboat.

But the ship was damaged—a shell had struck the lower deck. Hurried repairs of the steering gear were being made by a floating shop moored alongside. Ragozin was laid in a cabin on board this repair shop. The commander of the squadron paid him a visit after the ship's doctor finished his examination and reported that Ragozin's left collarbone had been splintered, with injuries to a nerve centre, and that an operation was necessary.

"So you see, my dear fellow," said the commander in the condescending tone used with the sick, "we'll be having to send you to the hospital."

When Ragozin lay motionless, the pain was not so unbearable, and he answered softly:

"I'm not your subordinate, Comrade Commander."

"We've been fighting for five years straight, my dear fellow. And you talk about subordination!"

"Well—I'm staying."

"Oh no you're not. We're obliged to send you away if there is any possibility of it. They'll give you a good overhauling out there."

"How are things out there—on shore?"

"Why on shore? The medics will tend to you on the hospital ship."

"It's the fighting I mean—on shore. . . ."

"Don't worry about the fighting. We'll take care of that. We'll see that you get shipped off before we open fire."

"What do you mean—open fire?"

"Cover fire. Have to cover our retreat."

Ragozin did not take his eyes off the commander. They were burning feverishly. It was clear that he had a temperature. He lifted his head, but immediately dropped it. With a grimace he asked:

"Retreat?. . . Strashnov!. . . What's that . . . retreat?"

Strashnov glanced through the half-open door and strode into the cabin.

"Lie down," he whispered. "Don't worry, everything's all right."

Ragozin interrupted with a groan:

"What are you trying to kid me for? Nursemaid!"

He was silent for a moment, then said dully:

"I guess I can bear it. ... How can everything be all right once we're retreating?"

"What of it?" asked Strashnov, somewhat offended. "Didn't we drive them away from Saratov? Didn't we keep them off the Volga? Didn't we slash off their fingers at Elton Lake when they stretched out their hand to the Urals Cossacks?"

"Drop the consoling," sighed Ragozin, and closed his eyes.

On leaving, the commander whispered to Strashnov:

"Go for the medical orderlies. We'll put him in the starboard boat."

The doctor directed the carrying of the wounded man and the placing of the stretcher in a hammock swung from pulleys. The sailors gathered round. There was a spurt of steam, and the rope slowly became taut. Strashnov tested the stretcher, to see that it would not collapse in the hammock.

When the sailor bent over him, Ragozin slightly raised his right hand. Strashnov pressed it gently.

"Yes," he said.

"That's how," answered Ragozin.

"All right," agreed Strashnov.

The rope grew more taut, the hammock rose, and Strashnov guided it toward the railing.

"Easy, easy," he said softly, and the sailors relayed to the quarter-deck: "Easy, easy."

When he was about to push the hammock over the side, Strashnov noticed that Ragozin wished to say something. He stayed the rope for a second.

"Help them here... to make repairs," said Ragozin quickly.

"Teach a Volga man to fish!" snorted Strashnov.

"Too bad you're not a Volga man...."

"Let her go!" called Strashnov in a loud voice.

He gave the rope a push and called to Ragozin, already lost in the shadow of the ship's side:

"Us folks from the North can fish as good as your Volga fellows any day! Goodbye, Pyotr Petrovich! Hurry and get well!"

"Hurry and get well!" echoed the sailors leaning over the rail to peer into the darkness below.

Two minutes later the motorboat pushed off. It curved noisily away from the *October* and headed for the middle of the river. The yellow reflection of its light still gleamed on the water when the flotilla opened artillery fire to cut off the advance of the Whites to the north.

31

Lisa was married to Anatoli Mikhailovich in the middle of September.

On a rainy evening, two cabs drove up to the Kazan Church, and Lisa, gathering up the skirts of her white dress (her first wedding dress made over), stepped out of one of them and entered the church yard. For a second she glanced through the iron grating at the steel band of the Volga, the same Volga she saw every autumn, and in some surprise thought to herself that in just the same way flowed on the life of the former Lisa. She entered the church with the same feeling of surprise that she was that Lisa.

Slender candles were burning behind the lectern in the centre of the church, but the corners were in shadow. It seemed that the mystic rite about to be performed would take place in the darkness, whereas something very ordinary would take place in the light.

Vitya had never been to a wedding before. The solemn significance of the ceremony was impressed on him by the reserved radiance of his mother's face and the important mien of Anatoli Mikhailovich (probably adopted to indicate that he was now Vitya's father, and not merely Anatoli Mikhailovich). But when they held a crown over

454

the head of Anatoli Mikhailovich and began to lead him round the lectern with Vitya's mother, likewise crowned, on his arm, Vitya found it very funny. Under that gilded crown set with paste jewels, Anatoli Mikhailovich looked amazingly like Tsar Nikolai, and Vitya began to giggle softly. Somebody pulled his sleeve. He turned, and caught sight of two little boys like himself who had run in from the street and were standing at some distance watching Anatoli Mikhailovich.

Vitya backed up and wormed his way through the standing spectators. Then he put his hand over his mouth, and gave vent to his laughter.

When the spell was over, he became aware of the coldness of the stone column against which he was leaning. He moved away.

A tall, naked old man with a white beard extending to his very toes looked down from the column through the dusk. His glance was piercing and hungry. Vitya moved still further away. He felt that he had misbehaved. And suddenly he became worried by the strange and frightening contrast between Anatoli Mikhailovich in the crown, and the naked old man with the hungry look. Throughout the rest of the ceremony he pondered the matter, his eyes fixed on the saint.

But on the whole, Vitya liked the wedding. He rode both ways in a cab—to the church and back again. Both of the trips were interesting. Among the guests were people invited by Anatoli Mikhailovich whom Vitya had never met before. They grew merry at the table and began talking in tatters.

"Well, we'll have a try at it now, all right... smack down!..."

"Um-m-m!... Marvellous!..."

"What's the flavour?"

"Oh, mint? Well, if that's the case... then, of course!"

"Lemon's not bad, either."

"But it can't be compa-a-red!"

Suddenly they all became vocal at once, like leaves under a blast of wind:

"Come now!"—"But let me finish!"—"Quiet!" —"Just a minute!"—"Hold on there! We'll never get anywhere at this rate!"—"But that's exactly what I was saying! Exactly!"—"Oh, no you don't!"—"Let me finish! This is impossible!"— "So that's that!..."

Then the gust passed over and the leaves quieted down. The guests began to blink languidly, hang their heads, and break the long pauses with vague grunts and sighs. Those with a gift for oratory gave expression to profound ideas.

"Allow me to draw your attention to the following fact," argued Oznobishin, slightly gesticulating with his ladylike hand. "The forbidding of one type of behaviour inevitably encourages its opposite. To forbid animosity means to preach love. In denouncing cruelty, we approve kindness. Now imagine that, on the contrary, we began to denounce kindness. What would that lead us to?"

"Brutality," cried one of the guests gloomily, raising his head, only to drop it again.

"But who is denouncing kindness?" asked the student (he had been invited because of the calcium injections he had given Lisa). "Take the measures instituted for health protection for example, which. . . ."

"Do you call that kindness?" laughed Lisa. "Sticking a needle this long right into your arm!"

She looked very pretty in her wedding clothes, and she knew it. It irritated her a bit that the guests should be getting tipsy and talking all kinds of nonsense which distracted Oznobishin's attention from herself, apparently forgetting that this was a wedding and therefore should be brimful of happiness. Only her son was sufficiently attentive, looking at her in admiration more often than anyone else. She filled his wineglass with sweetened beet juice.

"You must drink a toast to me, to yourself, and to Anatoli Mikhailovich," she said, happily watching him gulp it down, after which he flushed and gazed rapturously up into her face.

Yes, it was a real wedding, in spite of the fact that they had ridden in a cab instead of their own carriage, were drinking beet juice instead of champagne, and had no music or new clothes. The spirit of elation, if not quite triumph, was expressed by every object in the room—or at least, so it seemed to Lisa.

The party soon broke up, for the guests had to reach home before the curfew. When they were gone the house became filled with the clatter and bang of a hasty cleaning up.

When everything was put away, Anatoli Mikhailovich sat down alongside of Lisa on the divan. He took her hand in both of his, and his devoted look, tinged with slyness, said that now they had achieved their heart's desire: they were one family, and had a home, a burrow, a shell in which they could snuggle up to each other for protection against the storms besieging humanity.

"How rich I am! Everything that is yours, is now mine," he said after a stretch of silence. "Thank you."

"It has long been yours," answered Lisa.

"But now it is mine, once and for all, with nothing held back. Like in the ancient title deeds, when land was sold '... including all grain—new-sown, and ripened, and threshed.' "

They heard someone cough outside the door. Anatoli Mikhailovich got up.

Matvei, the old man who was their neighbour, stood shuffling in the hall, trying to make up his mind to knock. It seemed that some man insisted on seeing Elisaveta Merkuryevna, in spite of Matvei's explanation that it was scarcely decent to intrude just after a wedding. Perhaps it was one of the guests who had returned? No, it was a stranger, who refused to give his name.

Lisa heard the whispering and went out into the hall. She was immediately alarmed and asked to have the man shown in.

A minute later Anatoli Mikhailovich led the stranger into the room.

He was a short fellow, of no certain age and shy manners; a streak of white passed through his dark hair, and he was badly in need of a shave. He glanced furtively about the room as he played with the brim of his straw hat and ran his fingers over the buttons of his coat to see that all of them were fastened. Apparently he feared that his appearance might be held against him.

"May I...?" he asked softly, once more running his eyes over the walls.

"What is it?" asked Lisa, unconsciously assuming the same undertone.

"Are you Elisaveta Merkuryevna?"

"Yes. Please state what you wish."

"Begging your pardon for coming at such an inconvenient hour—I am only discharging a duty assumed on promising your father to get in touch with you."

"You have come from my father?"

"If you are indeed the daughter of Merkuri Avdeyevich. . . ."

"Yes, I am the daughter of Merkuri Avdeyevich Meshkov. Have you come from him? From Khvalynsk?"

"I am from Saratov."

"But you were . . . you have been to Khvalynsk?"

"It was just chance that led me to meet your father—as unexpectedly for him as for. . . ."

"But you have seen him? What has happened to my father?" cried Lisa in a loud voice, impelled by sudden fear to step forward, but actually falling back and clutching the hand of her husband. She clearly perceived a harbinger of evil in this small, respectable-looking man with his clerkish tongue, and everything within her rose to meet the blow, and it seemed that only the hand of her husband, which she kept pressing ever more tightly, could give her sufficient strength to withstand it.

"It was not in Khvalynsk that you saw Merkuri Avdeyevich? Then where could it have been?" asked Oznobishin, stroking Lisa's hand.

"As I have already said, I am from Saratov, and had no intention of leaving the city. But, due to circumstances over which I had no control, I went away not very long ago—it would be more correct to say I was taken away—to no great distance, and, fortunately, for only a short time."

"But you wished to tell us about Merkuri Avdeyevich," said Oznobishin.

"Quite right. About the chance circumstances which brought us together. I had the misfortune to be taken out to the main stream. Does that mean anything to you?"

"To the main stream?" repeated Oznobishin, although he apparently understood without asking, for his face immediately fell, and he threw a quick glance at Lisa.

"What is that?" she asked, also understanding, but unwilling to admit it as yet.

"On the barge," explained the man tactfully. "I was taken out to the barge. And today I was released when the unfortunate misunderstanding was cleared up. I was released at Pokrovsk, and from there I reached Saratov by ferry and hurried

461

to find you without wasting any time. In fulfilment of my promise."

"He is—there?" asked Lisa, drawing herself up, so that she seemed to visibly grow.

"Begging your pardon, I grieve to admit that at the present moment Merkuri Avdeyevich is on the barge."

Lisa slumped against her husband. He put his arm about her and led her over to the divan.

"I trust that you will forgive me, but I have come as a man of my word and in the interests of your father, with whom I was confined out there. He asked me to let you know how precious every minute is to one in his unfortunate situation."

"Every minute? What for?" said Lisa, this time actually not comprehending.

"Your father has fallen into bad company. Judging by what you yourself have just said, he, along with other prisoners, was brought down the river from Khvalynsk. Merkuri Avdeyevich did not mention this to me. On arrival, they were left on the river. That is, they were transferred to the barge, since this floating jail was nearer than any other. Actually the party in which he was included consisted of only one other person, but a bad person, as Merkuri Avdeyevich informed me. This person was, begging your pardon, a former gendarme. Apparently bearing the well-known name of Polotentsev."

"My God!" cried Oznobishin, with a flutter of his hands.

"On the barge we learned that soon after his arrival Polotentsev departed for the land of the blessed" (here the man made a crooked grimace somewhat resembling a smile) "where there is no more weeping and lamentation—heh, heh! Or, as we say, his appointed time expired."

"Be good enough to tell us about my father," said Lisa with unexpected severity.

The man seemed slightly taken aback, but continued in the same pompous style:

"Merkuri Avdeyevich is in the greatest alarm about his fate, which he fears depends on the investigation of Polotentsev's case."

"My father could not have had anything in common with a gendarme," said Lisa curtly.

"A fact of which there can be not the slightest doubt—that is, for you and me. On the basis of my personal observations I have come to the conclusion that the inclinations of your father could lead him to nothing more reprehensible than extensive praying. Merkuri Avdeyevich prays incessantly. But at the present moment, as my own experience has convinced me, our lives are in the hands of fate."

"What?" asked Oznobishin.

"In the hands of fate. And Merkuri Avdeyevich begs you to do everything in your power to help him, for anything may happen at any moment, even to the extent of...."

Here the stranger glanced furtively behind him.

Vitya silently came out of the next room and stood looking at him with angry challenge in his eyes.

"Is grandad alive?" he asked roughly.

"Yes," said the respectable-looking gentleman, seeming to cringe beneath the boy's gaze. "I can definitely affirm that Merkuri Avdeyevich was still on the barge when I was released this morning."

"I know that barge on the main stream," said Vitya resolutely. "We saw it that time we went to the sands with Arseni Romanych. It's anchored out there. Arseni Romanych said counterrevolutionaries were locked up inside. But grandad's not one of them! Come on, mother, let's take a boat and go get him!"

"Be quiet, Vitya! Leave the room," said Anatoli Mikhailovich, but Lisa quickly held out her hand to her son.

"Come here," she said.

She drew Vitya toward her.

"And so I have done my duty," concluded the stranger, placing his hat over his heart and clicking his heels politely. "And I would advise you to act with haste."

"I don't know how to thank you," said Ozno-bishin. "Only thanks is hardly the word ... if you understand ... for such news. ..."

"Don't think of it! I myself was quite non-plussed as to how to prepare you for it."

"Prepare us? For what?" cried Lisa in a sud-den outburst.

"Begging your pardon—not to prepare you, but to lead you to take measures for the rescue of your father. I have no motives other than my kind re-gards for Merkuri Avdeyevich. I was touched by his humility. A worthy man! I have always re-spected him."

He raised a finger to his lips:

"Just between ourselves, of course: while Mer-kuri Avdeyevich was in business, I was the man-ager of the neighbouring shop. So I remember you from old times, Elisaveta Merkuryevna. And I hope you succeed in rescuing your father."

Once more he placed his hat over his heart and bowed. He made a separate bow to Vitya.

Anatoli Mikhailovich saw him to the door and tried to make no noise as he returned.

He found Lisa in the same position in which he had left her. She sat with her arms around her son, staring hard into space. She looked severe in her close-fitting white dress. Anatoli Mikhailovich sat down opposite her and crossed his hands. For a while everyone remained motionless. Then Oznobishin leaned forward, trying to catch Lisa's eye.

"There may be difficulties if Merkuri Avdeyevich is mixed up with—with that Polotentsev," he said with some concern.

Lisa turned on him the same wide eyes with which she had been gazing into space.

"Does it make any difference whether he is mixed up with him or not?"

"The fact of such a connection is a circumstance legally aggravating the guilt."

"What talk can there be of guilt?" asked Lisa in surprise.

"Of course, Lisa," said Oznobishin, hastening to counteract the impression his words had made by assuming a gentle tone. "I am not speaking of guilt; I am as certain as you are that Merkuri Avdeyevich is guilty of nothing. I am speaking of the difficulties that may interfere with our efforts on his behalf."

"Why think about what may interfere? We must think about how to help him as quickly as possible."

"Of course, of course! But in seeking the right path, we must take into consideration whatever difficulties may arise. In order to avoid them. Isn't that true?"

"But I'm telling you I know the exact way to the barge!" cried Vitya impatiently, as though wondering how they could fail to understand him. "Arseni Romanych has a friend who's a boatman. Uncle Matvei knows him too. We'll take a boat and I'll show you...."

His mother cut short his speech by pressing his head to her breast.

"You haven't thought of Ragozin, have you?" she asked her husband, seeking the answer in his face.

Vitya jumped out of her arms and cried happily, before she had a chance to draw him down again:

"I thought of Ragozin, mom—honest to goodness! Pavlik and I went to see him. And he did every single thing we asked him to. For Arseni Romanych. Pyotr Petrovich will fix things up right away. He knows grandad."

"No, my little hothead, you're still a bit too young to serve as an advisor," said Anatoli Mikhailovich with a smile which for a second distracted attention from Lisa's question.

Ever since Oznobishin had heard the tidings of this unexpected messenger, he had been thinking about Ragozin. He realized that he must immediately take measures to help Meshkov, that full responsibility for this help fell completely on his shoulders, that it was a ticklish, and probably hopeless matter, but one which could not be evaded however ticklish or hopeless. He was afraid that the situation would have a bad effect on Lisa's health, which was not yet any too good, and for that reason he knew that he must act all the more resolutely in order to support her hope that everything would turn out all right. But he was no less frightened by the thought that his efforts on behalf of Meshkov might be interpreted by the authorities as efforts on behalf of Polotentsev as well, once Meshkov was accused of having connections with him. At the same time he felt that the hour had come for him to repay Lisa and Meshkov for the solicitude they had shown when he was in jail. It seemed that his honour was being put to the test. But he clearly recognized his helplessness. He was certain that in his position of a former official, once suspected of having tried to hide his past, it would be foolish to expect the authorities to do him any favours, or even to heed his requests. And he convinced himself ahead of time that nothing good would come of his efforts. He knew only one person whose influence might help in setting Meshkov free. That person was Ragozin. But in his memory lingered the vision

468

of Ragozin as he had appeared the day Oznobishin had met him on the street after slipping on the piece of watermelon rind. He remembered him as hard, and unbending, and mocking, as he had said: "That is not an easy thing to do. I don't accept services." Nor could Oznobishin forget the fear and hesitation with which he had then approached Ragozin, dreading that his theft of the paper from the archives had been discovered. Ever since he had stolen the paper and thrown it into the Volga he had been haunted by a morbid fear that another such incriminating paper might turn up. After all, the past could not be wholly destroyed; bits of it were lurking somewhere, and suddenly they might come poking up through some little crack into the light of day. What would happen then? A lawyer's supersensitivity to the law, and that captiousness which he had once applied to other people, now was turned against himself, robbing him of sleep. He had a horror of once more facing Ragozin.

These thoughts and apprehensions, this fear for himself, for his wife, and for that life upon which he had just hoped to embark and which was put to so great a test before ever initiated, had kept revolving in his mind and heart while he listened to the cumbersome speech of the man with the straw hat, and they continued to revolve with greater insistence now, while Lisa waited for an answer to her question.

Suddenly Vitya again liberated himself from his mother's arms and said with quiet distress:

"I forgot, mom: Ragozin isn't here any more. Pavlik said Pyotr Petrovich was a naval commissar now and had gone away. Maybe Pavlik was lying," he added despairingly, then lapsed into silence. "But he said Pyotr Petrovich had gone away with the fleet...."

"What a misfortune if that is really true!" put in Oznobishin hastily.

But Lisa had read the answer to her question in her husband's face before he made this exclamation. She had not been able to trace the entire course of his thinking and feeling, but she had read what was most important for her to know: she had read that he was afraid to intercede for her father, and that he was ashamed to admit it.

She gave a slow, bitter smile.

"Behold my grain—new-sown, and ripened, and threshed," she said, shaking her head and looking her husband straight in the eye.

Unable to withstand the rebuke, he threw himself at her feet, tearing her hands away from her son, to whom she persistently clung, and began to kiss them feverishly, muttering the while:

"Don't despair. We'll make every effort, we'll succeed somehow. We'll try some other means—find some other person to help us. . . ."

"I've already found such a person," she said.

He was taken aback. Her quiet, even glance expressed condescending forgiveness.

"Who?" he asked.

"Izvekov."

This was the first time Lisa had spoken this name for many, many years, and she spoke it now with a strange quietude.

Oznobishin got up. Some distant association rose in his memory, connecting that name with Lisa—some expression seen on her face years ago —an expression of childish embarrassment, or even fright, lending it the particular charm which had attracted him on meeting her on the street, or in the Prosecutor's office, or at a student ball—he could not recall just where. At the same time he immediately remembered that the name of Izvekov was connected with the name of Pyotr Ragozin, and with the deplorable business which might rise to the surface again if he were brought into contact with Izvekov.

"That's a good idea, Lisa!" exclaimed Anatoli Mikhailovich, pacing the floor in order to prevent Lisa from coldly reading his thoughts, as well as to avoid seeing her unnatural calmness, which was beginning to get on his nerves.

"An excellent idea. Unquestionably we must begin with that—going to see Izvekov."

"I shall go alone," said Lisa.

"I'll go with you, mom!" interrupted Vitya again. "I know Izvekov. When we were on the sands with Arseni Romanych...."

"Oh, you and your Arseni Romanych!" snorted Oznobishin. "Enough, if you please! What help can we expect from that saint of yours!"

"He's no saint," said Vitya, offended. "He doesn't even go to church, if you want to know, so there!"

"Come, I'll turn down your bed for you. Time you went to bed long ago," said Lisa, leading Vitya out.

Anatoli Mikhailovich continued pacing the floor with his mincing steps. Somewhat more slowly, but just as insistently revolved the thought that here he was, helpless in the face of this misfortune falling so unexpectedly on his head—before he had even had a chance to settle in his dovecote. Ah yes, the hours following his wedding had been spent quite differently than Anatoli Mikhailovich had planned.

At dawn, when he glanced with inflamed eyes through the window, he could see no more in the

472

darkness of night, for the air was cold, and the windowpane had become frosted.

In the morning he offered to accompany Lisa, but she declined his offer. He kissed her goodbye, and was offended by the unresponsiveness of her lips.

Her plan was simple enough: she would go to Izvekov's office like any other person, applying to him merely because of the position he held. She was not going to the Kirill to whom she had once been dear. She was going to the Secretary of the City Soviet, to that Comrade Izvekov whose name she had read in the paper when he had returned after nine years' absence.

At that time she had told herself that she must not meet him. Mentally taking apart and putting together the letters spelling his name, Lisa had sat motionless over the newspaper article in which it appeared, reading it over and over with dimming eyes and pounding heart, telling herself the while that the Izvekov whom she had loved no longer existed, so it was impossible to meet him, whereas the Izvekov of whom the newspaper wrote had nothing to do with her, so there was no reason for their meeting.

Now as she made her way to him she likewise kept insisting that she was going to see the Secretary of the Soviet, and not Kirill. But just as her heart had denied that this was some alien Izvekov when she had read his name in the paper, so now it denied that she was going to see some unknown secretary named Izvekov, whose help she needed.

If she had not counted on finding that the Secretary was indeed Kirill, who would recognize her as Lisa and fulfil her request for the sake of their former relationship, why had she not applied to some other secretary, or to the Chairman of the Soviet, or to any other person holding a responsible position? The fact was that it was Kirill to whom she was applying, in spite of the fact that she kept telling herself it was not.

But when she reached the Soviet she was told that Izvekov had returned to the city only that morning and had gone directly home. It was uncertain when he would be at the office.

Once out on the street again, Lisa stopped beside a front garden. The acacias had not yet turned yellow, but the leaves were dry and faded. Instead of murmuring in the breeze, they rasped harshly. Lisa broke off a branch and began to pinch off the leaves with her nails, letting them fall to the earth. Suddenly, as in childhood, she began to count off the leaves, deciding thereby whether she should wait for Izvekov or go to his house. Quickly she tore them all off. It came out that she should go to his house.

ing for Izvekov—he was at the front. This frightened Lisa, though on second thought she remembered that at the Soviet they had told her of his return.

She almost ran to the trolley. Time was flying, and every minute was probably more precious now than it had ever been in her life. . . .

Izvekov was at home. As he changed his clothes he gave his mother a brief account of his experiences on the expedition, remaining silent in respect to aspects of the trip which particularly preyed on his mind and might upset Vera Nikandrovna.

"Can you imagine how it all happened?" he cried through the closed door while his mother was setting the table. "Dibich was to have put in his appearance at eight o'clock in the morning. He didn't show up. At nine I sent a messenger to find his house. At ten the fellow galloped back to report that he had found Dibich's house, but Dibich had not been there either in the morning or the evening."

"Who told him that?" asked Vera Nikandrovna, gripped by her son's emotion.

"The messenger? What do you mean, who? His mother told him, the mother he had been so anxious to see."

"What a dreadful thing! Just think of it—his mother!"

Kirill came out of the room, pulling at the belt of a new tunic. He looked very youthful after a wash and a shave, and wearing that new outfit, somewhat resembling a school uniform.

"I almost behaved like a coward later," he said quietly.

"When?"

"I thought I should not have the courage to go see his mother."

"How could you not go?"

"That's just it. But there was another circumstance. . . ."

Without finishing the sentence, he walked over to the open window and stood in front of it in silence.

"Sit down. Everything's ready."

"I haven't told you what followed," he said, turning around. "I took some soldiers and set off down the road along which Dibich should have returned to town. When we reached the monastery we found the militia there already. A monk who was acting as watchman in the orchard had found his body early in the morning. It seems that the monks had heard a shot in the evening, but had been afraid to enter the woods. They took us to him. He was lying head down on the path where it descends to the orchard. Choked by his own blood. The wound was in his chest."

478

"What beast could have done it!" said Vera Nikandrovna, propping her head on her hand in a simple feminine gesture.

"I don't suppose he lived long. They shot him some three steps away from where he was lying, under a clump of maples. Traces of blood were found on the path. Red Army men and the militia surrounded the hill, and by dinner time the bandits surrendered. There were only four of the skunks. They had taken Dibich's horse and gun. They said they had hidden at the edge of the woods for the purpose of robbing the monastery. Suddenly Dibich appeared, and they shot him from the bushes."

"You mean to say it was just chance!" exclaimed Vera Nikandrovna, as though it was the element of chance in Dibich's death which most shocked her.

"Just chance," agreed Kirill with a frown, "but a chance which might have been foreseen."

Again he became silent, and, contrary to his wont, stood there with drooping shoulders and hanging head.

"I've already poured your tea. It will get cold."

"It was my duty to have foreseen it," said Kirill.

"What?"

"I should have foreseen the possibility of such a chance."

"How could you, under the circumstances which you yourself described?"

"That's just it. The circumstances. With bandits everywhere. When we ourselves had been sent to catch them. What right had I to let Dibich go off alone?"

"But—he himself.... And besides, you weren't his superior. You couldn't have prevented his going, could you?"

"I had no right to allow it. I even suggested it myself. My idea. Sent him off."

"But you meant well, Kirill," said Vera Nikandrovna, gazing into her son's eyes compassionately.

"Meant well," he exclaimed, jumping up and going over to the window once more. "Why did I later lack the courage to tell his mother that I had meant well? Wanted to do him a favour. Why did I find it shameful and terrifying to go see her? In wanting to do him a favour I became soft and sentimental, and they killed him. In the final analysis, am I not to blame for the fact that they killed him? What do you think?"

"I think it is foolish for you to torture yourself. You cannot assume responsibility for such an accident—for such a tragic accident. You cannot rebuke yourself for having wanted to do something good and kind."

"Something good, as a result of which a good man perished. I know such goodness. Goodness on the impulse. Senseless, thoughtless, unreasonable. Just because it is pleasant. Pleasant for you yourself. So that others will think how kind you are. Well, I turned out to be kind. I had the pleasure of doing someone a favour. And that person is no more. And what a person! If you had only known him, mother!"

He sat on the window sill, leaning out to breathe deeply of the coolness of the morning.

Presently Vera Nikandrovna said:

"If a person always stopped to consider the possible consequences of his good deeds, generous impulses would always be stillborn. I remember what you once told me about Dibich. Had he stopped to consider back there in the tsarist army, he might have found it his duty to arrest you for spreading defeatist propaganda at the front. But he didn't."

Kirill made no answer. After a brief pause, she asked:

"How did Dibich's mother receive you? Did you help her in any way?"

Kirill returned to the table. A pained and tender smile slowly came into his eyes.

"Why do you ask? How could his mother receive me? Aren't you a mother yourself?"

"To be sure," said Vera Nikandrovna, dropping her eyes. "Everything is only too clear."

They were exchanging casual remarks when they heard a knock. The door was opened haltingly, as though by a child, and Vera Nikandrovna rose from the table expecting to see one of her pupils. Suddenly it swung wide open.

"Is it you, Vera Nikandrovna?" asked Lisa in a loud voice, looking at Kirill, unable to tear her eyes from him, though the movement of her body indicated that she wished to approach his mother.

She was very pale, and the polite smile she forced to her lips only emphasized her awkwardness and made her face seem more unnatural. Her first words, undoubtedly prepared beforehand, had come as ringing as a cry, but her voice fell as she murmured:

"Forgive me for coming. . . ."

"Lisa? . . . Elisaveta Merkuryevna?" interrupted Vera Nikandrovna, also turning to look at Kirill.

He rose on hearing that name, and only then realized who this woman was.

". . . for coming uninvited," ended Lisa, still looking at Kirill.

She looked at him as one looks at a person in whom one finds what is expected, yet who is astonished by the fact that, in spite of a long separation, the person remains the same, as though life's

482

vicissitudes had no power to change him. Kirill seemed the same to Lisa not only in his very essence, as expressed in his glance, and the unforgettable features of his face, but even in his clothing—in that tunic with the leather belt which seemed an exact duplicate of what he had worn in the past.

He also looked at Lisa. She was all new to him, but with the newness of a remodelled building, the innovations of which only emphasize the passage of time.

He was the first to go over to her and hold out his hand.

"I have come to see Vera Nikandrovna," she said, feeling the coldness of her own fingers in the warmth of his.

"Then do you want me to leave?" he asked with a youthful smile.

"No. I also want to see—you," she admitted, embarrassed almost to tears.

"So I am the one to leave?" laughed Vera Nikandrovna.

Taking her hand in greeting and retaining her hold, Vera Nikandrovna led Lisa over to the table.

They began to speak about things intended to help Lisa overcome her embarrassment—about the fact that Lisa had grown thin and was not very well; that Vera Nikandrovna had seen her twice at the theatre a long time ago, when Lisa had been plumper; that Lisa's son had already grown into a big boy whose acquaintance Kirill had made during the fishing trip—a splendid youngster, the image of his mother; and about her second marriage—was it true, and who was her husband? (This topic, of course, was broached by Vera Nikandrovna.)

"I have married one of my colleagues at the office. A notary. Actually the notary's assistant," she hastened to add.

"What name do you go by now?"

"My old one. . . . The same as my son's."

"And your husband's name?"

"Oznobishin."

"Oznobishin?" asked Vera Nikandrovna. "Oznobishin," she repeated to herself, getting up and going into the other room.

"Oh, please don't go away," said Lisa, stopping her. "I should like you to. . . ."

"I shall be right back."

And so Lisa was left alone with Kirill.

For a brief second there was silence, and this frightened Lisa. Both of them thought of their past; both of them saw it again with utter clarity, and Lisa felt that she would never find the courage to touch it with words—this past, now revived by some miracle. Kirill came to her aid with a question whose directness and tactfulness sobered her:

"You have probably come to me about some pressing matter, haven't you?"

"Forgive me for deciding on such a step. It isn't for myself alone. You won't refuse to help me, will you?"

"Only you mustn't be apologetic."

"You are the only one who can help. I am petitioning for my father."

She paused, expecting him to ask questions. But he was silent, and it seemed to her that his eyes darkened.

"I have just learned that my father was arrested. That he is in jail. On a barge. Did you know that there was a jail on the main stream?"

He made no reply.

"What am I saying? Of course you know," she said, ashamed of her naïveté and wondering at his silence. "I don't know how long my father has been there."

Once more she waited. Some elusive change took place in Kirill as she watched him. But the change was incontrovertible; already there was almost nothing left of the Kirill she had beheld a moment before. She discovered lines in his face, especially one deep furrow between his straight brows. She immediately said to herself that that was as it should be: after all, she had not come to Kirill at all, but to some secretary whom she did not know.

"I don't even know when my father was taken," she said more resolutely. "Late last night I was told of his arrest by a man who had just been released."

"Which means," said Kirill at last, turning his head slightly to look out of the window, "that you don't know for what he was arrested either."

"I cannot imagine what he could be guilty of. Or where he could have been arrested. At the beginning of August I saw him off to Khvalynsk. Since then I have heard nothing from him. He didn't write. Perhaps he never reached there. I can't—I am simply at a loss to imagine what could have happened to him. It must be a dreadful mistake."

"People don't land on the barge by mistake," said Kirill, still looking out of the window.

"At a time like this? But that isn't important. Perhaps you are right, perhaps it was not a mistake. But there on the barge he is exposed to the danger of many mistakes being made. You cannot deny this. And I must. . . . We. . . . You are in a position to help him. I beg you to do so."

Slyly and clumsily she moved toward him, stressing the urgency of her request with this ges-

ture. He became only the more alien, and this
undermined her hopes, making her feel that her
emotion was reduced to bare words.

"It is necessary to know of what a person is
guilty before seeking to aid him. And the estab-
lishment of guilt is the duty of the courts. What
can I do in a case like this?"

"You can find out whether he actually is guilty.
Perhaps there is no guilt at all. They will not
tell me this, but they will tell you. The very fact
of your asking will be of great help."

Again he was silent. Then she said with irritation:

"They are obliged to explain everything to
you. You represent the government. That is why
I am appealing to you."

He quickly fixed her with the yellow beam of
his bold glance.

"Is that the only reason you came to me?" he
asked.

In that penetrating golden glance and the challenge of his confident young voice, she once more
recognized Kirill. She could not answer, for all of
her strength was concentrated on withstanding this
glance.

"Why did your father go to Khvalynsk?"

"That had long been his desire. He wished to
end his days there."

"Among friends?"

"On the contrary, he sought seclusion. He wished to enter a monastery. To become a—monk."

She blushed in pronouncing this word, and for some reason was ashamed, but suddenly it seemed that she had discovered the answer to the puzzle, and she said with unexpected boldness:

"I am convinced that that is why he is being punished. I am certain of it. Because he wanted to enter a monastery. But it is cruel to persecute a person because of his beliefs. He is an old man. It is too late to make him over. And he is not one to lend himself to being made over. I know him only too well. He has his weaknesses and his oddities, but he is an honest man. You cannot forbid his thinking as he pleases."

"Perhaps you don't know him as well as you think you do," said Kirill casually.

Lisa's breath came in quick gasps from her effort to convince not only Izvekov, but herself as well, of the truth of what had unexpectedly dawned on her.

"But you don't know him at all!" she remonstrated.

"You can hardly say that. I know him slightly— at least from his attitude toward you. From the role he played in determining your fate."

"My fate!" cried Lisa in protest. "I answer for that more than anyone else. But it is only natural that I should have been brought up by *my* father, and not by anyone else, and that he should have brought me up in his own way. Does he answer for my fate? Yes. There was a time when he answered for it. But before whom? I shall not call him to account. Can it be that you would act as his judge?"

"I have already said that I am no judge. For that reason I cannot help. And if you do not wish to judge him, how can you defend him without knowing of what he is guilty? It would be foolish to think that he had been arrested simply because he was religious."

"I do not hold him to account for my fate. I do not harbour a grudge against him. Now he is in trouble. And he is my father."

Suddenly she cried out:

"My father—do you understand? Is it possible that you would not defend your mother if she were in need of your defence? Have you no heart?"

"Heart?" repeated Izvekov quietly, getting up seemingly surprised by some idea which her words prompted. "Father, mother, brother ... these words sound like an incantation, and we accept them as primitive people accepted charms. But—you had a husband—Shubnikov. Would you have sprung to his defence also—simply because he was your husband?"

She was taken unawares both by his pronunciation of that name and by the rebuke suddenly sounding in Kirill's quiet voice. It seemed to her that now had begun the conversation which she had so often imagined to herself long years ago, when she had still lived in anticipation of meeting Kirill again and of explaining to him a marriage which she could not explain to her own self.

She tried to answer calmly (she kept reminding herself of her vow not to become upset, and to speak with Izvekov calmly, like any ordinary petitioner).

"Yes, when Shubnikov was still my husband I would have come to his defence. I probably would do so even now, for he is the father of my son."

"Why such blindness? Don't you hear the witchcraft in those words—husband, father? Behind the words stand people, and behind the people—their deeds. Cain also bore the name of brother."

"What are you accusing me of?" asked Lisa indignantly. "Of the fact that my relatives are my relatives? That they are near and dear to me?"

"Accuse you?" he said with a puzzled smile, as though pricked by the charge.

"It is not my fault that things turned out as they did in our lives," said Lisa quickly, also getting up. "Our fate does not depend on us. And it was not I who sent you down the path leading away from me."

He stood motionless. She realized what she had said and drew her hand across her brow, as though wiping away a spell of dizziness.

"Never in my life have I accused you of anything," said Kirill. "You acted as a free agent, because you were free. The relationship we bore to each other in our youth did not fetter either you or me. All the more reason why it should not fetter us now."

"Forgive me. I said that only because you began to speak of my marriage. At the time I considered myself bitterly punished for lacking the strength to wait for you or to follow you...." (She raised her head and looked at him almost wrathfully.) "But now you seem trying to prove to me that I would have been even more bitterly punished by your cruelty had I followed you!"

Again Lisa raised her hand to her forehead, as though his increasing astonishment had brought her back to reality. Turning her head, she caught sight of Vera Nikandrovna standing in the doorway.

"Quite unintentionally I overheard your conversation," said Kirill's mother. "Do not take offence. After all, you came to see both me and my son, isn't that so?"

"I placed great hopes in you," said Lisa with weary submission. Her strength was exhausted, and she seemed incapable of further outbursts of indignation or of pleading.

"I understand everything," said Vera Nikandrovna, cautiously approaching Lisa. "Your request needs no explanation. And Kirill will forgive your reproaching him with hardness—even with cruelty."

She glanced at her son as though prompting him to confirm her words. He did not respond.

"But it seems to me that you are wrong in resurrecting the past," she continued. "The past is a poor helpmate. It cannot be forgotten anyway. And you have only brought more clearly to my mind the memory of how Merkuri Avdeyevich refused to help Kirill when he was in trouble. Or of how you and I knocked futilely at the icy walls behind which Oznobishin then sat—if he is the same Oznobishin. . . ."

"Good God!" whispered Lisa.

"Do not think I am trying to reproach you with that past," Vera Nikandrovna hastened to say, afraid that Lisa would not give her an opportunity to finish. "But do people who have drunk to the dregs the shameless cruelty of the past, and are now ready to give their lives to wipe it out, deserve to be accused of heartlessness?"

"No, no," interrupted Kirill firmly. "That is not true. I have no desire to avenge myself on anyone."

"Of course, Kirill. I know that you are incapable of acting on personal motives," replied his mother with happy pride.

"Ah, to think!" cried Lisa in her extremity. "Was it to be so cruelly tested that I came here? Do you imagine it was easy for me to come to you— to you!" she repeated, starting toward Izvekov. "Tell me candidly that you refuse to help me, and I shall go."

Lacking the strength to take that last step toward Kirill, she grasped a chair to sit upon, but her listless body slipped past it onto the floor. She did not fall completely. She checked herself on her knees and remained thus, as though this had been her intention, and raised her arms to Kirill.

Quickly he grasped her by those outstretched arms, and Vera Nikandrovna rushed over to help Lisa to her feet. But at that moment the room rang with another frightened voice, which no one had expected:

"Oh, what has happened?"

Everyone turned toward the door, which had stood ajar ever since Lisa's entrance.

Annochka stood in the hall, her hands on the doorjamb, her body strained forward as though she had checked herself while running at full speed.

Kirill immediately dropped Lisa's hands—she was standing now—and ran to meet Annochka.

But the latter swept past him to Vera Nikandrovna, kissed her quickly over and over again, and turned her enormous eyes on Lisa. Only after she had greeted her did she speak to Kirill.

"Have you come home?" she asked, then turned back to Lisa. "Vitya told Pavlik about Merkuri Avdeyevich. I know everything," she said in a surge of sympathy tinged with childish dread. "Haven't you learned the details yet? Don't worry, I'm sure it isn't as serious as it seems. Everything will be all right if the proper measures are taken." She looked at Kirill. "I suppose you have promised to help, haven't you, Kirill Nikolayevich?"

He answered with carefully chosen and precisely enunciated words:

"I have promised Elisaveta Merkuryevna to find out what her father is accused of."

"And to do everything possible to help him?" asked Annochka in a tone of affirmation.

"And to help—if that is possible," said Kirill with the same precision.

Lisa looked at them both uncomprehending. For the first time during those few bitter moments she saw in Kirill not the two separate persons she had imagined, but a fusion of the never-to-be-forgotten Kirill, and a new, unapproachable Izvekov. And she saw Annochka's eyes shining not only with sympathy for her, and not only with childish dread, but also with happy, almost ecstatic triumph.

Lisa suddenly straightened.

"I am going. Forgive me. Goodbye."

She bowed her head without looking at anyone.

"Alone? I shall go with you! You are so upset!" cried Annochka.

"It isn't necessary, thank you. I am in a hurry."

"I won't let you go alone," interrupted Vera Nikandrovna. "You must compose yourself. I shall see you to the trolley."

Lisa kept on towards the door; Vera Nikandrovna overtook her and placed her arm in hers, and they went out together.

Kirill smiled at Annochka uncertainly and in some surprise.

"Lisa has changed," she said.

"Very much."

"I feel sorry for her, don't you?"

"Very sorry."

He stood opposite her without moving, awaiting other questions. She looked up from under knitted brows.

"I had intended coming to see you as soon as I arrived," he said, groping for her response.

She kept probing him with her eyes. He moved closer.

"Didn't you know that I had returned?"

Suddenly she grasped his fingers and pressed them to her breast in a womanly impulse, conscious that they lost their harshness under her touch.

"Of course I knew that you had returned. That's why I came running," she said softly.

Kirill dropped his head on her breast, and for the first time during that week of fearful, uninterrupted strain, he felt his whole being relax.

*   32   *

Kirill involuntarily stopped as he entered the hospital ward. They had told him that Ragozin's injuries were not serious, but the sight of Pyotr Petrovich was disarming: his bed was moved away from the wall to accommodate an apparatus supporting his left arm, which extended at right angles to his body and was heavily bandaged, the bindings covering his neck and shoulder and part of his chest as well.

Without moving the bandaged part of his body, Ragozin waved his other hand and winked at his visitor.

"How do I look moored down here?" he said. "Don't worry, I'll soon be weighing anchor. Everything's all right to starboard."

His eyes twinkled in a warm smile.

"Pull up a chair. Greetings."

Kirill carefully pressed his fingers and sat at some distance, so that it would be convenient for the sick man to see him.

"When did it happen?" he asked, nodding at the bandages.

"Be a week tomorrow. Near Tsaritsyn."

"They told me. This would be the right time to bring you a basket of treats," said Kirill with an apologetic smile. "Rotten of me, but I had no time. I arrived only this morning."

"Thanks, but you needn't worry about me. I'm kept well supplied."

"In a cast?" asked Kirill, again nodding at the injured arm. "Bone broken?"

"I'm still young. It'll heal in a jiffy," answered Ragozin, keeping his smile.

He was embarrassed by what seemed to him shameful helplessness. Furthermore, the appearance of Kirill brought to the surface the anxiety which Ragozin had suppressed, but which had been growing within him from day to day. And while each of them distracted the other with questions about their personal experiences, avoiding the vital theme which made them kin, it became harder and harder for Ragozin to conceal his anxiety.

This was particularly true when he learned about the defeat at Tsaritsyn and the cessation of assault operations by the special striking force. His anxiety grew on learning the situation about other fronts, though he knew that this information was not complete and could not explain the general course events had taken.

Ragozin, and Kirill Izvekov, and hundreds and thousands of other Soviet military men on the same rung of the ladder, obtained their information about what was happening mainly from the sources available to that rung, viz.: the activities in which they themselves participated, the newspapers which could supply only part of what they wished to know, the meetings held to discuss the news in these papers or whatever instructions sent from the centre were not secret, and the rumours of plans being drawn up by the staffs and kept in absolute secrecy. Both Kirill and Ragozin understood (as, in his own way, did any man, regardless of the rung on which he stood), the general idea of what was happening in Russia and the obvious reasons for the minor events which they themselves could observe. But the major event of the civil war as a whole could be perceived only in its result, and the main reasons for the changes which took place in the course of this major event remained unknown to them until they became known to all.

It was as though Ragozin and Kirill were fighting on one street of a city under siege, and the houses and barricades of that street cut off their view of innumerable other houses and streets. They knew only that on those other streets men were also fighting behind barricades, and if rumours came that one section of the city had fallen, they could not understand why it should be so, since their street was keeping up the fight, and those in command asserted that the city was not to be surrendered.

Realizing that their information was incomplete, Ragozin and Kirill nevertheless based their judgment of events on this information, involuntarily creating their own reality, which sometimes lagged behind, sometimes leaped ahead of what was actually happening.

Thus on the day on which Kirill visited Ragozin in the hospital he was still debating the question as to whether Mironov would be able to join Mamontov's corps, which was retreating from Voronezh in the direction of the front line, whereas on the preceding day the remnants of Mironov's forces had already been surrounded in the Balashov uyezd and Mironov himself captured by the Oka Gorodovikov Cavalry Division, part of Budyonny's corps. Both Kirill and Ragozin were concerned most of all about events on the Southern front, and in discussing them, they still drew their conclusions from the situation which had allowed the Red Army to open up the August counterattack on that front.

Actually, by this day in the middle of September, the situation on the Southern front had radically changed.

The counteroffensive, opened in August according to the plan of the command of the Southern front and of the Supreme Command, had ended in defeat. The special striking force which had reached the northern borders of the Don region and been defeated on the left flank in the vicinity of Tsaritsyn, found itself facing united forces of White Don Cossacks, who were determined to stop the penetration of the Red Army into Cossack territory at any cost. The supporting group, operating to the right of the striking force, had suffered defeat even earlier and been thrown back beyond the positions from which it had begun its advance in the middle of August. At the same time, Denikin's Volunteer Army drew up its main forces in order to aim a blow at the north, in the direction of Kursk-Orel and Voronezh.

Ragozin and Kirill knew of Denikin's "Moscow" instructions (his July plan of attacking Moscow) and they prognosticated White operations according to their knowledge of these instructions.

But Denikin's September plan of attacking Moscow had little in common with his July plan. According to the "Moscow" instructions, all of Denikin's armies were to march on the capital simultaneously in four main streams, three of which were to consist of Cossack armies while the fourth was to be his Volunteer Army. According to the plan adopted by Denikin in September, the drive was to be effected principally by the Volunteer Army, supported by Shkuro's volunteer cavalry and Mamontov's Don Cossacks. To the Cossack armies Denikin entrusted the guarding of the borders of the Don region, without making any great inroads into non-Cossack territory.

In drawing up his new plan, Denikin bore in mind the fact that, while the Cossack armies were reluctant to fight beyond their own borders, they furiously defended Cossack lands in the hope that later these lands would be turned into counterrevolutionary "autonomous" White Cossack territory. He entrusted to the Cossacks only this defence task, which they ably fulfilled, while entrusting the attack on Moscow to the Volunteer Army, consisting mostly of tsarist officers who were eager to reach the capital and restore the monarchy. In doing so, Denikin profited by the mistake made by the Commander-in-Chief of the Red Army in planning a drive on Novorossiisk across the Don and Kuban steppes without ensuring the defence of the Moscow direction, which was of primary importance to Soviet Russia.

Ragozin and Kirill were not aware of Denikin's new plan, nor of the mistakes of the Red Army Command of the Southern front, nor of the fact that the Commander-in-Chief insisted on carrying out the plan of a counteroffensive aimed at Novorossiisk in spite of the fact that this plan had proved its infeasibility as early as August, and that the situation on the Southern front had radically changed.

They could not know that four days before the opening of Denikin's drive on Kursk, the Revolutionary Military Council of the Republic had heard and approved the report of the Supreme Command, in which it had been stated that "the Kursk-Voronezh direction is not, and never has been, the main direction," and that "a shifting of the focal centre from our left flank (i.e., from the Don Steppes) to the Kursk-Voronezh direction would mean a giving up of the initiative which we have just wrenched from the hands of the enemy and subordinating our operations to the will of the enemy." They did not know that as a result of approving this report at a moment when the forces of the Volunteer Army were drawn up for a blow in the Kursk direction, the Commander-in-Chief sent the command of the Southern front instructions saying that "The basic plan of attack for the Southern front remains unchanged: the main blow is still to be delivered by a special group ... whose task is the wiping out of the enemy in the regions of the Don and the Kuban."

Without knowing these instructions of the Commander-in-Chief, or the plan of Denikin, they could not realize that in insisting on once more crossing the Don regions to strike at the Kuban, the Supreme Command was indeed subordinating our operations to the will of the enemy, since the enemy could well count on the defensive activities of the Cossacks. Ragozin and Kirill wanted only that the success of the Red Army which had been interrupted be restored as soon as possible and that the Whites be defeated.

But both of them knew that just before they met here in the hospital, that is, in the middle of September, after the defeat at Tsaritsyn, the initiative had been taken out of the hands of the Red Army, and neither of them could understand how this could have happened, considering the victories gained in August. They also knew that in far away Siberia, the routed, retreating army of Admiral Kolchak had suddenly launched a counterattack near Petropavlovsk at the end of August, as a result of which two Soviet armies of the Eastern front were forced back two hundred versts beyond the Tobol River. This too seemed incomprehensible. And finally, the most menacing circumstance was the fact that Denikin's Volunteer Army had, in one concentrated blow, broken through Soviet lines at the junction of two armies on the central sector of the Southern front, and was rapidly enlarging the breach and advancing on Kursk.

The accumulation of all this information fed the anxiety which Ragozin had so far hidden in the depths of his soul. During Kirill's visit he was aware that Izvekov sensed his mood, and responded with the same suppressed anxiety. It was inevitable that they give expression to their feeling that something was wrong, but neither could make up his mind to begin such a conversation. The crisis had not yet been called by its true name. The staffs of the armies and of the divisions made an effort to reflect the mood of the command of the Southern front which, along with the Commander-in-Chief, tried to paint the crisis as only a temporary setback. For that reason, Ragozin and Kirill could not see the crisis as a palpable fact; they merely sensed it and expected it to reveal itself in some impending event or by the intervention of some perspicacious, powerful force.

And even later, when accumulating events in the autumn obviously threatened the Red Army's Southern front with catastrophe, only to turn into a decisive defeat of Denikin—even then Ragozin and Kirill failed fully to understand the causes that brought the Southern front first to the brink of disaster and then to triumphant victory.

Only history could fully reveal these causes, and among the facts it brought to light was the one that gave the first impulse to a change in the course of the civil war in the south.

It was at just this time (when Ragozin and Kirill were suppressing their fears for the Southern front; when Denikin was speedily developing his drive on Kursk; when the Supreme Command of the Red Army was calling the enforced cessation of the counteroffensive by the striking force "the completion of the first phase of the plan," the failure of the manoeuvres of the supporting groups "a hitch in operations," and Mamontov's devastating raid an "illusory success" of the enemy) that Lenin wrote a letter which was an indictment against those responsible for the defeat of the Red Army.

The letter was addressed to one of the members of the Revolutionary Military Council of the Republic, who was at the same time a member of the Revolutionary Military Council of the Southern front.

Lenin wrote:

"... It is poor tactics to keep offering us reassurances. It turns into the veriest game of 'Reassurance.'

"Actually we have reached a point of stagnation—almost disintegration. ...

"... Stagnation of operations against Mamontov. Obviously we are too late time and time again. Too late with the troops brought to Voronezh from the north. Too late in shifting the 21st Division to the south. Too late with machine guns. Too late with communications. No matter whether the Commander-in-Chief went to Orel alone or with you— nothing was accomplished. No contact was made with Selivachev,* no watch was placed over him, in spite of direct orders issued long before by the Central Committee.

* Selivachev: A former colonel in the tsarist army who was in command of the Red Army groups entrusted with rendering a supporting blow in the August counteroffensive on the Southern front.

"In the final analysis, stagnation of operations against Mamontov, and stagnation of operations by Selivachev (instead of your promises of 'victory' day after day, accompanied by childish drawings— remember those drawings you showed me? I said at the time: 'You've forgotten about the enemy!').

"If Selivachev runs away, or the commanders of his divisions turn traitor, the Revolutionary Military Council of the Republic will be to blame, for it slept and offered reassurances instead of doing things. It is necessary to send the best, the most energetic commissars to the south, and not a bunch of sleepyheads.

"We shall be too late in organizing troops too. Autumn will pass—Denikin will strengthen his forces, receive tanks, etc., etc. Things can't go on this way. This lazy tempo must be changed to a lively one.

"... Apparently our Revolutionary Military Council of the Republic 'gives orders,' without bothering or not caring to check up on how they are carried out. Perhaps this is a common fault of ours, but in military matters it is nothing short of disastrous."

Even after the sending of this letter (three days after Lenin wrote it), the Commander-in-Chief continued to await the outcome of events

on the Don direction, demanding "sharp manoeuvring" from the striking force designed to
bring the right flank out upon the bank of the
Don.

Only three days later, after Kursk had already
fallen, did new interference on the part of Lenin
lead to the sending of reserves to the threatened
region of Orel. Even this, however, did not mean
that the Commander-in-Chief admitted his mistake
in stubbornly insisting on seeking salvation only
on the Don steppes.

Ragozin pulled at his moustache and narrowed
his eyes on Izvekov, in the expectation that the
latter would speak about that which was most important. Kirill, on his part, waited for Ragozin to
broach the subject.

A makeshift curtain stitched together out of
bandage, stirred at the window. A hornet which
had become trapped in the room buzzed angrily
against the windowpane. Orderlies shuffled past
the door in soft slippers.

Some three months before, when this had been
a convalescent home and Kirill had come here to
see Dibich, the building had not created the impression of a hospital. The atmosphere had been
cheerful, as though it gave promise of better things
in store. Now that the home had been converted
into a hospital it seemed to be on the alert, and its

very silence suggested that people were having a hard time of it, and one must be circumspect.

"Don't be angry with me for not looking up your son," said Kirill, "I had no time, but I shall do it now, while you are in here."

"Ah, yes," answered Ragozin, smiling again and squinting slyly at the ceiling. "But wait a bit—just a bit.... This is no time for personal business. People have no time to think about even their own kids these days, let alone other people's. We'll tend to it later."

"Oh no, I'll do it all right. I'm not trying to get out of it," insisted Izvekov a bit testily.

"All right. Don't get huffy. I heard you had some pretty tough experiences yourself. Tell me about your expedition."

"Did you know that fellow Zubinsky?"

"Who is he?"

Kirill told him the story about the attempted sabotage.

"You were lucky he didn't put a bullet in your back," said Ragozin.

"I didn't show him my back."

"And right you were. Plenty of trouble arises from the fact that we turn our backs on these so-called military experts. Maybe our city military commissar is also an ex-officer?"

"I don't know."

509

"Have to check up on him. Why should he have sent Zubinsky along with you? May have had some ulterior motives, eh?... What do you think about affairs in the south?" asked Ragozin suddenly.

"What south?" enquired Kirill, feigning innocence.

"Near Kursk. Looks like we didn't learn anything from our experience with Mamontov. They tried it once—it worked. Why not try it a second time? It's about the Whites I'm speaking—about the Whites."

"It may turn out even worse than it did with Mamontov."

"That's what I'm saying. One fine day these ex-officers we've got as our military experts will go opening the gates to the enemy, and then where will we be?"

"But we can't blame everything on military experts. And not all of them are the same. Take Dibich, for example—didn't I ever tell you about him? He was commander of my company."

"Did they kill him?"

"Yes. I can't get him off my mind."

Kirill became lost in thought for a moment, and then, as though the time had come to summarize their relationship, he began to recall each of his meetings with Dibich, including the last one on the path under the clump of maples, when Dibich could no longer respond to his comrade's despairing glance.

Not once did Ragozin interrupt the sad tale. When it was over he rubbed his bald spot briskly and said:

"You can't help grieving over a good man, and that's the truth."

"Grieving!" burst out Kirill. "It's all right to grieve, but what I want to know is whether we have to answer for him or not?"

"Answer for him?" repeated Ragozin, lapsing into silence. "Yes, looks like we had to answer for him too.... Once things turned out like that ... hm. Yes, we have to answer for him."

Kirill gave a wry smile.

"How? By repenting? Answer for him by repenting?"

"Repenting in your own heart is not a bad thing, I should say. Why not? For self-perfection. Quite commendable. But so far as your personal responsibility is concerned—repenting is not quite enough, I should say."

"That's what I'm asking you: what does it mean to answer for somebody?" said Kirill with a shade of irritation.

"It means a person must give account. A person is called to answer for the loss of a loyal man.

How, and through whose fault did it happen? That's what you must make clear in reporting on how you carried out your assignment."

"In other words, you think I am to blame?" asked Izvekov, gazing intently into Ragozin's face.

"What do you think?"

Kirill nodded without speaking.

"According to the letter of martial law, the dead man was probably more to blame," continued Ragozin. "Had he any right to leave his company in the middle of an operation? After all, he was the commander. According to the regulations, he's to blame. But you can't hold dead men to account. He's squared his debt. But you're alive, thank goodness. Dibich left with your permission, didn't he? From the Party point of view, you're also a commander. And so it turns out—although of course, according to the letter you're innocent enough—but according to the spirit. . . . Well, you see. . . ."

"Thanks. That's the way I see it too," said Kirill quickly, hastening to free himself of this burdensome thought. "I have another question to put to you. Or perhaps it would be better to say, a request. . . ."

He hesitated after so bold a beginning, for as soon as he began to clearly formulate his request, he realized the difficulties involved. He forced a smile.

"Well, then, you'll have to listen to another story. I haven't worn you out, have I? I'll be brief."

As soon as Kirill spoke of Meshkov, Ragozin began to twist his head on the pillow, and every unbandaged part of his body also twisted impatiently under the sheet, so that one became aware of the hugeness of his frame, and of the discomfort he must be suffering lying there on that bed. He lacked the patience to hear the story of the Meshkov gold to the end.

"Bah, the measly soul of a merchant!" he exclaimed. "So he deceived me! Oh, how he pretended! 'Not a single coin,' he said. 'You can turn out my mattress if you don't believe me.' But it was his pillow needed turning out. So he fooled me, the old fox! And with all that humility of his! What do you intend doing about it, eh?"

He kept lifting and dropping his head on the pillow as the exclamations escaped him.

"The confiscated money has been brought to Saratov," said Kirill, "and Meshkov himself is on the barge."

"That's where he belongs."

"Probably, if the court finds it a suitable place for him. But before he comes to trial I wanted to ask your advice, Pyotr Petrovich. Meshkov's daughter came and asked me to do something for the old man if it was possible...."

Kirill became silent. Ragozin stopped twisting and cast Izvekov a sidelong glance that seemed to go right through him.

"Want to act the patron saint?" he remarked after a pause.

"Something like that," laughed Kirill with a shake of his head.

"That's what it would be all right. I took that holy man of yours at his word and he made a fool out of me. You plan to pull him up out of the hole he's gotten himself into, and he's probably wondering how he can push you down in his place."

"But I helped put him in."

"You put him in, and now you're pitying him."

"No I'm not. He'll get what's coming to him. But I don't want it to be more or less."

"Afraid of a little overmeasure? Want some Solomon to be his judge, eh? You judge him yourself. You're ready to answer for Dibich—answer for Meshkov too."

"I've done my duty."

"Whose do you intend doing now?"

Kirill shrugged his shoulders. He could find no answer, but objected to Ragozin's retorts.

"You don't understand. I have no intention of letting Meshkov off. But I promised his daughter to find out just how his affairs stand and what he is charged with."

"Suffering for the daughter's sake?"

"She's suffering for her father's sake."

"What's she to you?"

"There you go!" exclaimed Kirill in vexation, adding stubbornly, in a tone suggesting that he wished to put an end to the conversation: "You simply tell me who can supply this information. You know better than I do."

"Go ahead and do whatever you please. I'm not your teacher, and I don't intend to aid and abet such a scoundrel."

"But you *are* my teacher, once you keep lecturing me as if I were a little child. How have I been aiding and abetting Meshkov? Don't I realize that by his very nature he's our enemy, even if his intentions are not malicious?"

"Fine speeches you're making."

Kirill looked at Ragozin. An ironic smile flickered beneath his tangled moustaches. But no, it was not ironic; it was slyly affectionate—a sort of smile Kirill had never before seen on his lips.

It was as though Ragozin were ashamed, yet delighted to smile in this sly way.

"Here comes my market basket," he said in a voice as strange as his smile, looking straight ahead and trying to lift himself on his pillow.

Kirill followed his eyes.

Into the ward came a lean, long-legged boy with a large forehead and eyebrows climbing to his temples. The expression of concern and curiosity in his eyes contradicted his general carefree air. He was still a child, but he gave a hint of the awkwardness heralding adolescence. Suddenly that awkwardness of long legs and arms seemed very familiar to Kirill.

"Put the basket in the corner for the present," said Ragozin, "and come make the acquaintance of Kirill Nikolayevich Izvekov."

"Ragozin," said the boy without bowing, thrusting up his chin and poking out his hand.

"Vanya," said his father softly.

"I see," said Izvekov, again turning to Pyotr Petrovich. "So you found him?"

Ragozin's present smile seemed even more unexpected to Kirill. In addition to the sly affection it expressed, there was something ingratiating about it, like the smile of a doting grandmother. It was remarkably becoming to this baldheaded man, who seemed suddenly older, and at the same time it was so incompatible with Kirill's former conception of the stern, slightly ironic Ragozin, that he burst out laughing. Pyotr Petrovich also laughed in some embarrassment. The ward became filled with this good-natured laughter; only Vanya remained serious, gazing disapprovingly at his father and his new acquaintance.

"Sit down," said Ragozin, moving his legs under the sheet to make room for his son on the edge of the bed. "Looks like it's my turn to do some story-telling, eh?"

"How did it ever come about?" asked Izvekov.

"Vanya and I have a pet ship—the gunboat *Risky*. Remember how I helped overhaul it? Well, Vanya shipped off on it."

Ragozin began his tale, trying to make it brief, but in his mind arose hundreds of details which were infinitely dear and held great significance for him.

Pyotr Petrovich had met his son on the hospital ship the day after he had been removed from the *October*. The hospital ship, filled with wounded, had then been despatched to Saratov.

By that time the pain had eased up a bit, though Ragozin still suffered from the sensation that he was enveloped in a fog which his thoughts penetrated intermittently and with great difficulty. Thinking was not only difficult, but unpleasant, for it led merely to a recognition of the failure of their operation and fruitless searchings for the cause of this failure.

Up to the day on which Ragozin had been wounded, he had been constantly accumulating battle experience, and he lived with the sense of gradually attaining new heights. Instinctively he was aware of having acquired a new ability which he made no effort to define or name—the ability to make correct mental estimates. His foresight was developed as never before, and he unerringly knew what must be done at the given moment. He seemed to have achieved an elevation from which he could easily direct the aiming of the weapon which the masses had taken into their hands.

And just at that moment, all that Ragozin had accomplished seemed unaccomplished: the attack had ended in retreat, and he was oppressed by the consciousness of his own complete helplessness.

In one of those moments of intermittent mental activity, the nurse entered his cabin to say that there was a boy from the crew of the ship who wished to see him.

Later Ragozin realized that he had been impressed not so much by the actual meeting with his son as by the fact that he had known this meeting would take place the moment the commissar of the *Risky* reported to him about the youngster who was to be put on shore. When the nurse announced the boy from the crew, he immediately decided it was the same one he had ordered put on the hospital ship rather than on shore. He recalled the boys who had bartered watermelons from the boats near Bykov Khutor, and the explosion of the shell in the water, and the frightened splashing of the oars, and his fear for the rowers, and his fury, and the fact that his fear and fury merged with his longing for his lost son. Now he had no doubt that it was his son he should see, for the boy from the crew could be none other. This certainty brought a healing flow of blood to his brain, dispersing the fog which had dimmed his reason, and driving away the pain, which lurked somewhere off in the distance.

The conversations held with his son on shipboard had been brief (the doctors did not allow the boy to remain long with the wounded man), but Ragozin went over every word a hundred times in his mind, where they glowed with undiminishing brightness.

"Why did you run away from my house?" asked Pyotr Petrovich when Vanya stood leaning against the door of the cabin, a bold, but frightened culprit.

"Turned out to be a good thing I ran away."

"Why a good thing?"

"Now I can take care of you—like a man nurse."

"Oh, thanks. So you think you'll be my nurse . . . but—do you know what you actually are to me?"

"Yes."

"Oh, you do, do you?"

"I knew back there already—at your house."

"And still you ran away."

"Ahuh."

"Is that all you can say—'ahuh'?"

"What else?"

"I'm asking you why you ran away, once you knew who I was."

"What if I *did* know?"

"What do you mean—'what if I *did* know?' "

"Nothing special."

"Do boys usually run away from their fathers?"

"Plenty of them."

"Maybe from bad fathers. But I want to be a good father to you. I'm glad I found you. Are you glad?"

Vanya placed his hands behind his back.

"If they'd told me then that you were a commissar . . . but I asked, and they said you just added up figures. Like the bookkeeper in our Home."

"A bookkeeper. Humph. What's wrong with being a bookkeeper? I know a bookkeeper, now—Arseni Romanych. All the fellows like him."

"He's no bookkeeper. I know him too."

"What is he then?"

"He's something like an artist."

"So that's where your taste runs!" smiled Ragozin. "I guess you're right when you say that—he is like an artist. Well, you'll study and become an artist too."

Vanya was silent. Ragozin impatiently awaited his response.

"If it's not in you—don't make any difference how much you study," Vanya said at last.

"Ability comes with study."

"I've seen people that study for all they're worth. But I can draw just like that!"

"You don't say!" was all Ragozin could exclaim as he studied the little braggart in amazement.

He already foresaw that the development of their relationship depended upon the desire of his son to study, and the next time they met he broached the subject again. He thought that what he considered most important and indispensable in life, was most important and indispensable in his son's life as well, and he was upset by discovering that Vanya had an entirely different point of view.

"If you study hard and learn to work well, you can be of some service in life."

"What's that?" asked Vanya, apparently not understanding.

"How shall I explain it to you. . . . Have you ever been to a museum?"

"Yes."

"Did you like the pictures?"

"Ahuh."

"In other words, by their work the artists did you a service. Through their pictures, do you understand?"

Vanya gazed intently through the open window of the cabin. The Volga was coursing past—he could hear the water surging beneath the wheels of the huge boat and see the green waves heaving away, laving the shore and etching the sand with foam.

"That's no service," replied Vanya, and his serious face became impenetrable, as though he alone knew what service was.

"What is it then?"

"That's just making you jealous—jealous that *you* didn't draw it. That *yours* don't come out like that."

"That's it," exclaimed Ragozin happily. "Making you want to do something as well as others have done it. So that people will admire your work as you admire theirs. Don't you see that that is being of service?"

"Funny how you bishop it," laughed Vanya.

"What's 'bishoping it?'"

"Like a monk."

"What do you know about monks?"

"Back at the Home we used to run to the bishop for sugar. He'd give everybody a piece and then start bishoping: 'Run along and play, children, in peace and concord; listen to the words of your elders, and may the Lord give you His blessing.'"

Vanya gave an apt imitation of the bishop's unctuous speech.

"And what would you do?" asked Ragozin with a smile, though he was a bit taken aback.

"Nothing. Eat the sugar and come back for more. He'd give it to us and start bishoping again. . . . But you're a commissar," Vanya wound up reproachfully.

The next time they met Ragozin tried approaching the subject from a different angle.

"Who'll supply you with paper and pencils if you don't study? You don't mean to drop your drawing, do you?"

"Whenever I need anything I manage to snitch it," answered Vanya unhesitatingly.

"Well, now. . . ."

"Who's going to wait until they hand things out? Never get anything that way. I snitch whatever I need to make my pictures."

"That's called stealing, brother. Did you ever think of that?"

"Pencils?" asked Vanya with starting eyes.

"Pencils or anything else. Time to get rid of those wayward manners of yours. I'll supply you with everything you need."

Vanya sulked for a moment before saying, in a crestfallen manner:

"Well, if you've got so much of everything—suits me."

Suddenly carried away by his emotion, he used an intimate tone with his father for the first time, saying reassuringly:

"But don't worry, if there's anything you don't have, I'll manage to crib it somehow."

His father was shocked and delighted by this outburst, which revealed both the distortion of the boy's outlook, and the spontaneous generosity of his nature.

These were the things Ragozin remembered as he recounted to Kirill the story of how he had found his son on the Volga.

Vanya sat at his father's feet gazing with detachment at the smooth white ceiling. This was the second time he had brought his father a basket of food packed by Ragozin's landlady, and he knew that he would carry half of the contents back with him: Ragozin was stubbornly solicitous about his boy's well-being. Vanya was aware of the place he occupied in his father's heart. He regarded this affection as a weakness peculiar to grownups, but was inclined to accept it condescendingly, and even accepted the caresses of this big man, who had been wounded in battle and now needed looking after.

"He and I have decided to live together," said Ragozin, with an approving glance at Vanya. "And do you know what conclusion I have drawn from all this, Kirill? I have had plenty of time to think things over, lying here. It gives us great joy to know that we are moving toward our goal. But it seems to me this joy would be even greater if we found that this goal, which in the main still lies before us, was being achieved bit by bit in the little things already won. Do you get my point?"

"More or less," smiled Kirill.

"I'm not much good at abstractions. I have a practical approach. So I simply ask myself: do we want to change human relations in the future? Obviously we do. Then it seems to me we ought to search for signs of this change in our present life, so that a bit of the future may come to life in the

525

present, understand? How shall I put it? Embody our ideas in living beings, so to speak. In human relations. Give these ideas practical expression. Otherwise we'll get absorbed in our dreams of, let's say, a Communist society when actually there is no such society as yet. And we'll become so used to worshipping a mere dream, that we'll gradually become estranged from human beings. Isn't that true? We must find what we want right now. Find just a bit of the future in the people of today. And make contact with these people as though they had already become our ideal. And if everybody would act like that, we could realize some of our dreams for the future right here and now. Sow our seeds, understand?"

"I understand. But we can't apply this recipe to all people. Especially now. Remember your saying to me: the times determine the policy?"

"Of course. You've got to find a person who already bears a bit of the future within him. In his work, in his service to society, or something else. And use him to learn on. Put your ideals into practice on him. You've got to find people," repeated Ragozin, once more resting contented eyes on his son.

"You're right," exclaimed Kirill. "I remember Chernyshevsky saying almost the same thing: bring the future nearer, was what he said; transfer as much as possible from the future into the present."

"See? Ideas stand firmer when you find somebody else supporting you," said Ragozin, winking merrily at his son.

Kirill also turned to Vanya.

The boy gave a delicious yawn.

"How was it you abandoned your comrade and went off to join the fleet?" asked Kirill, restraining a smile. "Pavlik Parabukin told me how you let him down."

"It wasn't my fault. The sailors fooled me. Pavlik knows. We've made up already. Him and me wanted to come see you."

"What for?"

"To complain."

"What about?"

"His father."

"What has his father done?"

"He makes paper bags out of Arseni Romanych's books."

"Arseni Romanych?" exclaimed Ragozin, raising his head from the pillow only to let it down slowly, with a grimace of pain.

"Arseni Romanych gave his books to some library. And the library sent half the books to the Old Goods Department. And Pavlik's father is making paper bags out of them. Pavlik saw it himself."

"What do you think of that, Kirill, eh? You better drop in and have a look," said Ragozin, who had gone quite limp. "Arseni Romanych's library—that's no joke. It'd be a sin on our souls to hurt Dorogomilov."

"I'll run over right now," said Izvekov, getting up. "I've been wanting to pay a visit to the learned Parabukin for some time. Don't worry about it."

He lifted Ragozin's hand from the bed. Pyotr Petrovich held on to Kirill, as though searching for something to say in parting.

"You seem to have a fever. I've made you talk too much."

"I'm all right. A bath makes you clean; talk makes you keen."

Still he did not release Izvekov's hand.

"If you hear any news, let me know, will you?"

He drew Kirill closer.

"One of the comrades is supposed to come see me. I'll ask him to find out about that business of yours. He's in a position to."

"What business of mine?"

"The business Meshkov's daughter came to see you about."

He gave an insinuating smile and pushed Kirill away.

"You're crazy," laughed Kirill.

"It's not about Meshkov I'm concerned. His song is sung. It's his daughter. Maybe she's got a bit of that future in her—your future, eh?"

"Crazy as a loon," laughed Kirill again, colouring up and retreating to the door. "You're right in thinking that there's not a vestige of that future in Meshkov. But he may be of some use in the present. Believe it or not, he identified Polotentsev for us."

"The gendarme? Not really! And you didn't tell me about it! Well, that's a service all right, no denying that!"

"I'll tell you all about it another time. Hurry up and get well."

"You going straight to the Old Goods Department?" called Ragozin when Kirill was already out in the corridor.

"Straight."

"Find me something to read. And don't forget those bookshelves of yours either."

The Old Goods Department was part of an organism bearing the name of "The Gubernia Council of People's Economy," the brain of which found cramped accommodation in the hotel "Astoria," whose façade, built according to the canons of contemporary art, graced the main street. One could hardly say that in importance the Old Goods Department represented one hemisphere of that brain. But in extent it indeed represented almost a whole hemisphere, and for that reason it could not be quartered along with other departments in the "Astoria," but found accommodations in a neighbouring building along the main street—a sort of independent brain, as it were.

Here the most varied types fluttered about like birds on the wing. And still they were incapable of coping with all the tasks of the Old Goods Department. At the head of each of the organization's branches stood a separate organization with its staff of fluttering employees. The foundation of this complicated structure was represented by its shops for shoemaking, capmaking, soapmaking and paper bagmaking. The lower one descended from the heights to the foundation, the less became the fluttering, so that on reaching the vats where soap was made, or the benches where woollen boot tops were stitched out of discarded uniforms, one met very few people and found things very quiet.

This many-branched organization was stamped with the contradictions of the times.

Its various enterprises, united under a huge management, deserved nothing more than a modest burial. The workmen pegged away without the slightest hope of advancing beyond the century-old technique of their ancestors. The capmakers boasted no instruments other than needles, scissors, and flatirons; the carpenters—hammers and saws. And indeed, what else was needed to make a cap out of an old army coat rescued from the rag bag, or a stool or a coffin out of an unseasoned pine board? None of the people fluttering through the rooms of the ultra modern hotel disturbed their brains with thoughts of modernizing the workshops of the Old Goods Department.

But while these workshops deserved nothing better than a modest burial, their hour had not yet come. However feeble their efforts, they were yet indispensable. At that time economic life had disintegrated to an unheard-of extent, a fact openly recognized as one of the most serious threats to the revolution. Every piece of soap and scrap of paper, every shoe sole which would serve for even a week, every button which would briefly hold together one's tatters, assumed fantastic value.

This no doubt explained why, in spite of the antiquated technique of the workshops belonging to the Old Goods Department, their output was so highly valued, and why such numbers of people fluttered about trying to fan the breath of life into this organism, postponing its complete decease.

Izvekov did not immediately discover the headquarters of the paper-bag industry. The shops and storehouses of the Old Goods Department were scattered from the Volga to the Monastery Settlement, occupying old granaries, packhouses, rickety mills in the old section of town, cellars and stalls at the bazaar. Kirill asked where Parabukin was employed, but his name was not so renowned that any office clerk could immediately place him.

Tikhon Platonovich sat behind ply-board partitions forming a little cubbyhole between two large rooms, one of which contained old newspapers and magazines, the other—secondhand books which had not yet been sorted. A hole in the wall connected the paper-bag shop with the newspaper room.

Human shadows moved among the piles of papers. Every once in a while could be heard the rustling of newssheets stirred by a draught. The smell of fresh glue, mouldy leather, and damp calico, suggesting the odour of a stagnant pond, was wafted from door to window.

After drinking down the nondescript liquid supplied by Mefody Silych, Tikhon Platonovich put his cup away in the drawer of his desk and gave his attention to his friend.

"What you trying to tell me about Tsvetukhin! He's like a twin brother to me. I know him better than my own self," said Mefody. "He's a martyr, same as me. But he doesn't show it. His pride keeps him from bowing his head. His genius hasn't hatched yet. Keeps pecking at the shell. Can't break through. So he goes on suffering. I'm a mere amoeba compared to him. Even if I am an actor. I'm an actor too."

"In an eggshell too," added Parabukin.

"I'm not denying it. Humbly admit it. I'm not proud—just vain. It's not so hard for me. It's harder for him because he's a genius. What stands in his way? Posing. Poses at having principles. What principles can an actor have? If he acts well—there's all his principles. If he acts bad—principles won't help. We had a tragedian once—a rum devil he was. Not a single principle, but he set the whole theatre sobbing. Got to work with your feelings in our trade, brother. Egor wants to understand too much."

"He'll be the ruin of my Annochka," sighed Tikhon Platonovich bitterly.

"Who you talking about?" said Mefody offended. "You're talking about Hamlet. Phooh, you grub! He's not one to play around with his girls. It's purity he demands from them. He teaches his pupils to have souls like crystal. I grovelled at his feet for two weeks until he let me join his studio. Talent, he says, demands two things: cleanliness and sobriety. Anyone who drinks up his talent, he says, is a thief. He robs the people of what nature has given them, for talent is presented to all through the medium of one. People would be a hundred times happier, he says, if talent wasn't given to drunkards. Stop drinking, he says, and you can join my troupe. But if you don't stop, then you can go to the devil. I've got young people to answer for."

"What about himself? On the water waggon?"

"That's just it. There am I, grovelling at his feet and saying to him: why should you throw an extra drink up to me, Egor, after all the liquor you and I have consumed together? And he answers me: Tsvetukhin's no drunkard. Once I drink, he says, I drink with joy. A feast. A holiday. I know very well my drinking isn't serious—just for the joy of it. If you drink in despair, that's letting yourself get out of hand. Then he flares up. It all comes from thinking yourself a genius, he says. All drunks think they're geniuses. They can't say a word without boasting. Always trying to be smart, to be different, to be original. Not artistic, he says. Get the point?"

"Raked you over the coals all right."

"Why me?" said Mefody, again taking offence. "I'm a simple person. A mere bottle. Without any pretentions. Consume my liquor like any other proletarian.'

"Call yourself a proletarian? Father Mefody!"

"Why not? I'm part of propertyless Russia, that's what I am. It's on people like me the country rests. Caryatids!"

"Car-ya-tids!" sang Parabukin mockingly.

Suddenly his face straightened, he ran his fingers hastily through his hair and struggled to get up.

"Where's the guardian of all these riches?" asked Izvekov in a loud voice, opening the ply-board door and glancing into the cubbyhole.

"Comrade Secretary," said Parabukin, pulling at his short blouse, stroking his beard and moustache, clearing his throat, and wondering what else he could do in such an awkward position.

"We expected you long ago," he said. "Allow me to introduce Mefody Silych, a member of Tsvetukhin's dramatic studio, one of my daughter's colleagues, so to speak. A caryatid."

"Is that your name?" asked Izvekov in some surprise.

"More in the metaphorical sense," said Mefody with a solemn bow.

"I seem to have interrupted your meal," observed Izvekov, retreating before the inexplicable odour. (As he glanced at Mefody's broken Socratic nose, he thought to himself that here was a type outshining Parabukin.)

535

"Just a bite during the recess," explained Tikhon Platonovich hastily. "Nothing much. Can't be particular these days."

"What are you doing with Dorogomilov's library?"

Relieved that one delicate subject had been glossed over, and fearing that another might arise, Parabukin took himself in hand to the extent of offering his guest a wobbly chair.

"Thank you for deigning to visit our antique shop."

"Show me which of Dorogomilov's books are here."

"I suppose my Pavlik's been telling tales. You can be sure there's no truth in them. He's always butting in where he don't belong."

"Show me where the books are. I should like to see them."

Together they moved down the lanes and alleys between towering stacks of old papers. Parabukin spoke incessantly in his role of guide.

"Not a book have we received from Dorogomilov. We got them all from the reading room where he sent his library. More trash than anything else. They sent all the trash to us. Magazines, newspapers, books on accounting. Not bad raw material. Part of it'll go for paper bags, part for envelopes. The stronger paper will make good office folders. Here, for example, is a pile of Dorogomilov's stuff. Pavel rummaged through it, the little monkey."

Kirill took a bound journal off the top of the pile. It was a printed report issued by the city management some twenty years earlier.

"What paper, eh? Howard!" said Parabukin, narrowing his eyes as he rubbed the glazed paper between his fingers.

Kirill took up another journal. It contained a report of the city Theatre Committee and a record of the city's income from and expenditures on the theatre. The season to which the document referred was a memorable one for Kirill: it was the year in which he had last attended the theatre—with Lisa. On the morning following the performance, still under the influence of her presence, Kirill was led into the yard of the jail.

Involuntarily his fingers listed through the journal. Suddenly they stopped. At first he did not realize what had arrested his attention. At the end of the page he read that the manager of the theatre objected to the city's appropriating a certain sum from Tsvetukhin's benefit performance. The name of Tsvetukhin was printed in large letters.

Kirill tossed away the journal.

"But where are the books?" he insisted.

"The books are kept apart. In the treasury, so to speak. This way, if you please."

They went into the adjoining room. Books were piled almost to the ceiling, in strange formations, like a mountain range, with peaks and canyons and jagged slopes.

Kirill slowly cast his eye about this chaos. Here was life, honour, fame, he recalled. Wealth, ecstasy, inexpressible happiness! Profound love for humanity!

"All the books go through a scientific process," muttered Parabukin, kicking back a thick volume that threatened to unbalance him. "Research. Sorting."

"Hm," murmured Izvekov.

"Experts decide what is of value and what, according to the instructions, can be called trash. Now come here, if you please. Against this wall we have all kinds of religious writings—Greek Orthodox, Roman Catholic, German Lutheran. Good bindings."

"Was that one of the experts having a bite with you?"

"No, he's my personal friend. A highly educated person—anticlerical and knows Latin. An old hand at art, beings as he's an actor. But they send us big specialists to pick out the books on art. One of them even found a book he himself had written here. Called *What is Chiaroscuro?* Ever read it? Egor Pavlovich Tsvetukhin does the selecting of books on the theatre."

Izvekov quickly interrupted him:

"But I want to see Dorogomilov's books."

"Over by the door. Something less than a cartload. A feeble sort of literature. No bindings worth speaking of."

"Please leave me to myself."

"Just as you say," exclaimed Parabukin happily. "See what interests you. Plenty of people have been pleased with their pickings."

Kirill remained alone. From time to time street noises came through the window, and the open pages were occasionally stirred by a breeze. One book pulled out of the pile upset others, which came sliding and tumbling down. The silence was comprised of those discrete noises, seemingly meditative, which create so perfect an atmosphere for solitude.

Kirill stooped to pick up a book and remained crouched there motionless, turning pages and occasionally exchanging one book for another.

If one judged Arseni Romanovich by the collection of volumes found here, his personality would indeed seem perplexing. His books had accumulated over a period of dozens of years, during which time he had given himself up to all sorts of enthusiasms, from watchmaking and photography, to the history of philosophy and ship designing. Here were books on Buddhism, gymnastics, fruit canning, Russian religious sects, and fish breeding. Among cheap leaflets lay a thick volume of the theory of numbers, like a barge among rowboats. Suddenly Kirill came across a German translation of the adventures of Casanova, a French translation of Hoffmann with engravings by Gavarni, and the first Russian translation of Don Quixote.

On every title page of this pot-pourri, the owner had written his signature and the date on which the book had been purchased (probably at the secondhand book stalls in the market). For Kirill, Dorogomilov remained the enigmatic creature toward whom he nurtured an antipathy—"Shaggy Locks," whom as a child he had always avoided meeting by crossing to the other side of the street. How could this man have won the friendship of Kirill's father? Perhaps because of Arseni Romanovich's strange range of interests—chance interests, cluttering up his life like barnacles on a ship's bottom. If you could view such a ship's bottom under the water, it too would look queer. Actually, what of interest could be found in a person who took pleasure in signing his name to every leaflet? The book lover who had roused

Kirill's reverence for the written word had once said: "A man has a right to sign his name only to a book which he himself has written."

Kirill picked up a heavy volume of Solovyov's *History of Russia* and, taking hold of all the pages, let them slip through his thumb with the gesture of a book-buyer checking whether all the pages were intact. He caught glimpses of pencil notes in the margins. Kirill turned back and found certain lines sharply underscored. They were extracts from Pugachov's charter promising his followers land and fields, seas and forests, money and provisions, lead and gunpowder and eternal freedom. In the margin was written: "Thus it shall be."

Someone had pondered over the splendour of these magnanimous words; someone wanted others to ponder these words; someone was expecting this promise to be realized. Could it have been Dorogomilov?

Kirill put the book to one side. Presently he added to it a volume of Leo Tolstoy which had been banned in tsarist Russia. Then he left Dorogomilov's pile of books and moved to another.

He found Shchedrin's *Gubernia Sketches*. This remarkable work lay alongside of a manual containing instructions for weaving rugs and textiles. He put Shchedrin with his other selections. Then he found Ibsen's plays (only two volumes—the set was incomplete). These he also annexed. As he penetrated deeper into the mountains, he came upon Lombroso (in rather a bad state, with broken corners). This work, dealing with genius and insanity, had long been discredited, as he knew, but he had never read it. It would do no harm to read what had been discredited too. His eye fell upon an old binding bearing the name of Beltov. At first he passed it by, but then returned to read the title: *Concerning the Development of the Monistic View of History*. Plekhanov. A quarter of a century old. Apparently the volume had already been laid aside by someone else. It was lying in too conspicuous a place. But Kirill could not do without Plekhanov. Plekhanov was not Lombroso.

Suddenly he came upon Shakespeare. Four exquisite volumes—gold on black leather—in excellent condition. He opened them up. Never before had he seen such bindings. The paper of the flyleaves was as fragile as silk and embellished with birds and flowers which were neither blue nor brown, but blue and brown together. A tiny silver thread arabesqued among the birds and flowers. "They would be nice for Annochka," was his first thought. "Annochka can borrow them from me," was his second.

The Shakespeare volumes had certainly been put aside before Kirill came. They were piled neatly along with some other fine volumes. But who could have come here to select books? Who appointed the experts, the specialists, the sorters? Surely Kirill had as much right to help himself as they. Perhaps he had even more right. However that might be, for the present he would add the Shakespeare to his other books.

He began to hurry. There were so many books that if he lingered over each of them, he would get nowhere. He imagined what his shelves would look like, filled with these books. It was most important to select his future library with a definite system. He must first find works on basic subjects. But he was not free to select whatever he wanted. He was merely wandering through this labyrinth and taking the best of what came to hand. For the present he must be content to appropriate whatever he could not resist. "I'm as bad as Dorogomilov, damn it all," he thought, but consoled himself by saying: "Later I can throw away what is superfluous."

He became greedy. He kept adding more and more treasures to his pile. Unconsciously he found himself calling them "his books." He kept making mental notes such as: "This book on education will interest mother," or "I'll give this to Ragozin to read."

Twilight came. He had difficulty making out the letters. He was alone. Not once did anyone come to disturb him. This was utter self-oblivion. He dug deeper and deeper into the mountains, tunnelling through them in the hope that he might find some name dear to his heart hidden in their depths. Slipping his hands under the bottom of a pile he had selected, and pressing down on the top with his chin, he would stagger over to his original heap, which kept growing and growing. Then he would find a new corner and begin climbing from ledge to ledge, browsing on the slopes, scaling peaks, sliding down embankments. His hands became slippery with dust. His throat became lined with this fine, sweet, ticklish dust, making him cough.

Finally the hills and mountains merged into one general heap; it became impossible to read; the pale patches of the windows offered the only relief to the darkness.

Kirill shook himself and went over to his newly-acquired wealth. "My God!" he thought. "How shall I ever cart them all away? I'll have to hire a horse." He stood there for a second as though wondering how it had ever happened, and what kind of books he had collected. His head was swimming and he had difficulty keeping his balance.

Suddenly the sound of a march came through the window. Rough voices, accompanied by the

544

measured tread of boots, came down the street in
irresistible crescendo:

> Brave-ly
>   we to battle go,
> For the power
>   of the So-o-viets. . . .

Kirill wiped his forehead on his sleeve. He did
indeed feel dizzy, and a shudder passed through him.

He pushed the door open with both hands, almost knocking down Parabukin, who retreated in
fright.

Tikhon Platonovich was holding up a little
lamp, which gilded his beard and hair.

"I was bringing you a lamp. It's dark already.
Did you find anything suitable?"

"No," said Kirill. "Later. Goodbye."

"If you wish, we'll send the books to you. Only
leave us your address."

"Never mind. Goodbye," repeated Kirill and
almost ran through the strewn papers to the door.

*   33   *

There are problems in art which seem to be
solved only because experienced artists have grown
accustomed to them and to assuming that they
have been solved. If a young artist approaches a

mature one with these problems, he is not offered a solution, but is merely referred to the experience which comes with maturity. Experience takes the place of a solution, since none exists as a general law, but is sought by every artist for himself and for his time.

As soon as Annochka Parabukina stepped onto the stage, she found herself encompassed by dozens of such problems, like trees in a forest. Among the puzzles and perplexities loomed one question which she considered so important that the answer had to be immediately found.

The question was: what sources should an actor draw upon for creating a role having little in common with his own life and personality?

If Annochka Parabukina had to play the role of Annochka Parabukina, the problem would be simple: Annochka would merely step from life onto the stage, remaining her own self.

But Annochka had to play the role of Luise, from *Love and Intrigue*. Annochka had never seen Luise. That is, when just a little girl she had seen Luise on the stage of the Folk Theatre playing in Servier Park, at the edge of town. But that was Luise as played by an actress. Annochka could not possibly have known Luise Miller who lived in the eighteenth century in some German duchy.

Why did they say that the theatre represented life? What life? A life nobody had seen? How should Annochka act? Like the actress in Servier Park?

When Annochka put this question to Egor Pavlovich, he answered without a moment's hesitation.

"Luise is *you*. Act yourself."

"How?" asked Annochka very seriously. "How can I? I wear a short skirt and walk like a trooper. Luise wore hooped skirts."

"As soon as you put on the hoops, everything will fall in its proper place. Remember only one thing—*you* are Luise."

"What about my hands and arms? Could Luise have had such long ones?"

"Certainly. Don't think about them. Think only about your love for Ferdinand—that you might have been happy with me—that is, with Ferdinand, but that I—that is, Ferdinand, made you unhappy. Think of your feeling for me."

"I do nothing but think. You try thinking a bit."

"Tsch, tsch," chuckled Tsvetukhin with a smile, letting her know that even so charming a maid must not forget that she is a mere pupil.

This embarrassed her, but the earnestness of her desire led her to lift her hands imploringly:

"Am I to blame that I don't understand? It seems to Luise that there is no way out of her situation, but I could easily find a way out. In other words, she is not like me."

"Wonderful. You are Luise to perfection. That's just the way she wrung her hands when imploring Ferdinand. Remember that."

"But I would never throw myself at his feet. Not for anything in the world! I wouldn't try to hold him back. I'd let him go. He'd be sure to come back anyway," she ended vixenishly.

He gazed into her face with the air of a fond and delighted admirer.

"Listen, honey, try to find in Luise at least something of what you yourself have once lived through."

"But if there is nothing in her which corresponds to what I have lived through?"

"Very well," he corrected himself. "Don't search for anything about her which resembles you. But find something within yourself which resembles her. However slightly."

At the same time he asked himself: "How can she understand Luise's despair if she herself has never loved and never experienced despair?"

"Furthermore," he added, "the creation of a role is partly technique."

They were alone during this conversation, which took place after a rehearsal in the club where the studio was quartered. They were standing at the window of a dusty hall with chairs lined upside down against the walls.

"To illustrate my point, I shall weep for you if you wish," said Tsvetukhin with a smile.

He glanced out of the window. A fine rain was falling. Mud glistened on the cobblestones of the street. A drayman with the skirts of his kaftan tucked up into his girdle was goading on his jade with the reins. The load was too much for the poor creature, whose hoofs kept slipping on the round pates of the cobbles. As it stumbled along it jerked its head on its skinny neck, which seemed escaping from the yoke.

Annochka saw Egor Pavlovich's black eyes gradually expand and begin to shine as though lacquered. Then the upper lids trembled and a thread of moisture appeared along the lower ones, gathering into transparent drops which grew, until they overflowed and trickled slowly down his cheeks.

Egor Pavlovich was weeping as he gazed out into the street.

"Don't!" cried Annochka impulsively. Tears had sprung to her own eyes.

He wiped his face with his handkerchief.

"Now I shall show you how I can pale, if you wish."

Grabbing Annochka's hand, he clamped his fingers about it and thrust his body away from her. She saw his limp lower lip and half-open mouth. The colour drained from his face; his features became pinched and lifeless.

With difficulty she freed her hand from his grasp.

He laughed, delighted with the success of his lesson.

"Do you know what that is? It is the resurrection of grief once suffered, the resurrection of fear once experienced."

He looked down at her expectantly from lofty heights.

"You must experience life. And then revive this experience. Your body will do the rest. It must be as responsive to your emotions as an instrument in the hand of a musician."

She did not like the expectation in his eyes.

She realized that this did not answer the question as to what Luise should be like. But she was astonished by the knowledge that one could exercise one's emotions like a pianist his fingers, and by means of the "technique" acquired, rouse similar emotions in others.

She tried summoning tears at will. When left alone, she made herself recall moments when she had cried. But this did not make her want to cry now as she had cried then. Nothing came of her efforts.

But on awakening one night, Annochka began to think of her mother. In the most minute detail she recalled those dead hands warmed by the sun, with the needle pricks in the finger tips. So vividly did she remember the touch of her cheek on those work-roughened fingers that she was overwhelmed with self-pity. She discovered that her pillow was wet, and guessed that she had been crying in her sleep. Once more she called up the vision of her mother's hands, and again the tears flowed. She wiped her eyes on the pillowcase, and after lying there for a while, fell asleep, oppressed by a sense of guilt.

In the morning she again thought of her mother—of her mother's hands—and again she wept. She was ashamed to be making such use of her mother's memory, and she even feared the blasphemy of repeating the process of recollection. But repeat it she did, and in spite of her fear and shame, she was happy to discover that she could always achieve what she wanted: as soon as she recalled how she had kissed her mother's hands, the tears sprang to her eyes. She began to implore her mother's forgiveness and to assure her that her tears were profoundly sincere.

What, indeed, was Annochka to do if she had suffered no great pain other than parting with her mother, and if the memory of this was the only thing which at any moment could cause her to weep? She built up her "technique" on her mother's memory, but this was in the name of art, than which nothing was more sacred to her.

If she wished to become an actress, she would have to repeat one and the same emotion a hundred times over on the stage, and she realized that she could not make herself love or hate some character a hundred times over if this love and hate were not reduced to some technical reaction. She must develop "technique," and so far the only source which had been pointed out to her was reality—the knowledge of life she herself had accumulated. She had not yet learned of the love of an actor for his role (so far she had played only one role, and that only once), and did not know that an emotion which perhaps an actor had never experienced in real life could involuntarily be roused in him thousands of times by a role which was dear to his heart.

With all the strength of her being Annochka wished to become an actress. In her fancy she had many times traversed the long path leading to the realization of her dream. Perhaps it was the ordinary, common-place path imagined by every girl who aspired to become an actress, but for her it was unique and foreordained. And exquisite memories were associated with it.

After having arranged Annochka's admittance to the gymnasium, Vera Nikandrovna forbade her going backstage. Obedience was made difficult by the fact that Olga Ivanovna sewed costumes for the theatre and sent her daughter to deliver the work.

"If you want me to help your daughter with her schooling, you must put a stop to it," insisted Vera Nikandrovna.

It was easier for Olga Ivanovna to obey than for Annochka. The mother dreamed of having her daughter get an education, but the daughter found backstage infinitely more interesting than the classroom. However, the influence of Vera Nikandrovna held sway.

As Annochka grew up, the lure of the theatre assumed a new form: the mysteries of backstage were indeed intriguing, but even more intriguing were the mysteries revealed on the stage, where one beheld the magic of life being created before his very eyes.

In this respect too Vera Nikandrovna was demanding.

"It is just because the theatre reveals the workings of the human spirit that every visit should be an event," she said. "You can't glance into the human spirit casually, like into a tearoom, can you now? You must enter the theatre as though it were a temple."

With pedagogical consistency, she extended these precepts to books.

"To glance through a book is not to read it. You must read a book as though hearing someone's confession. Penetrating deeply into it. Only then will it fully reveal itself to you, so that you can discover its full beauty. Just as you can never appreciate the beauty of a forest by observing it from a distance or walking along the edge without penetrating its depths, so you can never achieve the joy of knowledge which a book can bring you if you do not learn to give yourself up wholly to it."

As she said this, Vera Nikandrovna smiled so tenderly and shook her head so convincingly that Annochka felt ashamed of herself, for it was true that she did not give herself up to serious reading, and that she was ready to run to the theatre at any time of the day or night, if only for a minute. Yet despite this seeming casualness, the theatre remained a temple for her. Indeed, it embraced all the temples of all the world, and lured her like life itself.

554

And so, as time passed, it became necessary to replace demands with advice, and finally advice with a resigned smile.

Annochka graduated from school at a time when all the traditions of the old gymnasium had not yet died. One day the woman who had formerly been her teacher of philology and was now teaching literature, approached Annochka at the end of the lesson, and after first complimenting her on her composition, asked softly:

"Parabukina, do your folks allow you to write with the new orthography?"

She wanted her pupil to hang on to at least something from the good old days.

But already boys had appeared within the walls of this once girls' gymnasium; already a School Director had taken the place of the Preceptress; no longer did a teacher of scriptures pass from classroom to classroom making the sign of the cross; and finally, on their own initiative the girls invited a professional actor to coach the performance of *The Minor* which they intended staging.

This was a break with the old tradition according to which the play presented by the graduating class was always coached by the teacher of philology. And this break was effected by Annochka Parabukina.

At the head of a group of girls as nervous as herself, Annochka called on Egor Pavlovich Tsvetukhin.

The girls' visit was unexpected, and it took him some time to make himself presentable. Tsvetukhin accepted their coming as homage from theatre fans, a thing which had become quite rare at that time.

He had been sitting in his night shirt over a cup of cold tea, brooding unhappily as he cleaned the makhorka out of his pipe. He had just put out the drunken Mefody, who had come to ask for money and to complain that his head was as foggy as on a blue Monday.

From the other room came the sounds of Agnia Lvovna clearing her throat and trying her voice. A year before she had returned to Egor Pavlovich for the seventh time, in the hope of at last setting up a happy home based on mutual fidelity. He listened inimically to her tobacco-hoarse contralto and remembered the years gone by when he had referred to Agnia Lvovna's eyes as orbs, and her mouth as a rosebud. At that time her prettiness had been nature's own, if a bit oleographic. Agnia Lvovna made a pleasing impression, and stage managers kept offering her jobs. until her lack of talent became generally known.

Agnia Lvovna was something non-essential to

the life of Tsvetukhin, yet she had been attached to him like something essential throughout his youth. When she had first left him, he had tried to give her no further thought, but she made this impossible. As a result, he not only came to like her less and less, but to dislike her more and more. Yet he was unable to force her to leave him once and for all, since her desire not to leave him was more insistent than his desire to have her go.

Agnia Lvovna belonged to that obsolescent category of wives who are comparatively happy when they lead their husbands on a leash like a lap dog—but only comparatively happy, because they become extremely irritated if the lap dog pulls too strongly at the leash, and they begin to weep and tear their hair and grab for the smelling salts if the leash breaks.

Egor Pavlovich did not answer the demands of such a dog-fan. His searchings and inventions made of him a dreamer, a type not given to finding happiness in submission. Perhaps a chain would have held him more effectively than this leash that he yanked and shook and tore. But the charms of Agnia Lvovna were not sufficient to forge a chain. She could only mend the flimsy leash, fastening it again and again about his unruly neck.

With the passage of time, nothing was left of Tsvetukhin's searchings but old hobbies and a certain restlessness. The violin was abandoned, since his fingers lost their elasticity quicker than they acquired virtuosity. He lost interest in his dreams of new flying machines, since the progress made in aeroplane designing during the war left all of Tsvetukhin's once bold concepts far behind. To prevent falling asleep evenings over his fruitless mathematical calculations, he took to playing solitaire.

There remained only the theatre.

Egor Pavlovich was sincerely and ardently devoted to his art. Above everything else he wished to be an innovator in the theatre. But here too time dulled his ardour. His flight turned into a run, his run into an even stride, and even this stride was sometimes checked by indecision.

Tsvetukhin often argued with actors by force of habit, rather than conviction. His stage experience taught him customs and conventions which solved problems more simply than any innovation could. Gradually he adapted himself to the ponderous inflexibility of routine, and with growing indifference sinned against his true nature. His older colleagues had long since slid down the hill of routine. They did not even consider it reprehensible if an actor remained indifferent to the great purposes of art.

"Don't try to teach us," said his elders. "Just show us what you can do. We'll follow your example if we find it to our liking. Didn't we once take example from actors like Sarmatov and Orlenev?"

The first thunder of revolution sent Tsvetukhin's spirit soaring. It seemed that the new epoch would do for man what had been beyond his own poor strength. Tsvetukhin imagined that he could immediately convert the whole theatre to his ideas. But there were few who cared to listen to him. They were too used to hearing his challenging speeches. They considered him as queer as ever, and would not concede that his platform was born of the revolution. So they met him with the same old retorts:

"You're talking about what *ought* to be, brother. But art is what *is*. Got to show us something first. Who knows what will come of those ideas of yours? An actor's a doubting Thomas—won't believe what he hasn't seen with his own eyes."

It was necessary for him to tread an unpaved road. Or perhaps to strike out across virgin soil.

Thus Egor Pavlovich was sitting brooding over his fate and listening to the hated contralto, whose every aspect he found forced, unnatural and affected. She loved to become kittenish, curling up on the sofa with the knees of her peg legs poking up

559

like pyramids. She imitated actresses with hail-fellow-well-met manners of slapping their friends on the back, swaggering along with their hands on their hips, embracing everybody like long lost friends, and exchanging resounding kisses. She did all this with the vulgarity of a fishwoman, and everything in Egor Pavlovich rose up in protest.

He was just about to interrupt the vocal exercises by knocking on the wall, when the girls arrived.

He hastily threw on a bathrobe and straightened up the room, before letting them in. The girls crowded in the doorway, lacking the courage to cross the threshold of their idol's temple.

It is amazing what a physiological influence worship wields over an individual. Every joint in the body of Egor Pavlovich sang as he saw the girls' flaming cheeks and their bright eyes, which they dared not so much as wink. It was as though some intoxication coursed through his veins, bringing him cheer. It was a tall, graceful, youthful Tsvetukhin who stood before these maids, and not at all the Tsvetukhin who had been playing with his spoon and fighting down the spleen occasioned by Agnia Lvovna's singing.

Annochka, the initiator of this undertaking, spoke as befitted the head of the deputation:

"We have come to you, Egor Pavlovich, as students of the graduating class of school number. . . ."

He smiled graciously and encouragingly, grasping the intention of the students long before Annochka reached the invitation for him to be present at one of their rehearsals and then perhaps help them stage the play.

"*The Minor?*" he said, lifting his head as though about to nod to an old acquaintance. "And which of you is to play Sophia?"

"I am," answered Annochka with a boldness contradicted by a blush.

"Ah, you . . ." said Egor Pavlovich, leaving his words hanging in the air.

He had not seen Annochka since the revolution, and now she seemed even more unexpected than when he had once met her during the war— after an interval of several years. Then he had found her already a young girl in a high-school uniform, and could not imagine that this was the same Annochka with flaxen pigtails who had once hung about the greenrooms and run out to buy cigarettes for the actors.

He immediately agreed to visit the school. He sensed the prospects which might be opened by his contact with these frightened and ecstatic maids who scarcely knew to what they were aspiring.

Furthermore, he was goaded to consent by a keen curiosity about Annochka. Ecstasy burned more brightly within her than within her friends, and she struggled more boldly with her timidity.

After working a while at the school, he became convinced of the correctness of his intuition. His every word was law for these young folks. They unquestioningly accepted any interpretation he gave of the characters from *The Minor,* and tried to fit their feet exactly into the footsteps of their teacher.

To be sure, the only thing revolutionary about this production was the novelty of such contact and the absence of all the harness incumbering actors hitched to the theatre. Here sincerity was not labelled naïveté. These maids still exclaimed "How I cried!" unashamed of the spontaneity of their reactions and unaware of the fact that under such circumstances sophistication demanded that an actress say, with a crooked smile: "I simply bawled, my darling!"

Naturally the performance of *The Minor* was like any other school play, even to the hilarious accident. When Madame Prostakova was running up and down the stage at the end of the fourth act, her skirt extinguished the kerosene lamp in the prompter's box, causing the prompter to give a loud sneeze.

But during rehearsals Tsvetukhin experienced a new zest for work and realized that at last he had found fertile soil for his ideas.

He decided to form a troupe composed primarily of young people who as yet had had no stage experience. He knew he would be charged with becoming an amateur, but this did not frighten him, for he also knew that the greatest discoveries in art had been made as a result of the searchings of amateurs.

Annochka supplied the strongest stimulus to the new undertaking. There was no doubt in Tsvetukhin's mind that she should go on the stage. Her sharp elbows, slender neck, and dangling arms indicated that she had not fully matured. But it was just this youthful awkwardness which gave a strange vitality to her portrayal of Sophia the minute she donned the costume. She was almost too vivid, and her facial expressions changed almost too swiftly—from embarrassment to sullenness, from mockery to severity. But on the stage this liveliness was transformed into emotion: her mockery became sensitivity to her partner; her shyness—purity; her sullenness—thoughtfulness.

Egor Pavlovich was unaware of how his admiration for Annochka's talent changed into adoration of the owner of this talent. During the rehearsing of *The Minor* and later, while going through the complicated process of organizing the dramatic studio, Egor Pavlovich experienced a renascence. He had known such moments earlier in life, but this time it seemed inexpressibly fresh, like spring suddenly discovered in full bloom. Everyone except Annochka herself, who was much too engrossed in her work, was aware of the fact that Tsvetukhin followed her like her shadow.

It was a motley troupe that Tsvetukhin gathered together. Experienced actors were added to uninitiated young people. The studio had the good fortune to obtain the patronage of a military club, and this meant bread. The actors came to rehearsals with sacks on their backs; even Egor Pavlovich had a ration bag which he kept ever with him. It was with donations of millet and dried fish that he pacified Agnia Lvovna, who complained that even in "their own troupe" her talents were ignored.

Egor Pavlovich himself was willing to live on air, rehearsals, and his daily walk with Annochka, when seeing her home. When one day he put on a Russian blouse embroidered in red flowers, and Annochka exclaimed "How becoming!", he swore to wear the blouse all his life, without ever taking it off. He grew younger, and it was as if he were rehearsing the role of Ferdinand for the first time, though actually he had played it years before and had derived much joy from it.

He had chosen *Love and Intrigue* as their first performance because this romantic piece was highly popular during the revolution, surcharged as it was with passions people had hesitated to give rein to in the old days. The experienced actors found in the play nothing more than a collection of roles that had been played over and over again and were now destined to be played once more, and they did not overexert themselves, curious only to see what would come of Tsvetukhin's efforts with these youthful amateurs.

As soon as Annochka demonstrated her talent, people came to her with all kinds of advice. One expounded on the French school, another on realism, a third on Stanislavsky, while a fourth simply pointed out the indispensability of a euphonious stage name.

"What kind of a name is that, child: Parabukina!" exclaimed an actor who specialized in old men's parts. "Just think how it'll sound when they start shouting from the gallery: '... bu-u-u-kina!'"

"A person's deeds embellish his name," said Annochka, becoming pedantic to hide her hurt.

"They embellish it to be sure. But go ahead and try to embellish your name if it's Wagtail. You need something more elevated—like Para ... bella, Para ... cella.... Something like that: We had a case once: a fellow playing the hero. He could make

565

your heart stand still. But the public would have none of him. Why? Didn't like his name. Stupkin! So he moved to another town. Acted like a ham. Turned even his own stomach. But the public went into raptures. Why? Changed his name. Sylvester!"

Mefody, who had been listening to the conversation, tried to console Annochka.

"Don't listen to him! Call him an actor? A waiter, that's what he is! Always trying to hand out advice, like the serpent with the apple."

"I simply can't understand, Annochka!" said Agnia Lvovna. "Why is Egor Pavlovich such a bug about memorizing lines? What's left for the prompter to do? I remember reading in some French novel—Balzac, I think—about a young star named Florina. Her greenroom was packed with admirers, and she chased them out just before it was time for her to make her appearance on the stage. The bell was already ringing. 'Get out!' she said. 'Give me a chance to read my role and try to understand what it's all about.' Just think, after the bell had gone! Trying to understand what it was all about just before she stepped on the stage! There's an actress for you! And here you are studying and studying for months on end! It's not commas and periods you want to act. It's something else. Have you got that something else? We'll see, darling!"

All these loyal soldiers of the stage, who had spent their lives lined up at the gates of Fame, lavishly offered their advice to this poor novice, and if Annochka did not lose her head in this welter of advice, it was only because she placed Egor Pavlovich above everyone else and tried to listen only to him, if anyone.

Perhaps he was incapable of explaining the theory of acting, or how to play Luise Miller when you are Annochka Parabukina, but he was a true artist, and therefore experience took the place of explanations. He offered Annochka solutions which he himself had found, and only time could tell whether she was capable of understanding them and whether she wished to accept them.

Finally, at the end of October, the play was ready.

* 34 *

The play was ready.

They performed it in the regiment barracks next to the university. The huge hall, which had not yet been heated, was filled from end to end with new recruits in army coats and sheepskins, some of them—the patrol guards—with rifles in hand. But among the audience there were also many civilians, who had not feared to cross half the town in the darkness and cold for the sake of an event which the name of Tsvetukhin made intriguing. It goes without saying that the first rows were reserved for the families and friends of the new actors.

Parabukin, who had never before sat so close to the stage, deported himself with painful respectability. He had buoyed up his spirits with only the tiniest sip before leaving, a fact which he had carefully concealed. But he was the first to become conscious of the heat in the overcrowded hall, and began to pat his forehead with a neatly folded pocket handkerchief.

Dorogomilov had been ailing all fall, but he could not resist the boys' pleadings that he be present. His little friends sat squirming on their chairs, now stretching their necks to make sure they could see everything, now twisting their close-cropped heads about to view the hall. Their eyes were already shining with enthusiasm, brightly reflecting the electricity which the club had been supplied with for the occasion.

Lisa and Anatoli Mikhailovich were sitting off to one side, where they could keep an eye on Vitya without being observed by Vera Nikandrovna. Lisa did not wish to be conspicuous. She was agitated by her surroundings, which did not entirely resemble a theatre, but called forth innumerable associations.

Vera Nikandrovna had saved a place for Kirill, who arrived at the very last minute, when the lights had already gone out and conversation had ceased.

Just before that, Annochka had been glancing out into the hall through a tiny slit in the curtains. Egor Pavlovich had told her to choose some face in the audience which pleased her, and then to play only for that person.

"I always act for some particular person," he said, "and imagine that the individual of my choice will be my judge and deliver my sentence."

She ran her eyes over dozens of faces, unable to decide on any particular one. She was having a peep into the world. A peep into her own future, which she was now going forth to meet. Her heart pounded.

Suddenly she saw Kirill making his way down the aisle. At that moment the hall was plunged in darkness. She became faint with terror and would have collapsed, had not Ferdinand approached at that moment and whispered in her ear:

"Enough, Luise. Time to begin."

The action of *Love and Intrigue* absorbs the audience from the very first act, the more so if the audience is unsophisticated. The story presented on the stage is immediately comprehensible to all, and arouses interest at once by plunging straight into the action.

569

The fact that the actors are wearing waistcoats and powdered wigs and slippers with gold buckles does not estrange them from the audience. The unusualness of their appearance only whets interest in what is happening to them. The significance of a play lies deeper than the masks.

Whose heart could resist the ardour of that youth, or the love of that maid, a love so pure and innocent and longing for expression that it defied concealment? Whose blood did not boil at the sight of that wrathful father, accusing his wife of indulging the dangerous attachment of their daughter? Who was not familiar with those villainous lords, willing to destroy the happiness of others for the sake of their own greed?

Beyond the walls of this barracks hall—out in the town—beyond the town—throughout the whole vast land—a struggle was being waged against violence by those who had been the age-old victims of this violence and now had risen up to secure their liberation. The Red Army men filling the hall found echoes of their own feelings in the adventures depicted in this bourgeois tragedy. There on the boards, violence was rampant. Here in the hall, violence was hated. The hall was filled with a thirst for justice. On the boards, justice was being violated, and the unrestrained sympathy of the audience swept in a wave across the footlights.

No, Luise's sufferings were not in vain. She was not alone in her contempt for brute force, in her proud disdain for those in power, nor even in her grief and loneliness. The soldiers of the revolution, seeking truth in all aspects of life, demanded truth from the theatre as well. They found an element of this truth in the defenceless girl, and the more elevated were the sufferings of Luise, the more willing were they to extend her a helping hand.

The silence in the hall was as profound as that of the fields on a moonless night. The strongest emotion of all those which gripped the observers was astonishment—astonishment that these painted figures in coloured waistcoats and lacy caps were living as intensely as real people.

From the stage poured streams and rivers and oceans of words which did not resemble any of the words used by ordinary people, yet their magic conveyed ideas comprehensible to all.

The pompousness and stiltedness of Ferdinand's exclamations could not keep the public from sympathizing with the graceful, impassioned Tsvetukhin when with youthful lavishness he poured his vows of eternal love at the feet of Luise.

All of these soldiers wrapped in greatcoats and coughing into their fists so as not to disturb their neighbours, trembled lest they miss a single syllable pronounced by Tsvetukhin's velvety voice. Each of them translated Ferdinand's cabalistic declaration into his own tongue, and perhaps thought that someday he too would speak the words of the hero: "Let mountains rise between us—they will serve only as a stairway by which I shall attain the embrace of Luise! The storms of hostile fate only fan the flames of my passion; danger only enhances the charms of my Luise!" And perhaps each of them dreamed that some day, someone like Luise would answer him in a torrent of terror and passion: "Enough! I implore thy silence! If thou couldst know! . . ."

This Luise with the difficult name of Parabukina scratched in ink on the bills won the audience by her maidenly simplicity, sincerity, and suffering. Here was the true Luise. But perhaps this was only an illusion. Perhaps her emotion actually stemmed from her fear that she would not be able to cope with a task so brazenly assumed. But her fear of the audience was in some inexplicable way swallowed up by another fear—the fear roused by her desperate, ill-fated love.

Lisa followed the acting of Annochka with envy and amazement, scarcely believing that this was the same girl who, when Lisa was already tasting the delights of the theatre and dreaming of it as of the highest joy earth could hold, was growing up unnoticed, like an inconspicuous wayside plant. Ah, how the plant had grown and strengthened! This was no child. This was a woman on the threshold of her blossoming. Where could Annochka have learned those flowing gestures? Who had taught her to wear those old-fashioned gowns with such grace? Could it have been Tsvetukhin? She was acting with Tsvetukhin. With Tsvetukhin himself. Annochka, who as a child had timidly referred to him as "the dark one." How would Lisa have acted with Tsvetukhin? Surely she would have made a good actress—with her proud walk and her lovely face. But it was the plain and awkward Annochka who had become the actress. While Lisa would probably live and die in sad obscurity, an ordinary provincial woman. But was not that all for the better? Perhaps fate had spared Lisa humiliation. In ordinary life she retained her charm; on the stage she might have been insignificant. Who could tell? Had not the gods been generous in allowing Lisa to continue worshipping the stage in secret, as most women worship it?

For a second Lisa withdrew her eyes from the play and sought Kirill.

His body was tense and leaning slightly forward. In the rosy light from the stage his face seemed paler than usual, and was etched sharply against the shadowy background. From such a distance it was difficult to define his exact expres-

573

sion, but it was clear that Kirill was gazing at Luise.

The astonishment experienced by the audience was apparently conveyed to him as well. But he was astonished not by the performance as a whole, but by Annochka alone. How could he have failed to see the dominant, most important aspect of her personality: her talent! Her nature was incomparably richer and more gifted than he had imagined. When he thought about her, he realized there was no one with whom she was to be compared.

A tender smile crept slowly over his face and lingered there. The sufferings depicted beyond the footlights were too sincere and innocent to leave even a hardened heart untouched.

When Luise jumped up off her knees and wrenched herself from the arms of her father, rushing after Ferdinand with the cry: "Stay! Stay! Where art thou going? Mother! Father! He is abandoning us at such a moment!" Kirill strained forward and cleared his throat in order to smother a strange sound rising in his breast. He remembered how he had laughed that night when he had watched Annochka through the window and heard that tortured cry, which had first frightened, then amused him. "Stay! Stay!" But now he had no desire to laugh. His emotions brought him closer to Annochka than he had been on that evening, when he had first embraced her. In the effort to hide his feelings he kept leaning further forward, until he was on the very edge of his chair. This made it all the more convenient for Vera Nikandrovna to observe him from where she was sitting settled back, constantly shifting her gaze from Annochka to her son. All possible doubts in her mind were dispersed by what she saw.

The second act ended in a triumph, and the audience began to call for the actors, who came out holding hands, and their happy excitement seemed to be transmitted to the curtain, which billowed like the sea behind them.

While bowing, Annochka sought Kirill with her eyes. Suddenly her dazzling smile vanished. She saw a Red Army man approach Izvekov and whisper something in his ear. Immediately Kirill rose and followed the Red Army man to the exit.

The audience continued to applaud and to call out the names of the actors. Annochka caught a young voice crying "Para-bu-u-kin-a!" She found the sound impressive and even musical, despite that long-drawn "u-u-u" in the . . . b-u-u-kina. But this sudden disappointment prevented her from experiencing the full joy of her first success. Kirill had not glanced at her, and probably he had left the club altogether—after all, he had more important things to think of than amateur performances!

For the fourth time the actors had joined hands,

575

the hero pulling the heroine along with the whole troupe in their wake, when the Red Army man who had just led Kirill out of the hall appeared in the wings.

"May I speak to you a moment, Comrade Tsvetukhin?" he said.

The few words he spoke led Tsvetukhin to abandon his intentions, and in a second everything changed.

The stagehands stopped shifting scenery and stood expectantly, hammers and pliers in hand. The rumpled prompter crawled out of his booth; the fire inspector left his post; extras in the gendarme uniforms of some fierce government came straggling up. The actors were chagrined, for the applause in the hall had not yet died down.

"Don't go away, comrades, don't go away!" cried the producer's assistant, waving a dog-eared copy of Schiller over his head.

"The entire troupe!" ordered Tsvetukhin.

"Shall I put out the lights in the auditorium?" shouted the electrician across the length of the stage.

"Line up in a semicircle, comrades, in a semicircle," said the bustling assistant.

"What's happened? Are we to be photographed or what?"

"Call the make-up man! Call Maria Ivanovna!"

"Actors up ahead! Closer! Closer! Luise in the centre! President! Hofmarshal! Closer together!"

"What we going to do, sing?"

"Comrades stagehands! Get in line! Where you going?"

"The right-hand spot! The spot's gone out!"

"A meeting? What about?"

"Give a long ring in the auditorium. Who's at the bell?"

"Ready, Egor Pavlovich! Everybody's here!"

Tsvetukhin swept the troupe with his eye, took his place in the very centre of the semicircle, and nodded to his assistant.

"Let her go!" cried the latter, lifting the tattered Schiller over his head and sweeping it down as a signal.

Slowly the curtains parted.

The audience began to settle down in a hum of conversation and a burst of renewed applause. Nobody knew just what was going to happen, and many accepted the unexpected ceremony as an expression of the troupe's gratitude for such a warm reception. Everything was new these days: the public did not know old theatre traditions, and the theatre made no effort to preserve them.

But suddenly Izvekov crossed to the centre of the stage and held up his hand. Everyone became quiet.

"Comrades," he said, in a loud, strained voice which in no way resembled the modulated voices of the actors. It was so unexpected that everything theatrical seemed to fall away, making room for something totally different.

"We have just received a telegram stating that we have won a tremendous victory on the Southern front."

Once more a hum passed through the hall, dying down at once.

"The Red Cavalry troops of Comrade Budyonny have completely routed the White Cavalry Corps of Mamontov and Shkuro near Voronezh. Voronezh. . . ."

They did not give him a chance to finish. It was not a hum, but a storm which swept the hall now. The cries seemed to be vying with the clapping, the stamping of feet with the pounding of rifle butts against the floor. Red Army men jumped up first from the back rows, then from the front ones, and came crowding down the aisles toward the stage.

Kirill again raised his hand and moved closer to the crowd, which reluctantly quieted down.

"Voronezh has been cleared of the enemy. Tremendous trophies have fallen into our hands. The Whites are fleeing."

Once more he was interrupted by youthful cries of "Hurrah!" and another outburst of applause. It

578

seemed to Kirill that the myriad faces of the crowd merged into one beaming smile.

"We are expecting to receive details any minute. The telegram states that the enemy is still being pursued. We are licking Mamontov's Cossacks and Shkuro's volunteers. This, comrades, is the beginning of their end. Denikin will surely be defeated. He and all that he stands for will be done away with for all time. The Red Army is digging them a bottomless grave. Long live the glorious Soviet workers' and peasants' cavalry!"

This was a challenge to rapture, and rapture ensued, rocking the building, through which the roars echoed and re-echoed, wave after wave.

All the civilians sitting up front also rose from their seats. Pavlik, followed by Vanya and Vitya, climbed up on their chairs. Arseni Romanovich held his hands over his head, and his grey locks shook in rhythm to his clapping. For some reason Parabukin waved his neatly folded handkerchief. Lisa kept her eyes on her son as she applauded, waiting for him to turn around so that she could nod him off the chair. Even Oznobishin circumspectly beat his fingers against his little palm.

The actors crowded around Izvekov on the stage, breaking up their semicircle. They kept up the ovation, preventing Kirill from retiring backstage. His khaki tunic struck a jarring note amid the colourful costumes of the 18th century—the satin ribbons of the Hofmarshal, the lace and chiffon of Lady Milford, descendant of the Duke of Norfolk, the silks and velvet of the President. Izvekov alone displayed his own dark hair in this encirclement of powdered wigs. And he felt as awkward as though he were the one in trumpery, while everyone else was in ordinary attire. To cover his embarrassment he thrust his hands into his pockets, but immediately pulled them out to offer his hand to Tsvetukhin—why, he did not know. He gave the latter's fingers a quick grip, and then, even quicker, squeezed the hand of the happy, laughing Annochka.

It seemed to him that this caused the applause to increase, and he felt that his gesture had caused the audience to shift its attention from the news of victory to the actors, and this was unforgivable. He turned and left the stage.

Annochka overtook him. Still laughing, she said in a loud voice:

"I suppose you won't stay to see the rest of the play after such news."

He stopped, and for the first time saw at close hand her powdered neck and bare shoulders and lacquered lips and the deep blue of her eyes, which seemed to have run over and smeared her long lids. But from behind all this, Annochka looked at him with her wondrously clear glance—the same Annochka he always saw in his mind's eye—the Annochka whom no make-up could mar or embellish, and who was waiting tremulously for his answer.

"No, I shall stay to the end. I shall only go to the telephone every once in a while. In that room over there."

He waited. He could not tear himself away from what he beheld beyond the make-up, as beyond a frosted windowpane.

"You are wonderful," he said.

She moved away slightly.

"Put someone on duty at the telephone," she said.

"I must be there myself."

"Then put somebody in your place in the auditorium, so that they can report to you what a mess I make of it."

"I shall go out only during the intermission." He smiled.

Her expression contained not a shade of caprice or coquettishness—she simply doubted the seriousness of his promise. The other actors watched them from a distance, and a stagehand shouted. "Make way!" Kirill nodded and left.

Tsvetukhin immediately approached Annochka.

"What did he say?"

"He likes it," she answered casually.

While the play was on she could not see Kirill (in general she was afraid to glance into the hall), and during the intermissions his seat was empty. Thus she did not know whether he had kept his word or not.

Once the performance had started rolling smoothly, it rolled on to the end without mishap. Indeed, it was received with growing enthusiasm. Perhaps the elation incident to the news of victory affected the audience, for it became more receptive than ever, clapping unsparingly. But the actors attributed their success solely to their own efforts, and carried on well, and with self-confidence.

The curtain calls at the end of the last act were stormy and repeated. The audience rushed toward the stage. The actors applauded Tsvetukhin. He applauded the troupe, and took Annochka by the hand to lead her forward. There was no counting the bows made to the public.

Parabukin stood proudly awaiting congratulations. Arseni Romanovich was the first to shake his hand vigorously.

"What do you think of that, now?" he said. "Great promise. A real star, discovered right here at home. Inborn talent, so to speak. And all Tsvetukhin's doings. Splendid!"

Tikhon Platonovich wiped his brow with his handkerchief, which had long since become damp

and had lost its neat folds. He nodded his head and
cleared his throat importantly. Catching his son by
the sleeve and fishing him out of the crowd, he
bent down and said to him:

"You and me are millionaires now, Pavlik!
Egor Pavlovich will shower gold on that sister of
yours!"

With a slow glance Lisa followed Annochka as
she came and went before the footlights. And at
that moment Lisa had no thought either for Oznobishin, who was waiting for her patiently, or for
Vitya. Still she kept asking herself where that slip
of a girl had found the courage to enter such a con-
test and emerge the victor? And still she discovered no answer. Suddenly she noticed Kirill standing almost next to her.

Straining forward, he was staring over Vera
Nikandrovna's shoulder at the stage. His lips
twitched. Apparently he was trying to be a severe
judge, but his emotions were running away with
him, and through this conflict glinted sparks of
joy. Conscious that he was being watched, he turned
around, and coloured on meeting Lisa's eye. He
went over and greeted her.

"I see that you too are delighted with Annochka," she said.

"It seems to me that we have witnessed the
birth of a new theatre. I had no idea that Tsvetu-

khin would be able to do anything like it. Just look at the reception the Red Army men have given them!"

"Especially Annochka, isn't that true?" insisted Lisa.

"Yes," said Kirill evasively. "But it's easy to act for such an unspoiled audience."

"I don't agree with you. Everything has to be made so obvious."

"Not at all. The people are sufficiently intelligent," he said. "But you are right in the sense that it is always easier to leave things vague."

The hall was still noisy, and they spoke in loud voices, standing so close together that their shoulders almost touched.

"I'm glad that I met you."

"So am I."

"I lacked the courage to come and thank you."

"For what?"

"For helping father. He has been home for the last two weeks."

"He ... oh, yes: I understand. Only I had nothing to do with it."

"That's not true."

He laughed.

"Why should I accept other people's laurels? It was all the doings of Ragozin. He knew your father."

"But that's not true. I heard rumours that Ragozin had interceded. My husband went to thank him, but Ragozin said he knew nothing about it and almost put my husband out of his office."

"No fooling with Ragozin," laughed Kirill again. "He's not one of your patron saints either. In general, I don't think your father has anyone to thank in particular. Apparently he got whatever punishment was coming to him."

Lisa moved her shoulder as far from Kirill as the crowd permitted and silently looked him in the eye.

"As usual, you fulfilled your filial duty and have a right to be content," he said, "what else do you want?"

"What's that? Old scores?" she asked bitterly.

"It's—the truth," he answered dryly and glanced up. "Apparently the actors aren't coming out any more. Time to go home."

He hastily took his leave.

It had indeed become quieter in the hall, though many were still clapping, and for the last time Tsvetukhin appeared, holding Annochka by the hand.

She looked as though she were still dizzy from success. Her smile had become fixed and her bows wooden. With growing alarm she kept searching for Kirill, and with growing disappointment retired behind the curtain.

At last she ran to her tiny dressing room—a corner partitioned off by plyboard, and almost fell onto a chair, covering her face with her hands. The dreams of her most sacred moments of solitude had been realized—she had played the main role and been a success. And here she was, feeling nothing but weariness, and a dull sort of misery. She was on the verge of weeping with exhaustion.

She had just taken a deep breath when the door shook with pounding, and was immediately flung open.

Tsvetukhin rushed in. He snatched off his wig and swung it by the tail like a trophy. Only a step away from Annochka he opened wide his arms.

"You darling! Here, let me kiss you!"

All her weariness vanished. She jumped up, overturning the chair, and threw her arms about his neck. He embraced her and kissed her lips. Then, tearing himself away, he cried:

"Once more, my adorable actress! Once more!"

She herself kissed him. Again his mouth sought her lips. She tried to withdraw, but he held her head in the crook of his arm. She wrenched away. He spoke quickly, and very softly.

"Once more, honey.... Quickly!"

She gazed at his strange eyes—dark and fearful.

She stooped to pick up the chair and sat down at the dressing table with her back to Tsvetukhin. In the glass she saw him wipe his forehead, which was sharply divided into two parts—the upper part, swarthy and crowned with greying dark hair; and the lower part, orange with paint, which emphasized the wrinkles.

"Please leave me, Egor Pavlovich. I have to change."

Tsvetukhin remained standing there for another moment. Suddenly he swung his wig as though to throw it away, turned on his heel and went out, carefully closing the door behind him.

Annochka sat motionless. All of her exhaustion returned, robbing her of the strength to lift her hands to remove the hairpins holding her cap. At the border line between the noise of the hall and the lonely silence of backstage, she sensed the beginning of a new and sinister life.

Suddenly she heard a woman's voice. Annochka recognized it and began to undress.

"Well, where are you hiding, darling?" sang Agnia Lvovna in her hoarse contralto. "Here we are, come to congratulate you, and you've hidden yourself away!"

She broke into the dressing room, grabbed Annochka from behind, and began to plant kisses on her ear, neck, and cheeks.

"There's no denying it, no denying it!" she exclaimed between kisses, "you were simply too sweet for words, and with such artistic temperament! Really, I would never have believed it! To be sure, you still lack sufficient inner fire. But how can this be expected from such an infant! That's the truth, darling, don't take offence. And then, of course, you haven't yet mastered any particular school. I'd been on the stage four years before I played Luise. What a furore! Unforgettable! And you expect everything right from the very start! Naturally your interpretation can't help being superficial! But that's nothing, nothing at all. Don't be discouraged, and for goodness' sake, don't dare think of crying! The most important thing is that you were simply sweet, and you got it across to the public. The school will come with time. As for the fire. . . ."

Here Agnia Lvovna pressed her flaming cheek to Annochka's ear:

"Don't think of giving in to Egor Pavlovich in this respect!"

"How could you!" cried Annochka, starting away.

"Ah, my child, do you think I don't know him? He'll be coming to kiss you presently. And then he'll begin complaining about his fate. He'll say that I terrorize him, and that you are the only one who can put an end to my tyranny over his ruined life. Don't believe him. That's all nonsense. He's just an old Lovelace, and if I didn't keep him in check, he'd never be Tsvetukhin. He'd always be running after some girl. But I have made a genius out of him!"

Annochka attempted to protest and even got up, trying to free herself from this furious entanglement of words, but Agnia Lvovna pressed her hand over Annochka's mouth and whispered with exaggerated stress, like a snake charmer:

"Remember! I'll wipe you off the earth if you melt under the entreaties of my Egor."

At that moment Agnia Lvovna gave a laugh and resumed her contralto.

"It's too early to become conceited, darling! There's a whole crowd waiting to see you. Like Wise Men come to worship, with your father at their head. And you don't even want to give them a peep at you! Look! Be nice to them. Well, I'm off to see Egor Pavlovich."

There was no crowd, but Tikhon Platonovich and Pavlik were indeed standing in the corridor gazing at Annochka. In some mysterious way Parabukin had managed to have a drop. Probably he had brought a flask just in case he was deeply moved, which in fact he was.

"Annochka! My precious daughter!" he gasped

as he entered. "Couldn't believe my own eyes! Was it really you? Even dropped a tear or two. I admit it. Went right to my heart. Whose heart? Parabukin's. Goliath's. You have brought your father back to worthy living. Accept a fond parent's profound gratitude."

He bowed and embraced her.

"For your sake I am ready to spend the rest of my days travelling from theatre to theatre. Wherever you go, I go too. I'll be your curtain boy. I'll press your costumes, if you wish. And I shall turn Pavlik over completely to your care. Yes, yes. You shall be a mother to him. Poor mother didn't live to see this happiness. How she would have wept!"

"All right, father, go along. Wait for me to come out."

Tikhon Platonovich shook a sly finger.

"It's not for me to wait for you. Somebody else is doing that. At the door, when I entered. . . ."

He swayed closer to Annochka.

". . . Comrade Izvekov! Himself."

"Where?" Annochka almost shouted.

"Come along, I'll show you," said Pavlik eagerly.

But she ran out without a glance at them, flying down the corridor until she reached the entrance to the hall. There was no one there. Softly she opened the door.

At the edge of the stairway separated from the hall by real hangings, Kirill was pacing like a lion in a cage—three steps up, three steps down.

"Aren't you ready yet?" he asked happily, on seeing her.

"Where have you been?" she said, scarce able to breathe.

"Here all the time."

"I didn't see you."

"But I saw you. That's as it should be. Hurry and take off your make-up. I want to see you home."

"Don't let me keep you waiting if you're in a hurry."

"It's only because I want us to have more time together."

She seemed not to hear him, and in a sudden burst of childish despair began to pour out hurt, reproachful words.

"Go on, go on if you're in such a hurry ... I never thought you would wait for me, that you could take so much time from your work. Go on back to your work. Why do you keep standing here?"

He pressed her hands.

"Darling, darling," he repeated with a helpless smile. "On such a memorable day!"

591

It was as though she were returned to consciousness. Never before had his voice trembled so with emotion.

"It's just because of your happiness, isn't it? Tell me it is. Don't. Don't, Annochka!"

Tears still stood in her eyes, but she was filled with rejoicing. She grabbed Kirill's hands and pressed them in her turn.

"Just a second. I'll be right out," she whispered hurriedly and rushed off.

On the way to her dressing room she tore off her wig along with the cap.

"Go along without me; someone else will see me home," she said to her father and Pavlik, at the same time delaying them with brief orders to her brother:

"My apron. Unfasten my apron. Now the hooks. The top ones first. Hurry up. Don't be afraid. Push them from both sides and they'll open of themselves. Oh, what a clumsy creature! All right, I'll do it myself. Go on, get out. . . ."

She pulled Luise's dress over her head and, after smearing her face with vaseline, dived quickly into Annochka's usual garments. She wiped off her make-up on a towel and shook off her slippers in the manner of little children. The lacing up of her shoes took the most time—this stupid new fashion—cloth tops laced to the very knee. But at last her tortures were over. She threw on her coat, grabbed her beret off the rack like catching a ball, and ran out. Luckily she met no one.

The audience had already dispersed and the streets were empty when Kirill led Annochka into the darkness of the autumn night. They had to go around the huge barrack building, and on reaching the corner they saw the lights of a waiting automobile.

"A machine?" she exclaimed with undisguised disappointment. "One minute and then goodbye again?"

He took her arm.

"Drive slowly to the old cathedral," he said to the man.

That meant crossing the entire city.

A wind was blowing, but it was not cold in the machine. The glass separating the front and the back seats reflected their every movement as they sat down, and then Annochka caught a glimpse of Kirill's head close to hers. Their images vibrated in the glass, and Annochka could not tear her eyes away from that vague, trembling reflection. A prickly thread of air streamed through a crack in the door; something under the seat whistled on one high note; the motor purred sleepily.

Now, after the strain, fear, hope, and suffering of the day, and the triumph, loneliness, insult, injury, tears, and happiness of the evening, a strange peace settled over her. It was as though after fainting someone had tucked her in bed with the tenderest solicitude and whispered soft words in her ear. She was not even surprised at the change, so completely had she relaxed. Everything seemed perfectly natural, as though she had ridden next to Kirill hundreds of times, and hundreds of times his body had touched hers from knee to shoulder as it was now touching it, and this was as it should be, and she wanted nothing more, only to go on riding and riding without end.

They met no one on the way, nothing could be seen beyond the windows, and never once did the driver blow his horn. The endless stream of fresh air blew into her face, and it seemed that it was this stream of air whistling on that high note.

When they reached the centre of the city and the machine glided over the asphalt like an iron over a board, Annochka said quietly:

"Tonight I remembered how we students used to sit up in the gallery of the theatre. There was one actress who was our favourite. You weren't here then, Kirill Nikolayevich."

"Kirill Nikolayevich?" he repeated, half in jest.

She paused a moment. Then, taking Kirill's hand and pressing it gently where it lay on his knee, she continued:

"You weren't here then, Kirill. So you didn't know her. When her interpretation of Katerina or Pribytkova threw us into transports, we all wanted to be exactly like her. And now I should like everybody to be exactly like me—feeling exactly what I am feeling now."

He did not answer. Simply turned and gazed at her. The machine rolled on and on almost without a quiver. Then the asphalt came to an end and the reflection in the glass began to shake again.

"Did you like Tsvetukhin?" she asked.

"Yes. He was much better than I had expected. I developed a dislike for him after one performance. That was before my exile."

"Perhaps I shall soon leave his troupe," she said after a long pause.

Kirill silently studied her face and wondered what she would tell him. She did not look at him.

"He wants to teach me something besides art," said Annochka, turning quite away from him.

"I guessed as much," he answered quickly, adding more slowly, and in a tone which seemed to confirm his own question: "But surely he will not have the opportunity?"

She shrugged her shoulders.

"Where do we go from here? To the left or the right?" called the driver through the glass.

"Stop."

Kirill opened the door. The pointed belfry of the cathedral stood black against the dark sky. A wind from the Volga advanced in a broad curtain.

"Let's get out."

They found themselves on the square. They were conscious of a dank, pungent odour comprising the mire of the shore, fusty hawsers, tar, machine oil, and rotting wood.

"How good!" said Kirill, tightly gripping her arm.

They began to slowly descend the embankment. Two or three buoys winked in the distance. Here and there little boats struggled against the current, their lights now flashing, now fading, as though brushed with tears.

They stopped before reaching the very shore, and before them extended the vast expanse of water, shining in spots with a leaden glow. They could hear the lapping of little waves, while the wind caused a rasping of the boats overturned on the embankment.

Annochka retained her tranquillity, responding to Kirill's embrace by nestling closer to him.

"As I look into the darkness," said Kirill, "I see innumerable lights and a multitude of people, and I hear countless voices talking on and on without pause."

"Why is it that whenever we speak of what is fine, we think of the future?"

"In order to advance to something better."

"But don't we sometimes have that something better in the present? As I gaze into the darkness, it seems to represent something very good to me. And I want nothing better."

"Nor I," he said, tightening his hold of her.

"And it seems to me I have never before seen such a night."

"Nor I."

"And the wind has never blown so."

"Never."

"And everything so quiet."

"What a pity to have to leave it."

"Must we so soon?"

"A pity. An inexpressible pity. But we must."

"When will this end?"

"What?"

"This insufferable 'must.' "

"Listen to me. And answer me. I need your answer. Will you give it?"

"Yes."

"This is what I want to say. There can be no flight into heaven without an earth. One must take off from solid ground. At present we are winning for ourselves this taking-off place. Right now. We are building the flying fields of the future. It will be a long and difficult task. Perhaps the most difficult man could undertake. We must forget all comforts. If necessary, we shall dig the earth with our bare hands, rake it with our fingernails, stamp it down with the soles of our feet. And we shall not cease our labours until the flying field is ready. We have no time to rest. Sometimes we have no time even to smile. We must hurry. Perhaps this labour has made us hard and stern. Sometimes it seems to you yourself that you have become the sort of bogeyman mothers frighten their children with, so cantankerous have you grown. No, I mean it. But I cannot change. I shall pound the earth until it is hard enough for a take-off. So that later we can climb to heights undreamed of. The vision of those heights is with me always—do you believe me? All the while I'm filling the holes and levelling down the ruts, I've got my eyes on the heights. I see people new, and different, and better, and me along with them. And actually there is nothing of the bogeyman in me at all, do you believe me?"

While he was speaking Annochka kept moving away, the better to distinguish his figure in the darkness, and when he finished she smiled at the seriousness with which he mentioned the bogeyman.

"Do I believe what? The bogeyman?"

"You asked when it would end. I don't know. Not soon. Yet it might be very soon."

"I don't understand."

"You don't see the end of my 'must' because it is not yours. If it became both yours and mine, you would not find it so important to hasten the end."

"It wouldn't come any sooner because of that, would it?" she smiled again.

He also smiled.

"A bit sooner. There'd be one builder the more.... And that's just the question I wanted to ask you. Do you want to build the flying field along with me?"

"I thought we—had already begun?" she answered softly, glancing up at him and then turning her eyes away.

He laughed, turned her about, and began climbing quickly.

He took her home, saw her through the yard, and parted with her—"Till we meet again—soon!"

Parabukin and his son put in their appearance right after she entered the room. She wished to be alone, but her father began his congratulations all over again. The cold air had made him more tipsy than ever.

"I beg your pardon, daughter, but I never thought it would turn out like that. How, thinks I to myself, can she ever hope to attain such heights!

An actress! Tikhon Parabukin's daughter an actress! No, thinks I, it'll be something half rate—neither fish nor fowl. But there I sat and heard all the compliments the public paid. Even pointed me out—the actress's father. Congratulations, daughter, you've sure done me proud!"

He clapped his hands.

"And I hadn't much confidence in Egor Pavlovich either, sinner that I be. What's he ranting about, thinks I. Watch out something don't happen to that innocent girl of yours! But tonight he showed he was doing right by you. Making a celebrity out of you. Congratulations!"

"Don't be too hasty with your congratulations, father. They'll be needed later."

"I get you. You mean I'll be needing to congratulate you on your career as an actress? I get you."

"On my career and—something else."

Tikhon Platonovich did not at first grasp what she was hinting at, and kept marking time with his compliments and congratulations. But all of a sudden he seemed to understand, and collapsed on a chair as though struck by thunder.

"Pavlik!" he cried. "Come here! What did I tell you? Didn't I tell you Tsvetukhin would shower gold on her? That's what I said all right. Tell Annochka that's what I said. And now Egor Pavlovich wants to marry our Annochka. Right? Have I guessed it?"

Suddenly he stopped.

"But how can he do such a thing, eh? He's got one wife already. What's it to be, a divorce? A divorce, I'm asking you?"

"Don't jump to conclusions," said Annochka. "Time to go to bed."

"What do you mean—jump to conclusions? What are you asking me to congratulate you about then? Jump to conclusions! Don't try to fool me. I've been seeing things for a long time. Don't you think I've got eyes? Am I blind or what? Blind?... Wait a minute. Impossible!" he shouted, jumping up. "Is it Izvekov?"

He dropped his fists on the table and laid his lean, flat body across it with his starting eyes fixed on his daughter.

She laughed gaily and went into her own room to undress.

"So that's what it means to have an engaged daughter, Tikhon Platonovich!" he roared through the door. "As long as you needed him you showed some respect for him. But now you can throw the old fellow overboard! He's the one put you on your feet, made you a place in the world, and now you shove him out with a ha-ha-ha, eh? And who's to feed your brother? Maybe you think your Comrade Izvekov will, eh? Those Izvekovs have been pulling you away from your family all your life. They want everything their own way. Want to teach everybody. First it was the schoolteacher tried to teach me, and now her son thinks he will, eh? Oh no, you first try getting a job, and then you can ha-ha-ha all you like!"

For a long time Annochka heard her father's grumbling, but its dubious meaning soon ceased to penetrate her mind.

For a long time before she fell asleep she seemed to float in a dreamy half-consciousness, during which fragments of the events of that extraordinary evening were drawn and withdrawn like cards in the hands of a fortuneteller. With her tired brain she tried to sort the evening's gains and losses. But a conglomeration of impressions swam before her eyes, and in this conglomeration it seemed that Izvekov was walking down her dream with her, while a tiny Tsvetukhin was waving his powdered wig after them from some dark, enormous pool far, far away.

The last sound which came to her was the moan of her father as he tossed on his bed:

"God forgive me, bastard that I am!"

Annochka had noticed that as he aged, especially since the death of his wife, Parabukin's fear of God seemed to increase.

35

EPILOGUE
TO WAR SCENES

During the equinoctial storms of September, the Whites, in developing their general drive in the South, captured the Kursk region. The Kutepov Corps, made up of picked infantry divisions comprised entirely of officers, fanned out to the north, the northwest, and the northeast. The Kornilov division moved on Orel; the Drozdov division on Bryansk; the Alexeyev and Markov divisions on Elets. The cavalry corps of Shkuro, uniting with Mamontov's troops, set out toward Voronezh for coordinated action with the left flank of the Don Army.

Orel fell in the middle of October, and the army of Denikin started marching on Tula, thus threatening a city which was the main arsenal supplying the Red Army with cartridges, rifles, and machine guns.

The danger to Moscow increased with every day.

This period represented the culmination point in the successes won by Denikin's "Armed Forces of the South of Russia," as well as the point of highest tension in the struggle of the Soviets against counterrevolution, fought on the fronts of the civil war.

The year of 1919 was such a strain on Russia, that had the people broken under the calamities heaped on them by history, they would long have been deprived of that new life for the sake of which they had fought the great Socialist Revolution.

The famous "expanses," so often quoted as bringing salvation to Russia whenever the country was invaded by her enemies, this time fell almost entirely into the hands of counterrevolutionary governments and foreign interventionists. At the height of the civil war, only that part of European Russia surrounding Moscow remained in the hands of the Soviets.

Russia lost not only her Far East and the vast territories of Siberia, but at one time she lost the entire Urals and almost the entire Volga region. She lost her entire southeast, including Turkestan; the whole of the South, including the Caucasus, the Kuban, the Don, and the Donets basin. She was cut off from the Ukraine and Moldavia, from Byelorussia and the Baltic lands. She was deprived of her lake regions, and of all of her northern territory. Not an inch of sea coast lying in any of the four directions of the compass remained to her.

The bulk of the wealth of a great nation derived from these vast outlying territories. By 1919 the counterrevolutionaries had seized Russia's basic supplies of wheat, oil, and coal; they had seized Urals ore, the cotton grown in Central Asia, the pastures on steppes and mountains, the forests supplying timber for industry.

In place of the wealth which had been wrested away, the inner provinces of Russia, including her two capitals, were left with nothing but cold and hunger.

And now in this autumn of 1919, the enemy was straining toward Moscow from the south, and toward Petrograd from the west and the northeast.

After the failure of the first spring drive opened by the Entente and ending in the defeat of Kolchak in the east, the capitalist powers planned a second crusade, by means of which they intended to put an end to the revolution in one fell blow. According to the cover-all plan of Churchill, British Minister of War and main initiator of this crusade, operations were to be undertaken by the united efforts of fourteen states, including, among others, England, the United States of America, France, Japan, Italy, Finland, and Poland. This bloc of fourteen Powers soon revealed its inefficacy. There were four main reasons helping to bring this about. First, the defeat of Kolchak demonstrated the growing strength of the Red Army. Secondly, most of the small countries on which the Entente had counted for carrying out its plans, preferred seeking some advantage for themselves from the national policy of the Soviet government, which declared the right of all peoples to self-determination. Thirdly, the attempts of the West-European interventionists to have their own soldiers seize Soviet territory resulted in rousing discontent among these soldiers and the protest of their own workers, as expressed in an increase in the number of strikes in the countries of the interventionists. Fourthly, these very governments could not find a solution to the contradictions characterizing their relations with Russia, a fact demonstrated by the conflicting foreign policies of France and Britain: the French wanted to restore a strong and "indivisible" Russia to stand as a permanent threat to conquered Germany, while Britain insisted on the partition of Russia in order to prevent her offering any threat to Britain's colonies in Asia.

The united blow dealt by all fourteen of the anti-Soviet states which Churchill, instigator of the intervention, had dreamed of, proved unfeasible, and the Entente had to content itself with rendering the strongest possible support to the counter-revolutionists within Russia. They placed all their hopes in Denikin, making him the central figure of the second crusade of the Entente against the Soviets.

For six months the "Armed Forces of South Russia" were uninterruptedly supplied with all types of armaments, arriving through the ports of the Black Sea. According to Denikin's own statement, by the middle of September the British had sent him more than five hundred and fifty guns and about one million seven hundred thousand shells. They had also supplied a hundred thousand rifles, a hundred and sixty-eight million cartridges, and two hundred and fifty thousand uniforms. The United States, hand in glove with Great Britain, sent Denikin another hundred thousand rifles and an enormous quantity of uniforms. Tanks and aeroplanes arrived. Pounds and dollars poured into Denikin's coffers.

At the same time the home armament plants, which were the Red Army's only source of supply, could not fulfil the demands placed on them by the war. By spring the manufacture of rifles and cartridges had fallen to one-third of the 1917 output. During the first four months of 1919 the production of shells was only one-fifth of what it had been. This was the result of the general economic disintegration, as well as of the lack of raw materials, the recruiting of workers for the front, the unprecedented mortality from typhus epidemics and famine. Bread rations for the urban population at that time were only one-fourth of a pound a day.

How, then, could it have happened that Denikin's White Army was defeated and wiped out? How could Soviet Russia have issued the victor when deprived of all its outlying territories, all of its raw materials, and almost all of its wheat, and when the enemy, armed to the teeth, had brought the Red Army's most important front to the brink of catastrophe and threatened to capture Moscow?

At the end of September a plenary session of the Central Committee of the Russian Communist Party decided to despatch Stalin, then a member of the Revolutionary Military Council of the Western front and head of war operations on that front, to the Southern front.

On the day following the passing of this decision, Stalin was appointed a member of the Revolutionary Military Council of the Southern front, and in the beginning of October he arrived at staff headquarters in the village of Sergievskoye.

The chaos reigning among the command, the retreat which had turned almost into flight, and the demoralization of operations control, did not prevent Stalin from quickly grasping the situation at the front and exposing the causes of the approaching catastrophe. While the army continued withdrawing to the north under pressure of the Whites, Stalin worked out a new strategic plan of attacking Denikin from the region of Voronezh in the direction of Rostov, moving through Kharkov and the Donbas.

At new Staff Headquarters in Serpukhov on the fifteenth of October, two days after Kornilov's troops captured Orel, Stalin wrote a letter to Lenin containing an exposition of this plan.

In the briefest possible form this letter presented a merciless criticism of the old plan of attacking Denikin through the Don regions and the Kuban in the direction of Novorossiisk—a plan still stubbornly insisted on by the Commander-in-Chief. This criticism was followed by an explanation of political reasons justifying the Stalin strategy. And finally, the letter offered operative solutions to the tasks presented by the new plan.

In analyzing the situation on the Southern front, Stalin asserted that fundamental changes had taken place since the adoption of the old plan, based as it was on the summer withdrawal of southern forces to the southeast. Stalin defined the three basic forces of the Southern front and compared their present positions with those held during the summer. These forces were the Eighth Army, which was now "directly facing the Donets basin," Budyonny's Cavalry Corps, and the Lettish

39—670   609

Division, which had been transferred from the west to the south.

In this letter Stalin asked the question: "What makes General Headquarters insist on the old plan when the former disposition of forces on the Southern front no longer exists?"

To which he supplied the following answer:

"Apparently it is nothing but stubbornness, or perhaps factionalism—thickheaded factionalism, which represents a major menace to the Republic. . . ."

In reporting that the Commander-in-Chief had again issued instructions to advance from Tsaritsyn in the direction of Novorossiisk, Stalin pointed out just wherein lay the danger for the Red Army of an advance ". . . through the Don steppes over territory which perhaps our flyers would have no difficulty in covering, but which our infantry and cavalry cannot possibly wade through. There is no need to prove that this (proposed) wild campaign through territory with a *hostile* population, at a time when the roads are *absolutely impassable,* can end in nothing but catastrophe. It is not difficult to see that this march on Cossack towns (as recent experience has amply proved), can only cause the Cossacks to rally round Denikin in defence of their territory; can only present Denikin in the role of saviour of the Don; can only mobilize Cossack armies to serve Denikin; in other words, can only strengthen Denikin.

"For this reason it is essential to lose no time in substituting this plan, which practical experience has already abrogated, for a new plan based on delivering the main blow at Rostov, proceeding from Voronezh through Kharkov and the Donets basin. First of all, we shall be crossing territory whose population is sympathetic, rather than hostile, a fact which will facilitate our advance. Secondly, we shall acquire a railway of first importance (the Donets) and the main artery feeding the army of Denikin—the railway line from Voronezh to Rostov (without this line the Cossacks will have no means of receiving winter supplies, for the Don River, along which the Don Army is supplied, freezes over, while the East-Donets road from Likhaya to Tsaritsyn will be cut off). Thirdly, our advance will cut the army of Denikin into two parts, one of which, the Volunteer Army, we shall leave to be devoured by Makhno, while the other, the Cossack armies, will be under threat of attack from the rear. Fourthly, we shall have an opportunity to set the Cossacks against Denikin, who (Denikin) will attempt to transfer the Cossack units to the west in the event of our successful advance, a transfer which most of the Cossacks will oppose if by that time we have raised the question of making peace with the Cossacks, of carrying on peace negotiations, etc. Fifthly, we shall acquire a supply of coal, while Denikin will be left without this supply.

"There must be no delay in the adoption of the new plan, for the Commander-in-Chief's plan of disposing our regiments threatens to reduce our recent victories on the Southern front to nought, to say nothing of the fact that the latest decision of the Central Committee and the Government—'All for the Southern Front'—is being completely ignored by General Headquarters, and in actuality has been cancelled.

"To be brief: the old plan, already cancelled in practice, should under no account be revived— this would place the Republic in danger and unquestionably serve the cause of Denikin. It must be substituted by another plan. The present situation and given conditions not only make the time ripe for this, but insistently demand such a substitution. Then the disposition of our regiments will be entirely different.

"Without this, my work at the Southern front becomes meaningless, criminal, superfluous, a fact which gives me a right—or rather, makes it my duty—to go anywhere else, perhaps to the very devil, but under no circumstances to remain on the Southern front.

YOURS, STALIN

The new plan was fully approved and adopted by the Central Committee of the Party, and Lenin wrote an order to field headquarters immediately countermanding the out-of-date instructions of the Commander-in-Chief.

Thus was opened a new page in the struggle with Denikin—a page which spelled doom to the entire White movement, to the entire counter-revolution. Stalin not only worked out and proposed the strategic plan for this struggle, not only succeeded in having it adopted, but directed its execution from beginning to end, leading the fight to a victorious conclusion.

The practical realization of this plan demanded exceptional effort and determination.

The Southern front had to create its initial groupings almost entirely from units already on the battle line. It was necessary to stop the retreat and re-group forces in order to immediately switch over to a counteroffensive.

Simultaneously with the carrying out of this task, the front was purged of inefficient workers. Their substitution by energetic leaders selected by Stalin brought new people to many positions, including a new Commander-in-Chief of the front.

As Voroshilov later wrote, this measure represented one of the main conditions which Stalin submitted to the Central Committee before accepting his appointment to the Southern front: "... a whole group of leaders whom Comrade Stalin considers incapable of creating the proper morale among the soldiers must be immediately recalled from the Southern front. ..." It was impossible to raise the morale of the troops while they were headed by the former staff. In a letter to Lenin sent from the front, Orjonikidze described the army staffs at that time as "something unbelievable— something bordering on treason. ..." He wrote that on the Southern front "the attitude among the units is that the Soviet cause is already lost and nothing can be done to save it." It would have been impossible to cement the forces of this front without first purging its ranks of traitors.

Responsibility for the extensive preparations preceding the putting of the plan into operation fell on Stalin. In recalling this period, Voroshilov wrote that Stalin "... did not sleep nights; all his time was spent in organizing; he took the entire leadership into his strong hands; he tore down, and was merciless, and—created a turning point; saved the situation."

The whole of Soviet Russia helped the Southern front achieve this turning point which decided the fate of the young state. A "Party Week" of mobilization brought the front twenty thousand Bolsheviks, ten thousand members of the Komsomol, thirty-six thousand workers. During the first half of October the army received over a hundred companies of new recruits, numbering as many as twenty thousand. Two thousand political workers joined the ranks of Red Army men. The desire to put an end to Denikin was so urgent that the Baltic sailors, despite the critical situation near Petrograd, sent another thousand sailors to help the south, while many Komsomol organizations set out for the south in their entirety, leaving notes on the doors of their headquarters saying: "Committee closed. All members gone to the front."

Due to the influx of popular reserves, bringing new strength to the tired troops, the fighting qualities of the army were restored with unprecedented speed. On the main sector from Voronezh to the Donbas, the Eighth Army (which, along with the adjacent cavalry corps of Budyonny on whom it relied for support, constituted the main force operating here) removed one division after another from the fighting line, reinforced them within a few days, and sent them back with new energy. Within a week the army's numerical strength had tripled. The enormous task of replenishing the troops of the Southern front and regrouping them for a counteroffensive was completed in record time.

According to Stalin's conception, the plan of attacking Denikin on a strategic scale involved two phases: the cleaving of Denikin's forces in two—the Volunteer Army and the Cossacks; and the subsequent defeating of each part separately. The carrying out of the first phase depended on the fulfilment of two operative tasks. One of them was to breach Denikin's line on the Voronezh direction and emerge in the Donets basin. The other was to deter the advance of White forces on Moscow, for which purpose it was necessary to launch a counteroffensive on the Orel sector.

A week before Stalin submitted his strategic plan to Lenin, he signed an order issued by the Revolutionary Military Council of the Southern front providing for the formation of a striking force which was to operate against Denikin's army at Orel. This striking force played an outstanding part in the initial battles which marked a turn in the tide of events on the Southern front.

Just when the Whites had cleared the road to Tula, and it seemed that at any moment Moscow might become the target of Denikin's big guns, an end was put to the successes of the Volunteer Army.

Even before Kornilov's troops took Orel, the Revolutionary Military Council of the Southern front issued an order that the striking force, made up of units which had been transferred from the Western front, was to launch a counteroffensive against the enemy's main groupings operating in the Orel direction. The blow was to come from the west and be aimed at the southeast, against Kornilov's flank, and its purpose was to cut off the Orel-Kursk railway behind enemy lines.

The Whites had large forces at their disposal. After breaching the Soviet front at the junction of two armies, they took the city of Kromy, southwest of Orel. The battles were fierce. The Whiteguards realized their decisive significance, and did not spare their best officer regiments. The troops of Drozdov tried to advance west of Kromy to the north; Kornilov's troops defeated the Soviet divisions defending Orel from the south, and forced units of the Red Army to withdraw from the city.

This was an exceedingly tense moment for the striking force, whose flanks and rear remained exposed. Clamped between the troops of Kornilov on one side, and of Drozdov on the other, it became exhausted by prolonged battles. On the fourth day of the fighting the group, advancing at a slow pace, reached the neighbourhood of Kromy.

Since the troops of Drozdov, in trying to reach Bryansk, had dislocated the left flank of the troops to the west of the striking force and threatened Kromy from the right; and since at the same time the troops of Kornilov, after feigning an advance along the road to Tula, turned to deal their main blow at Kromy from the left, the command of the Southern front decided to act against both enemy groupings simultaneously. The striking force was ordered to advance in diverging lines, sending its main forces against the troops of Kornilov at Orel, while other units of this same group were to move against the troops of Drozdov at Dmitrovsk.

This operation led to prolonged and bloody battles at Dmitrovsk, where units of the striking force fought with fluctuating success. But in the course of three days of fierce fighting near Orel, the main forces of the striking force dealt a severe blow to the Kornilov division. As a result of these battles, the Red Army surrounded Orel on three sides—the north, the west, and the southwest. Having exhausted their reserves, the Whites were forced to withdraw Kornilov's troops from Orel along the only free road leading to the south.

The liberation of Orel strengthened the Red Army's confidence in its superiority over Denikin's army, which had seized the city only a week before. The Whites were showing signs of exhaustion, and it became clear that the Soviet command was taking the initiative into its own hands.

Yet the capture of Orel did not mean that the situation along the entire central sector of the Southern front had reached a turning point. Denikin was still active; his Volunteer Army was making desperate efforts to preserve the advantages gained in recent victories.

The fighting at Kromy continued to rage.

Along a thirty-kilometre sector of front the Drozdov troops opened an attack on the city from the southwest, and at the price of terrific losses, broke the resistance of Soviet riflemen and recaptured the city. On the following day the defenders of Kromy, along with additional forces assigned to them at this time, drove the Whites out in a gallant attack. But twenty-four hours later the Drozdov troops again moved forward, forced one point of the defence, and threatened the Soviet forces with encirclement, as a result of which the latter retreated to the north. For the third time Kromy was in the hands of the Whites.

Two weeks of unabated fighting drained the reserves of the striking force and scattered its units over an enormous front. The Whites, on the other hand, after their defeat at Orel, concentrated all their forces against the central sector of the Southern front in the hope of defeating the striking force piecemeal and again taking Orel.

Stalin foresaw the intention of the enemy and issued orders to work out a plan of action according to which both armies, operating on the central sector, should clearly define the directions in which they would attack the Orel and Kromy White

619

groupings, and should advance in massed groups, rather than scattering their forces. Stalin explained the idea behind his operative tactics in a direct-wire conversation with Orjonikidze:

"During the last few days the enemy has managed by clever manoeuvring to break up the striking force into separate regiments and fight them one by one. Our last instructions are aimed at giving you the opportunity to unite these regiments into a single group and wipe out Denikin's best regiments—I repeat 'wipe out,' for that is exactly what must be done. The taking of Kromy by the enemy is something which can be rectified. The main task is to prevent the striking force from being broken up into regiments, and to attack the enemy in a united mass and in one definite direction; the other units, approaching from the south, will offer you every possible support."

The reference to the "units approaching from the south" was not an empty promise prompted by the desire to encourage the soldiers. Stalin gave his instructions over the direct wire to the Revolutionary Military Council of the Army on the right flank of the front in the small hours of October 25. But on the preceding day a brilliant victory had been won by the forces operating along the main direction according to the Stalin plan: units of Budyonny's cavalry and of the Eighth Army took the city of Voronezh. This made it possible to attack the Volunteer Army from the rear, and to offer decisive support to the prolonged struggle on the central sector of the front.

The fighting near Voronezh was of quite a specific nature. It was cavalry fighting on a large scale, and it left no doubt in the minds of the Whites that their superiority in this type of warfare was coming to an end.

In the beginning of October, after the taking of Voronezh, the cavalry corps of Shkuro moved to the north. It was supported by Mamontov, who made raids on regions occupied by the Eighth Soviet Army. The northern (right) flank of this army was exposed, so that the White cavalry could make deep inroads into the territory of the Southern front.

The only force capable of opposing Shkuro and Mamontov was Budyonny's Cavalry Corps.

But there still existed the old instructions, according to which this corps was to proceed to the Don region.

Perceiving the danger of Shkuro's reaching the north, Budyonny turned his cavalry about, and, even before the fall of Voronezh, rushed forward in the hope of an encounter with the enemy's cavalry. This bold and responsible decision was fully justified by succeeding events.

Soon the Revolutionary Military Council of the Southern front ordered Budyonny to defeat the enemy's cavalry in the region of Voronezh and help the Eighth Army reach the Don as quickly as possible. Budyonny immediately concentrated his corps northeast of Voronezh.

In preparing his units for this operation and finding out the groupings of the Whites, Budyonny resorted to a stratagem. He connected up with Shkuro's telegraph line and sent a sham order to the First Cavalry Corps. The order spoke of preparations for a drive on Voronezh, with the main blow coming from the southeast, whereas actually the blow was to be dealt from the northeast. The staff of Shkuro's cavalry accepted this "Red order" which they thought they had intercepted, as a true one.

Fearing to lose the initiative, Shkuro went into attack with twelve cavalry regiments. One of Budyonny's two divisions was hard pressed until the other came to its aid by attacking the enemy in flank and rear. This manoeuvre decided the outcome of the engagement. Budyonny's forces defeated a division of Kuban Cossacks, wiped out a White infantry regiment, and pursued the fleeing enemy to the eastern borders of Voronezh.

After that Budyonny again regrouped his cavalry corps. His main forces were concentrated to attack Voronezh from the north. The remaining units were given the task of approaching the town from the southwest. All the artillery and an enormous number of machine guns were concentrated in the region occupied by these units.

Early in the morning of the day of the final battle, a storm of artillery fire was loosed on the city, while one of Budyonny's divisions dismounted and crossed the Voronezh River. The main forces of the Whites were gradually drawn into the fighting which broke out in the eastern section of the city. Meanwhile, the main forces of Budyonny's First Corps appeared to the north and northwest, and came rushing down on Voronezh. The blow took the Whites off their guard. Shkuro was left with no alternative but to order a retreat. His cavalry abandoned their cannon and machine guns and made a dash for the Don.

On the next day Stalin sent the following telegram to Lenin:

"The cavalry corps of Shkuro and Mamontov, which the Entente and Denikin took such pains to create as the main bulwark of counterrevolution, have been completely smashed in battles at Voronezh by the cavalry corps of Comrade Budyonny. Voronezh has been taken by Red heroes. A count is now being made of the vast number of trophies captured. At present we know that we have captured all the enemy's armoured trains bearing names of generals, including that of General Shkuro. We are still pursuing the fleeing enemy. The halo of invincibility created around the names of Generals Mamontov and Shkuro has been trampled in the dust through the valour of the Red heroes of Comrade Budyonny's Mounted Corps.

Revolutionary Military Council
of the Southern Front

S T A L I N."

A day after the defeat of the Don and Volunteer Cavalry at Voronezh, the striking force, which had transferred its units from Orel to the region of Kromy, again took the offensive. In two days of fighting the Red Army defeated Kutepov's corps on all three sectors of the Orel-Kromy-Dmitrovsk front, thus putting an end to Denikin's "march on Moscow." In a night attack the striking force drove the Whites out of Kromy; the division west of the striking force routed the troops of Drozdov and entered Dmitrovsk; divisions operating to the left of the striking force smashed the troops of Kornilov near Orel and advanced south along the railway.

A general retreat of the Whites began along the entire central section of the Southern front.

At the same time the successes of the Soviet cavalry multiplied with every new battle. After forcing the Don River and dealing another major defeat to the cavalry of Shkuro, Budyonny drove the enemy back to the railway junction of Kastornaya in the direction of Kursk. Here, in the middle of November, during a blizzard marking the advent of an unusually early winter, he again delivered the Whites a smashing blow with combined cavalry and infantry forces.

The retreat of Denikin's volunteers assumed the nature of headlong flight. Under such conditions the pursuit of the enemy by the cavalry, now transformed into the First Mounted Army headed by Voroshilov and Budyonny, was of decisive significance. The regiments became filled with fighting spirit and confident in victory. Every advance of Soviet forces made more evident the advantages of Stalin's strategic plan of attack.

The main blow, issuing from the region of Voronezh, brought the basic army group (coordinated cavalry and infantry) from the northeast to the southwest, into the Donets basin. At the same time, a blow from the region of Orel opened the way for the right-flank army to advance southward, through Kursk on to Kharkov.

As these military tasks were fulfilled one after another, the Red Army enjoyed the growing successes ensured by the basic idea of the Stalin strategic plan. In the Donets basin the victories of Soviet troops were facilitated by the unanimous support of the workers. One result of these victories was that the Mounted Army, which operated at the point of proximity between the Don and Volunteer armies, was now advancing toward the Azov Sea by the shortest possible route. And this in turn ensured the accomplishment of the task set by the first phase of the plan, viz., the cutting of Denikin's forces in two: the Volunteers, who were driven back to the Crimea and the Western Ukraine, and the Cossacks, who were pressed into the regions of the Lower Don and the North Caucasus.

In November and December Denikin suffered defeat on the enormous spaces between the Dnieper and the Volga. The Red Army was gloriously liberating the Ukraine. Now the Southeastern front began to move forward. Approaching from Astrakhan, the army commanded by Kirov attacked a group of White forces in the North Caucasus. Complete victory over the "Armed Forces of South Russia" was drawing ever nearer. By the end of December Stalin could already sum up the results of the first stage of the struggle. He did this in a long article entitled "The Military Situation in the South."

Calling to mind the failure of the Entente-organized Kolchak campaign from the east, Stalin said that the plan of this expedition had been "outlined in a letter written by Denikin to Kolchak which we found in the spring of 1919 on capturing Grishin-Almazov's headquarters. 'The most important thing is not to stop at the Volga,' wrote Denikin, 'but continue fighting on to Moscow, heart of Bolshevism. I hope to meet you in Saratov....'"

But Denikin was not destined to meet Kolchak in Saratov or anywhere else. Kolchak was defeated east of the Volga, and his troops fled beyond the Urals. "Soviet Russia remained safe and sound," wrote Stalin.

At the height of the successes of the Entente's second (southern) campaign, Denikin's forces were confident that they would triumph. They planned to be in Moscow "no later than the end of December—by Christmas, 1919," as General Mai-Mayevsky announced after the capture of Orel by the Whites. But by Christmas the Volunteer Army, with ranks thinned to half their original number, was driven back beyond Poltava and forced to flee from the Donets basin. It was the industrial magnates of this very Donets basin who in October had offered a prize of one million tsarist rubles to the regiment of the Volunteer Army which first set foot in the capital. "This time Russia also remained safe and sound," repeated Stalin, adding:

"The failure of the counterrevolution was this time so unexpected and sudden that the victors in the war against imperialist Germany, the old Entente wolves, were compelled to announce publicly that 'Bolshevism cannot be defeated by force of arms.' And the discomfiture of the fakirs of imperialism was so great that they were unable to discover the true causes of the defeat of the counterrevolution, and began to compare Russia now to 'quicksand' in which 'the best of generals' must inevitably sink, now to a 'vast desert' where death necessarily lies in wait for even the 'best troops.' "

In the main section of his article Stalin analyzes the causes that led to the defeat of the counterrevolution and dwells at length on two of them, as the most important.

Stalin names as the first reason for the defeat of the Whites the insecurity of the rear of the counterrevolutionary troops, which he explains by the social nature of the Denikin-Kolchak government which formed those troops.

'Denikin and Kolchak threaten Russia not only with the yoke of the landlord and capitalist, but also with the yoke of British and French capital. A Denikin-Kolchak victory would mean the loss of Russia's independence, the conversion of Russia into a milch cow for the British and French money-bags. In this sense the Denikin-Kolchak government is a most antinational government, a government most opposed to the interests of the people. In this sense the Soviet government is the only people's government and the only national government, in the best meaning of the term, for it brings not only the emancipation of the working people from capital, but the emancipation of all Russia from the yoke of world imperialism, the transformation of Russia from a colony into a free, independent country."

Hence the inevitable conclusion drawn by Stalin that the Denikin-Kolchak troops could not have that passionate desire to win and that enthusiasm without which victory is impossible.

"The Denikin-Kolchak rear is crumbling, undermining the mainstays of the front, because the Denikin-Kolchak government is a government of bondage for the Russian people, a government most distrusted by the broad strata of the population."

Stalin pointed out that the second reason for the defeat of the Whites was the geographical demarcation of the areas of the revolution and the counterrevolution which became indicated at the beginning of the October Revolution and were fully defined in the course of the civil war. The outlying position of the counterrevolution—therein lay its "fatal, inevitable drawback," and therein also lay the "inevitable advantages" of the revolution, which held a central position in inner Russia.

"Inner Russia with her industrial, cultural and political centres—Moscow and Petrograd—and with a nationally homogeneous population, mainly Russian, has become the base of the revolution. Russia's outlying regions, on the other hand, chiefly the borderlands in the east and south, possessing no important centres (industrial, cultural, or political), with an extremely heterogeneous population, consisting of privileged Cossack colonizers on the one hand and of disfranchised Tatars, Bashkirs, Kirghiz (in the east), Ukrainians, Chechens, Ingushetians and other Moslem peoples, on the other hand, have become the base of the counter-revolution."

And further Stalin reveals the disadvantages to the counterrevolution and the advantages to the revolution accruing from this geographical demarcation.

"For the success of the troops operating in an epoch of fierce civil war it is absolutely essential that the human environment in which they find themselves be united, for it is from this environment that the troops draw strength and sustenance. Such unity may be either national (especially in the early stages of the civil war) or class unity (especially in the advanced stages of the civil war).

No lasting military success is possible without such unity. But that is just the point that the borderlands of Russia (in the east and south) do not provide, either in respect to nationality or class, nor can they provide Denikin's and Kolchak's troops with that minimum of unity of the human environment without which (as I have said above) no serious victory is possible.

"Indeed, what *national* unity can there be between the national aspirations of the Tatars, Bashkirs, Kirghiz (in the east), Kalmyks, Chechens, Ingushetians, and Ukrainians (in the south), on the one hand, and the hundred per cent Russian autocratic administrations of Kolchak and Denikin, on the other?

"Or again: What *class* unity can there be between the privileged Cossacks of the Urals, Orenburg, Don, and Kuban, on the one hand, and all the rest of the borderland population, not excluding the Russian 'non-Cossacks,' oppressed and exploited from time immemorial by the local Cossacks?

"Is it not obvious that troops made up of such heterogeneous elements are inevitably bound to fall apart at the first serious blow dealt by the Soviet armies, and that every blow is inevitably bound to increase the gravitation of the non-Cossack elements in the outlying regions of Russia toward the Soviet Government, which utterly renounces imperialist ambitions and is willing to satisfy their national aspirations?

"In contradistinction to the borderlands, inner Russia presents an entirely different picture. Firstly, she is united and welded nationally (Great-Russians make up nine-tenths of her population). Secondly, the achievement of the class unity of the human environment (from which the Soviet front and rear draws strength and sustenance) is facilitated by the presence of the Petrograd and Moscow proletariat, which is popular among the peasantry and rallies the latter closely round the Soviet Government.

"This, incidentally, accounts for the wonderful contact between the rear and the front in Soviet Russia, a thing the Kolchak-Denikin government could never boast of. The Soviet Government need but issue a call for aid to the front, and Russia will at once put in the field a whole array of fresh regiments.

"Herein, too, lies the source of that amazing strength and unparalleled resiliency which Soviet Russia usually displays in critical moments.

"Here also one should look for the explanation of the fact, incomprehensible to the enlightened shamans of the Entente, that the counterrevolutionary troops, when they reach certain limits (the limits of inner Russia!) inevitably suffer disaster...."

Thus Stalin, while still directing the constantly expanding operations to defeat Denikin—in the days before the Soviet forces had reached Rostov, the final goal of the first stage of the great strategic plan—on the heels of the first victories over the counterrevolution in South Russia, explained the causes of these victories and the profound reasons why the entire movement of the Whites was historically doomed to failure.

With reference to the situation on the Southern front as it was at the time the article was written (late in December), Stalin said that "the cornerstone of the entire further advance of our armies southward" was laid by the first decisive successes of the Soviet infantry in the fighting at Orel and in the Kromy-Dmitrovsk area, and the first decisive successes of the Red cavalry in the fighting at Voronezh.

The Southern front and, following it, the other civil war fronts in the south owe these successes to Stalin entirely, in every respect—political, strategical, operational and in the matter of directing the entire machinery of the armies. Orel and Voronezh were the first of the levers which turned the tide of events in 1919 in favour of Soviet Russia and dashed the hopes the Entente powers reposed in Denikin's "march on Moscow."

Mamontov, with his Don Cossack raid, and Kutepov, with his incursion of crack officer divisions, were the White generals who had reached the limits of inner Russia and even crossed beyond them. They came short of Tula by a matter of a hundred and fifty or two hundred kilometres—the former on the southeast, the latter on the southwest.

The upshot of the Entente-organized Denikin campaign into the interior of Russia was that the peasant masses resolutely gave their support to the Soviets. At the most crucial moment they took their stand for the revolution against its most dangerous enemy—Denikin. The upshot of that campaign was that the workers not only "put in the field a whole array of fresh regiments" to help their army, but raised red partisan banners in the territory under the Whites. Not only where the Soviets were in control, but also in those parts of the country ruled by the Whites, the people implicitly believed in the truth of the revolution and placed their trust in their best, soundest, and strongest section, the working-class section of the population. They were confident that it was just this section of the population, the proletariat, that would direct all life along lines fair to the masses.

That was the historic reality; it was the law of history on the basis of which Stalin built up and carried out his plan of victory.

In the very beginning of January the Mounted Army breached Denikin's front, inflicted on his forces a crushing defeat at Taganrog, broke down the desperate resistance of the Whites at Rostov and captured that city.

The Volunteer Army was utterly routed and ceased to exist as Denikin's main force. Denikin now assigned the role of his main force to the Cossack troops. It was to them that he looked for salvation, on them that he pinned his last hopes.

But that was already the new year 1920, a new year of our Lord, as old folks would say—a new landmark in the progress of young Soviet Russia after it had triumphantly scaled the peak of the civil war in the no ordinary year of Nineteen Hundred and Nineteen.

* 36 *

One morning at the end of November, Pavlik asked his sister for money. When Annochka asked him what he needed money for, he admitted that this was not the first time the boys had pooled their funds to buy milk for Arseni Romanovich.

Thus it became known that Dorogomilov was ill. Annochka told Kirill, and he told his mother.

"Don't you think we ought to help him?"

"Probably," answered Vera Nikandrovna.

635

Kirill detected a slight hesitance in her tone. He himself had difficulty in deciding what attitude to assume toward Dorogomilov.

"Ragozin has the greatest respect for him."

She was silent. He realized that you could respect a person without liking him. It seemed superfluous to add that Annochka considered Dorogomilov an extremely kindhearted person. Vera Nikandrovna had heard this from Annochka herself. There could be only one answer: other people's opinions had little to do with your own attitude toward people. Too personal had been the relations between the Izvekov family and Arseni Romanovich for any third person to bring about a change of attitude. And indeed, was such a change necessary?

"The whole thing happened so long ago, and the facts are so obscure, that it would be foolish to hold anything against the old man now," said Kirill.

"I have long since ceased to hold anything against him. And even in the past he roused in me only painful memories. Nothing else."

"Maybe we should assure him of this?"

"I shall speak to Annochka. If she agrees, we shall go see him together."

"Of course she'll agree," said Kirill impulsively, catching himself with the realization that only

Annochka could speak so categorically about herself.

All fall Dorogomilov had been ailing. He could not define any particular illness. He simply was not himself. His indisposition had come upon him just when he had intended to exchange his frock coat for an army tunic, when he had begun to make enquiries as to possible employment in some military organization, when he had parted with his library.

He had felt the first attack of weakness on the day when his books had been hauled away. Two carts had come at once, and before they were fully loaded, half his shelves were empty. Grey dust swirled about the room as though in protest at being disturbed. When the books had been removed from one side of the longest shelf, the whole thing collapsed. A cloud of dust rose to the ceiling and the mice ran squealing over the heap of books.

Unable to bear the sight of such destruction, Dorogomilov lay down on the divan. Once on his back, he became more keenly aware of his weakness. His arms and legs were trembling. He did not get up when they came for the rest of the books.

He had donated his beloved library to a newly-opened children's reading room. He could think of no better fate for the collection he himself had made for the children. Furthermore, by giving away his books he had hoped to simplify the carrying out of his vague, but courageous decision. Yet when the books were gone he suffered from a loneliness he had not experienced in years. He became more indifferent to events which formerly had stirred him to the depths of his soul. Perhaps that was because the danger represented by these events seemed to have passed over.

The boys continued to visit him, but he suspected that they had lost interest in coming to his house now that the books were gone. He had to bring about a reconciliation between Pavlik and Vitya because Pavlik was in favour of the reading room, while Vitya was against it.

More and more often Arseni Romanovich had spells of ill health. Many things had undoubtedly served to bring this about—poor food, the cold and dampness of autumn, and most of all—old age. And then suddenly he was taken with pneumonia.

Vanya Ragozin, his latest admirer, told his father about this misfortune. A doctor was sent, a cartload of wood was delivered, and the boys took turns nursing the old man.

For Dorogomilov, the nights became longer than ever before, the apartment larger. His illness dragged along sluggishly. He suffered nothing but weakness and sharp pains when he coughed. But he was worn out by insomnia.

His thoughts turned to trifles. He would fix his eyes on one of the hundreds of articles cluttering up his study and begin endless reminiscences. All these articles, once essential, remained attached to his life like the tail of a comet. They all had their separate biographies, and he would lie there and figure out how many years he had owned those scissors which were now so much the worse for wear that nobody but himself could have found any use for them. But in his hands they served equally well for performing surgical operations, pulling out nails, and even affording a musical accompaniment when he clanged them together in rhythm to his pensive rendering of "The Danube Waves."

Suddenly he would recall some particular book whose individuality depended less upon its contents than upon its connection with some definite life situation, or upon the details of its biography: where it had been bought, on what particular day, by whom it had been published, where it stood in his library, and why it had never been read to the end.

Arseni Romanovich rarely read a book through, just as he rarely carried through any of his innumerable projects. He would try his hand at making something, discover that he could do it, and—drop the task for something else. He would take up a book, go into ecstasies over it, fall to musing, and—put away the book. It was as though his own imagination supplied the endings, and he remembered books by their beginnings, as a person is remembered by his face. For that reason the world of his things and his books was an unfinished world, a world without end. This fact made it impossible to comprehend at the present moment why an end had come to this endlessness. The books were gone, probably the things would also go, and then he himself would go.

By the day on which Annochka and Vera Nikandrovna came to see him he had become extremely weak. But their visit roused him to feverishness. He became talkative and his fidgetiness returned, though it could express itself only in his face and hands. He kept his eyes fixed on Annochka, stealing only sly glances at his other guest. Vera Nikandrovna sensed that he was waiting for her to speak. But she could find no words. She was shocked by the sight of this old man with the hot, rosy face crowned by a halo of white hair.

Annochka opened the conversation simply enough with the remark that he must find it boring to lie here all by himself. He denied it as hastily as his lack of breath permitted.

"I am never left alone. My boys are always fussing about."

After catching his breath he continued more slowly:

"Solitude is dreadful if nobody wants you; if you stand on the street and everyone passes you by.... It is wonderful if you have your own corner to which you sometimes retire and close the door for a brief rest, apart from those who need you."

"When you get well," said Annochka, "you can lock all your doors against us and rest to your heart's content: but for the present people must come and take care of you."

"But I am quite satisfied. Your Pavlik takes care of my stove. Vanya Ragozin washes the dishes. They are trying very hard."

"Boys don't understand anything. What you need is a woman around. We'll see that you get one, won't we, Vera Nikandrovna?"

Dorogomilov glanced frightenedly at Izvekova.

"Dear me! I am already getting my strength back. I must go to work."

"Your work will wait," said Annochka somewhat imperiously.

A smile lighted his inflamed eyes and he said with an old man's playfulness, and a bit apologetically:

"I'll be going to the front yet."

"Like Pavlik," laughed Annochka.

"And then I shall settle down to some poetic occupation."

"Excellent. What, for example?"

"Angling."

"That's no occupation—that's just a means of killing time," laughed Annochka.

"Why? You can even earn money angling."

"Fishing, but not angling."

"Fishing is all right, but angling is more poetic."

He was becoming tired. His cheeks paled and his eyes grew sad.

"Do you think secondhand booksellers will be dispensed with in time?" he asked unexpectedly.

"Those who sell books at the market?"

"Old books."

"Would you like to become a bookseller? Better to be a librarian."

"Oh no. A bookseller is better. If there is some book he loves, he will give it only to someone who loves it even more. . . . A librarian must satisfy everybody's taste."

"All right, you'll be a bookseller," exclaimed Annochka glowingly. "And I shall come and browse through your books."

"Bring Pavlik with you. You must encourage . . . little boys . . . to love. . . ."

It was becoming more difficult for him to talk, and he seemed to be growing delirious.

Vitya entered and sat down in the corner, watching the women sternly. They got up.

Vera Nikandrovna quickly pressed the hand of Arseni Romanovich and bent over to say the only words which could express her conviction that he would never get well:

"When you get well, come see me and Kirill. Do, please."

"So you came at last . . . good," replied Dorogomilov weakly, frowning and squeezing together his trembling eyelids.

He died one night not long after that, alone in his incongruous apartment. Vanya Ragozin found him in the morning. Vanya was not afraid of dead bodies—he had seen them more than once in his short life. Furthermore, Dorogomilov wore the same expression of beneficence, though his right hand was clenched in a fist, as if he were threatening somebody, or had just shaken hands. Vanya stood by his bedside for a moment, then rushed to break the news to his father.

Strangely enough, the funeral of this lonely man was attended by a rather large number of people. Among them were young people of all ages, from little boys to youths in military uniforms or faded student caps. Most of them remembered each other from childhood days. But among those who followed the coffin to the cemetery were also many grownups who did not know each other, but were joined for a brief hour by some common experience. Naturally there were the relatives of Dorogomilov's beloved boys, among them Lisa, Parabukin, and Annochka. Ragozin was also there, walking just behind the hearse. He had helped arrange the funeral, which was not such a simple matter at that time.

The usual question of passers-by in the old provinces—"Who is being buried?"—was rarely heard in those grim days. There were many deaths, and the funerals were all alike, excepting that some coffins were unpainted, while others were painted red.

Yet the length of the procession aroused the curiosity of passers-by, who could not make out why the burial of such a humble citizen should have attracted such a large number of people.

"Who was he, a teacher?"

"No, an accountant, or something like that."

"Why so many youngsters in the procession?"

But the women of the town immediately guessed who had died.

"Dorogomilov? Old Shaggy Locks, eh?"

"The very one."

"Crazy, he was."

"Uh-huh. So his time's come too!"

Thus was found a valid explanation of why there were so many people, for a crazy man always arouses greater interest than an ordinary person.

At the cemetery the people crowded about the grave. Though there was a strong wind and a light snow, the people stood with bared heads—even the little boys, who ignored their parents' admonitions to put on their caps. For some reason it was expected that the moment of final leave-taking would be marked by something special, and everyone pressed closer on seeing Ragozin mount the mound of earth alongside of the grave.

For a second he said nothing. Naturally almost a head taller than anyone else, he became clearly visible to all from his position on the mound, and his bald head with curly strands blowing about his temples and the back of his head, drew all eyes.

"A man has died who was known to many of our townsmen," he began quietly. "He was known to his colleagues at the office where he worked for thirty-five years. He was known to the children with whom he loved to spend his leisure. He was known for his indefatigable labour, for his humble character, for his love for children. But he was little known for one aspect of his character which was probably most important, and it behooves us to speak of this now."

Pyotr Petrovich glanced at the red coffin, along the lid of which the wind was driving snowflakes. He lifted his head still higher and raised his voice:

"Arseni Romanovich Dorogomilov was a dreamer. All his life he dreamed of the future, of the great future of mankind, and he laboured inconspicuously to help create this future, because he believed in it, and could not help making his contribution.

"Many people now know that during the tsarist regime a society called 'The Beacon' was formed in Saratov. It had an educational purpose and worked openly. At the same time, some five years before the revolution, a strong underground organization of Bolsheviks was formed. The sisters of Vladimir Ilyich Lenin worked in this organization at that time. Workers and artisans soon grew to love their Party, and during the war we were already publishing a Bolshevik paper openly. It was sent throughout almost the whole of Russia. It was read in Byelorussia, in Moscow and in Petrograd. But the gendarmes closed it down. Then the Bolsheviks found another means of keeping in contact with the masses. They made use of the society called 'The Beacon,' forming within it a Party unit. 'The Beacon' became a legal screen for revolutionary work carried on in factories, study groups, and the garrison. At the beginning of the revolution, the enormous results of this work made themselves felt. Thanks to our propaganda, the garrison of some sixty thousand soldiers played an outstanding role in the revolutions of February and October. Our Party Committee was elected at a meeting of Bolsheviks held on the premises of 'The Beacon' soon after the February revolution. . . ."

It seemed to Vitya, who had been listening attentively, that Pyotr Petrovich's speech had wandered too far off the subject of Arseni Romanovich. The crowd had pressed him tight against the cross marking one of the graves, and he twisted his head uncomfortably to read a metal plaque:

"Here lie the remains of the village of Korochka Olga Rodionovna Kalinnikova. May the Lord receive her soul in peace and settle it in the land of the blessed." And then another one painted in bright blue letters underneath a cherubim: "To Vera from mama and papa."

Vitya did not spend much time pondering over the remains of the village of Korochka—this was not a serious problem. Apparently the remains of this geographical location were somehow connected with the deceased Olga. Purely a question of form. But the land of the blessed set Vitya to thinking. He could not decide what land they should ask to have the soul of Arseni Romanovich settled in, what lands existed in general, and where and to whom they should apply, if not to the Lord himself. It was a serious problem, for on its solution depended the inscription to be placed above the grave of Arseni Romanovich. Probably the land of the blessed would do for him as well as for the remains of the village of Korochka, and yet there might be some better place. Pyotr Petrovich would probably touch on this important question in his speech. Once more Vitya began to listen.

"Arseni Romanovich helped the revolutionaries even before the founding of 'The Beacon,'" said Ragozin. "But after the Party unit was organized within the society, he was in permanent contact with it. His apartment became a secret meeting place. He hid underground workers in his house. Revolutionary literature was sometimes stored among his books, behind all sorts of trash which he deliberately collected for the purpose of camouflage. He did all this so artistically that for long years he led the secret police by the nose, and not one of the revolutionaries entrusted to his care was ever caught. For the sake of secrecy he never became a member of 'The Beacon,' a society which shone as brightly for him as for many others. Among those of us gathered here are several old Party members who remember the prerevolutionary work of the deceased.

"Comrades, I would not say of Arseni Romanovich that he was a mighty beacon shining in the night, pointing the course to sea-going vessels. But he was a buoy, whose little lantern burned steadily to show the bend in the river. Everyone who sailed down that river to the sea of the future saw the lantern gleaming despite wind and storm, and continued on his way confident that he was not alone— that someone was concerned for his welfare.

"Now we have all reached that sea, and while remaining the future, it has also become the present. Its extent is limitless, and it will still be troubled by many winds and storms. But now the beacons shine with equal light for all, and the way is open to all.

"I began by saying that Arseni Romanovich was a dreamer. That is true, and children, who themselves are dreamers by nature, sensed this better than others. To be sure, the dreams of Arseni Romanovich were vague. The children whom he loved contributed to them their own desires, their own visions of the future. We Communists cannot allow ourselves to dream formless dreams, for we wish not only to dream, but to build a glorious future. And it is impossible to build without clear purposes, without a definite pattern. But our pattern includes the vast spaces of the sea essential to dreams. The vast spaces which lure the innocent fancy of a child, demanding a world of justice, beauty, and happiness. It is for us to dream with the ardour which attracted the children to Arseni

649

Romanovich. We must learn from him what true enthusiasm means. But we must show our children the correct path to our dreams. Along that path they will fearlessly tear down everything which stands in the way of our purposes, our plans for the future. Our children will go forth to meet Communism along with the young people now fighting in defence of the Soviet Republic.

"Let me end these farewell words to Arseni Romanovich with a promise. Not long ago I heard some of our sailors saying that when passing through the Red Sea, stokers found it cooler in the ship's hold than up on deck. Just so the difficulties suffered in fighting for the new world seem easier for a Bolshevik to endure than the bourgeois stagnation of the old world. We shall not abandon our furnaces in order to rest up on deck; we find the deck more stifling. And we promise our friend Arseni Romanovich that while feeding the furnaces, we shall continue to dream, and will teach our children to dream—the children he loved so dearly. We shall teach them not to lose sight of the beacons pointing the way to the future."

In one long step Pyotr Petrovich descended the mound.

He was followed by two other orators. But their speeches were brief—everything had already been said. And now the wind had grown stronger, the snow had increased, and people were huddling together for protection.

The grave had not yet been levelled with the ground when the gathering began to disperse. The trolley did not run all the way to the cemetery; it was necessary to go as far as the university on foot. The snow came blowing across an open field in front of the cemetery, swirling up like a swung lasso and spiralling about the telephone poles. In places the earth was bare, stripped by the wind. The snow was driven against the blocks of log houses, which sulked darkly against the white sidewalks.

Frozen from standing at the grave, the little boys thrust their hands up their sleeves or into their pockets and scurried ahead of their elders.

"How time flies," said Vera Nikandrovna to Annochka. "Isn't that Lisa's son with Pavlik?"

"Yes, that's Vitya."

"And what a fine big chap Pavlik has become."

"Sometimes I can hardly believe that I was once his nursemaid."

Annochka laughed.

"What are you laughing at?"

"Remember the story with the chocolate?"

"Chocolate?"

"Before the war. Don't you remember how you once gave Pavlik a bar of chocolate on his birthday? Mother told him to share it with me. After a bitter struggle with himself he finally said: 'All right, mother, I'll give Annochka a tiny wee bit.' 'Why a tiny wee bit when you have so much?' asked mother. 'I'm afraid she might choke over a big piece,' he answered."

They both burst out laughing, but the laughter abruptly broke off as though they suddenly remembered they were coming from a funeral.

Annochka crooked her arm in front of her face to protect it from the wind as she said casually:

"Why didn't Kirill Nikolayevich come?"

"I'm sorry he didn't. Ragozin's speech would have helped him understand his father's friendship with Dorogomilov. Kirill intended to come, but something turned up unexpectedly at the Military Commissariat."

Annochka lifted her eyebrows, but said nothing, only quickening her steps to catch up with the boys who were running too far ahead.

They were pattering along in a group in the middle of the road, leaning into the wind, exchanging brief words interspersed by long silences.

"Can't my father make speeches though, Pavlik?" said Vanya.

"Uhuh," agreed Pavlik, adding after a moment's thought: "But it's too bad he said that about the trash. My father was tickled to death."

"What was he tickled about?"

"Nudged me in the ribs and said: 'See? Comrade Ragozin agrees with me. Arseni Romanovich's books are nothing but trash.'"

"Well, let him. Who cares? Your father!"

It seemed to Vitya that Pyotr Petrovich had not said the most important thing about Arseni Romanovich. The most important thing was that Arseni Romanovich was no more, and there never would be and never could be another his equal.

"What'll we write about Arseni Romanych?" he said.

"Write where?" asked Vanya.

"On the cross."

"That's right," said Pavlik with concern.

"On the cross!" scoffed Vanya.

"What's wrong with that?" said Vitya, accepting the challenge.

"Arseni Romanych won't have a cross. He'll have a tombstone without any cross."

"Of course—a tombstone—a great big one," agreed Pavlik.

The three of them rubbed their ears in turn.

"Hey, fellows, look! A muzhik on a sledge!" shouted Vitya.

"The dunce! Not enough snow to cover a pebble, and him on a sledge!"

"Here's what we ought to write," said Pavlik in

deep concentration. "Just 'Here lies our Arseni Romanovich,' and then the names."

"What names?" asked Vanya.

"Well, yours and mine, and Vitya's and some others."

"Where'd you ever get that? Nobody ever signs their names to a tombstone. I lived in a cemetery a whole summer, so I know."

"What if you did? We'll sign our names if we want. Who can stop us?"

"What does it mean—the land of the blessed?" asked Vitya.

"Guess you saw that on some cross, didn't you? I know," said Vanya.

"Was it on a cross?" enquired Pavlik.

"It's all those priests," went on Vanya supercil- iously. "Resurrection, the land of the blessed, and all the rest of it. Bishoping. Nothing but a lot of bosh. Once they dig you in, there's no resurrecting."

"That's right," agreed Pavlik. "Once you're done for, you're done for for good."

"What about on Mars?" asked Vitya sceptically.

"On Mars! Well, what about it?" said Pavlik with a shrug.

"You didn't read what I did, so you don't know."

"You must have read backwards," said Vanya. "The people on Mars aren't dead. They're alive."

"Uhuh," agreed Pavlik. "Only they're called Marsists."

"Here's how it should be," continued Vitya. "Here lies . . ." (he paused, wondering whether he should say anything about "remains," or geography) " 'Here lies Arseni Romanovich, the best man in the world.' "

He glanced uncertainly at his comrades. Pavlik considered it a good version. Vanya was not particularly pleased.

"We ought to draw something and then carve it into the stone," he observed.

"A picture?"

"Uhuh."

"What kind?"

At this point the boys were overtaken by Ragozin, who laid heavy mittened hands on their shoulders.

"Frozen?"

"No," they chorused, taking to rubbing their ears again.

"We were just talking about what to write on the gravestone, Pyotr Petrovich."

"Well, and what did you decide?"

Once more they began arguing and offering new suggestions. Finally they made Pyotr Petrovich say what kind of inscription he would write.

"It seems to me we should just write: Arseni Romanovich Dorogomilov—Revolutionary."

"And nothing else?" asked Pavlik, chagrined.

"Nothing else."

"Nothing else," agreed Vanya. "That's just the thing!"

"Just the thing!" chimed in Pavlik. "Arseni Romanych would be glad, wouldn't he?"

Vitya became silent and thoughtful. It seemed sad that they should write only one little word about such a man as Arseni Romanovich.

The boys kept up with Pyotr Petrovich, trying to match their stride to his, and soon they reached the square, where a crowd of people were waiting for the streetcar.

It had become very cold and the storm was growing fiercer with the quick descent of night. But the boys waited patiently with the grownups in the cold and snow, ever more frequently rubbing their ears and squinting through the blizzard at the vague contours of the university buildings.

* 37 *

Kirill and Annochka saw each other every week after the first performance of *Love and Intrigue*. They had arranged to meet on the day of Dorogomilov's funeral.

It seemed to Kirill that thay met very frequently—that is, that they could not possibly meet more frequently, so difficult was it for both of them to extricate themselves from their work for two or three hours at a stretch. It was, of course, more difficult for him than for her. Annochka once said to him when they were fixing the hour of their next meeting:

"But don't you have a schedule?"

"A schedule of what?"

"Of when you're busy and when you're not."

"When I'm not?" he laughed. "Something unforeseen always turns up then."

His levity was not for long.

"The unforeseen is a rather important aspect of our work. Sometimes the most important. It teaches us to foresee."

"Then is there hope that someday you will learn to foresee on what day you can properly visit me?"

"Properly?"

"Yes. Not for just a minute."

She was amused by the seriousness with which he accepted her remark.

So far Kirill had never broken an engagement with Annochka—or rather, he had always let her know ahead of time if it was necessary to postpone it. But on that day he was unexpectedly sent to address a meeting outside of town. He counted on returning by the appointed hour, but everything interfered.

The meeting was summoned with the purpose of enlisting volunteers for the cavalry troops. People were crowded shoulder to shoulder in one of the dreary buildings of a military settlement on the hills. Everyone was standing. The audience consisted of Red Army recruits, employees from the settlement, inhabitants of the Monastery Settlement, workers from the brickkilns scattered over this section.

Izvekov spoke from a platform that heaved under his steps. He was in the habit of walking when he spoke. This helped him to take himself in hand and collect his thoughts, which flowed on in rhythm to his stride. He was oblivious of the jumping of the table covered with red bunting.

He spoke easily. The events he mentioned were of themselves sufficiently interesting to hold his audience. He told them about the victories in the south, about the flight of the defeated Yudenich to Whiteguard Estonia, the new offensive in Siberia against Kolchak—all the fronts of the civil war were in unprecedented motion, but this time they had been set in motion not on the initiative of the counterrevolution, as had been the case two or three months earlier, but by the concentrated will of the Red Army. It swept forward with its banners flying, giving back to Russia her distant borderlands.

There was something demanding, sullen and watchful in the hundreds of eyes that followed Kirill; it was as though his endurance and knowledge were being put to the test. But he doggedly paced back and forth under their scrutiny, stopping himself at the turnings, stabbing the air occasionally with his fist—evidently to thrust his point home. As for his knowledge, it proved to be so thorough that when he began to enumerate the victories of the Red cavalry, brows cleared, there was a relieved shuffling of feet and a murmur of voices followed, along with a crackle of applause: the meeting had evidently decided that Kirill had passed the test.

Kirill wound up by saying that the enemy had been disgraced, smashed and put to flight, but that he was not yet destroyed, and that in order to finish him off the ranks of the fighting men needed new strength. And he called on his hearers to join the Mounted Army; he called on cavalrymen, old and young, and machine gunners, experienced and novices, with horses and without—all who felt strength in their arms, all whose hearts burned with hatred for the Whiteguards and loyalty to the cause of the liberation of the workers and peasants.

He expected that volunteers would respond at once to this appeal. But instead the men began to put questions, and a few asked for the floor.

A bewhiskered Astrakhaner with yellow stripes on his wide trousers climbed on to the platform. His speech was at first less eloquent than loud, and he held his audience not so much by what he said as by the volume of his voice. There were Cossacks and Cossacks, he said; there were the general's lackeys and dyed-in-the-wool kulaks and shopkeepers; but also there were Cossacks like himself. He was a real Cossack, whose palm was his drinking cup when life demanded. The meeting listened to him with evident mistrust, but he wound up by saying something that quieted them down and caused sympathetic glances to follow him back to his place.

"A real Cossack," he said, "has a healthy respect for the Red cavalry. Nowadays the Reds are the only ones who are true to their colours. They stand staunch in the face of the enemy, all alike and no exceptions. Those in the front and those in the rear. They don't play hide-and-seek. But there's another side to the picture. What side is that? Let me tell you. Who was the first to put the Urals Whites to flight? Vasili Ivanych Chapayev. He may not have been a Cossack, but he could outride the best Cossack by a whole length. And where is Comrade Chapayev now? At the bottom of a Urals river below Lbishchensk. Why was he allowed to get killed? Why didn't his men protect him with their bodies? Why couldn't they get him out of Lbishchensk in time? What if he did want to get a slash at the Whites himself! He ought to have been protected like the eagle protects its own. And then we would have him with us safe and sound today. We haven't got so many Red atamans; they're only beginning to appear. We've got to have service regulations that will make every man stand true to his colours, and that each man should get the protection he deserves for his services to the Red cavalry. We've got to take care of our atamans. That's my proposal to the comrades."

This speaker was followed by others, and then men began to speak straight from the floor without raising hands or asking the chairman's permission. Kirill realized that all this was taking the meeting too far from the business in hand.

He asked for the floor again, answered the questions that had been raised, and said that the speaker had been right about Chapayev. Chapayev's comrades had not taken proper care of him, nor had Chapayev himself thought of his own safety; it was necessary to be on the lookout day and night

661

since in no other war that had ever been fought had there been such a merciless and treacherous enemy as the Whites.

"The heroic death of Chapayev is mourned by all Soviet Russia, and it is a particularly grievous loss for the Volga whose son he was. Yet there is something in Chapayev's death that makes him akin to our legendary national heroes. Like Vasili Buslayev he knew neither hesitation nor timidity in the face of death. Like Yermak Timofeyevich he met his end swimming across the river he had made glorious by his deeds of valour. Other heroes will come to take his place. And the more men flock to our army and our cavalry, the sooner will these leaders appear. They will come from the ranks of the people, from your seasoned ranks, comrades!"

Kirill went over to the table, picked up a sheet of paper and raised it above his head.

"Who wants to join a new fighting squadron to support our victorious cavalry? I declare the list open, and I myself will be the first volunteer for the Mounted Army. Who's next, comrades? Step up."

He stuck the pen into the inkwell. The table shook under his elbow and the pen cut through the paper against the soft backing of bunting. The meeting applauded loudly as he signed, and when volunteers began to climb onto the platform and form a line at the table, the applause grew louder.

Kirill called out the names of the men who enlisted, and all those seated at the table shook hands with the volunteers, who moved away with an air of solemn exaltation and earnestly persuaded others to follow their example as they climbed off the platform.

When he signed the list Kirill knew that he would be going to the front in any case, and not later than the following morning. The paper from the War Commissariat already lay in his pocket. But he felt that not to have signed would have been impossible in the face of those whom he had urged to do the same. The personal initiative essential for any undertaking was more patently necessary here than in any other case. In signing first, Kirill had acted on the impulse, prompted by an inner conviction that this would start things moving.

When he had taken the step and saw that he was not mistaken and that everything began to go smoothly, he felt a sense of elation as if he had earned public approval of a decision which for him was already fixed and irrevocable. The general feeling of uplift, which had been absent at first and which was hardly to be expected from such a heterogeneous crowd, was communicated to him. True, most of the enthusiasm came from the new recruits

663

who, almost to a man, demanded to be transferred from the infantry to the cavalry. But their youthful fervour inspired many others.

Kirill left the meeting with that feeling of intense satisfaction that is brought by the consciousness of having accomplished something important. Thinking that he would not be late for his appointment with Annochka, he climbed happily into the car. But they were hardly on their way when they had a blowout.

The blizzard which had been rising since the late afternoon had now gotten into full stride. Winters that start too soon nearly always begin with vicious snowstorms which tear and harass everything on the surface of the earth, piling up snowdrifts in the lowlands and licking the last blade of grass off the hills. Dust, as hard and stinging as ground glass, is whirled with the snow. The very houses shiver and groan under the pressure of the wind. Everything is bent and bowed; everything trembles and whistles in uncanny polyphony.

As he stepped onto the road, Kirill was almost knocked off his feet by the door of the car, swung back by a gust of wind. The snow swirled malevolently around him as if about to entwine him in its white shroud and roll him, bound hand and foot, over the snowhills together with the wind that swept low over the ground. The driver gave vent to the finest epithet in his treasured collection reserved for breakdowns, and reached for the jack.

Kirill thought of taking cover inside the car, but suddenly changed his mind and announced that he would walk the rest of the way rather than stand and freeze in the field.

He raised the collar of his overcoat, thrust his hands into his pockets and with his head bent against the wind, set out down the middle of the road. His surroundings were unfamiliar and he was not sure which part of town the road would lead to. It was as dark ahead as around him. The cold penetrated deeper and deeper under his coat, the wind now blew open its skirts, now flung them tightly around his legs or wound them between his knees. His step grew less sure and steady.

Kirill's exhilaration gradually vanished. He felt annoyed with himself for not having warned Annochka of the possibility of his being detained. Added to this annoyance was an uneasiness that had disturbed him for the past few days, indeed ever since he had known that he was going to the front. He had put off telling Annochka and his mother in the hope that the briefer the leave-taking, the easier it would be for all concerned. Now it became clear to him that this had been a brutal thing to do, that Annochka was bound to reproach him with heartlessness and disregard for her feelings, and that he would indeed have nothing to say in his own defence.

Through the stinging swirl of the blizzard Kirill saw the warm light of the little room where he yearned to be now and which was still so far away. Every moment brought some other detail of that room to his mind, and his annoyance at himself mounted.

The wind buffeted him rudely in the back. For an instant he had the sensation of going downhill, and he was reminded of the slanting floor in Annochka's room: one of the walls in the building where the Parabukins dwelt had settled. He had a vision of the woven tablecloth that resembled a honeycomb; the magazine reproduction of Quinji's *Birch Grove* on the wall; the brown and yellow straw flowers stuck behind the photograph of Annochka's mother; the cone-shaped, paper lamp shade with one side burnt a chocolate brown; the lid of the sewing machine reverently covered with a linen towel bearing the embroidered inscription: "When the family's together all is well"—all these details of a home that had already become dear and familiar to him passed before his mind's eye, and amid these surroundings he saw Annochka sitting on the bed, her blue eyes staring out of the frosted window: "He didn't come, he didn't come." He pulled down his cap, bent his head lower against the blast, drew his collar over his ears and quickened his pace.

Of course it did not require much imagination to visualize from afar every corner of the simple room, and every movement of Annochka in it. Waiting for him she had not only sat on her bed (exactly as Izvekov had pictured her); she had moved from place to place twenty times over, sitting down only to get up again and run to the door or to the window and hearken to the groans and howls of the blizzard, fearing that they might drown out the sound of Kirill's knock.

On returning from Dorogomilov's funeral, she had put up the samovar in order to warm up properly. With unwonted alacrity she had allowed Pavlik to visit Vitya. Tikhon Platonovich had announced that he had some business of state urgency to attend to (and how could she object to state business even if she did not believe for a moment that her father was speaking the truth). She was only too glad to be left alone.

An hour later she was wearing her prettiest dress and the whole place was neat and tidy, and she had the samovar going again so that Kirill might also have something hot to drink when he came. Outside the blizzard howled savagely, the wind sought out microscopic cracks in the window and whined through them like a host of mosquitoes.

The time dragged on agonizingly and Annochka began to despair. She turned over in her mind everything Kirill had ever said to justify or explain his preoccupation with his work, his duty, or anything else bearing on the difference between his life and hers, his responsibility to people, to the revolution, to the epoch—oh, there was no end to the things that obliged Kirill to live a life all his own, so utterly different from the commonplace, trivial life of Annochka.

Why had she never before thought about the meaning of all his excuses, those imaginary accidents that had often prevented their seeing each other all through the summer and autumn? How could she have failed to notice that he was irked, burdened, encumbered by these meetings she waited for, these promises which she extracted from him—that he should come, that he should ignore those unforeseen duties that stood like a barrier in their path? Oh, of course, his duties were important, she realized that. They were of state urgency. Izvekov was not Parabukin. He would not prevaricate. There was no need for him even to exaggerate.

But if that were so then the gulf between Kirill's momentous concerns and Annochka's petty ones would never be bridged. On the contrary, it could only grow wider and deeper. Did that mean that

Annochka would become an even greater burden to Kirill, and that she would be doomed to still more of this fruitless waiting, waiting for him to condescend to allot her a moment of his valuable time and to favour her with his precious attention?

Why, indeed, should he consider himself to be privileged in that respect? Was not her time every bit as valuable as his? Had it been easy, for instance, for the sake of this wretched rendezvous with Kirill, to miss the reading of the new play in which Tsvetukhin promised her a part? To stay away from the theatre where she was expected, the theatre in which she had just launched on a work that had obsessed her thoughts from childhood? Was that not a sacrifice? And what was Kirill doing? He was deceiving her. He had deceived her. He had not come.

But perhaps he would still come. Perhaps he had been detained by something exceptionally urgent. After all, so many big things were happening these days. And he was such a big man. He was doing such important work. How could one compare his work with the reading of a play in which Annochka might not be given any role at all? She had hurt Tsvetukhin too much for him to give her any role. She ought to consider herself lucky to love such a remarkable man as Kirill and to be loved by him.

He did love her. Of course he did. He had simply been detained. He would not deceive her. He would be here any minute. What ought she to do for him? Ah God, she was ready to do anything, anything for him if only he would come! But he would not come. He was two hours late. No, two hours and four minutes. Four minutes! Dear God, what could she do to make him come? Heat the samovar once more? It was cold. The chimney was howling like a demon. But the samovar was cold. Kirill Izvekov was cold. Gracious, what nonsense she was thinking!

She split some kindling and threw it into the samovar, went back and sat down on the bed. With her elbows on her knees she held her head in her hands. Perhaps it would be better to lie down. Her forehead was afire.

And suddenly Annochka bounded from the bed and stood motionless, listening. A knock at the door. Yes, she was not mistaken. A rapid, insistent knocking.

He had come.

She ran out to the door and raised the latch with one swift movement. Out of the darkness a figure stumbled toward her, plastered with snow from head to foot and bent under the blast.

"Quick, quick!" she murmured, throwing open the door of the inner room and straining with her other hand and her knee to prevent the wind from slamming the outside door. Barely managing to cope with the latch, she rushed back into the room, stopped in the doorway, and nearly cried out.

There before her, pulling off his heavy overcoat and shaking the snow off onto the floor, stood Tsvetukhin.

"Damn it all! Knocks you clean off your feet! Hello honey. Alone? That's fine."

With her back pressed against the cold doorjamb, Annochka stared at Egor Pavlovich round-eyed. The dismay that seized her at that moment distorted her features into a grimace of helplessness and fright.

"Got the samovar going?" Egor Pavlovich was saying, wiping the rime from his brows. "A glass of something hot is just what I need. My, but it's nice and warm in here! Waiting for your family to come home?"

He patted her hand uncertainly.

"Aren't you well? Why weren't you at the reading of the play? I've just come from the theatre. Took it for granted you must be sick."

At last self-possession returned, and she replied to all his questions at once—yes, she hadn't felt very well after coming home from the cemetery, and that was why she had stayed home. Pavlik and her father should arrive any moment.

"Ah yes—Dorogomilov," he exclaimed. "Poor chap. I also wanted to go to the funeral, but the devil only knows all the business cropped up. He was a queer bird all right. A rarity. One of a vanishing tribe. But you seem to be out of sorts."

She busied herself with the tea things—the refuge usually resorted to by hospitable hostesses who wish to hide their feelings from uninvited guests.

Tsvetukhin took her by the hand and made her sit down opposite him.

"Listen, Annochka, I came because I had to speak to you."

He looked at her resolutely, but his lower lip trembled with something like injury.

"You and I must have it out. The way things are now ... because of your behaviour...."

"My behaviour? Why, have I been behaving badly?"

"It seems to me you're the best one to decide that—whether it's good or bad to rouse people's curiosity about yourself—an unwholesome curiosity—on the part of the whole troupe."

"I have roused it? On the part of the whole troupe? And an unwholesome curiosity at that?"

Annochka shifted her chair away from him.

"Please don't talk like that," pleaded Egor Pavlovich. "It's not like you. Yes, unfortunately the curiosity is about you too."

"And who else?"

"You act as if I didn't exist."

"Egor Pavlovich, have I offended you?" Annochka asked in sudden earnestness, lowering her voice.

"Offended?" Tsvetukhin cried, and now his voice sounded with the undisguised chagrin which makes a man a trifle ridiculous and hence annoyed with himself. "It is more insulting than offensive to know that people are whispering and sneering at you behind your back."

"Egor Pavlovich!"

"I don't mean you. You don't do any whispering. But all the others do. I'm certain that you don't fully realize what is happening, and so I don't take offence. Forgive me, but I feel that I have to explain things to you. If you yourself don't see—or if—if you are doing it the least bit intentionally after all...."

"Honestly I don't understand what you're talking about," said Annochka, brightening up a bit.

"How can that be? For a whole month you have been treating me with the coldest formality.

Forgive me, but that is terribly petty. 'How do you do,' 'goodbye,' 'thank you,' and that's all. What sort of an attitude is that? People can't help noticing. If you were a person used to stirring up intrigue, no one would pay any attention to it. But after all, you are my pupil. Everyone is curious to know what is going on. They sense that there must be something between you and me. Something wrong —or perhaps right. Can't you appreciate the position you put me in?"

"What if I do?" said Annochka slowly, staring fixedly at Egor Pavlovich. "What if I am doing it a bit intentionally?"

He stood up, ran his hand through his hair and began pacing the floor with a measured step.

"I refuse to believe it. I know you too well. You'd have to have someone else's heart in your breast to do a thing like that."

She was silent, hearkening to the voice of her agitated heart to discover whether it really harboured any feeling that was not her own. But no, no.

"No," she said with unrestrained emotion. "I wanted to keep my independence. I was hurt—terribly hurt for you that time—after our performance. Hurt—and ashamed."

"But I too wished to keep my independence!"

cried Egor Pavlovich almost imploringly. "Can it be that you still don't see. . . ."

She too got up.

"Oh no, I see everything. I saw it all of a sudden and was afraid that perhaps Pastukhov had been right—last summer."

He began shouting in a voice that was scarcely recognizable.

"Pastukhov! That fine gentleman who hasn't said a sincere word in his life! Nothing but posing and affectation! Remember how he boasted that he wrote only when inspired? The other day some actors came from Kozlov and said he was scribbling texts for animated cartoons. He disgraced himself when Mamontov was there and now he's trying to show that he's converted and willing to do anything. Had to get down off his high horse!"

Egor Pavlovich stopped short, as though ashamed of having let himself go. He straightened his tie and took a step or two before he continued in a calmer tone, though with the same irritation:

"It's strange that you should have come to share Pastukhov's opinion of me. You yourself called his words vile."

"I remember. But I only came to fear that he might have been right."

"But how—how could he have been right?"

"Egor Pavlovich, whose fault is it that I remembered his words?"

He strode over to Annochka and seized her hands, seeking to draw her toward him, and began to speak with such fervour that she could neither stop him nor object even by a gesture.

"Listen, listen to me! Who has contaminated you? Who has managed to give you such a low opinion of actors? I can see that these are not your own ideas. I could understand and forgive your coldness, your suspicion, even your dislike, if we had met only yesterday. But you know me so well. I have done a lot for you, Annochka, but I am ready to do ever so much more because of my feeling for you. How can you not trust me? Have I ever deceived you in anything? Never in my life have I had a more pure, a more genuine attachment to anyone. You bring me new life, do you understand? A new future. Why should I hide my hopes from you?"

"But how can I help myself, when . . ." exclaimed Annochka, trying to interrupt him.

He would not let her speak.

"Wait! Answer only one question. Look at me — look, I tell you. Do you believe me when I say that I have never adored anyone as I adore you?"

"But this is torture—forcing me to speak when I cannot."

"You cannot? All right. Wait. Wait with your answer. I shall not press you. I am patient—oh, how patient!" said Tsvetukhin bitterly.

"I shall not try your patience," she said in a fit of stubbornness.

"Wait. No decision for the present. Nothing final. You yourself will be convinced. You will come to understand and appreciate this suffering."

Her chin began to tremble, and it was difficult to tell whether she was struggling with laughter or tears.

"To suffer ... and then to relive the suffering ..." she murmured, as though to herself.

"Oh, that there should be such cruelty in an innocent young heart!" Egor Pavlovich sighed in despair, pressing her hands still more tightly.

"Let me go. Don't you hear? Someone is knocking," she cried, wrenching herself free and running out.

She paused to listen and hurried to the outside door. Above the howling of the blizzard she distinctly heard a loud impatient knocking. As soon as she lifted the latch the door flew open by itself, someone entered the hallway, and Annochka knew at once that this was Kirill.

"I'll close it. Run inside or you'll catch cold," he said in a voice hoarse from his battle with the storm.

677

She rushed back into the room. Tsvetukhin was standing against the window with something almost martial in his bearing. She lifted her hand as if to prepare him for a surprise, but dropped it at once as Izvekov entered.

He was fumbling at his coat buttons with his numb fingers. The snow fell in lumps from the folds in his sleeves. He stamped his feet to shake the snow off his boots, threw down his coat, glanced at Annochka, then at Tsvetukhin, and tried to smile. But his face, stiff from the frost and flaming red, remained immobile.

"This is the limit! Real February weather!"

He quickly proffered an icy hand to both of them, went over to the round iron stove, hugged it close for a few seconds and then turned and stood with his back against it.

"Had you given me up, Annochka? Are you angry? I was at the Soldiers' Settlement. We had a blowout and I walked all the way from the cemetery."

"All the way from the cemetery!" she echoed and turned to glance at Tsvetukhin as if calling on him to share her amazement.

" 'A wanderer belated, comes knocking at the pane,' "* quoted Egor Pavlovich, stealthily tap-

* Pushkin.

678

ping on the window at his back and pretending to be listening to some mysterious sound.

"Is that you?" said Annochka softly.

"It's me," he answered in a frightened whisper. "Why, were you expecting some other wanderer?"

Kirill laughed. Bending over the samovar, he blew the ashes off the top, lifted it and carried it over to the table.

"Do the honours, Annochka!"

"Frozen?" she asked him, brightening up, and again she looked at Tsvetukhin as much as to say: you can see for yourself on what familiar terms we two are!

Kirill invited Tsvetukhin to take a seat at the table but Egor Pavlovich refused: he had to be going, he had only looked in for a moment to make sure Annochka was not sick.

"Sick?"

"We had a reading of a new play tonight and Annochka was supposed to be there. But she didn't come. She has never missed a reading before."

"Why didn't you tell me?" Kirill said to Annochka. "We could easily have met some other evening."

The three exchanged glances and, unexpectedly for all of them, Annochka ran into the next room and burst out laughing like a naughty child caught in a prank.

The injured look returned to Egor Pavlovich's face—at such moments he stuck his lower lip out too far and held it pressed in distaste against the upper lip.

"You must not let Annochka have her own way too much," Kirill said, suppressing a smile. "She has a tendency to be self-willed."

"Yes, there is still something of the child about her," Tsvetukhin said severely. "Of course, it is a wonderful thing to be natural. But you cannot create art only by being natural. Art is primarily work, work, work" (he bore down irritably on the last word). "It demands all that a person has to give. Private life must be relegated to the background, must be subordinated" (he viciously chopped the word into pieces—sub-or-din-a-ted) "if one wishes to dedicate oneself to the service of art. This must be accepted as a law."

"I share your views," said Kirill with a gravity not unmixed with mockery. "And it is my earnest request that you insist on Annochka's strictly observing this law."

He paused. With lowered brows he kept his eyes fixed on Tsvetukhin.

"I should not like anything in Annochka's private life to interfere with her work. Especially in my absence. If I go away."

Annochka came in from the other room. She was holding a sheet of paper, and with each step her hands dropped lower.

"If you go away?" she said softly.

He lacked the courage to answer directly, and passed it off with a jest.

"Well, just in case. Into whose care could I entrust you more safely?"

She sensed his evasion and smiled, still on her guard.

"Here you are scolding me, both of you, but I work much better when I'm praised than when I'm scolded. Egor Pavlovich, may I boast a little?"

She handed Kirill the paper.

It was a certificate of honour, elaborately inscribed in red, yellow, and blue letters, presented to Luise Miller by the fighting men of the cavalry detachment (Annochka had played her only role seven times over in the club). The authors of the certificate spoke of the actress who had pleased them in terms customarily applied to the dead— they praised her virtues with a lavishness that excluded the possibility of it being within her power ever to disappoint them. They wrote that her acting had shown them what the poor had had to endure at the hands of the tyrannical monarchy. They assured her that such splendid performances as *Love and Intrigue* had strengthened their resolve to fight for complete victory over the bourgeoisie. They called Comrade A. T. Parabukina superb, incomparable, and declared that although some of them had seen the play twice, they would be only too glad to see it many more times. And they invited A. T. Parabukina and the other actors to come and visit them at the front, where "... you will show us your proletarian art, and we in our turn will grind the reptile Denikin into the dust." And beside nearly every signature penned by the admirers of Annochka's art was added some remark such as: "Till we meet again," "Visit us at the front," and even "On to Rostov!"

Kirill studied the fantastic flourishes that covered the paper, perceiving the peculiar significance of the message contained in these earnest, heartfelt words. He reached into his pocket and produced a pencil.

"What are you doing?" Annochka cried and rushed over to snatch the paper away from him.

"I also want to sign it."

"Oh no. You mustn't. I shan't allow anyone to make fun of it. I intend to keep it for always."

Holding the paper out of her reach, he got up and turned his back, placing it against the wall while he signed his name in the upper corner.

"Oh, why did you do that!" she exclaimed almost in tears.

"In the first place I too want your theatre to go to the front," he replied as calmly as he could. "And secondly, I have as much right as anyone else to sign this certificate."

"Nothing of the kind—just because you happened to see the play. And now you're making fun of it all."

"No, this happens to be my cavalry unit. I have been placed in charge of it and am taking it to the front. We leave tomorrow morning."

Annochka stood motionless staring at him. Kirill's face, red from the frost a moment before, quickly paled. He seemed overwhelmed by the effect his words had on Annochka. He pushed forward a chair for her.

Tsvetukhin cleared his throat and gave a loud sigh.

"Yes indeed, that would be splendid. We should like nothing better than to go to the front. That's our dream. But what about our repertory? So far we have only one play. And a rather elaborate one. To be sure, we could reduce the scenery to a cyclorama. Simplify it, cut it...."

He waited anxiously for a reply. His vibrant voice was much too loud for this tiny room.

"But we'll do our best, won't we, Annochka?"

"We'll do our best," she repeated absent-mindedly.

"And so you're leaving tomorrow?" continued Tsvetukhin in the same jarring voice. "Against Denikin, eh? Well, the only thing I can do is wish you luck. For myself, I can promise you that we shall go on working to the best of our ability."

He gave Kirill's hand a vigorous shake and began to put on his coat.

"You need have no fear about Annochka. I know her virtues and her weaknesses, and I shall always be exacting. Very exacting. Goodbye. If we need your help, I hope you won't refuse it—I mean the theatre. We are allies, you know."

"I'll see you out," said Kirill.

His movement toward the door seemed to bring Annochka to herself. She sprang forward to stop Kirill, and herself went into the hall with Tsvetukhin. In the darkness he muttered a few despairing words.

"I see how it is, honey. Well, there's nothing to do about it. You'll always be the same to me. I hope you'll be happy. Only...."

A gust of wind carried his last words into the blizzard as he crossed the threshold.

Annochka slammed the door and ran back into the room, coming to a standstill in front of Kirill. It was clear that she was struggling to reconcile herself to what Kirill had told her, but could not.

"The only, only thing I ask of you is not to always break such news all of a sudden like this," she said bitterly.

He held out his arms, but she seemed not to notice this gesture betokening his sense of guilt.

"Why? Why always at the last minute?"

"I thought it was better so."

"In order to avoid spending an extra hour with me?"

"In order to avoid talking about what is clear without words."

"In order to make it more painful?"

"In order to shorten the pain."

"Don't you think that is cruel?"

"Too often courage is called cruelty. Why should you make the same mistake? The only thing required for our complete happiness now is courage."

She answered him with a look revealing unfathomed depths of womanliness, and strangely enough he accepted this as the pledge of courage he had awaited. They sat down together on the edge of the bed. He held her hands and gazed into her eyes.

The roar of the wind outside the window emphasized the utter silence within the room. They heard each other's breathing, and the crackle of the flame in the lamp, and the mosquito-drone of the wind through the cracks, and the cheerful ticking of the cuckoo-clock on the wall. It seemed to Kirill that Annochka had now found the reconciliation which only so recently had seemed impossible.

"When you judge my actions, darling, always try to be a bit older than your age. I beg this of you."

"It seems to me I have always been older than my age. But why do you ask this of me?"

"I have no right to do only what is pleasant for myself or for those I love. I must answer for my actions, do you understand? I must answer for them."

"I understand—that is not so difficult. You must answer to everyone else. But not to me?"

"To you too, in so far as that is possible," he answered, smiling good-naturedly. "It's funny, but on the way here I was thinking that I should have told you sooner about my leaving."

She squeezed his fingers.

"So you repented?"

"Perhaps it really was thoughtless of me."

"But must we forever weigh everything we do?"

Without answering, he bent down and placed his cheek on her palm. With her other hand she stroked his wiry hair that needed a cutting. He raised his head and once more gazed into her eyes.

"Ah, dear . . ." she whispered.

He kissed her. For some time she was silent, and then her face was lighted by a new, bewildered smile.

"Are you thinking now about what you are doing?" she asked, still softly, turning upon him her huge, darkening eyes.

He kissed her again with added fervour. She withdrew and lifted her sensitive chin to indicate the window.

He jumped up, went over to the table, and in one breath blew out the light.

* 38 *

The storm subsided during the night.

The December day was barely dawning when Annochka left the house. The street was strangely quiet. Along the pavements the snow lay in rippling waves, like sand dunes. The streets were bare in the middle and only here and there at the edges stood lopsided snowhills with sharp glistening crests. Crows perched silently on the black trees.

The serenity of the town after the blizzard did not allay Annochka's agitation, but rather intensified it. She was in a great hurry.

At the station sleepy, impatient people kept pouring in from somewhere and disappearing somewhere, crowding together suddenly only to be swallowed up again. The doors swung back and forth, with loud thuds and groans. The hissing of locomotives sounded now far off, now so close by that they seemed threatening to break into the station building.

Annochka stood in the main hall under the far window near the platform as she and Kirill had agreed the night before. She waited for a long time and her eyes grew weary gazing into the milling throngs surging from exit to exit.

When he did appear she did not recognize him for a moment. He wore a sheepskin jacket that reached to his knees, white *valenki*, and a Cossack cap of some brown, short-haired fur. He looked clumsy and he rolled rather than walked up to Annochka.

"At least you won't freeze," she said with a smile.

He took off his fur mittens and stuck them under his arm in a soldierly gesture.

"If you had told me sooner that you were leaving I would not have come here emptyhanded," she said.

He took her hands and stroked each finger.

"For me they are never empty," he said.

For a moment they gazed into each other's eyes.

"The men have boarded the train. It's at the platform. We'll be leaving soon."

"Already?" she said softly, lowering her eyes.

"Let's go," he said.

He took her by the elbow and steered her out onto the platform, where they walked down the length of the train. Clouds of steam rose from the doors of the cars, icicles hung from the roofs, and the freight cars smelt of horses.

"Is it a long way?" asked Annochka.

"The last car."

"Let's not hurry."

They heard neither the shouts nor the singing, nor the dashing chords of the harmonica. As they walked on and on, they involuntarily slackened their pace.

At last they saw Ragozin with Vera Nikandrovna beside him. They all stood there for a while, speaking of trifles. Then the whistle of the engine blew. Louder and more strident grew its fearless voice, making the very air shudder.

"Well," said Kirill's lips. He looked at his mother and embraced her.

Then his eyes turned to Annochka. He took her in his arms and kissed her fiercely again and again until her lips hurt.

Then he tore himself away and glanced again at his mother. Vera Nikandrovna smiled and nodded to him. He stepped over to her. She pressed his head to her breast and—just as the whistling broke off—she said in a secretive whisper: "I shall take care of her. Never fear."

She continued to nod. The past night had brought the lines on her face into sharper relief and it was suddenly evident that she was growing old.

Kirill turned to Ragozin. The train was already moving. They both ran after the car whose platform was crowded with soldiers. Kirill jumped onto the step.

"I'll be following you before long!" Ragozin shouted as he bared his head.

"You see to your health first, Pyotr Petrovich! Take care of yourself! Goodbye!" Kirill had time to reply, looking over Ragozin's bald head.

Annochka stood motionless with her arm upraised. Kirill waved his mittens. It was only then that both he and she noticed what a crowd of people had come to see the train off. Almost instantly they lost sight of each other amid the forest of waving hands, caps and kerchiefs.

People's voices which had drowned out the sound of the train's motion at first, quickly died down, and the rumble of the wheels now reached Annochka from afar, growing fainter and fainter.

This is the worst moment in parting with a loved one—this second when the train leaves, when the last car disappears from sight and suddenly you are overcome by a sense of the physical loss of some being who belonged to you, who but a moment back was near enough to touch, and now is beyond your reach.

Ragozin and Vera Nikandrovna were aware that they both felt the poignancy of that moment and that Annochka felt it too. But they were struck also by the conflict of emotions they read in Annochka's face; she seemed to be not only overwhelmed by the pain of separation but to be facing some new ordeal. She was pale and seemed about to collapse.

"Come along," said Ragozin, offering his arm to Annochka with studied cheerfulness and exaggerated gallantry.

"Perhaps we ought to sit down for a while," Vera Nikandrovna suggested with concern. "And then we can go to my place."

"Thank you, I cannot," said Annochka, "I have to go.... Oh, Vera Nikandrovna, it would be so good if you could come with me!"

"Of course, my dear, if you wish. But where must you go so urgently?"

"To the hospital."

"The hospital? Do you feel ill?"

"No, no. It's my father. He was taken to the hospital last night."

"Why, what's the matter with him?"

They halted in the middle of the now half-deserted platform, and Annochka gave a hasty account of what she had learned about Tikhon Platonovich the evening before.

Soon after Kirill had left her, Pavlik came home. He was accompanied by a man he had met at their gate who happened to work with Parabukin. After working all evening at the Old Goods Department, this man had braved the blizzard to find Parabukin's house and bring bad news about Tikhon Platonovich.

It turned out that on returning from Dorogomilov's funeral, Parabukin had shut himself up in his cubbyhole with his friend Mefody in order to hold a wake. After a time they had emerged in high spirits and Mefody had announced that the wake had been disproportionate to the grief they both felt at the loss of such a man as Arseni Romanovich Dorogomilov. Whereupon they had both gone out, evidently in search of the missing proportion. Some three hours later, when this man had finished his work and was preparing to leave, a telephone call came from the hospital. Tikhon Platonovich and Mefody, it appeared, had been picked up on the street and taken to the hospital with symptoms of stomach poisoning.

It had been too late to go to the hospital in the storm, and so Annochka had decided to wait until morning.

She wound up her story by saying that she had been unable to sleep all night. Naturally, no one need know that to her anxiety for her father was added all that she had experienced in that brief evening so full of conflicting experiences— from the torment of loneliness to her talk with Egor Pavlovich, from the shock of the news of Kirill's departure to those minutes which made Annochka and Kirill belong to each other forever.

Ragozin settled the matter: "I have a cab here. It can take you wherever you have to go. If you need help, let me know."

The two women set off at once for the hospital. On the way Vera Nikandrovna asked but one question—had Annochka told Kirill about her father's mishap?

"No, why should I? There was no time for him to do anything and it would have been an added weight on his mind."

Vera Nikandrovna, who held Annochka around the waist, pressed closer to her, and thus they sat throughout the long and painful journey, with the cab now getting stuck in the snowdrifts, now diving into the ruts between the cobbles.

Annochka kept herself in hand, deriving strength from silence. She endured the long ordeal at the hospital, her whole body tensed with the effort of self-control, her face pale and impassive.

There was a great deal of waiting to be done because every person Izvekova and Annochka approached had many duties to attend to at once. Nurses and doctors hurried down the corridors, stopping or being stopped to answer the questions of anxious visitors. To be in the hospital was part of the profession of these doctors and nurses, a job they had been at day in and day out all their lives. But for those who came here owing to the illness or death of relatives and friends, the experience was untoward, harrowing, and often an irreparable misfortune. Those who worked in the hospital were of the opinion that everything was being done for the patients, and to them the anxiety of the visitors was exaggerated and annoying. The visitors, on the other hand, were firmly convinced that everything was *not* being done for the patients, and the imperturbability of the hospital workers alarmed and irritated them. Here, just as in a courtroom, one could see only too plainly the difference between a person's attitude towards that which affects him personally, and that which affects others.

The young lady at the desk looked over the entries made in the registry book the night before and confirmed the fact that Tikhon Platonovich and Mefody Silych had indeed been brought here and sent to ward number so-and-so. They could enquire about the patients' condition at the Information Office. The Information Office, after consulting the night register, stated that both patients had been placed in the said ward in a serious condition, temperature such-and-such. No information had been received as yet concerning their condition that morning, but this could be learned by calling the nurse attending the ward and asking her to find out from the ward doctor. It took them a good half hour before they could locate the nurse. When she appeared it was to inform them that when she had gone on duty that morning no new patients had been reported to her. She undertook to make enquiries from the senior nurse or at the doctors' room, but on the way there she paused for a long time in the doorway of the Information Office in full view of Annochka and Vera Nikandrovna to gossip with another nurse, showing her a hole worn through one of her felt boots. It was another half hour at least before a nurse appeared with a tiny red cross on her apron and said that both patients had been moved during the night from general ward number so-and-so to a private ward number so-and-so, and that no one was allowed to see them. If they wanted to find out about the patients' condition before the Information Office received the morning data, they would have to get permission from the chief of the department, but that was impossible at the moment because he was making his morning rounds. The head doctor could also give the necessary permission, but he happened to be in the operating room.

The nurse went back to the door through which white uniforms were continually passing in both directions, but before she reached it she turned back and pointed out a thin man with gaunt shaven cheeks.

"There's Ignati Ivanovich," she said. "Ask him. He's the head of the department."

She went up to him herself and said something. He glanced at Vera Nikandrovna and Annochka, shook his head, and continued his conversation with a woman who was continually interrupting him with questions and twisting her fingers. Presently a young girl approached him from the Information Office and proceeded loudly to deny having received some book from someone. Together they disappeared into the Information Office. Their voices raised in argument issued from the little window through which information was given, and it was obvious that they were arguing about the same book the girl denied having received from anyone.

"Ignati Ivanovich!" came through the little window, "surely you don't think I'm making it up?"

At last Ignati Ivanovich reappeared and was about to go straight out of the door when he noticed Annochka and Izvekova and turned to them.

"You have come about Parabukin?" he asked in a confidential tone. "Are you relatives? Ah, your father."

His eyes kept wandering toward the door through which he had been about to pass, and he seemed to have difficulty making himself speak.

"Yes, yes," he said at last, and his tone implied that Annochka and Vera Nikandrovna already knew what he was about to tell them. "Yes, at seven o'clock. Died."

"What ... so suddenly?" Vera Nikandrovna managed to say, as if endeavouring to grasp the meaning of her own words, and she seized Annochka awkwardly by the arm so that it was impossible to tell whether she wished to support her or was herself seeking support.

"Well, it was not exactly sudden. He lived for ten hours. His heart was quite strong. Although he evidently had been indulging for some time? Powerful constitution."

"But he was not alone?" Vera Nikandrovna was still groping for the right words.

"Yes, the other one too. Weaker. An asthenical type. An hour or two earlier. Also a relative of yours? No?"

He subjected Annochka to closer scrutiny and said consolingly:

"Don't take it too much to heart. It is much better this way. Had they survived, they would have been blind. Methylated spirits."

He looked furtively at the door again.

"Where is he?" Annochka asked in a lifeless voice.

"You will be allowed to see him after the autopsy," said the doctor.

He began to tie the tapes on his left sleeve, pressing his wrist against his stomach.

"Excuse me, I must continue my rounds. You ought to sit down. I shall send someone to you."

He bowed to each of them and moved away with the springy step of an athlete, going through the door that had been beckoning to him all the time.

Annochka and Vera Nikandrovna sat down on

a bench. They did not look at each other, but sat close together, shoulder to shoulder, finding their only support in this proximity.

They were approached by the nurse with the tiny red cross who had informed them that they could not see the patients. She handed Annochka a small slender glass half full of a strong-smelling liquid.

"Drink this. You must," she said persuasively and as calmly as if there were not the slightest incongruity between what she had said before and what she was saying now.

Vera Nikandrovna took the glass and raised it to Annochka's lips. Annochka swallowed the medicine obediently.

Her face was as immobile and bloodless as before. It was not so much that she was unconscious of what was going on around her, as that she was indifferent to it, as if for her there was no longer any difference between the necessary and the negligible, the important and the trivial. She looked absently at the girl from the Information Office who was again shouting excitedly to someone through the window:

"I've never seen it, I tell you! Think I'm making it up, or what?"

And with the same absent air Annochka listened as Vera Nikandrovna sought for words of sympathy in an effort to rouse in her the desire to submerge her sorrow in action.

"Don't be afraid, I shall be with you. And we both have friends. We are not alone."

But in spite of Annochka's apathy and indifference to her surroundings, there was a tiny glimmer in the depth of her eyes indicating that frantic search for reason characteristic of the mentally sick. At this moment she was as liable to succumb to weakness and fall ill, as to discover hidden reserves of strength sufficient to give her confidence in herself for the rest of her life.

With this tiny glimmer she perceived the most poignant moments of the day that had passed; she seemed to hear the clatter of wheels over rails, to see the last car of the train slipping into the distance, and to hear a voice saying: "Try to be a little older than your age," and another voice: "His heart was quite strong." There was a certain coherence in this incoherence, albeit the one excluded the other. It was as if Annochka's soul were split in two, and one part, departing with the last car of the train, would go on living for years to come, while the other, remaining in the hospital, had departed from life forever.

She smiled with an infinite sadness.

"You know, Vera Nikandrovna," she said as

though making a sudden discovery. "Kirill was really very fond of father."

Vera Nikandrovna pressed Annochka's hand to her bosom, in a rush of maternal feeling.

"How right you are. You do not even guess how right, my dear."

"Father was really a very kindhearted person," said Annochka with the same sadness. "He was only unfortunate."

"You will have the happiness he missed."

"Why are we sitting here?" said Annochka, with a sobbing sigh as though she had wept refreshing tears. "We must do something. Let's go see Ragozin. And then Egor Pavlovich. Mefody Silych has caused him plenty of bother today."

"Yes, let us be going. We are not alone, we are not alone," Vera Nikandrovna reiterated.

They went out into the cold, and this was like physical return to reality. Again the wheels of the cab alternately rattled over the cobblestones and screeched in the snow. The city was still quiet, not yet recovered from the blizzard. And with every house, every block further from the hospital, Annochka had a clearer vision of the railway car crossing boundless white fields, and of herself inside, sitting opposite Kirill, reading his thoughts in the clear gaze of his golden eyes.

Naturally his thoughts were about Annochka. He could not leave her there alone; he took her along, carried her with him in this car, in this long train rolling across the Russian plain.

At some distant siding, as he stepped out of the car, his eyes dazzled by the brilliance of the sun-bathed snow-blanketed steppe, Kirill recalled what Tolstoy had said about travellers: during the first half of the journey one thinks of what has been left behind, at the point of departure; during the second half, of what awaits one ahead, at one's destination.

As the train sped on, Kirill made contact with his numerous fellow travellers. This was no ordinary train whose passengers are thrown together by chance and scatter again as soon as they reach their destination.

The troop train was like a small bustling town on wheels. And as the inhabitants of a town are bound into a community by the same roads, the same rivers and the same earth, so the travellers on board this train were united by a common purpose that transcended the bounds of the train and its movement. And the unity of their interests lay more in the fight for the future they were about to wage than in the daily round of feeding men and horses, playing cards and checkers, smoking and singing and climbing out of the train at sidings where they were detained by a closed semaphore.

Kirill grew more and more conscious of belonging to this town on wheels; more and more often his thoughts turned to the work awaiting him at the front and returned less and less frequently to the Saratov he had left behind. It was this fact that led him to recall Tolstoy's observation, and he realized that as the day advanced, even thoughts of Annochka occurred less frequently. Yet this caused him no concern. Annochka was merely retreating to the inmost recesses of his heart where he knew she would dwell as long as his heart beat.

The troop train took the route via Balashov and Povorino. There were the holdups and stoppages inevitable in a zone immediately behind the front lines, and only on the third day were the sites of recent great battles—Voronezh and Kastornaya—left behind. Winter had arrived in earnest; a continual blizzard hid the traces of sanguinary battles under a blanket of snow, and only the railway stations and villages along main roads wore the mourning of charred buildings and heaps of rubble.

At last the detachment became part of a cavalry brigade formed of replacements, wherewith Izvekov's main assignment—to take the echelon to its destination—was completed. He bid farewell to the Volga men and moved on further south where the First Mounted Army was operating.

The day he arrived at Novy Oskol the place was in the grip of excitement. Flags fluttered over the houses, mounted men dashed up and down the roads, and through the wide-open gates of the yards one could see saddled horses and knots of dismounted men. Groups of children bundled up in warm clothes ran up the streets followed by adults, all headed in one direction—out of town.

After repeatedly asking for directions and failing to find anyone who could tell him where he should go, Kirill bumped into a young commander in charge of a group of Red Army men who were engaged in trying to get a huge, cumbersome desk through the front door of a house. The door was narrow and the men tried carrying the desk sidewise, legs first, then squeezing it through upright.

"Pull the legs out," shouted one of the Red Army men. "We'll knock them back once we get it inside."

"Go ahead," said the commander, looking away with a hopeless gesture. His eyes lighted on Kirill, and he frowned as if the latter were to blame for the desk.

"What are you doing here, Comrade?"

Kirill told him what he was looking for, but this only increased the commander's displeasure.

"Let's see your papers."

By the very tone of the reply Kirill could tell that if he had not hit upon the right address he was not far from it. He produced his papers. Without removing his thick gloves, the commander gripped the documents in his fist and set to examining them with an air of stern concentration while the desk crunched like a gigantic nut being cracked. Then he turned around, saw that both desk and Red Army men had disappeared, and forthwith returned Kirill's papers cordially.

"So you're from Saratov? Never been there myself. Had occasion to be in Tsaritsyn, though. With Comrade Voroshilov. . . . Let's go inside."

He proved to be one of Voroshilov's orderlies who had been sent to Novy Oskol on a billeting mission. From him Kirill learned that a joint sitting of the Revolutionary Military Councils of the Southern front and the First Mounted Army had been held in a neighbouring village. Stalin, who had come from Serpukhov, where front headquarters were located, had addressed the sitting on the tasks of the First Mounted in the further realization of the plan for the defeat of Denikin.

Mounted Army formations had been concentrated in the vicinity, and a major review was scheduled to be held near Novy Oskol (one brigade from each division remaining in action at the front).

"Want to come along? I'll have a sleigh here in an hour," the orderly said.

The more he talked the more hospitable he grew. Evidently he really had been put out by the trouble the desk had given him. Now, however, when everything was going smoothly and he was supervising the disposition of the furniture in the petty-bourgeois parlour, carrying out flowerpots and rehanging the pictures, he felt right in his element and became more communicative.

"Well, let's go. Your appointment will have to be approved by Comrade Voroshilov in any case. And that goes for your report about that detachment of yours. In other words, there's plenty of time. You'll see what our divisions are like. They'll take your breath away."

He hesitated.

"What do you think, shall I leave this where it is or have it taken down?"

He nodded dubiously toward a soot-darkened oleograph depicting a *boyaryshnia* in old Russian headdress.

"Why does it bother you?"

"Well, there'll be commanders and commissars coming here to report to the Revolutionary Military Council."

"What of it? That's a Makovsky, after all."

"The devil knows about this art. You never can tell in advance."

They both laughed, each for his own reasons. That swift intimacy which springs up so quickly between soldiers at the front and often is as quickly forgotten, but which sometimes develops into a lifelong friendship, was already asserting itself.

By the time they set off for the review, Kirill and the orderly were friends. The blunt runners of the sleigh emitted an incessant high-pitched screech as they plunged into and slowly climbed out of holes in the road. The men were now thrown forward toward the dashboard, now jerked against the back of the seat, their conversation shifting tempo accordingly.

Immediately beyond the town limits spread the boundless steppe, intersected here and there by rolling hills and long tongues of swirling snow licking above the sugar-loaf expanses. It was the brightest hour of the winter's day, but the low-hanging snow clouds gave it a leaden hue.

In the distance Kirill discerned the dark segmented lines of cavalry on parade, the subdivisions spread out like railway ties over an enormous territory. A black ribbon of people stretched in the foreground, and as the sleigh drew nearer it began to overtake increasing numbers of hurrying latecomers.

When Kirill and the orderly reached the crowd and climbed out of the sleigh, it was no longer possible to push through the multitude of spectators to the central point where red banners were flying and where a place had been reserved for those who were to review the parade. The two climbed back into the sleigh and drove along behind the crowd, looking for a place where there were less people.

Reverberating cheers came from the distance and the wind brought intermittent strains of music. The inspection had begun—members of the Revolutionary Military Council were riding past the divisions on parade and greeting the various units.

Having at last found a convenient place and pushed into the front row of spectators, Kirill cast a glance at the steppe spread before him. Directly ahead and to the right, it rolled on and on to merge with the horizon, hardly a spot breaking its smoothness except for tiny pencils of telegraph poles showing indistinctly through the ragged swirls of snow far away in the distance. To the left was the cavalry; on closer scrutiny you could make out in the forward line a strip of horses, and above it a strip of riders, and here and there a banner billowing out in the wind.

The music and the cheering ended, runners began dashing about, medical orderlies appeared with arm bands on their sleeves and kits slung over their shoulders. When this momentary animation subsided, Kirill saw a handful of men on horseback accompanying a sleigh approaching from the left down the line of spectators toward the centre.

"They're coming," the orderly said, nudging Kirill with his elbow. Almost at that very moment, however, the group of riders galloped so close to the front row of onlookers that they all but merged with it, and Kirill could not make out anything ahead, although he stepped a full pace in front of the crowd around him.

Immediately after came the brassy blare of trumpets, while somewhere in the distance barely audible words of command rang out. But all that happened far to the left of him and was nearly swallowed up by the steppe, and Kirill realized how far away he stood from the centre of events. He was annoyed at being off here on the sidelines; he wanted to be in the centre of things, but in spite of the feeling of annoyance his spirits rose in joyous elation at the sight of the distant wall of troops tensely awaiting the signal to move, and especially at the sight of the snowy expanse that seemed to be subordinated to these ranks of people.

The commands died out, and in the silence of the steppe you could hear the wind lashing the ground and the hard particles of snow rustle as they swept along.

A band struck up somewhere near by. It was a stirring cavalry march expressing a playful sort of valour, and its rhythm was set by the prancing of a well-trained steed. And gradually, after the band had struck up, a hollow rumble approaching in subterranean reverberations intruded upon the march strains: the cavalry had gone into motion, the review had begun.

It was a specific, unprecedented kind of movement that bore as little resemblance to marching as the flight of pigeons to the walking of man.

The divisions came in numerical order, and the parade was opened by the Fourth. The leading squadron set off at a trot, but went into a gallop almost at once. The men raised their sabres above their heads. The standard-bearer, bending low in the saddle with the flames of the banner sweeping over him, held his staff lowered like a pike,

so that it cleaved knife-like through the frigid air, while behind him poured the squadron in an irresistible onrush through the wide-open doors of space.

To the heavy rumbling was added the ring of the frozen earth, which responded like a myriad of tambourines under the iron-shod hoofs cutting through the blanket of snow. The cavalrymen cheered. The squadron was now in full gallop, and the pounding hoofs sent the snow flying and falling in cascades.

With breath-taking speed the first wave surged to the spot whence the march strains had come a moment before. Now, however, the music was swallowed up by the ring of the earth, the cheers of the mounted men, and the pounding of hoofs. The people, overwhelmed for an instant by the avalanche sweeping past them, responded with cheers and shouts, and everything merged in a solid peal of thunder.

Kirill caught a fleeting glimpse of a glowing face with a flash of bared teeth; a yellowish fur cap; the up-thrust head of a coal-black horse with twisted jaws fiercely grinding on the bit; the glint of sabre blades waving in the air; a sudden view of a huge black boot digging a spur into a horse's flank and as sudden a vision of the bloodless face of a youngster pressed close to a chestnut mane.

Barely had Kirill's eye picked out all this from the swirling white cloud than the squadron had already receded far to the right and another was thundering down from the left to replace it in a tumult of shouting and cheering, a beating of hoofs and a snorting of frenzied horses.

Thus squadron after squadron bore down on Kirill in motley array—in sheepskins and greatcoats and quilted jackets and Cossack *poddevki* and British uniforms captured from the Whites. With rifles over their shoulders. In caps and hats and hoods and cloth helmets. Riding all kinds of horses. The only uniformity to be found was in the flash of the sabres flourished above their heads and the ring of the good Russian steel.

"The Sixth! The Sixth Division's coming!" Izvekov's comrade shouted in his ear.

Kirill was already watching the Sixth's standard-bearer drive the lowered tip of his flagstaff through the headwind when a dark ball separated from the last squadron of the Fourth and rolled in the powdery snow.

"Man down!" came the shouts. "He'll be crushed! They'll trample him!"

The fallen horseman was lying on his back some ten paces from the edge of the crowd, and a few yards away his mount was thrashing the air with its hoofs, struggling to regain its feet.

Kirill sprang forward and the next moment was bending over the man; he seized him by the arm and began pulling him over the snow. The horseman's other hand was caught in the sword-knot, and the sabre, thrust deep in the ground, refused to part with its owner. Kirill wrenched it from the ground and again set to hauling the man. He heard the standard-bearer career by and the first squadron of the Sixth thunder down on him. Just then a medical orderly rushed over, and together they picked up the heavy burden and carried it to safety. The frightened horse had found its feet and a line guard had dashed up and led it aside a fraction of a second before the oncoming squadron arrived. As it was, the mount of the right-flank trooper struck the riderless horse such a blow on the hind quarters that the animal nearly lost its balance and trampled the nearest onlookers.

All this happened in the twinkling of an eye, and so eager were Kirill and the orderly to watch the parade that they dumped the rescued man in the snow the minute they reached safety.

The man came to from the jolt. He was a sturdy chap in Cossack uniform of the kind worn in the First Mounted by "non-Cossacks" from the Don and men of the Red Cossack units. His head was covered by a natural cap of shaggy blond hair; whatever headgear he had had was now being trampled by the passing squadrons. He raised himself from the ground and surveyed the crowd with a dazed look; his hand felt quickly for the sabre Kirill had returned to the scabbard, and then like a taut spring he leapt to his feet, buried his fingers in his tousled mane and shouted at the top of his voice:

"Mashka! Where's that bitch Mashka?"

Over the shoulders of the crowd he saw his mare, nodding its spotted nose in consternation. He dashed over to the animal, gave it a swipe between the eyes with the edge of his hand and seized the reins, jerking them from side to side, as he shouted:

"Damn your hide, why did you have to do a thing like that, eh? You lousy Whiteguard!"

This incident was soon forgotten in the excitement of watching the flying squadrons.

"The Eleventh!" shouted the orderly ecstatically when ranks of formidable-looking horsemen in Budyonny helmets hove in sight. The uniformity of this new headgear seemed to make their abandon even more striking, their onward sweep more irresistible, their cheering more fierce, as though they were going into deadly attack.

From the moment Kirill leapt to the assistance of the fallen trooper his mood of exaltation changed to a keen sensation that he himself was taking part in this parade. He was no longer a spectator watching squadron after squadron flash by; he himself was riding an invisible steed in the thick of the army. The difference was that whereas all the other troopers rode past the throngs but once, Kirill rode past with every squadron, with every trooper. His face was flaming, his blood was on fire, and he breathed quickly.

The review proceeded at lightning speed and was over in something like a quarter of an hour, during which time practically two-thirds of the total strength of the First Mounted Army passed before its leaders.

The people abandoned all semblance of order when the parade was over and rushed for the centre of the reviewing line. Once more you could hear the music. Banners fluttered in the wind. Isolated riders set off in various directions through the crowd.

"Look straight ahead," Kirill's companion said to him, keeping close to his side. "See that white horse? There, in the group of horsemen coming straight at you. See?"

Kirill could not see for the crowd that milled in front. Then a banner was carried past, and after it, another.

"To your right, look to your right! Quick!"

Kirill now saw the group withdrawing at a trot in the wake of the divisions. He tried to make out the separate riders, but they kept close together and he could not get a good view of any of them. He heard people around him crying out:

"Budyonny, Budyonny!"

The orderly pulled Kirill to one side.

"Look, in that sled! Stalin! It's Stalin!"

For a second Kirill had a clear view of the man in the sled—he was wearing a greatcoat of coarse army cloth and a fur hat resembling a helmet. The turned-down earflaps concealed his face.

The sleigh, a light Russian one of the kind that had brought Kirill in from town, quickly sped out of sight, offering only a fleeting glimpse of the carpeted back seat.

As Kirill followed the receding sleigh with his eyes, he was aware that the orderly had said something to him. But when he looked around there was neither the orderly nor the orderly's horse and sleigh—he had abandoned Kirill in the open field even more readily than he had picked him up in town.

Kirill laughed and was glad to join the crowd walking back to town.

As always at moments of spiritual uplift, the working of his mind became an actual sensation.

His physical perceptions merged with that ceaseless cycle of thoughts and impressions revolving in his mind. The monotony of the scene and the regularity of his step only enhanced this unity of thought and feeling, and he found walking a delight.

Kirill did not mentally dissect the experience that had impressed itself so deeply on his mind. He carried it with him whole and complete.

In the course of this pleasant walk across the steppe, his memory turned again and again to the last impression it had registered. It had seemed modest enough; the flash of the carpeted seat as the sleigh turned and drove off, the man in the sleigh, his shoulders in an army greatcoat, his fur cap covering the whole of his head.

By this time the Southern front had come to associate Stalin's name with the sweeping drive launched against Denikin. This name was spoken not only at staff headquarters, but throughout the army. There were cavalrymen who remembered their first meeting with Stalin in the Salsk steppe as far back as the summer of 1918. A little more than a year had passed since Stalin smashed Krasnov's Cossacks at Tsaritsyn, and there were a great many commanders and commissars in the South who could tell the Red Army men about the revolution's early battles for the Volga. Now the name

"Stalin" had spread to all armies and all fronts. After Stalin's telegram reporting victory at Voronezh, his name resounded on every front, acquiring for the entire Red Army a new purport as the hallmark of military genius. The final words of this telegram were imprinted in Soviet Russia's memory: "The halo of invincibility created around the names of Generals Mamontov and Shkuro has been trampled in the dust through the valour of the Red heroes of Comrade Budyonny's Mounted Corps."

Most Communists, Izvekov included, were aware that Stalin's role in the struggle waged on the civil war fronts by no means exhausted his activities since the October Revolution. Yet in spite of himself, Kirill came more and more frequently to regard Stalin as a military man. While thinking of the July events in Petrograd, he recalled that it was Stalin who had suppressed the counterrevolutionary uprising of the Krasnaya Gorka and Seraya Loshad forts in Kronstadt. And when he thought of the Soviet cavalry, it came to him that it was Stalin who had signed the order of the day on the formation of the First Mounted Army. While Stalin still remained for Kirill a great Party leader, he had already become for him, as for all Red Army men, a great Soviet military leader.

plenishing the glass with a liquor as black as ink and thick as molasses.

"Move up, Comrades. Give the Volga man a chance," the orderly said.

Someone poured out a glass for Kirill. The smell of the food brought him a keen realization of his hunger. He was given a formidable-looking hunting knife, with which he cut off a heel of bread. Someone asked him where he was from. Kirill downed the whole glassful at one gulp and caught his breath before answering. So the talk started.

After the meal Kirill looked over the rooms in the cottage. The orderly had told him he could stay here for the night, and in the morning everything would be straightened out. But the few beds in the place and the kitchen benches which had been pushed together were all occupied by sleeping men.

Kirill returned to the parlour where soldiers were coming and going, crowding around the table for a quick snack, as at a railway station. In a corner he found an old easy chair with loose springs. He unbuttoned his sheepskin and sat down. Warmth and fatigue soon made him drowsy.

As he closed his eyes Kirill told himself he would surely write a letter as soon as he had rested up a bit. He selected the thoughts and impressions which he felt must be written down in order to prevent their being crowded out by teeming new impressions. The first letter which he conceived was to Annochka. Then he added one to his mother. He kept beginning by saying that he felt wonderful here, though he could not explain why he felt so wonderful and wanted them simply to take him at his word. Yet he sought an explanation for his elation. He thought he would tell them how he had been overwhelmed and carried away by the roar of the cavalry charging across the steppes. The whole world had resounded with this roar. It was the onward march of history. And his present elation was due to the fact that he, Kirill Izvekov, had added his small but loyal step to this thunderous stride. As soon as he said "the march of history" he realized that he was writing neither to Annochka nor to his mother, but to Ragozin. All three letters now merged in his mind into one. But with a supreme effort he separated the letter to Annochka from the others and decided that he would remind Annochka of the talk he had had with her a long, long time ago, when they had met for the first time at his mother's place. And he clearly visualized this meeting, remembering how his mother had smoothed an unruly lock of hair on Annochka's forehead and smiled at her. Kirill would remind Annochka of his talk with her about art, and the fact that he loved art. And he would write that he felt wonderful because the poetry of living could be felt in all its fulness only here where he now was—only here, and nowhere else. Gradually his perceptions became veiled in mist, and it seemed to him that he was lost in deep thought, but actually he was sunk in deep, peaceful sleep.

It was probably the silence that awoke him. A trooper wearing a high fur hat was sitting at the table chewing a piece of fatback. Another was asleep on the floor, his head resting on his forearm. The dry wick in the lamp was spluttering, on the verge of going out.

Kirill buttoned up his jacket and went out. The wind had died down, the temperature had dropped considerably, and the sky was bright, with a half moon riding high. The snow sparkled in the nocturnal brilliance, and the white road, which seemed to be climbing up and up, beckoned the onlooker to venture forth.

There were two or three other men who had come out for air and were now standing motionless admiring the winter night. The silence, nearly complete, was broken only by an occasional horse snorting noisily in its sleep somewhere in the distance.

A Red Army man shot out of the sentry-guard-
ed house and set off at a run. The snow crunched
under the thumping of his felt boots. The man disappeared into the cottage, only to re-emerge a
minute later.

"Hey, comrades!" he shouted, "is there anybody here by the name of Izvekov?"

Kirill responded.

"Come along, you're wanted!"

He led Kirill past the sentries.

The large room where he had been with the
orderly earlier in the day was now crowded. Commanders and commissars stood along the walls,
others were seated on the window sills and around
the table. Kirill paused at the door. Several lamps
of different shapes shed a steady light on the
scene. Kirill's eye was drawn to a large-scale map
of Southern Russia on the wall behind the table.
The small flags pinned on the map and the brack-
ets, ovals and arrows entered on it in red and
blue pencil were evidence of its purpose. On
the table was a samovar and the same simple
fare Kirill had found in the neighbouring cottage.
The colourful wine bottles were now empty. The
collection of dishes had been pushed over to
the edge of the table. Supper was obviously over.

The men along the walls and at the windows
were talking in low voices, while those around

the table were listening to the quiet conversation of a small group hidden from Kirill by a lamp. The room was full of tobacco smoke, which hung in blue clouds around the lamp chimneys.

Kirill stepped forward in order to get a better view of the men at the table. Just then the orderly appeared at his elbow.

"Come and be introduced," he said, for some reason speaking into Kirill's ear, although his voice was quite loud enough.

As they approached the table he gave Kirill's sleeve a tug and addressed a military man who was standing with his back to them.

"Comrade Voroshilov, here is the man from Saratov I reported to you about."

Voroshilov turned, looked quickly at Izvekov, and said: "Good evening, Comrade Commissar."

"I'm afraid I'm not a commissar, Comrade Voroshilov," Izvekov replied.

"How is that? From what I have heard, you could be given a brigade at any time!"

Kirill said nothing. In responding to the greeting he had snapped his heels together forgetting that he was wearing felt boots; the result was a clumsy movement that embarrassed him.

"Well, you've been in the saddle sometime or other, haven't you?" Voroshilov asked.

"I have."

"And how was it? Could you hang on?"

"I could."

Voroshilov smiled with a slight nod.

"Well, come along."

They moved over to the group engaged in conversation at the table. The commanders were crowding about someone who was talking unhurriedly. Voroshilov parted the circle of those who were standing. Kirill followed him.

In the centre sat Stalin and Budyonny. One of the men was recounting something to them, leaning forward with his elbows on his knees, speaking without gesticulation, choosing his words in the manner of one accustomed to being listened to.

Stalin darted keen glances at him, exhaling cigarette smoke from beneath his dark moustache.

"Right after Voronezh," the man said, "I sent Mironenko out on the heels of the Whites. He's a former non-commissioned officer—a Donbas miner. I ordered him to reconnoitre with his brigade, to find out in what villages the Whites were, how long they'd been there, what forces they had, and all the rest. He was to report back without delay as soon as the assignment was carried out. I waited for an hour—two hours—three. Midnight came and still there was no word. Finally, in the small hours of the morning a messenger came with a report. I opened the envelope and looked—only two lines: 'The enemy is fleeing in panic in the direction of Rostov.' And Rostov was five hundred versts away!"

Stalin laughed. Lighting a fresh cigarette from the butt of the previous, he said gaily:

"When you're that anxious to get to Rostov, you don't care much about tactical reconnaissance!"

Several voices joined in the conversation.

"It's getting hard to enforce service regulations," said one. "Recently I ordered the regular halt. Before I knew it they were reporting to me that the men were grumbling—too much time being spent on halts when we should keep driving forward."

"They're in a hurry to get home," observed another.

"Home?" asked Stalin casually.

"Most of the men in my unit are from the Don and the Kuban. They want to get back as quickly as possible."

With a quizzical smile, Stalin passed his eyes slowly over the group.

"In general I am for observing regulations. But frankly speaking, I too am against dragging out the halts unnecessarily. Haven't we, comrades, sat up rather late?"

He rose. All those who had been seated also sprang up, pulling their watches out of their pockets. Once more, this time with a serious expression, he surveyed the faces around him and said as quietly as before:

"I repeat: we must hurry. Let me wish you success again, Comrades Commissars and Commanders. Success that will mean the complete destruction of Denikin's armies. Today's review of Budyonny's cavalry showed that we have every reason to expect this."

Stalin shook hands with Budyonny and turned to go. Voroshilov stepped up to him.

"I should like to introduce a Saratov comrade to you, Comrade Stalin. He arrived with a mounted detachment for our new units."

Stalin greeted Kirill and began to ask him questions: how big was the detachment, what were the men like, were they well trained, how many days had they spent on the way, where had they detrained, and, finally, what was Kirill's name, had he served in the tsarist army, where had he worked, and what was the general frame of mind in Saratov.

"Enlistment of volunteers for the cavalry is continuing, people are joining eagerly," Kirill replied, recalling the meeting in the military settlement.

"That's fine. The Volga people are hotheaded, and hotheads make good cavalrymen," said Stalin. "By helping smash Denikin in the Donbas, the people of Saratov will remove all threat to their Volga."

He glanced at Voroshilov.

"We'll have to give this comrade an appointment in the First Mounted."

"I've already been thinking of giving him a brigade," Voroshilov said.

"Is that enough? He's young, but he seems to be experienced. And Volga people know their worth."

Stalin smiled at Kirill and held out his hand.

Everybody headed for the door. The hum of voices grew louder. The old floorboards in the hallway groaned under the heavy tread of the men.

Voroshilov, glancing around and observing Kirill's face in the dim light of a wall lamp, said:

"Well, young man, come and see me in the morning. And make it early."

The unexpected informality of address thrilled Kirill and reminded him of the extraordinary feeling that had pervaded him that day in his youth when on the Saratov uplands an old worker had called him "comrade" for the first time in his life and he had run into the hills to calm his emotion.

Kirill left the house in the cloud of vapour which poured with the men through the open door. Up the straight snow-carpeted road that seemed to lead ever higher and higher he set out with his new comrades for his soldier's billet in order, refreshed, to meet the coming dawn.

1945-1948

Printed in the Union of Soviet Socialist Republics

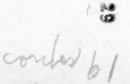